# Just one look, and I was on fire...

My eyes blinked open, then traveled up a pair of black pants, a firm butt, a belted waist and a well-filled-out black shirt. Ah, the Angel of Death, I realized, relaxing a little. He had his back to me as he spoke to someone on a walkie-talkie.

"Subject is roughly five foot six, slim, straight brown hair, hazel eyes—mostly green. Full lips." He paused. "Uh, really full lips. No tattoos...unfortunately."

Who the hell was "subject"? I wondered groggily. Me? Maybe creatures of the otherworld preferred to keep things all business. "Hello," I said.

The angel/demon spun around, and the crystalline blue of his eyes pierced me. I sucked in a breath, my hormones sizzling to life despite my condition.

"Hello, Belle. Glad to see you're awake."

The sound of my name on his soft, kiss-me lips was intoxicating. I fought the urge to reach out and trace my fingertips over that dark stubble dusting his jaw. I fought the urge to grab him by the neck and kiss the breath out of him. I fought the urge...oh, hell. Come to Momma...

# Gena Showalter

# Playing with Fire

tales of an 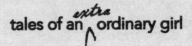 extra ordinary girl

HQN™

ISBN-13: 978-0-373-77129-5
ISBN-10:      0-373-77129-0

PLAYING WITH FIRE

www.HQNBooks.com

**Printed in U.S.A.**

Dear Reader,

In the past I've written about alien warriors turned to stone and cursed into a trinket box. I've written about dragon changelings, underwater worlds, a woman's journey to empowerment and an alien huntress who kills otherworldly bad guys. I've even ventured into the Goth high school. Why not write a book about my own life, I thought, and tell the world about my superpowers? It's time people know I can create fireballs from air, freeze my enemies into blocks of ice (be afraid, enemies) and blast slowpoke drivers with massive torrents of wind (be very afraid, slowpokes).

Okay, fine. I don't have superpowers. The book isn't about my life, but writing it was one hell of a ride. I was allowed to venture into the wonderful realm of supernatural experiments, paranormal abilities and (I admit) fantasies of sexy government agent Rome Masters—needless to say, I want him for myself. (Anyone up for a second story where a sassy heroine by the name of Gina/Jeanna/Genna battles Wonder Girl? No? Damn it!)

Anyway, to see what kind of story I'm working on next (this is one thing you do not need to fear!), visit my Web site at www.genashowalter.com and my blog at www.genashowalter.blogspot.com.

Here's to love, laughter and sexy men,

*Gena Showalter*

# Playing with Fire

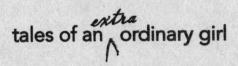

tales of an *extra* ordinary girl

Ordinary—*adj* [ME *ordinaire,* fr. L *ordinarius,* fr. ordin-, *ordo* order] 1: of a kind to be expected in the normal order of events: ROUTINE, USUAL. 2a: of common quality, rank, or ability. 2b: deficient in quality: POOR, INFERIOR. 2c: lacking in refinement. 3: Belle Jamison.

## Résumé of Belle Jamison (First Draft)

**OBJECTIVE:**

To find an exciting, exhilarating career with the opportunity for advancement and a low rate of employee dismissals

**EXPERIENCE:**

- Five years Remmie's Steak House—waitress
- Four and a half years Holiday Escape—maid
- May 18th—May 29th Harrison and Co. Books—dust patrol
- June 2nd—June 20th Kimberly Dolls—assembly line (heads)
- June 25th—July 3rd Rizzo's Grocery—cleanup, aisle 5
- July 19th—August 1st Hot House Flowers—funeral arrangement specialist
- August 11th—August 13th Professional clown (independent contractor)
- September 5th—September 30th Cutter's Gym—towel girl
- October 18th—October 31st Wisteria Elementary School—bus driver
- November 3rd—November 9th Donte Aeronautics—nuts and bolts finder
- November 10th—November 12th Jumpin' Jive Pre-owned Cars—odometer tweaker
- November 22nd—December 1st Beauty and Beyond Salon—hair sweeper
- December 14th—February 5th Cybernet Telemarketing—hang-up preventer

- Two month sabbatical Professional loafer
- April 6$^{th}$—present Utopia Café—coffee wench

## EDUCATION:

- Graduate of Wisteria High School
- Head cheerleader for the Fighting Trojans (Go team!)
- Voted best dressed
- One week at Groomers 'R' Us
- Four weeks at LaVonda's Divine School of Cosmetology

## INTERESTS:

Long walks on the beach, sunsets, romance novels, cold winter nights, paychecks, fine dining, shopping, naps, playing the lottery, men in kilts/uniforms/calendars, and massages.

## REFERENCES:

"If you do not enforce strict 'attendance' policies, Miss Jamison is the perfect candidate for your company."
                              —Mr. Ron Peaty, Manager of Utopia Café

"Please give my friend a job. Please."
                              —Miss Sherridan Smith, best friend

# CHAPTER ONE

ISN'T IT AMAZING HOW ONE seemingly innocent decision can change your entire life? For me, that decision came in the form of a grande mocha latte.

Allow me to explain.

The day began normally enough. Translation: I rolled out of bed thirty minutes late, rushed through a shower and hurriedly dressed in the standard black slacks and white button-up top every Utopia Café employee is required to wear. Unlike the other employees, I left the top three buttons of my shirt undone, revealing hints of the white lace (push-up) bra I wore underneath. Don't judge. Some people are mammarily challenged and need a little boost. Anyway, if I showed a little cleavage my pervert boss wouldn't care that I was late. Again.

He might even thank me for coming in at all.

Was it wrong of me to rely on the girls to get me out of trouble? Probably. Did I give a shit? Hell, no. In fact, I unabashedly adjusted them for ample display. I was single, twenty-four and determined to keep this job. Anyone who objected could blow me.

See, my dad suffers from massive heart problems and I'm the "responsible party" in charge of his bills, not to mention the one who finances his stay at Village on the Park, a nearby assisted living center. I would have loved for him to live with me (not that there's enough space in my one-bedroom efficiency), but it's best that he stays there. They have twenty-four-hour monitoring and make sure he takes his medications, which he "forgets" to do when left to his own devices.

Besides, he claims he's never been happier. The women there are "silver foxes," he says, and eager for masculine attention. Dare I mention those silver foxes cost more than high-priced hookers because my dad is always popping the Viagra he buys from his friends?

I'll do anything to ensure my dad's happiness, though, the way he unselfishly ensured my happiness throughout my entire childhood. So I desperately need to keep my current job *and* get the one I'm interviewing for after my shift.

*Can't be late, can't be late, can't be late,* I mentally chanted as I searched for my coffee-stained tennis shoes. I've spilled more cappuccinos on them than I've served to high-class snobs. Needless to say, I've served a lot of high-class snobs.

"Aha! Found you, you dirty little bastards." When had I put them in the refrigerator? I tugged them on, shivering as my toes grew numb from the cold.

Meanwhile, the clock ticked away more precious minutes.

I hastily applied blush, mascara and gloss. You'd think the need for money would inspire me to wake up bright and early every morning no matter the circumstances, but you'd be wrong. I was too tired to do bright and early today, even for a stack of greens. Last night I'd bartended a bachelorette party until 3:00 a.m. Me, a girl who knows nothing about alcohol. Sex on the Beach—sure, with the right man. Fuzzy Navel—uh, shower, anyone? Tom Collins—who the hell?

Of course, I'd pretended to be the expert I'd claimed to be in the interview, mixing anything and everything I could get my hands on. My drinks hadn't been the tastiest, but they'd certainly created the desired results. By the end of the evening, all of the women drunkenly swore they loved me and my "wicked nasty" concoctions.

The clock chimed the hour: 6:00 a.m.

"Damn it." I rubbed my tired, burning eyes—then froze when I realized the mascara hadn't dried. Freaking great. I probably looked like a boxer who'd lost the big match. As I scrubbed my face with a wet washrag, I watered my dry, brittle plants, multitasking to save time. What would it take to make the little green monsters thrive?

Finally ready to leave, I dug my keys out of the fishbowl. How many drinks had *I* sucked down last night? I didn't remember dropping my keys in the water. At least the bowl was presently devoid of fish. Martin, my betta, had kicked it a few days ago. Natural causes, I assure you.

"I hope you're rotting in the sewers," I said, looking down. No way he'd made it into heaven. The little snot had hated me, had always fanned his gills and hit the glass whenever I walked into a room. He'd been a present from my last boyfriend, aka the Prince of Darkness. Was it wrong of me to wish the ex had died with the fish?

No time to ponder the ethics of that dream now. I needed to go. Dressed? Check. Shoes? Check. Keys? Check. Résumé? Check. I'd stuffed it in my work pants last night in preparation for an interview today. Ugh. Yet another menial job. If only I could crawl back into bed, snuggle under the covers and continue my X-rated dream about Vin Diesel and an easy-squeeze tube of chocolate syrup. Double yum! Something about that bald head drove me wild.

*Stop daydreaming, woman.* I trudged to the front door just as the phone rang. Sighing, I raced into my bedroom. Probably my boss, Ron, but I wanted to double-check just in case. A quick peek at caller ID revealed it was actually my dad. Late as I was, I didn't even think about letting the machine pick up. I grabbed the receiver and held it to my ear.

"Hey, Daddy."

"Hey, doll. What'cha doing?"

"I'm headed off to work. Everything okay?"

"Fine, everything's fine." His deep, rumbling voice never failed to comfort me. "You work too hard."

"Ah, but you know it's what I live for," I said, and my voice held only truth. I'd never, never let this selfless man know I didn't like my job(s). He'd go off and get one of his own, the old teddy bear. Anything to take care of me. No wonder I loved him so damn much. "I'm not happy unless I'm working."

"Just like your mother, God rest her soul. Never did understand that mind-set, myself," he said. I pictured him shaking his head in wonderment. "I won't keep you. I just got to looking through old photo albums of you as a baby. I know you visited the other day, but I still wanted to hear your voice."

See? He's a sweetie. "Now you're trying to make me cry. But I'm glad you called. I missed you and your voice, too."

He chuckled. "Aren't we just a pair of mushy—"

"David!" I heard a woman call.

"Oh, hell," he said to me. To the woman, he grumbled, "Not now, Mary. I'm on the phone with my best gal."

"Did you or did you not kiss Janet in the gardens last night?" Mary demanded in the background.

"Double hell," my dad whispered. Then, "Oh, crap. I think she's wheeling her chair into my room." He paused. "I guess I should have resisted Janet's invitation for a stroll."

"I guess you should have," I said with a laugh.

"I have to go now. Love you, doll," he said.

"David!" Mary called, closer now.

"Love you, too, Daddy."

We disconnected, and I stared at the phone for a minute, a smile hovering on my lips. Shaking my head, I rushed out of my tiny apartment with only one wistful backward glance.

"Let's get this day over with," I muttered.

Outside, the dim spring morning proved wonderfully fragrant with the scent of magnolia, but oppressively hot, the air sticky with humidity. Ah, crap. I'd forgotten to bring a little towel to pat away any sweat. In a few minutes, my clothes were going to be plastered to my body. Oh, well. Nothing I could do about that now.

Not wanting to arrive at work hungry (hungry = bitchy and bitchy = fired), I stopped for a caramel glazed doughnut on my way to the bus station—and missed my bus. MARTA, Atlanta's premiere miss-it-and-you're-screwed transportation system, being what it was, the delay set me back another twenty minutes.

By the time I raced into Utopia, lines were long and winding. Customers were pissed about the wait and quite vocal about it. I yawned. I mean, please. Cry me a river, Richie Richersons. Jeez. Anyone who could afford a daily six-dollar cup of joe didn't need to be complaining about anything.

Ron, my boss, spotted me and gave me a you-are-so-dead scowl.

I squared my shoulders, thereby tightening the material of my shirt, and offered him a chocolate sundae smile, smothered in whipped cream and cherries. Hmm, whipped cream. That would fit nicely in my Vin Diesel fantasy.

Ron's gaze connected with the girls. He paled, looked away and crooked his finger in my general direction. Without glancing to see if I noticed, he pivoted on his heel, a silent command for me to follow him. Great. Freaking great. This didn't bode well.

Breathing deeply of the cinnamon-and-vanilla-scented air, I passed several men and women who were using the tables as mini work spaces, their computers, faxes and shredders surrounding them. I stepped into Ron's small, cramped office.

"You wanted to see me, Mr. Pretty?"

"It's Peaty, and shut the door," he said, his voice devoid of emotion. He plopped onto his chair, the cluttered desktop shielding his belly paunch. His black gaze remained lowered, not touching any part of me.

Shit.

Palms now sweating, I did as commanded. The smells of dust and cloying aftershave immediately assaulted me, wiping away any lingering hint of baked goods. Without waiting to be told, I claimed the only other seat in the room. A stiff, uncomfortable step stool I liked to call the Naughty Chair. File cabinets pressed close on both sides of me, making me feel pinned.

I studied Ron. He had thin lips, and right now those lips were pressed tightly together, barely visible slashes of pink in the contours of his rotund face. His sandy hair stood on end, as if he'd plowed his fingers through it one too many times. Lines of tension bracketed his eyes, and his brow was furrowed.

Ron had been pissed at me a *lot* these last few weeks, but he'd never radiated such disgruntled irritation. Such grim determination. I recognized the look, though. I'd gotten it from other bosses over the last year, right before they fired me.

I smothered a sigh. I hadn't always been a bad employee. For nearly five years, I'd worked as a waitress during the day and a maid during the evening. I'd made enough to pay for my living expenses and support my dad, as well as build a nice savings account—a savings account I'd used up during my (forced) hiatus, aka the two months that it had taken me to land this job at the café.

Why couldn't I hold back my restlessness anymore? Why couldn't I quash my discontent, as I had for so many years, and stop sabotaging my only source of revenue?

Though I didn't want to admit it, I knew the answer. I'd woken up one morning and realized life was passing me by, moving at high speed while I wallowed behind. Dissatisfaction had filled me—and had only grown since.

"I'm sorry for anything and everything I might have done," I said, when Ron opened his mouth to speak.

"You're late," he growled. "Again."

The fact that I didn't utter, "Thanks for stating the obvious," should have earned me major good-girl points. "I know, and I really am sorry." When his expression didn't soften, when he *still* didn't glance in my direction, my heart slammed against my ribs. "I worked another job late into the morning and had trouble waking up."

He stared at the wall clock just behind my head and adjusted his chocolate-smeared tie. "While I like the image of you lingering in bed—"

Sick bastard. Gross. Just…gross. I might have thrown up

in my mouth. And yes, I understand the irony here. *Yo* *brought it on yourself, Jamison. What else did you expect, un* *leashing the girls like that?* Suddenly hoping to hide then from view, I hunched my shoulders.

Wait, Ron's mouth was moving. He hadn't stopped talking.

"—that's just not a good enough excuse. I mean, I ca make an exception for it once, twice, but we've had this same conversation seven times now. And you've only worked here a few weeks."

"I'll be on time tomorrow, you have my word. I'll go with out sleep if necessary." Did I sound as desperate to Ron as did to myself? Probably. Damn it. I hated to let him see my desperation. Hated, hated, *hated*. The more desperate he knew I was, the more he could pull my strings and make me dance like a performing monkey.

He tapped a pen against his desktop. "That's what you said last time. This is a small, independent operation, Belle, and we rely on our employees to provide superior service to keep us in business."

"I *do* provide superior service," I gulped, adding, "when I'm here."

Frowning, he dropped the pen and pushed a hand through his hair, causing more of the sandy locks to spike straight toward the ceiling. "You think you're good with customers? Really?"

"Yes, really." I knew what was happening here. He teetered on the brink of firing me and was simply trying to work up the courage to utter the words. And, I realized with shattering fear, I might not be able to talk him out of it this time. By this point in our previous talks, he was usually sending me on my way with a stern (but perverted) warning

Had his irritation given him a supersonic determination no amount of sweet-talking persuasion could penetrate?

My eyes narrowed; my hands clenched into fists. I wouldn't allow him to get rid of me easily. Somehow, some way, I was going to penetrate that wall of nefarious determination. I could *not* lose this job. Lately very few businesses were willing to take a chance on me, so I could only imagine how long it would take to land another.

"Stupid jobs," I muttered.

"What was that?" Ron asked, his gaze sharpening.

Had I said that aloud? "Oh, uh, nothing." I straightened in the chair. "You were saying?"

He pushed out a sigh. "You have no people skills, Belle. Instead of smoothing ruffled feathers, you set them on fire."

"I'm telling you, I'm a good employee," I said through clenched teeth. And that wasn't a lie. Sure, I usually arrived late, always cussed, sometimes bitched and—and this is not an admission of guilt—(allegedly) borrowed from the stock room. But I worked weekends, holidays and overtime whenever possible. That counted for something, right?

"I can't believe you're making me do this." Ron flipped open a file and ran a blunt-tipped finger down the front page. "Complaint—server is rude and pushy. Complaint—server made tea instead of coffee. Complaint—server is rude. Complaint—server is rude. Complaint—server is rude. Shall I go on?"

"I don't let the customers yell and scream at me." Indignation gave me a sense of bravery, and I sat up even straighter, shoulders squared. Did people have nothing better to do with their lives than complain about a lowly server? "That doesn't make me rude, it makes me human."

"Jenni doesn't yell at customers even when they yell at her."

"Jenni is a brown-nosing moron."

Another sigh. "Belle—" Finally, his gaze landed on me and out of habit slid straight to the girls. He swallowed, his Adam's apple bobbing like a dinghy in a tidal wave. "Uh, what was I saying?"

I almost grinned, every muscle in my body relaxing. Penetration complete. And so much easier than I'd anticipated.

Being looked at was far different from hearing his sex-offender voice comment about me lingering in bed. *This* I could handle. "I believe you were about to tell me to get to work and never be late again. I planned to respond by telling you that you're the best boss in the world and I'll make you proud."

"Yes, I wanted to tell you to get to—" Eyes widening, he shook his head. "That's not what I meant to say," he said, a stern edge creeping into his voice. But he closed his eyes and pinched the bridge of his nose. He muttered something under his breath that sounded suspiciously like *brought down by a pair of pretty knockers.* "I should fire you, you know. Hell, that's why I brought you in here."

"I know," I admitted softly. I didn't mean to be such a disappointment to him. Honest. I just, well, I had always dreamed of being a— Wait. My eyebrows drew together. Even as a little girl, I hadn't been able to decide what I wanted to be when I grew up. I still didn't know. But being a peon stuck in a cycle of debt and endless servitude hadn't been, and still wasn't, part of my life's ambition.

Don't get me wrong. For my dad, I'd sign my soul over to the devil. Permanent ink. No "out" clause. Dad had toiled and slaved for years in construction, even when his weak heart caused him more pain than one person should ever have to bear. He'd worked so hard because he loved me, because he'd wanted me to have pretty clothes and take fun trips with my friends. But mostly because he'd wanted to make up for the car accident that had killed my mom when I was a toddler.

After I graduated high school, I had convinced him to quit, and I'd happily taken care of him ever since. I didn't regret it; truly I didn't, but my life had fallen into such a rut that sometimes I did wish for something extraordinary to happen to me. Something amazing, perhaps a little wild. What, I didn't know.

I frowned. No more wishing for things I couldn't have. From this point on, I would be a better employee. I would work harder, be less confrontational. Screw restlessness! Ron was giving me another chance, and I wouldn't let him down.

"I swear, Belle, you keep my ulcer in fighting form," he said darkly. He reached into his desk drawer, withdrew a packet of Tums and popped several in his mouth. "Why can't I be more like the Donald and just say it? You're fired. Boom. You're fired. So easy in theory." He sighed yet again, this one a dejected exhalation that made his shoulders sag. "This is your last chance. If you screw this up—"

"I won't. Swear to God." I didn't mention that I needed to leave a wee bit early today if I hoped to make my interview with Ambassador Suites, a nearby hotel. I'd bring up that little gem later. I'd double up my coffee-making or something to earn the early departure. "I'll be so good you'll nominate me for Employee of the Week. Maybe Employee of the Month."

"Yeah. Right." He popped a few more Tums and eyed the girls again. "I can't believe I'm doing this. Go. Open a register before I change my mind."

Grinning, I blew him a kiss, bounded out of my chair and raced to the door. Thank God for perverts.

I SPENT THE NEXT SEVERAL hours being a good little robot, smiling a sunshine-and-roses smile and waving customers to my register like a Miss America contestant. All under Ron's hawklike eyes. Once, I came close to bitch-slapping a woman who had the nerve to ask me if I moved that slow for everyone or if she was just special.

*You're certainly a special pain in my ass,* I'd wanted to say. But I didn't. I restrained myself from violence (see "bitch-slap" comment above), consoled by the thought that such an evil witch would surely acquire deep, deep wrinkles and lose all her teeth and hair before she kicked it.

My friend Sherridan—the only friend I had, really, since she didn't mind the fact that I had no free time—would have been proud of me for remaining silent and not launching myself forward, a catapult of retribution. When we were in grade school, she'd told me the devil on my right shoulder must have brutally strangled the angel on my left, destroying any hint of moral influence.

I plead the Fifth on that.

Speaking of Sherridan, she strolled into the café a few minutes later, spotted me and waved. She was talking on her cell. She was tall and gorgeous with blond curls and curves that went on forever, curves that were now encased in an emerald pants suit. She marched to me, bypassing the line to stand beside my register, and hooked her cell to her waist. "Hey, you," she said with a warm smile.

"Hey, back," I said, but kept my gaze on the customer and pretended to listen to her order. I loved when Sherridan visited me here. Technically, employees were discouraged from having guests, but lately it was the only time we spent together. "You look good."

"Thank you." She spoke over the frowning customer. "I'm showing a house later today and want to impress the buyer—who is half of the reason I'm here." She clapped her hands in excitement. "I got us dates."

"Dates?" Months had passed since I'd even thought the word, so it was foreign on my tongue. "Do you want cinnamon sprinkled on your half-caf?" I asked my customer.

"With twins," Sherridan said proudly. "Wealthy twins."

"Yes," the customer said through tight lips.

Sherridan didn't pause. "I think the older one likes me." There was a twinge of uncertainty in her voice.

"I'm sure he does," I said. "You're beautiful and smart." Sherridan liked to pretend she was confident, but deep down she needed reassurance when it came to men. She tended to fall for them quickly, become horribly needy and unsure, and drive them away. "I'm working that night, though."

Sherridan's grin slipped a little, and she narrowed her silver eyes suspiciously. "I didn't tell you—" her phone rang "—when."

"Sometime today on that drink," my customer said, drumming her nails on the counter.

"Doesn't matter about the day." I turned, grabbed a carton of milk and poured a measured amount into the proper container. "I'm always working."

"Leslie," Sherridan said to her assistant, "this isn't a good time. I'm in a meeting." She ended the call. "Belle, can't you take a day off? Just one? Please?"

A wave of longing hit me, but I didn't speak for several seconds as the milk steamed, buzzing loudly. When that tapered to quiet, I said, "I wish I could, Sher, but I'm interviewing for a second job later and I'll be working nights if I get it."

"Not another one," she said with a groan.

"Hey, server girl. Can I get an ETA on my drink? I'm in a mad rush, and you're taking forever."

My gaze sought and met the opposition's, my hazel against her brown. My impatience against her annoyance. She was a tall woman, tanned and toned, almost muscular, with leathery skin and hair as dark a brown as mine. But while my hair was long and straight (and, I like to think, silky), hers was short and frizzy, as if she'd left her perm rods in a thousand years too long.

"My name is not server or girl," I muttered under my breath. To her, I said loudly, "It'll be done in a second, sir. Oops, my bad. I mean, ma'am."

She scowled.

"Belle," Ron called warningly.

I gritted my teeth, nearly grinding them into powder, and prepared the stupid half-caf. All the while I chanted in my mind, *I will behave myself. I will behave myself. I will freaking behave myself.* On the bright side, at least Ron was overlooking Sherridan's visit.

"Well, I should go before Super Curls throws a fit," Sherridan said, ignoring my customer's scowl. She leaned over and kissed my cheek. "Call me if you change your mind about the twins. They have the cutest, tightest asses *ever* and if you married one—a twin, not his ass—all of your money troubles would be over." With that, she was off.

I handed Super Curls the coffee, but didn't get a thank-you.

"I'll have a skinny venti vanilla, please," my next customer said.

"Sugar free?"

His face scrunched in disgust. "I said skinny, not taste-less."

And so another hour passed unmercifully. I should have chucked my apron and left with Sherridan. "This isn't what I ordered," I heard. "Your fingers touched the rim, so I need you to start over and make me a new, uncontaminated drink," I heard. "You call this an espresso? I've had stronger water," I heard.

Did I complain? Did I mix anyone a swirlie (aka spit in their drink)? No and no! The continued restraint cost me, though. My stomach was a clenched knot of pain. My skin felt too tight against my bones. A tic had developed under my left eye. My back throbbed, and my feet ached—and not from standing too long. I was used to that. The ache was because I hadn't allowed myself to deliver a few much needed ass beatings.

If I didn't get Employee of the Week after this… Wait. I decided I'd rather have a break.

When I sent my last customer on her way, I glanced over at Ron, who had stopped watching me long enough to turn his attention to a woman who looked like she'd walked straight out of an X-rated pin-up. She sauntered past him, her red spandex halter top and shorts revealing more T and A than a *Penthouse* centerfold—not that I'd ever peeked inside one of *those* magazines (cough, cough). Ron adjusted his belt. I snapped my fingers to gain his attention, but the woman's thong-clad ass held him enthralled.

The bell above the door jingled, signaling the arrival of yet another group of patrons. Their eyes were feral, and I could tell they were desperate for their morning fix. If I didn't act quickly, I'd be stuck here a minimum—minimum!—of twenty more minutes, and I just didn't have another second of sweetness in me.

With a speed Superman would have envied, I began closing out my register.

"What are you doing?" Jenni, Employee of the Year—or, as I liked to call her, Bitch of the Millennium—demanded. She stood at the only other open register, a short, rounded-in-all-the-right-places blonde who drew male attention simply by breathing. She'd made her hatred of me known my first day on the job, tripping me every time I walked past her, handing me regular coffee when I asked for decaf.

Why she hated me, I didn't know. Didn't care, really.

"You're smart." I scratched my forehead with my middle finger, covertly flipping her off. "Figure it out." With her infuriated gasp ringing in my ears, I strode over to Ron and tapped him on the shoulder.

He jumped and clutched a hand over his heart as he whipped to face me. "Jesus H. Christ!"

"No, I'm Belle," I said drily.

"What do you want?" he grumbled.

"I'd really like to take my first fifteen-minute break. If that's okay with you, Mr. Pretty," I added sweetly.

"It's Peaty." He glanced at his wristwatch. "Fine. Whatever." His gaze slid back to the walking centerfold, now bending over to pick up the napkin she'd "accidentally" dropped, her shorts riding higher up her butt.

Shaking my head, I gathered the necessary items needed for a…hmm. What did I want? A mocha latte, I decided in the next flash. Yep. That sounded good. That's what I'd have. If anyone deserved chocolate, it was me.

"You're such a bitch," Jenni muttered, suddenly at my side to mix a chai tea.

"Your jealousy is showing," I uttered in a singsong voice. I poured two shots of espresso into my cup, then whole milk. I didn't do skim. "If you'd stopped sneaking bites of muffins, éclairs and cake slices you might have realized someone was due to go on break."

Jenni gasped. "I'll have you know I have low blood sugar. I *have* to eat."

"Right. I totally believe you and don't think you're delusional in the least."

"You're just begging for a piece of me, you know that?" she growled.

"I don't know what gave you the idea I've lowered my standards, but I assure you, I haven't. I want *no* part of you. By the way, you have a piece of dough stuck in your teeth." Latte completed, I skipped to an empty table. As I sipped the hot, deliciously sweet liquid (perfectly prepared, thank you!) I stared out the large storefront window and grinned. Ah, my little interlude with Jenni had revived my spirits, chasing away the tension brought on by forced charm.

Across the way loomed a pretty, obviously well maintained brownstone with steel-enforced, tinted windows. The bushes surrounding it were expertly trimmed and hedged. Flowers bloomed prettily in the spring sun, a pink, red and gold rainbow of petals.

But there were no signs, no advertisements to be seen. Occasionally I'd spotted a car or two in the parking lot, as I did now, so I knew people worked there. But I'd never been able to figure out what kind of business it was, had never seen an employee entering or leaving.

The place intrigued me. Always had. I'd thought about sneaking over there late one night and peeking inside, but usually fell asleep before working up the strength to leave my apartment. Perhaps it was a—

I blinked. What the hell? A tall, lanky man in a lab coat suddenly barreled out the front door of the brownstone at top speed, his eyes wide and wild, his white comb-over flapping in the breeze. One minute he wasn't there, the next he was. My back went ramrod straight, the movement swishing precious latte over the rim of the cup. I blinked again, as if the action could jump-start my brain into figuring out why he was running.

The man darted across the street, uncaring as vehicles honked and swerved to keep from hitting him. Two of the cars collided. Even from where I sat, I heard the squeal of tires and the grind of smashing metal.

My eyes rounded as two burly, scowling guys sprinted out of the brownstone, apparently giving chase to the harried, wreck-causing man—who was now racing inside Utopia as if his life depended on it.

The bell chimed and I shoved myself to my feet, spilling my latte further. I set the cup on the table and stared over at the man. Skin pale, features tense, breath emerging raggedly, he scanned the café wildly. His gaze bypassed me, then quickly snapped back. Across the distance, our eyes locked.

"Are you okay?" I called, projecting my voice over the inane chatter around us.

"Please, help me," he choked out. He sprinted toward me, shoving people out of the way and babbling, "They weren't supposed to know. They weren't supposed to chase me."

Some gasped. Some snarled, "Watch it."

When the man reached me, he gripped my forearms.

weat trickled from his brow; fear filled his dilated eyes. You have to help me," he said between shallow pants. They're going to kill me."

Kill? My mouth went dry; my blood mutated into ice, yet ot prickles slithered along my spine. "Stay here," I said. "No, ide. No, stay. Oh, hell. Do whatever while I call 911." His lasp tightened on me, but I tugged free and shouted to the eople around me, "Does anyone have a cell phone?" I'd iven mine up as an extravagance I could no longer afford. Anyone?" I leapt around the tables, but everyone purpose- ully avoided my gaze. "I won't use up your minutes, I swear. his is an emergency."

"I demand to speak with the manager," someone said, vanting, I'm sure, to complain about what had just happened nd demand free service.

I rushed into Ron's office and grabbed the phone. The 911 lispatcher answered after only two rings, and I explained vhat had happened. "A man was chased into this café," I ushed out. "He says someone's trying to kill him." As I poke, a woman screamed in the background. A male ;roaned.

"Help is on the way," the dispatcher promised.

Heart hammering, I disregarded her plea to remain on the ine, and tossed the receiver aside. I pounded back into the nain area and skidded to a stop. I'd only been gone a noment, but the café looked like a natural disaster had struck. Tables were overturned. Chairs were strewn in every direc- ion. Coffee slithered along the floor, a black river, with paper :ups and napkins floating in it like dead bodies.

Shaking and scared, the café's patrons and employees

huddled in a single corner. Only Ron seemed unafraid. His
arms were wrapped around Jenni, and he was copping a feel

The man in the lab coat had vanished. Was he hiding?

The two guys I'd observed chasing him were now in the
process of calming everyone down. A third male, whom I
hadn't seen exit the brownstone, stood at the doorway, preventing anyone from entering or leaving. He was young
probably in his mid-thirties, tall and muscled, with blond hair
and a face any male model would have envied. Perfect
chiseled and droolworthy. He watched the proceedings as if
mentally cataloging every detail.

"Everyone take a seat," he finally said, his voice firm, no-
nonsense. "Get comfortable. We're going to be here awhile."

"What's going on?" I demanded, since no one else had
spoken up. "Who are you?" Maybe I shouldn't have drawn
attention to myself, but there was no way in hell I'd just
blithely obey, perhaps walking to my own death.

"CIA." He frowned and flashed some sort of badge. "Now
sit."

*CIA?* My jaw performed a dance of drop and close, drop
and close. I'd seen agents on TV, of course, but never in real
life. Still, everything inside me screamed not to trust him. I
mean, Lab Coat's voice kept drifting through my head.
*They're going to kill me. They're going to kill me!*

But…what if Lab Coat was an evil man who needed
killing? Or what if Pretty Boy was lying and Lab Coat was
really the good guy? What if I confused myself to the point
of having an aneurism with all these internal questions?

*Think, Jamison, think.* Sit down. No, run. Sit. Yes, that's
what I'd do. No, no. I should run. As I continually changed
my mind, my right foot moved back and forth while the left

remained in place. Step, retreat. Step, retreat. Damn it! If I made the wrong decision, there was a very good chance tomorrow's headlines would read: *Local Idiot Found Dead.* "Victim's friend laments, 'If Belle had taken a day off like I asked, she'd still be alive.'"

My eyes slitted. "What happened to that guy? The one in the lab coat?"

Pretty Boy crossed his arms over his chest and pinned me with a dark, almost hypnotic stare. "That's none of your concern. Now," he said, speaking to the entire room, "I have questions, and you're going to answer me."

Those eyes...they were intense, commanding, a little scary. "I just called the cops," I gulped out. "If you hurt us, you'll be thrown in prison and become Big Daddy's bitch."

His gaze flicked to one of Lab Coat's pursuers, now our guard. He was a beast of a man, with a thick, black beard (were those peas between the hairs?) and more muscles than Arnold in his prime. "Take care of it."

Take care of what? Beast radioed...the cops? He spoke too quietly for me to hear what he was saying. Meanwhile, the other guard ushered everyone into chairs. Everyone except me, that is. Maybe I looked menacing and they didn't want to mess with me. Hey, it was a possibility.

But I didn't understand why they were content to remain in here instead of chasing Lab Coat. Or had they caught him and ushered him away while I was on the phone? Why question us, then, if they already had him?

"That man is a dangerous criminal," Pretty Boy told me. He must have realized that I wouldn't cooperate otherwise. "It's in your best interest to help us."

*Dangerous criminal*—the magic words of my capitulation. "All right, fine," I said grudgingly, deciding to give him the benefit of the doubt. He had a badge, after all. "But if anyone pulls a weapon on me, I'm going PMS on their ass."

"So noted," he said with a dry edge, completely unimpressed.

Thankfully, the table I'd occupied earlier remained upright. My latte sat on the surface, unharmed. I plopped down and lifted the cup to my lips, sipping. Warm and sweet—sweeter than it had been earlier, as if the chocolate had thickened. Mmm. I continued sipping, taking comfort from it.

Pretty Boy questioned us one at a time, writing names and answers in a notebook. How very detective he was. He asked everyone the same three questions: 1) What is your name and address? 2) Did you see the man in the lab coat? 3) Did he say anything to you or give you anything?

Pretty Boy spoke with me the longest and had more than the standard three questions for me. What had made me want to help Lab Coat—"the doctor," Pretty Boy called him, careful not to use his real name. Did we secretly plan to meet later? Had I ever met with the doctor before this?

I didn't bother lying. Actually, I wasn't sure I *could* lie to this man. Every time he turned those intense brown eyes on me, I felt compelled to share my deepest, darkest secrets. Not in a girls' sleepover kind of way, but an I'll-die-if-I-don't kind of way. Very weird.

And you know what? I didn't get any answers to *my* questions. What was his name? Why were they chasing Lab Coat? What made the man so dangerous? Was Pretty Boy going to eat the chocolate éclair he'd pilfered from the fridge? I was starved.

Finally, Pretty Boy and his men left, followed quickly by the customers. I'd expected him to threaten us if we told the press or cops—or anyone, really—what had happened, but he didn't. I'd expected the police to arrive (as promised), but they never did. I guess they really had been taken care of, which probably meant Pretty Boy was the CIA agent he'd claimed to be and Lab Coat actually was a criminal. I hoped I didn't get in trouble for having tried to aid him.

Left alone at last, I helped Ron, Jenni and the rest of Utopia's employees clean up the mess. Strangely enough, we worked in silence, not discussing the events. Maybe we were too scared. Maybe we were too confused. Maybe both. As I cleaned, I looked for Lab Coat but found no trace of him.

What a shit-infested day this had turned out to be. The only silver lining was when Ron decided to close the café for the rest of the day, giving me the opportunity I needed to escape to my interview—albeit late.

Maybe, if I was lucky, I'd be hit by a car and could sue for millions.

# CHAPTER TWO

BY THE TIME I REACHED the Ambassador Suites—without being hit by a car, damn it—I'd successfully forced the day's events to the back of my mind, to be considered and dissected later. Why not worry about it now, you ask? Because my head was about to explode into tiny Belle fragments, that's why. A sharp ache pounded in my temples and beads of sweat dotted my skin. My stomach pricked and burned as if I'd swallowed a thousand acid-coated needles.

Hunger pains, maybe? No, surely not. I'd skipped lunch, true, but I'd skipped meals before and never reacted this way.

I stumbled into the hotel's bathroom, the black-and-white-tiled floor spinning and making me dizzy. My eyes were normally hazel, a green-brown mix, but right now, in the mirror, they appeared a glassy emerald. Too bright. Dilated.

My hands shook as I splashed cold water on my face. But the liquid didn't trickle down; my skin seemed to open up and absorb every drop. It happened so quickly I would have missed it if I blinked. My pores screamed in protest, burning, burning.

A moan slipped from my lips. What the hell was wrong with me? Had I picked up a vicious, fast-acting virus after leaving Utopia?

God, I hurt everywhere, the pain growing stronger with

every passing second. My joints were swelling, and I was having trouble drawing in a decent breath. Straightening as best I could, I stared again at my reflection. Bruises had formed under my eyes and bright red spots of color painted my cheeks. My lips were pulled tight.

I looked liked a drug addict. In desperate need of a fix.

I could just imagine how a potential employer would respond to that: throw me out on my ass and post my picture all over the building with a notice that I was to be arrested if I set one foot inside the place ever again. Great. Freaking great.

A sudden cramp doubled me over, and I cried out. Breathe in. Breathe out. In. Out. Gradually, the pain subsided. I straightened again, my ears ringing loudly as blood pounded through them.

"Holy hell." *Just get the interview over with so you can go home and rest.*

Somehow, and God only knew how, I pulled myself together enough to walk into the interviewer's office with my head held high and my shoulders squared. An older man with thick silver hair and a stiff brown suit sat behind the room's only desk. He grinned when he spotted me, his eye crinkling at the corners. Kindness radiated from him.

"You must be Belle."

"Yes." I forced my lips into an answering smile. I wouldn't be able to keep up the facade for long. I realized that when the interviewer—what the hell was his name?—shook hands with me. The feel of his palm against my too-sensitized flesh nearly dropped me to the ground, huddling in a fetal ball and crying for the mommy I hadn't seen in more than twenty years. The contact, though brief, cut through me like a barrage of slashing knives.

"You're a little late," he said, glancing at his wristwatch, "but I think there's just enough time to get to know each other."

"Thank you. Thank you so much. I had an unavoidable delay, but I promise you now, I'll never be late again." Hurriedly I unfolded my résumé from my pocket and handed it to him, careful not to touch him.

*Ding, ding.* Let the interview begin.

OKAY, SO I TOTALLY BLEW the interview.

My ears had rung too loudly, and I hadn't been able to hear him. My joints had ached too fiercely, and I hadn't been able to sit still. My mind had neared explosion, and I hadn't been able to think of intelligent answers.

Disheartened and racked by intense, debilitating pain, I entered my apartment, tossed my keys onto the old brown shag carpet, locked the door and lumbered to my bedroom, stripping as I walked/crawled/begged God for sweet death. As I fell into the soft coolness of the bed, the entire horrific nightmare replayed in my mind.

> Interviewer: My, but you've worked at a lot of jobs.
> Me: Only recently. Before that, I was a maid—with the same hotel—for almost five years, as well as a waitress—for the same restaurant. But at each of my latest jobs, I assure you I've learned valuable lessons.
> Interviewer: What, uh, did you learn at the Kimberly Dolls factory?
> Me: I learned that it is not funny to put the Kevin head on the Kimberly body.
> Interviewer: Hmm. And at the pet groomer?
> Me: I learned that dogs and cats are to be respected

and not shaved to resemble lions. In my defense, the lion look is very popular with certain breeds.

Interviewer: I see. I'm curious about something. Were you fired from each of these jobs or did you quit?

Me: I prefer the term "let go." Fired just sounds so…mean.

Interviewer: Were you let go, then?

Me: Yes, but I can explain.

Interviewer: I'm listening.

Me: At Harrison and Co. Books, I completely misunderstood the return policy. A simple mistake, really, one anyone could have made. You see, I thought it would be totally fine to take the books home in my bag, read them and return them. You would have thought the same thing, wouldn't you? That's what return means.

Interviewer: Well, uh, hmm. What about Jumpin' Jive Cars? Why were you let go from there?

Me: Well, that's an interesting story. See, there was an unfortunate accident with one of the cars I borrowed. Totally not my fault. The lady in front of me didn't signal, and you know how important it is to signal when changing lanes.

Interviewer: Yes, that is important.

Me: Just give me a chance, Mr. uh, uh—

Interviewer: Mr. MacDonald.

Me: I'll be the best damn, uh, uh—

Interviewer: Maid.

Me:—maid you've ever seen. Maid! That's excellent. I told you about my five years of experience, didn't I? I'm great with people and even better with toilets, and that's the Belle Jamison guarantee. There's nothing more solid than that, Mr. MacRonald.

Interviewer: It's Donald.

Me: Why, thank you, Donald. You may call me Belle.

Interviewer: That's not—never mind. I have to be honest with you, Miss Jamison. We at the Ambassador are looking for someone more, well, grounded.

Me: I'm grounded. Totally. I spent most of my teenage years grounded.

Interviewer: Hmm.

Me: That was a joke. Promise. My dad didn't have the heart to ground me, even when I deserved it.

Interviewer: We need someone levelheaded.

Me: I can be levelheaded. One time I was shopping with my friend Sherridan, who will kill you if you call her Sherry, and she wanted to buy this very pretty, very expensive blue dress. Blue is totally her best color and it looked killer on her, but she'd already maxed out her cards and didn't have excess cash. I told her the dress made her ass look fat so she wouldn't put herself into more debt. A gal doesn't get any more levelheaded than that.

Interviewer: I'll make a note of that. Meanwhile, it was nice to meet you. I'll call you and let you know our decision.

Me: When? I really need this job. Really, really badly.

Interviewer: I'll be making calls in a few days.

Me: Okay, great. I'll keep my ringer turned on so you can reach me anytime. Really. Anytime is good. Well, except for tomorrow morning. I'm not feeling so great. And maybe tomorrow night won't be so good, either. And Saturday. But other than that I'm completely reachable.

Interviewer: That's…good to know. I'll have security show you out.

YEAH, LIKE Mr. Donald MacRonald was ever going to call me.

"Ouch, ouch, ouch." Groaning, I clutched a pillow to my stomach. I'd never been this sick. Not even the time Bobby Lowenstein planted a big wet one on me in the ninth grade and I woke up the next morning with lymph nodes the size of baseballs. Mono had sucked ass.

This sucked bigger ass.

Maybe I'd call Sherridan and make her come over and take care of me. As it was, I didn't have the strength to go into the kitchen and get myself a glass of water and eight hundred Tylenol.

I whimpered as another wave of pain assaulted me. My blood heated to boiling, burning like lava in my veins before chilling to ice. If I hadn't known better, I would have thought something was alive inside me, clawing its way through my every cell. Slicing me apart and rearranging my organs.

Forget Sherridan. I needed a doctor.

I reached for the phone, but my arm dropped onto the bed, too heavy to hold up. A strange but welcome lethargy suddenly flowed through me, lulling me into darkness, away from the pain. My eyelids closed and a black web wove inside my mind. Morning. I'd feel better in the morning.

# CHAPTER THREE

BY MORNING I WANTED to kill myself.

How many hours I drifted in and out of consciousness, I didn't know. One minute I saw sunshine streaming in through my windows, the next moonlight. One minute I shivered from cold, the next I sweated profusely. Awake I hurt. Asleep I hurt. Hurt, hurt, hurt. Everywhere. I was dying. I knew I was. I, who had never fallen in love, never owned a cat—or anything but an obnoxious betta—and never really *lived*.

This was it. The end. And it wasn't pretty.

You know how dying people claim to see a light at the end of the tunnel, or that their life flashes before their eyes? Lucky bastards! Why couldn't I be one of them? Instead I heard Ron's pervy voice tell me over and over that I was fired as I fell through a seemingly never-ending tunnel, the fires of hell licking at me on one side, snowballs slamming into me on the other.

In this strange la-la land, I'd watched my nightstand catch fire, orange-gold flames flickering toward the ceiling. Then I'd watched a rain cloud form above it and douse the flames completely. The hallucination had been so real I'd heard the crackle of burning wood, the patter of the water and the ensuing sizzle of dying embers. I'd even smelled the ashes.

Afterward, I'd spotted a dark angel/demon standing at the edge of my bed, watching me, waiting for me to die. His gaze had seemed to burn into me. Intense. Scorching. I had felt a strange sort of comfort in his presence, though, knowing I wasn't alone.

Now that I was awake, I wanted him with me again.

"Angel," I croaked, my wild eyes feverishly searching for him in the darkness. I needed a glass of water, el pronto. I think something had died inside my mouth and rigor mortis had already set in. When I earned no response, I tried again. "Demon."

Still nothing.

Had he left? Oh, he had. Bastard. He'd abandoned me.

I closed my eyes and a picture of him formed in my mind. He was severely hot—but he wasn't handsome, if that made any sense. He looked savage and feral, like something you should fear, yet couldn't because you wanted so badly to tame it. Hair as black as midnight framed his face, and his eyes were so blue they sparkled. I would have said they sparkled like sapphires, but there was a predatory glint in those eyes of his, dangerous and wild, nixing any thought of precious gems.

He was tall. Six-four was my guess. He'd been wearing black from head to toe, blending into the room's shadows. The scent of blueberry muffins, ashes and untamed jungle had wafted from him. I rolled to my side, burrowing deeper under the covers as another black web formed in my mind. He had to…

I must have fallen asleep again because the next thing I knew, my eyelids were fluttering open and taking in the sunlight. A long while passed before I was able to orient myself.

The room appeared hazy at first, everything slowly slipping into place as if someone had wiped my line of vision with glass cleaner. I saw my peeling ceiling…my yellowing walls…my brown shag carpet…my men's loafers…my— Men's loafers?

My eyes blinked open and closed, then traveled up a pair of black pants, a firm butt, a belted waist and a well filled out black shirt. Ah, the Angel of Death, I realized, relaxing a little. He hadn't left me, after all. Once again he was standing at the side of my bed. He had his back to me as he spoke to someone on a walkie-talkie.

"Subject is roughly five-six, slim, straight brown hair, hazel eyes—mostly green. Full lips." He paused. "Uh, really full lips. Small scar on left shoulder. No tattoos…unfortunately."

Who the hell was "subject"? I wondered groggily. Me? It sounded like me. Maybe creatures of the otherworld preferred to keep things all-business.

"Subject has stopped writhing, and her skin is no longer tinted green. The bruises under her eyes have faded. Subject seems to be on the mend."

His voice was low and sexy. I might be weak, but I wasn't dead—or was I? I shivered. My gaze swept over him once more. He was as deliciously tall as I remembered, and so wonderfully muscled I would have liked to wrap my hands (legs—whatever!) around his biceps. Obviously, he worked out. A lot. His shoulders were wide, his back broad and his ass total, quarter-bouncing perfection. I bet even Sherridan's twins couldn't compare.

"Are you God's minion or the devil's?" I asked, my voice weak and raw. I'd put my money on the devil. (If I had any money, that is.) God had probably banned me from heaven months ago, when I filled my ex the Prince of Darkness's apartment with rotten fish while he vacationed with the girl he'd dumped me for. (One rotten fish for another, you could say. Not that anything could compete with Martin.)

The angel/demon spun around, and those crystalline blue eyes pierced me. Hot, so unbelievably hot. I sucked in a breath, my hormones sizzling to life despite my condition. Seduction and danger poured from him. He had golden skin, a chiseled face with the shadow of a beard, and shaggy, wind-blown hair. The black locks fell over his forehead, almost shielding the arch of his brows. His nose was slightly crooked—from being broken one too many times?

"Hello, Belle. Glad to see you're awake."

The sound of my name on his soft, kiss-me lips was in-toxicating. I fought the urge to reach out and trace my fin-gertips over that dark stubble dusting his jaw. I fought the urge to grab him by the neck and kiss the breath out of him. I fought the urge…oh, hell. Come to Momma. I tried to reach out, but my arms were too weak and remained at my sides.

Maybe that was a good thing. He was the first man to enter my apartment in, well, too many months to think about (without crying), so I probably would have done a poor job of pouncing/licking/*consuming* him.

"Don't be afraid. If you'll answer some questions for me, I'll leave you alone," he said. "Sound good?"

Okay, so he wanted to get away from me as soon as pos-sible. I had to look like total crap. Before he escorted me through the gates of eternity, maybe he'd let me shower, brush my teeth, apply ten pounds of makeup, slip on a red teddy and mist myself with pheromone perfume. Not that I wanted to impress him or anything. Really. A girl just needed to make a good impression her first day in the afterlife.

"You falling asleep on me again?" he asked.

"No questions," I said. I'd answered enough of those when Pretty Boy had interrogated me. As I struggled to sit up, the ache in my head roared to full life. I groaned and flopped against the pillow. "I hate to break it to you, but you totally suck at your job. Don't just stand there looking sexy, take my soul already."

"Subject awake but not lucid," he said to the walkie-talkie. For a second, only a second, I thought I heard the beat of his heart. Steady at first, then gaining in speed. Or maybe that was *my* heart.

"If I'm asked to give an evaluation on the other side," I said, "you're going to score real low."

"You must be thirsty."

The moment he spoke, I realized just how dry my mouth was. "Yes," I rasped.

"Subject is thirsty," he said, then hooked the walkie-talkie, or whatever the hell it was, to his waist. He disappeared. That was the only way to describe it. He moved so silently, so quickly out of my room, he was like a puff of smoke. There one moment, gone the next.

He returned as quickly as he'd left and offered me a glass of water. I tried to sit up, but the feat proved impossible. Reaching out, he anchored his free hand under my neck and gently lifted my head to the glass. I drank deeply, the cool liquid soothing my throat, my stomach, moving through my over-heated blood.

Calluses covered his hand. My skin began to tingle. Umm, nice. So nice. My increasingly heavy eyelids fluttered open and closed as he eased me back onto the pillow and set the water aside. "Your evaluation scores just increased," I said hoarsely. Sleep. I'd sleep a little longer.

"We really do need to talk." He gave my shoulder a soft shake.

My brain wasn't functioning at optimal levels, but common sense finally slipped past the thick labyrinth of stupidity blanketing my mind. I jolted into total wakefulness. Could a hallucination help me drink a glass of water? Would an apparition have calluses? Would a messenger of death be able to physically touch me? No, no and no.

The stranger standing in front of me was very real.

Panic washed through me. "Get out," I demanded, my alarm making my voice scratchy. "Right now." I wore nothing more than the flimsy bra-and-panty set I'd worn under the Utopia uniform I'd stripped out of, and though my comforter shielded me from view, it could be ripped away at any moment. In my weakened condition, I wouldn't be able to fend him off if he decided to attack me.

"Relax." His voice was so soft and soothing, I barely heard him. "I'm not going to hurt you."

Liar! Why else would he be here? My panic doubled, and I groped the bedsheets for a weapon. Of course I found nothing more menacing than a few feathers from my pillow. Like those would stop a freaking dust mite.

The man crouched beside me, putting us at eye level. I studied his eyes so I could give a description to the cops, not because they momentarily hypnotized me. His irises were a work of art. Dark blue branched from his pupils and blended with the lighter blue.

"I need to ask you some questions, Belle."

"And I need you to leave," I said, weak but determined. "Now."

Ignoring my demand, he asked anyway. "Do you know how you got sick?"

"I don't have any money, and my husband will be home at any minute."

"You don't have a husband. Baby, stop and think for a minute. If I wanted to hurt you, I would have done so by now. I'm with the CDC, and I just need to know about your illness."

I shook my head to clear it, trying to understand. "Centers for Disease Control?" Okay, that made a little sense. And he *had* had plenty of time to hurt/molest me, but he hadn't. Still. How had he gotten inside my apartment? How had he found out I was sick? How did he know I wasn't married? "Do you have any ID?"

He flashed a badge, and the action reminded me of Pretty Boy. "Believe me now?" he asked.

"Maybe," I whispered. "What's wrong with me? Am I going to die?"

"There's a chance."

There was a chance? Seriously? My stomach bottomed out, and my jaw fell open. Why couldn't he have lied to me and let me have a few minutes of blissful ignorance? "You're really with the Chronically Diabolic Cockwad association, aren't you?" I muttered.

His lips twitched. "Yes, maybe I am, at that." He held up the walkie-talkie again. "Subject is alert and talking, lucid at last. Do you know how you got sick?"

Silence.

"Belle, do you know how you got sick?"

"What, you're talking to Subject now?"

"Yes."

I shrugged, the action only a slight lifting of my shoulders. "The normal way, I guess. A naughty little virus entered my body and started playing Russian roulette with my immune system."

His brows cocked. "Subject is exhibiting a strong sense of humor."

"Subject is getting pissed." I used the last of my strength to knock the walkie-talkie out of his hand. My arm collapsed at my side as the stupid black box landed on the floor with a thump. "What kind of virus do I have? How long do I have before I...you know, kick it?"

"Kick it?" His lush, kissable lips dipped into a frown as he bent to pick up the box. "Do you know anyone else who has this type of sickness?" he asked, ignoring my questions. "Someone you've been in contact with in the last few days?"

Someone I've been in contact with... Ohmygod! I sucked in a breath. Sherridan. And my dad. Had my dad contracted this horrible, probably-going-to-kill-me disease? I'd visited him just two—or was it three?—days ago. He'd seemed fine, but with his weak heart he wouldn't be able to fight off an infection this strong. I bit back a sob, my throat burning.

"I need to call my dad," I cried, "and find out if he's okay." I dragged myself to a sitting position, wincing as a tide of pain rolled through me. I stretched out my arm, the phone so near, yet so impossibly far. Couldn't...quite...reach... Desperation flooded me, so intense I shook with it. "If he's hurt—" I couldn't finish the sentence. *Get over here, you stupid thing.*

The phone flew at me on a mighty gust of wind.

As the force of the wind hit me, I was thrown backward. My body clanged against the headboard and the phone soared past me, past the bed, and thumped onto the carpet. Even the CDC man was knocked on his ass. Shocked, I looked at the phone, looked at the charred nightstand, looked at the phone, looked at the man. Wait. Charred nightstand? It had really burned? And where had that wind come from? Where the hell had that wind come from?

Confusion, shock and disbelief rocked me, feeding off each other, almost rendering me speechless. Almost. "Did you see that? Did you feel that wind?"

"Subject just asserted prototype four," he said into the walkie-talkie. A scowl darkened his features as he pushed to his feet. "I really wish you hadn't done that, Belle." He sounded resolute. A little angry. Completely menacing.

"Done what? I didn't do anything. Am I going crazy?" I covered my mouth with a shaky hand. "That's it, isn't it? The illness is making me insane." I paused. "Do you know if my dad's okay? Have you heard if David Jamison is sick?"

"Damn it." The man tangled a hand through his hair and shook his head. "Why the hell did you have to do that?" he said. "Why couldn't you just have been sick, like I hoped?"

"I don't understand. What are you talking about? What just happened?"

"Let me break it down for you, baby. You drank the formula, and now I have to neutralize you."

# CHAPTER FOUR

NEUTRALIZE ME? I blinked, the words registering like a flashing red light. *Neutralize me!*

The sexy man stalked toward me as he withdrew a syringe from his shirt pocket. His expression was detached as he uncapped the needle. My eyes widened in horror. I held out my hands, palms facing him in an effort to ward him off. A rush of adrenaline whipped through me.

"Stop!" I shouted. "Don't come any closer." What had I done to make this man want to hurt me?

To my shock, he stopped dead in his tracks. He frowned. Slowly, so slowly, he pushed his hands against the air, as if he were a mime trapped in an imaginary box. His features crinkled in confusion, and he pushed again, only to be blocked again. He scowled, anger chasing away his confusion.

Short locks of his hair billowed around his temples—more wind? In my room?—and he slammed a fist into the air. *Bang. Bang.* The sound reverberated in my ears. My mouth fell open. He had hit a solid object—a solid object I couldn't see. An invisible wall? No, not invisible, I realized in the next instant, my shock increasing. The air had somehow solidified, become dappled; opalescent waves rolled through it, rippling, sparkling with dust.

That wasn't possible. That simply wasn't possible. As I watched, the man threw his shoulder against…whatever it was, rattling its very foundation. What. The. Hell? I'd never seen anything like it, never heard of anything like it. Was I hallucinating, after all? No, no. That couldn't be right. This *felt* real. That meant the air was stopping him, really stopping him.

"Drop the shield, Belle." His tone was flat, as flat as his eyes.

Shield? "Drop" it? That meant he thought *I* was controlling it. Was I? Impossible. No freaking way. Except, there *was* a strange sensation in my hands. An unnatural warmth. A bone-deep tingling. I'd never experienced either one before today. "If I do," I said, trying to sound confident, "you'll *neutralize* me."

"We'll talk," he said.

"Hell, no. You're not with the CDC, are you, you liar?" *Escape,* I thought then. This was my chance to escape.

If I changed my body position, would I accidentally disrupt the…shield? I didn't know, but I kept my hands lifted and out as I scanned the bedroom. Though I hadn't noticed before, there was a black, ashy film over the carpet and the walls. They must have burned with my nightstand. "What did you do to my room?" I demanded.

"*I* didn't do anything."

*The room doesn't matter.* I looked around again, this time doing what I should have been doing the first time: finding a means of escape. The double windows led to a fire escape, but there was a broken ladder and a fifty-foot drop. No thanks. The air vents weren't big enough to fit a poodle through, much less a woman. No again.

My only other option was the door. The door he'd shut, I

realized. The door his big, menacing body now blocked. I'd have to get around him, as well as the shield.

Somehow I scrambled out of bed without the use of my hands and with a body weakened from sickness. The action was almost too difficult for me, but I managed, slowly scooting to the edge of the mattress. The man watched through slitted eyes as I stood. Wobbled. Righted myself.

"I'm not letting you leave," he said.

"You might not have a choice." I tried to scream for one of my neighbors, but the action caused my stomach to cramp, and I doubled over. Fighting past the pain, I quickly straightened and inched a step to the right. Instinct demanded I run, but I didn't have the strength. Already my legs shook and my unsteady knees threatened to collapse.

"Plan to walk outside in that?" His frighteningly electric-blue gaze swept over me, lingering on my breasts, between my legs, but his expression remained detached.

He did it on purpose, I knew, to rouse a sense of self-consciousness in me and keep me planted here. But I could have been naked, and I wouldn't have cared. People could look at me all they wanted, as long as I was safe.

He wasn't done, though. He looked me over again, abandoning the detachment in favor of heat. White-hot, exquisite heat. He licked his lips. "Nice outfit," he said, "but I liked you naked better."

As a shiver coasted along my spine, I paused and flicked a glance down at myself. Cool air kissed mile after mile of bare skin. Okay, I wasn't in the bra and panties I remembered. I now wore a skintight white tank that stopped at my belly button and heart-covered bikini panties. *I liked you better naked.* I almost—almost—leapt across the room and slapped him. He had undressed and redressed me while I was asleep and vulnerable. The bastard.

"Go to hell," I told him, moving another inch. Surprisingly, the shield moved with me, forcing the man to shift to the side, slightly away from the door. Maybe I *was* controlling it. But how?

I moved another inch. Another. Then...nothing. Though I wanted to keep moving, my body was suddenly petrified, bringing me to a halt. I drew in a shallow, panting breath. *Move. You can do it.*

"You leave this apartment," he said, "and you're dead." His tone was no longer cold, but as hot as his expression had become.

"Judging by that needle clutched in your hand, I'm dead if I stay."

"I'm the least of your worries, Belle."

"Excuse me if I disagree. Dead is dead." *Move!* One shaky leg managed to slide forward. Long pause, deep breath. Step. Pause. Another step, another pause. Good. *You're doing good.* But I knew, deep down, that I'd never make it out of the room at this rate.

Very deliberately, making sure I watched him, he capped the needle and placed it in his shirt pocket. All innocence, he held out his hands, palms out. "Listen to me, Belle. I'm all you've got right now."

"Save it. I don't know why you'd want to hurt an innocent, sick woman, but—"

"You haven't been sick. You've been changing."

I managed yet another inch, but my arms shook more with every second that passed; my knees knocked with such force my entire body vibrated. *Stay strong.*

"I'm not going to hurt you," he soothed.

"Yeah, right. I watch TV, you know. Every homicidal killer says that, especially when they're holding a syringe."

"I happen to mean it."

Yeah. Sure. He didn't deny being a killer, I noticed. "I bet the CIA and FBI are looking for you. You're probably known as the Phantom Needle and you've done this to hundreds of women."

"Think about what you're saying. Please. You would have heard about something like that on the news. I'm a government agent."

I shook my head and fought a wave of dizziness. "You targeted me because I was sick and too weak to fight you."

"Then why didn't I hurt you while you were sleeping?"

Good question, and one that gave me pause. "Why do you want to inject me? What were you going to inject me with? And don't say medicine. I won't believe you."

A muscle ticked beside his left eye. Instead of answering, he asked me a question of his own. "How do you think you're able to erect that air shield? I know you've never done anything like that before."

I managed one more step before my body once again froze in place. This time, however, I couldn't force myself back into motion. My muscles were like stone, heavy and hard. I ground my teeth together in an attempt to draw on a reservoir of strength I simply didn't have.

I wasn't going to escape, I realized with despair, and there was nothing I could do about it. A sense of helplessness bombarded me. Infuriated me. Scared me.

"You drank the formula," he said. "Whether you know it

or not, you drank it. You have powers now. Powers a lot of people want to exploit."

"*What* formula? I didn't drink anything. I swear."

"Denying it doesn't change the facts."

"I didn't!" As I shouted, my knees gave out. I collapsed onto the floor, yet somehow managed to keep my arms up. But the shield began to shimmer, no longer quite so solid. My heart tripped against my ribs, speeding up, then skipping a beat altogether. "I didn't," I cried weakly.

"You work at Utopia Café, do you not? A café that sits across from an unmarked building. A brownstone."

I paled, I know I did. My mouth went dry. I didn't nod, but then, I didn't have to. He knew about me. Had he followed me? Watched me?

Never taking his gaze from mine, he backed away from the shield, from me, and eased into the green velvet recliner in the corner of the room, unharmed by the fire that had evidently decimated my nightstand. I usually read books in that chair (when I had a rare, spare moment), sprawled out in my nightgown, bundled in thick covers.

I'd never again view that chair as a relaxant, though. He made it appear decadent. A place for carnality. His big body lounged against the curves, his legs stretched out in front of him. *You can sit on my lap,* his expression seemed to say. *I'll take care of you. I'll protect you. I'll pleasure you.*

Liar!

I might have believed him, if not for the needle sticking out of his pocket. Not to mention the unnerving intensity in his eyes. They were predator eyes. Eyes that watched and waited for the perfect time to strike.

"Release the shield, Belle. It's draining you. Release it and talk to me." Pause. "Please."

The "please" didn't sway me. But I was too weak and my arms hurt too much and death was beginning to look like a holiday. Really, he could kill me now and he'd only be putting me out of my misery.

I squeezed my eyes shut for a moment, drew in a deep breath and felt my arms fall to my sides. A part of me kind of expected the air shield to remain in place, to prove I wasn't the one controlling it. It did remain for a few seconds. Then it wavered again, like waves in an ocean dancing over a beach, only to disappear altogether.

For several minutes, I tried to pull myself up and out of this defeatist position. For several minutes, I failed. I ended up staying on the floor, leaning my forehead against the side of the bed. The coolness of the sheets helped alleviate the feverish burn of my brow.

My shoulders slumped as I gazed at the man. He didn't pounce. He remained where he was, utterly relaxed. "Want some help?" he asked.

"Don't come near me." I panted with exhaustion. God, why couldn't I sound strong? Menacing?

His dark eyebrows arched, but he didn't comment. Didn't point out that he could now do whatever he wanted to me. A long while passed, each minute more painful than the last.

"You wanted to talk to me," I said, just to fill the death-like silence that had enveloped us, "so talk. You mentioned a formula. Does this formula have a name? What was in it?"

"I can't answer those questions," he replied.

"Can't? Or won't?"

"Won't."

"Why?"

"It's classified."

"Let's see," I said, not bothering to raise my head. "I almost died from a formula you said I drank. You tried to 'neutralize' me because of it. And now you're telling me I don't need to know exactly what it is I allegedly consumed?"

"I'm not going to tell you specifics about the formula itself, but you can ask me something else."

Fine. I would. "When did I supposedly drink this formula?" Let's just see if he could formulate a believable answer.

His lips pulled downward in a tight frown, and he regarded me silently. I found his stare unnerving and strangely arousing. I knew I shouldn't be able to experience any type of arousal in my condition, especially toward this man. And this was the second time he'd made me feel this way! Had he shot me full of some kind of aphrodisiac while I slept? I wouldn't put such a lecherous act past the needle-wielding, clothes-changing bastard.

"Do you recall a man in a lab coat who stormed into the café a week ago?" he asked.

A week had passed? A whole week? The news hit me hard, dizzying, upsetting. So much time had passed, completely unnoticed by me. But despite the time lapse, I recalled that day very well. Lab Coat had swept into Utopia, created havoc, then left me and everyone else to clean up after him.

"Yes." I gulped. "I remember."

"That man is a scientist who ran off with a top-secret experiment, and he poured it in something you drank."

"That's impossible. That's stupid. That's—a mocha latte," I whispered, dazed. Dear Lord. After the chaos at Utopia had died down and Pretty Boy had begun questioning everyone, I'd chugged my too-sweet latte. I hadn't thought anything of it at the time. Now…I just didn't know.

"We weren't sure he'd given it to you. We hoped he hadn't, of course. Then you didn't show up for work, which led us to check on you here, where we discovered you were sick."

"We?" I asked, the word barely audible. There were more men out there like this one? More men who thought I needed neutralizing?

"My employer and I."

My blood ran cold. Was Pretty Boy his boss? If the CIA wanted me dead, I sure as hell was going to end up dead. "Do you work for the CIA?" I croaked.

"Hell, no. I actually don't work for the CDC, either. I work for an agency that you've never heard of. Paranormal Studies and Investigations. PSI. We're like ghosts. To the rest of the world, we don't exist."

So why tell *me?* I feared the answer: I'd soon be dead and couldn't tattle.

Okay. Did Pretty Boy work for this same agency, then? That guy had been Freaky with a capital *F.* I could totally believe him capable of ordering my death. Wait. Did I even believe this man's story? He'd already proved to be a liar, saying he was with the CDC when he wasn't.

"You said the formula was changing me. What kind of changes?"

"Do you really need to ask? You called forth the wind. You commanded the air to solidify."

"I didn't call it," I protested. "It just came."

"Did it?" His lip curled on one side, giving him a sardonic edge.

"Yes." The word held a layer of uncertainty.

"If everything goes as we think, you'll soon have power over the four elements. Air, fire, earth and water."

My eyes rounded. "You're saying I'll have powers? Superpowers?" No way. Now I *knew* he was lying to me.

"No." He gave one jerky shake of his head. "I'm saying you *do* have superpowers."

I rubbed my temple, trying to subdue a sudden ache. "I hope you realize how insane you sound. Superpowers are for movies. Superpowers are for comic books. They are *not* for real life or average girls who can't hold on to a job."

"Tell that to your superpowers," he said drily. "And FYI, you're not average anymore." As he spoke, he shifted in the chair.

I scrambled backward. Not that I got far.

"Whoa. Easy." Slowly he lifted his hands, showing me he held nothing. "I was just getting more comfortable."

I relaxed against the mattress again, saying weakly, "I don't want you to get comfortable. I want you to leave. You've overstayed your welcome."

"Sorry." Amusement dripped from his tone. "You're stuck with me."

"Because you have to neutralize me?"

"Yes."

I'd expected him to deny it, and that he hadn't, that he'd flat-out admitted he still planned to neutralize (kill?) me, should have panicked me. It didn't. He hadn't hurt me yet, and I wasn't going to allow myself to worry until he came at me again.

Besides, I did not want to believe him; I *couldn't* believe him. That would mean I had superpowers. That would mean

*I* had erected that air shield. That would mean something terrible truly had been done to me.

"I wish I could give you an antidote," he said, "but we don't have one. Yet." At least he sounded genuinely apologetic this time.

"There's no need to hurt me. Honest, I'm not a threat to anyone."

He snorted. "Very soon there's every possibility you'll be able to control the weather. You'll be able to start fires without any provocation. Cause floods, tornadoes. How is that not a threat?"

"I'm not going to do any of those things," I ground out.

"You will. You won't be able to help yourself."

"How do you know that for sure?" I had to make him realize exactly how foolish he sounded. "You said it was an experimental formula. That means you can't be one hundred percent sure of anything."

"Let's just say I've spent a lot of time with human lab rats and I know when trouble is coming." He paused, his eyes growing dark. "The man who has done everything in his power to control the formula will want to experiment on you when he discovers you actually drank it."

"Is he your boss?" Was he talking about Pretty Boy, as I'd suspected? "Because if he is, you can tell him I didn't drink a formula, I don't have powers and I need to be left alone."

"Hell, no, he's not my boss. And I can't 'tell' him anything. He runs OASS, Observation and Application of Supernatural Sciences, a nongovernment agency that's PSI's biggest rival. Just so you know, PSI is the home of the good guys." His brows quirked, and he grinned slowly. "Well, the better guys, at least."

If I'd had the energy to throw my hands in the air, I would have. I had to be the last sane person in the universe. "This is crazy!" I said. "You're an ass, he's an *O*-ASS. You're all asses!"

"Time will prove the truth of my words," he said with utter confidence.

A tremor slithered along my spine. His unshakable assurance did more to convince me than anything else had. Time *would* reveal the truth, and whether I totally believed his claim or not, I needed to be prepared for whatever was revealed. I might not believe this one hundred percent, but *he* certainly did.

"What—what kind of experiments are we talking about here?" I asked.

"Let's see. He's skinned people so he could later coat their bodies with metal, making them impenetrable. He's cut off their arms and replaced them with weapons. He's injected people with poison, hoping their bodily fluids would contain those poisons and kill anyone they kiss, anyone they screw. Oh, here's one you might enjoy—he's even fed people an experimental formula to give them powers over the four elements. Everyone—but one—who's taken it has either frozen to death or burst into flames."

God. Was he trying to warn me that I, too, would either freeze or burn? "I don't want to die," I told him. "And I don't want to be a human lab rat. I'm a person."

There was a brief flash of guilt in his eyes, then nothing. No emotion. "That's not for me to decide."

My chin trembled, and my eyes burned with moisture. "Why are you telling me all of this? If you had stuck with the CDC story, I might have cooperated with you."

"You deserve the truth," he said gently. "Or at least as much of it as I can tell you." His features softened, completely at odds with the underlying meaning of his words. I deserved the truth, but he was still going to hurt me.

So much for not worrying until he came at me. I tried to stand, tried to push myself up and run, but every ounce of my being protested and I ended up slumped over again. Fear beat through me. There had to be—ohmygod. My gaze was focused on my hands, which were folded in my lap. My eyes widened, becoming impossibly round. No. No, no, no. I blinked, but there was no change.

Ice crystals had just formed on the tips of my fingers. I'd watched them, watched the crystals form out of nothing, simply crystallizing from my skin. The cold didn't bother me, didn't affect me at all.

In that moment, I believed him. I believed everything he'd said, without any hint of doubt. I would control the weather, he'd said. Rain, snow…sleet. I would cause floods, fires and tornadoes, he'd said. People wanted to experiment on me, he'd said. *Ohmygod!*

"What's your name?" I gasped, hoping to drown out thoughts of ice and experiments. I rubbed my hands together for warmth and managed to melt the ice. I didn't tell him what had just happened.

"That's not important."

"I disagree. I like to know the names of the men who want to kill me. It's one of my little quirks."

His lips twitched. "Rome. My name is Rome."

An exotic name for an exotic-looking man. I frowned. Considering the reason he was here, I had no business thinking of him as "exotic."

"I don't want superpowers, Rome. I don't want to be in this situation," I added desperately. "Help me get my normal life back. Please."

"I can't. I told you that. The scientist who created the formula, maybe..." He shook his head. "Even then it's doubtful."

"I'm willing to try."

"Too bad. Dr. Roberts is missing and no one has been able to find the crafty bastard."

Dr. Roberts—I committed the name to memory. That harmless-looking man in the lab coat was the one ultimately responsible for my predicament. *He* deserved a horde of killers chasing him. "Tell me something. If you and your boss are the good guys, how can either of you consider hurting me? Destroying me?"

His lips lifted in a smile completely devoid of humor. "We do what we must to keep the world safe. That's our job. Sometimes good people do bad things, even unintentionally, and they must be stopped. If you're left on your own, you could cause one disaster after another. Hurt millions of people. Destroy—"

"I told you," I interrupted, determined to make him believe me. "I would never do those things."

"You wouldn't mean to, but..." He left the rest unsaid. "What's more, you could end up in the wrong hands. Enemy hands, and you could be used against us."

My eyes closed briefly, opened, then closed again, opened, and I stared at the carpet. My remaining strength (not that there had been much) abandoned me with lightning speed. Black stars winked over my vision, interlocking and slowly weaving together to form a solid wall I couldn't penetrate.

He'd won. Rome had won. Any moment now I would sink into total oblivion. He'd be able to do whatever he wanted to me then. Kill me. *Neutralize* me. I tried to fight the seductive call of sleep, but it proved increasingly potent. How could I do this? How could I fall asleep amid such danger?

If he possessed any type of remorse, any guilt, any hesitation in doing his job, I had to bring that into focus now. Before it was too late.

"Rome," I said, the word nearly undetectable. "Please don't hurt me. You won't only kill me, you'll kill my father. I'm all he's got. I pay his bills. He's too weak to work. Without me, he'll lose everything, will be destitute. Homeless... dead. Have you ever had anyone depend on you for their survival?"

Something almost tender flashed over his face, as if he *was* thinking of someone.

Maybe I imagined it, maybe I didn't. Either way, I didn't have time to think about it. Darkness consumed me in the next instant.

# CHAPTER FIVE

I SNAKED IN AND OUT of turbulent dreams—dreams that were hauntingly vivid. A knife flashed through my mind, its sharp tip glistening silver, then crimson. A huge black cat growled from the corner of my bedroom before leaping and attacking—me? Did it attack me?

Panic was beyond my grasp. At least I felt no pain.

The images were disjointed, seeming to happen all at once, yet an eternity apart.

I struggled against the violence, determined to tamp it out, but I had no control over the situation. I was completely vulnerable. Utterly helpless.

Rome's rugged face suddenly loomed over me, hazy, blurred. He appeared resolute and a little sad. "I'm sorry," he said, his voice penetrating and chasing away some of the darkness.

"Don't hurt me," I pleaded.

"If I don't, someone else will and they won't be merciful."

"Please."

"I must."

"No."

Pause.

He lifted tendrils of my hair and sifted it through his fingers. "You're as innocent as Sunny," he said gently. He sighed.

"Who's—" I felt a sharp sting in my arm and jerked. A burning river entered my bloodstream, racing through me. A drugging peace followed the burn, settling over me, infusing every part of my body.

Down, down I sank into another realm of darkness, a spiraling void. There were no solid anchors. No sense of time or place. Thankfully, the dreams were held at bay, evaporating as if they'd never existed. I floated over a blanket of clouds.

Then…nothing. Yet…everything.

How much time passed, I didn't know. I only knew pricks of light soon began to invade my mind. With the light came strength, and my eyelids fought to open. I needed to wake up; I knew I did. Something called to me. Beckoned. I stretched my arms over my head. My back arched, popping each vertebra of my spine. It felt good to move.

The scents of frying bacon and scrambled eggs blended with the sugary sweet fragrance of syrup, wafting to me like a summoning finger that promised to lead me straight into paradise. My mouth watered.

As I forced myself to full wakefulness, I gazed around the bedroom. Confusion seeped slowly into my consciousness. I don't know what I expected to see, but what I saw wasn't it.

A faux marble armoire rested against the far white wall. But…I didn't own an armoire. Sheer dark blue curtains draped the only window, curtains that should have been green. The old, ratty quilt I'd bought at a garage sale swathed the bed in a multihued sea of colors, but this mattress was different, softer than mine. Overhead, a ceiling fan whirled slowly, providing a light but welcome breeze.

I didn't have a ceiling fan in my room.

Where was I? In the last glimpse I'd had of my bedroom, black, ashy smudges had layered the carpet and walls. These walls were bare, peeling but clean. I shook my head, and my gaze landed on a junglelike corner of thriving plants, brilliant green and dewy. My plants were dry, nearing death.

Obviously I'd been moved. The man, the one who'd wanted to neutralize me, had brought me here. Yes. Rome was his name, and that's what he'd done. Too bad he hadn't been a dream. His harsh, savagely sensual face was too vivid in my mind; his threats still rang in my ears. My fingers still trembled from having held him off.

Shouldn't I be dead? I glanced down at my hands, turning them in the light. At the very least, shouldn't I have awakened in a laboratory, strapped to a table, with evil scientists doing things to my body they wouldn't do to farm animals? Instead, I felt well-rested and clean. I even tasted mint, as if someone had recently brushed my teeth. My hair and skin smelled fragrant, like jasmine body wash. I did *not* want to contemplate what that meant.

*Get up, Jamison. Get out of here before Rome returns.* Yes, yes. That's exactly what I needed to do. I threw a leg over the side of the bed.

"Good. You're awake," a cold, hard voice said from the doorway. "Not trying to escape, are you?"

Gasping, I whipped my head toward the speaker, my leg dangling guiltily in front of me. Rome filled the doorway, his arms crossed over his chest. He wore another black shirt, the sleeves rolled up, the button at his collar undone. Black slacks hugged lean legs.

He could have been a businessman if it hadn't been for his

I've-seen-the-worst-the-world-has-to-offer eyes, with those taut, determined lines around them. The gun holster hooked to his shoulder didn't help the image, either.

"Me?" I gulped. "Try and escape? Never."

"Liar," he said, yet there was no heat in his tone. "Now that you're up, we're going to eat breakfast and talk."

Eat? Talk? But… "Why aren't I dead?" My blood chilled. "Ohmygod, you're one of those crazy people who enjoys fear. You'll probably tell me all the ways you want to hurt me, making me scream and squirm for mercy, before you render the final blow."

He frowned, the action so menacing it propelled a shiver down my spine. "Don't scream. Don't even think about screaming. I'll have to knock you out, *then* knock out the neighbors."

I gulped at his fierceness. There was a silver lining, though. He'd said "neighbors"—that meant other people were around.

"You have five minutes to get your sexy ass in the kitchen," he said, turning.

Sexy? I nearly gasped. My mouth did fall open. He thought I was sexy when he'd only seen me at my worst? I quickly quashed the surge of pleasure that knowledge brought, and cursed myself for being a sex-starved idiot. "Did you take advantage of me while I was sleeping?"

He paused and flashed an are-you-kidding-me look over his shoulder. Then he strode away, disappearing down the hall and leaving me alone in the room. "Five minutes," he called.

*Or what?* I wanted to shout, but I was having trouble catching my breath. "Damn sickness," I muttered, because I refused—refused!—to blame my breathlessness on Rome.

I would *not* be attracted to the man who wanted to kill me.
Even I had standards.

*Escape, dummy. Escape!* He'd left me alone, the idiot.
Well, not alone, but close enough. If I could get out of the
apartment/house/wherever I was, I could get help from one
of the neighbors. I scrambled from the bed, a little shaky, but
stronger than I'd been since getting sick. I wore a tank top
and panties (different ones than before, damn it!), which
meant the neutralizing bastard had changed my clothes yet
again.

First stop: bathroom. I found it easily, since it branched
directly from the bedroom, and I took care of urgent business.
After that, I raced to the closet. The opportunity to escape
ticked like a time bomb in my brain as I grabbed the first pair
of jeans I found and tugged them on. They were mine, obviously brought from my home. Actually, several items from
my closet hung on the hangers.

As I hastily jerked a T-shirt over my head, my stomach
growled. How long had it been since I'd eaten? The bacon-
scented air smelled *so* good. I hated to admit it, but that smell
nearly tempted me to forget about something as minor as my
own impending murder, and stroll into the kitchen, sit down,
and gobble up breakfast.

Why did Rome want me to eat, anyway? To poison me?
"Most likely, the diabolical fiend." Or maybe he didn't plan
to let me eat at all. Maybe the food was for him, and I was
supposed to watch him eat it.

The man was an enigma, that was for sure, and I didn't
know what to think of him or his actions. Past, present or
future. He hadn't killed me when he'd had the chance. He
hadn't done anything damaging—that I knew of.

"Three minutes," Rome called from the kitchen.

"Go fuck yourself," I whispered. I grabbed the tennis shoes that rested on the shoe rack and tugged them on. They were mine, so they fit perfectly. I sprinted to the window, pushed away the curtain and took stock.

Okay, so. I was inside a tall, red brick building. Another red brick structure was right across from it. I glanced down, saw that the fire escape had a workable ladder, and grinned with relief. When I noticed people strolling on the street below, I almost clapped. Excitement rushed through me. Once I got outside, I could scream for help.

My fingers curled over the bottom of the window frame and shoved upward. Except…the window refused to open. *"Amph."* I put all my muscle into lifting the glass. Nothing happened. "What the hell?" I growled softly.

"I secured the lock," I heard. "Same with the rest of the windows. Same with the front door."

I bit the inside of my cheek, tamping down a scream of fury. His tone was laced with humor and held a splash of smug superiority. How had he known what I was doing, anyway? He couldn't see me. Did he consider me so lame that he didn't even have to check on me? Well, I'd show him.

Maybe I could throw something at the glass, shattering it, then leap outside. I only needed a few seconds, just long enough to get someone's attention so they could call the police.

"If you're thinking about breaking the glass," he called, "you should know it's thicker than normal and requires major force to render the slightest crack. If you're thinking about waving to someone below or across from us, you should know the glass has a film on the outside that prevents anyone from seeing in."

I didn't doubt the truth of his words. At closer inspection, I could see the density of the glass and the glint of a shade. "Thanks for the news flash," I said between clenched teeth.

"You're welcome."

Bastard. *Come on, Jamison. Think!* There had to be something I could do.

*You have power over the four elements,* he'd said. I didn't feel any different, didn't feel like a powerful being. But I'd already seen the proof. I'd caused ice to form on my fingers. I'd held the man at bay with some sort of air shield. Did I still possess those abilities?

Not knowing what else to do, I backtracked several feet from the window and held out my arms. I'd show that bastard what happened when he messed with a pissed-off woman. (I hoped.) I'd blow the whole freaking wall off, *then* climb down. (I hoped.)

"Wind," I said softly, not wanting to snag Rome's attention. "I summon you."

A few seconds passed. Nothing happened. Not even a slight breeze.

"Wind," I repeated with a little more volume. "I summon thee to thy master." A little dramatic, but…shit. Again, nothing. "I command wind to blow through that fucking wall!"

Once more, my efforts were not rewarded. Why wasn't this working? It had worked before. When I realized what I was doing, thinking, I shook my head. God, here I was, accepting the fact that I had powers. Who'd have thought *I* would ever end up in this situation? Ordinary Belle Jamison?

"You won't be able to do it." Rome's voice flowed like warm honey from directly behind me.

I drew in a sharp breath and stiffened. He'd moved so

silently, I hadn't heard him approach. Now his warm exhalations caressed the back of my neck. He was so close I could feel the heat of his body seeping through my clothes.

I gulped but didn't turn to look at him. Probably lack of courage on my part, but I chose to think of it as prudence. "If you strike me from behind," I told him, "you're nothing more than a coward."

"For the last time, if I had wanted to hurt you, I would have done so already. Now, put your arms down and we'll go into the kitchen to have our chat."

"Hell, no." Maybe I should have tried to run away just then. Maybe I should have turned around and kneed his balls into his throat. Oh, wait. That wasn't a bad idea. I spun, raising my knee.

Rome gripped my shoulders, twisting me back to the window before I could do any damage. He pinned me in place. "I don't think so. I didn't hurt you, so you're not going to hurt me. Understand?"

My gaze narrowed on the glass. "Why *didn't* you hurt me?"

He ignored my question. "You ready to eat?"

"No, I'm ready to leave you." At my sides, I shook my hands, increasing their blood flow. Wind, come on!

"Fine." He sighed. "Keep trying. Failure will be good for you." He released the pressure on my shoulders, and I was able to hold my palms out in front of me. "You'll realize that you can't get away from me, no matter how hard you try, and we can get down to business."

My eyelids squeezed tightly, and I visualized what I wanted: a gusting, torrential wind. Hard, pounding. Several seconds passed as I waited for something, anything. Was a slight breeze too much to ask for? Obviously. I got zilch. Nada.

"I told you." He tsked with his tongue.

"I hate when people say that." Irritation swam through me. Irritation and powerlessness, frustration and humming thrums of awareness of him—which only increased my irritation. "I wouldn't be standing here trying to blow this window to smithereens with my bare hands if it weren't for you."

He chuckled, a tender purr at odds with everything I'd come to think about him. "Stubborn," he said.

"Determined." How dare he laugh at me? Tendrils of fury began to replace my other emotions, burning them away. "Look, I've been threatened, taken against my will to an unfamiliar apartment and infected with some sort of formula. And there's no end in sight! I'll try to escape if I damn well—" My fingers caught fire and I screamed.

"Wonderful," he said drily.

"I'm on fire. I'm on fire!" Panicked, I waved my hands through the air. The flames only intensified. If I hadn't already been convinced I had powers, I would have believed it then.

Rome sighed. "Stop wiggling and take stock. Does it burn you?"

His words penetrated my mind, and I stilled. The panic receded (slightly), as did the flames. The dying fire produced heat on my skin, I realized, but somehow not enough to burn me. "No," I said, shocked.

He reached around me, running his fingers down my arms to my now-extinguished hands, then tracing a fingertip over each nail bed. A delicious shiver stole over me, warm and erotic, enough to lick tiny embers of sensation over my skin. Hot, like the flames. Maybe hotter.

"You're a menace to yourself, not to mention the rest of the world. No wonder the paras want you."

"Excuse me. The what-a's?"

"The paras. Para-agencies." When I made no reply, he added, "Agencies that deal with the paranormal, like PSI."

"Whatever. Those agencies can go to hell," I said, returning my attention to my hands. There were no burn marks, not a hint of redness. What struck me most, though, was how delicate they appeared next to Rome's. While mine were slender and olive-toned, his were thick and strong. A lovely tawny color. My nails were a little scraggly—I hadn't had the time (or inclination) to file them lately. His were perfectly buffed, obviously well maintained. Scars laced his palms.

"How did I start that fire?" I asked. "That was—that was…"

"Dangerous." He let out another sigh. "You're going to be more trouble than I anticipated."

"You don't know how I did it either, do you?" I felt like crying. "I set my fingers on fire, damn it. I don't want to do that ever again. Not ever!"

"But you will. You'll do worse before the day is out, I'm sure. These new abilities have already found their place in your chemical makeup. They've already changed you. While you slept, they were erratic and uncontrollable." His words were whisper-soft, a caress that traveled along my spine. "Now…"

"Now?" I prompted, my stomach twisting painfully.

"Now you must wield them, not they you. You must dominate them or they will consume you."

I tried to turn and look at him, but he stopped me by resting his chin on top of my head. Fine. He didn't want me to move, I wouldn't move. "How do you know they'll consume me?" I asked, remaining in place.

"Maybe I've been where you are."

My mouth fell open, and I instinctively tried to glance at him again. He applied more pressure to my head, keeping me immobile. "You can control the four elements, too?"

"No." He didn't elaborate.

I bit the inside of my cheek at such a cryptic nonanswer. He'd been where I was, yet he hadn't experienced the same thing. How? Why? I despised this puzzle; I *needed* answers. Rome was the only person I knew who understood what was happening to me. And so, unfortunately, this government agent who'd threatened to neutralize me was also my only link to sanity. And I didn't even know his last name.

"Help me understand, Rome. Please."

No response.

Tears gathered in my eyes as wave after wave of helplessness bombarded me. "I won't let you kill me, and I won't let you take me to a lab. I didn't ask for this to happen to me."

"But it did happen." His fingers became steel shackles on my wrists. "And just so you know, I didn't keep you alive—" He cut himself off. "I didn't keep you alive to watch you escape." A note of warning dripped from his voice.

Before I had time to act, before I had time to protest, he had my arms anchored behind my back, wrists tied together. The cord he bound me with was cool and firm, unyielding— and foreshadowed malevolence.

My heart slammed against my ribs. "Let me go! What are you doing?"

He gripped my shoulders and whipped me around, finally letting me see his face. His gaze pierced me with a fierceness that somehow managed to shock, frighten and rock me all at once. It darted over me, hungry, reading me, perhaps, before it went flat again, the light in it suppressed as quickly as it had flared.

"Your five minutes are up."

## CHAPTER SIX

FASTER THAN I COULD OFFER up a prayer of "strike this bastard dead" I was trussed up like a Thanksgiving Day turkey and tossed over Rome's shoulder. While he had me in such an undignified position, he tied my ankles with the rest of the cord.

"Put me down this instant!" I shouted, attempting to knee him in his midsection.

"Stop wiggling." He purposefully bounced me on his shoulder, cutting off my air when my stomach hit the sharp edge of his collarbone.

When I could breathe again, I muttered, "You're squashing my kidneys and my pancreas! Do you know how dangerous that is? Put me down before I sink into a coma."

"If you can point to exactly where your pancreas is located, I'll do as you so sweetly asked."

"It's—oh! Damn you. Put me down right now. I do not want my face in your ass."

He chuckled, that deep, seductive sound all the more potent because this time it held rusty layers of disuse, as if he didn't allow true humor in his life very often.

Keeping his stride smooth and easy so I didn't bounce on his shoulder again, he sailed down the short hallway and into the kitchen. He plopped me onto a bar stool. Without the use of my hands, I teetered precariously and almost tumbled to the floral linoleum.

"Now we eat and talk." He moved to the other side of the counter, heaping a plate with scrambled eggs and bacon.

I glared over at him, ignoring my grumbling stomach. "We *were* talking. There was no reason to tie me up like this."

"There was every reason." His gaze veered pointedly to my bound hands. "Call me silly, but I'd rather not be roasted alive."

I took some comfort in that and grinned smugly. "Afraid of me, Rome?"

He snorted. "Afraid of your inability to control yourself, more like."

Score one (or twelve million, but who's counting?) for Rome. I lost all sense of superiority, and my shoulders slumped. He was right. If I could catch my own fingers on fire without any provocation—that I knew of—what else could I do? I hated having powers.

The moment the thought filled my head, I blinked. Powers. Me. Would I ever get used to those two words used in conjunction?

"You're as likely to harm yourself as me," Rome said. He set the plate between us, scooped a portion of eggs onto a spoon and offered me the bite. "Open."

"Like hell—oomph!"

The moment I opened my mouth, he shoveled in the spoon. The jerk. The bast— Oh, this tasted good. So good. The taste exploded on my tongue, the flavor more defined than anything I'd ever experienced. I closed my eyes, enjoying the buttery delight. He'd seasoned them just right. Killer, neutralizer and master chef. Odd combination.

He cleared his throat, gaining my attention. His eyes were on the food, not me, so I couldn't read the emotion there. Like I could have, anyway.

"I have a proposition for you." His voice was a little scratchy.

I swallowed and opened my mouth for more. If the eggs were poisoned, I'd willingly die. His brows arched. "Bite," I said. "What kind of proposition?"

The heaping spoon trekked back to my mouth. I kind of liked being fed—and I didn't like that I liked it. Especially by this man. I frowned at him, just to make a point.

"The kind where I help you, then you help me."

Another bite. "Help me how? By putting me out of my supposed misery? By helping me save the world from my evil self?"

A flicker of anger sparked in his too-blue eyes, lighting them up. They quickly darkened again. "Will you stop that already? I didn't kill you, and I'm not going to."

"You came at me with a needle."

"I didn't use it on you."

"Yes, you did. I remember a sting in my arm."

He rolled his eyes. "I gave you a sedative to help you sleep. You were tossing and turning."

"That doesn't negate the fact that you did, in fact, try to neutralize me."

"Are you this unforgiving with everyone?" He stuffed a piece of bacon into my mouth. "A man makes one little mistake and you hold it over his head for eternity."

I nearly choked and had to force the chunk of salty meat down my throat. Once I regained my breath, I gasped, "One little mistake? Did you just say one little mistake? Is that what you said?"

"Yeah." His expression was deadpan, with no flicker of emotion—which I absolutely hated and which he was so damn good at. I scowled while he put a bite of egg into his mouth and chewed.

How could he remain so unreadable? He was like a light switch. If he wanted me to know his thoughts, he showed them to me. If he didn't, well, I got nothing.

"I'm finding it hard to believe you consider trying to kill me a little mistake. *Little* is forgetting to put the toilet seat down. *Little* is leaving your socks on the floor. *Little* is putting a dent in my car and pretending you didn't do it." I was growling by the time I finished my diatribe.

"Are you thirsty?"

I blinked over at him, momentarily rendered speechless. "That's your response to me? You ask if I'm thirsty?"

"I'll take that as a yes." He pushed to his feet and strode to the olive-green cabinets that perfectly matched the outdated green striped counter. At least this room didn't boast the same peeling yellow paint as the bedroom. Instead it had green polka-dotted wallpaper.

With the familiarity of a man who knew his way around, he reached inside and withdrew a glass. "Is this your place?" I asked.

"Hardly."

"Then whose is it? Does the owner know you're a criminal and holding me against my will?"

"For the moment, this is *our* place." He paused, his expression mocking. "I feel warm and fuzzy all of a sudden. I just realized it's like we're on a secret honeymoon."

Honeymoon of horror. "Did you kill someone to get this dump?"

A grin tugged at his lips. "Do you think this poorly of everyone or am I just lucky?" He procured a carton of orange juice from the fridge and poured some into the glass, the pleasant gurgle of cascading liquid the only sound for a moment.

I could have said the obvious: I only think poorly of those who want to neutralize me. Instead I asked, "How long was I out after you stuck me with that needle?" effectively changing the subject. I didn't really want to know what he'd done with the apartment's owner.

"A little over twelve hours." Instead of bringing me the drink, he gazed down at it, his hands circling the sides. I saw only his profile, so I couldn't read his expression. Not that he'd have one. I'd never met anyone who could mask emotions as quickly as he could. "Would it help if I apologized?" he asked.

I blinked. "For trying to kill me?"

"Trying to *neutralize* you."

"Same thing."

"No, it's not, but would it help?" he pressed. His gaze remained on the glass.

I didn't have to think about my answer. "No."

"Then I won't bother."

My jaw tightened, almost snapping. "Why did you spare me? You still haven't answered that."

Ignoring the question yet again, he finally turned toward me and closed the distance between us, eyeing me determinedly. "I'll tell you this. If I'd been totally serious about hurting you, you'd be dead. I could have broken that shield if I'd put any effort into it. I could have sliced your throat while you slept. I could have pumped you full of drugs and done anything I wanted to you."

I shuddered. Yes, he could have done all of those things. He hadn't. "Why didn't you?" How many times would he force me to ask?

He shrugged, but the action lacked animosity. "Open."

Obediently, I parted my lips. The cool glass touched the edge of my mouth a second before a rush of tangy juice slid down my throat. The vibrant flavor awakened more taste buds. God, I'd never had such a delicious meal.

Rome set the cup aside and spooned up a dripping, syrupy bite of pancake. "That other agency I mentioned before—OASS, the non-government-sanctioned one—won't hesitate to take you down. They'll strike first and ask questions later."

I swallowed, the food suddenly tasting like lead. "While I think it's great that the man assigned to kill me—"

"Neutralize you," he interjected through clenched teeth.

"Whatever. It's the same thing. And while I—"

"It's not the same thing. I only meant to knock you out."

"Yeah, but you wanted to knock me out for, like, ever."

He uttered a frustrated sigh. "I never planned to kill you."

Another bite. "Okay, then. Once you knocked me out for most of eternity, what did you plan to do with me?"

His cheeks darkened, and the fine lines around his eyes tightened. "I planned to put you into a coma—uh, deep sleep, and take you to my boss so he could experiment on you, then put you to work for him or lock you up. There. Is that what you wanted to hear?"

I didn't know whether he meant the words in truth or in jest. Either way, they sucked. "What made you change your mind? And don't sidestep the question this time."

"I checked. You weren't lying about your dad." For some

reason, he sounded accusatory. "You pay for his stay at th
assisted living center, and he can't leave it because of his reg
imented medications." Rome shrugged. "There's more to i
than that, but I'm not going to discuss it with you right now.

Did I believe him? Did I believe that he now meant m
no harm? "If you're so big on keeping me alive now, prov
it. Untie me."

"I don't think so."

"But—"

He cut off my words by stuffing more pancake into m
mouth. "You have no idea of the damage you can do. You
inexperience is dangerous."

I forced the food down my throat. "Inexperience? Uh
hello. In case you were wondering, this isn't a new job I ap
plied for. *No one* has experience with this."

His gaze narrowed on me. "You're likely to get more ex
perience than you're prepared for if you don't learn to slow
down on the emotional trigger. Have you noticed that bad
things happen when you get mad?"

"Are you saying the fire is caused by anger?" I ran m
tongue over my teeth. "Well, anyone would be quick to re
spond with fury if they woke up half-naked with a hired
goon at the foot of their bed."

"Hired goon." He laughed. "I like that."

"Excellent," I said drily. "Then you'll probably like Ra
Bastard, as well."

He didn't lose his amusement. "All I'm saying is that your
emotions go unrestrained. You don't try to tamp them down
in the least."

"I do, too! If I didn't, I'd have fed you your balls at our
first meeting."

"Ah, that kind of sweet talk really turns me on." Another grin, this one slower, more leisurely, spread over his features, softening his expression, making him look all the sexier, and giving him a charm I found irresistible.

I stiffened, not liking how attractive I found him. How stupid could I be? Apparently the more time I spent with him, the lower my IQ dropped. My eyes narrowed, and I worked at the cord binding my wrists, doing my best not to let him see my arms wiggle.

"Just so you know," he said, feeding me another spoonful of eggs. His countenance lost all traces of humor; his eyes went flat. "I'm not the only hired goon to show up at the foot of your bed. Someone broke into your apartment last night."

"What?" My back straightened.

"He tried to steal you from me." Rome's voice deepened, became utterly menacing. "I knew more like him would come, so I got you out of there as quickly and quietly as possible and brought you here."

I paused, my blood chilling at the thought of the danger I'd encountered and hadn't known about. I didn't doubt for a second that Rome was telling the truth about this. My dreams, I realized, hadn't really been dreams. They'd been real. Too real. I'd seen a man come at me with a knife.

But he hadn't killed me because…because… The answer clicked into place. Rome had killed him first. Rome had protected me. Up to this point, I'd been able to use sarcasm and humor to mask my fear; I couldn't now. This was real, in-your-face death. It couldn't be undone. Wasn't pretend.

"He tried to stab me," I whispered, going pale. "I remember seeing his weapon."

Rome blinked in surprise. "No. He tried to kidnap you. He tried to stab *me*. You know an awful lot for someone who was supposedly asleep."

"I only saw bits and pieces, but I thought...I thought it was a dream."

"No, no dream." He pinched a bite of eggs. "What else did you see?"

"There was a jaguar there. I saw—" My brow furrowed. "Surely I'm wrong. Surely there wasn't a wild animal in my apartment."

"No, of course there wasn't," he said, his tone leaving no room for argument. "You're blending your dreams with reality."

But the sights, the sounds had been so real. So vivid. *Uh, hello. If a jungle cat had been there, there would be signs. Like a gnawed-off arm.* "Who was the man?" I asked, my voice trembling.

"I didn't care to stop and ask his name. All I know is that his boss, Vincent, won't be pleased with the failure. Vincent will send more agents, and honey, trust me when I say you do not want them to capture you. I've seen what Vincent does to his victims. He'll test you, painfully, cruelly, in ways even my boss has outlawed. And then, if you're still alive, he'll force you by whatever means necessary to work for him."

Terrifying words, but Rome wasn't finished. "And don't think you can lie to him, tell him you'll work for him and escape. *His* power is making people tell the truth. No one can lie to the man. No one. And it's not because some women find him attractive," he added drily.

Attractive. Pretty Boy...Vincent. It made sense. I'd wanted to tell Pretty Boy all my secrets, I recalled. The pulse in my neck hammered wildly. "Isn't that what *your* boss wants to do to me? Test me, then make me work for him?"

"Not painfully, and not by force. You'll either do what he wants or be imprisoned like the other naughty supernatural beings."

"What kind of supernatural beings are we talking about?"

"Shape-shifters of every kind. People who can walk through walls or suck the soul right out of you. I believe I mentioned the people whose bodily fluids are so toxic they'll kill you if they even breathe on you. Shall I go on?"

I shook my head. All of those *things,* creatures, living weapons...yet... "Why haven't I ever heard of these people before, Rome? Why does *no one* know of them?"

"PSI is damn good at its job, that's why. We make sure the world remains ignorant about the paras. About scrims. About all of it."

Dear God. "Scrims?"

"Scrims are supernatural criminals. Vincent is a scrim because he inflicts unnecessary pain, he kills when he could lock away, and he enjoys doing it. But he also captures and controls other scrims—in fact, he's captured more than anyone else and any other agency, so the government caters to him. They allow him to live, turning a blind eye to his experiments."

It was too much to take in, almost unbelievable. "Are...are scrims born or made?"

"Some are born, some are made. The more experiments are done, the more scrims are born. It's a vicious cycle." His expression softened. "What I told you about the prison is true, too. Château Villain, as we've affectionately dubbed it, is very real, and you won't like it. A sassy little thing like you would end up as Venom's bitch."

"Venom?"

"She used to work for Vincent. Her saliva has deadly toxins, and if she kisses you..."

I swallowed.

"Vincent is one of the reasons PSI exists. Fixing the catastrophes he and his brotherhood of assholes cause is a full-time job." Rome canted his head, considering me. "Do you remember that big warehouse fire in Chicago last year? The one that killed forty-two people and was blamed on faulty wiring? Lie. Vincent was testing the four-elements formula. Like I told you, several people burst into flames."

I shuddered, and felt the vibration to the bone. "Why does he want people to control the four elements? Why kill them for it?"

"Think about it. He can cause a drought, then, if the price is right, he can save everyone with a rainstorm. He'll make money from it, exploit it, kill people with it. Control people with it."

My God. My mouth dried a little more with every word Rome spoke. If my hands hadn't been bound, I would have covered my ears so I wouldn't have to hear anymore. There was a villainous world out there I'd once thought could never touch or affect me. How wrong I'd been. I mourned the loss of such innocence.

"I'd already placed special locks and bolts on the doors and windows of your apartment," Rome said, "so the assailant shouldn't have been able to bypass them as silently as he did. He was good, and he was determined to get to you. Whoever else Vincent sends will be even more so."

"What did you do with the man's, uh, body?" I asked.

"I took care of everything and even cleaned your place. No reason to concern yourself with the details."

I was kind of glad he didn't elaborate. That was all I could handle at this point. Clandestine activities so were not for me.

Why had I ever despised my safe, normal, *average* life? More fool me.

Rome offered me another bite of eggs, but I shook my head. My stomach was now knotted and clenched, threatening to rebel. "I'm not feeling so hot," I said softly.

There was a long silence, then, "I think you're ready to hear the proposition I have for you." He settled on the stool beside me and turned mine so that I faced him.

At first I kept my gaze on the open gape of his collar. I liked looking at him a whole lot more than I liked thinking about bad guys and evil plans. Against the stark black of Rome's shirt, his skin looked deeply tanned, worshipped by the sun. A thin smattering of black chest hair peeked through. Not enough to notice without staring, but enough to tantalize. What would it feel like if I traced my hands over his chest? Allowed my fingers to roam, explore...indulge?

*What are you doing, you idiot?* I could not let myself be attracted to him. Him, a man who had just admitted to killing someone. A man who'd been okay with knocking me out. No matter how sexy he was, I. Could. Not. Desire. Him. Right? Right. Even though he'd saved me from a murderer, I didn't know if I could trust him fully.

"Belle?"

I blinked, snapping out of my internal conversation. "What?"

"I don't think you're listening."

My gaze jerked up to Rome's face. He was watching me, a curious glint in his bright blue eyes. Several strands of inky hair had fallen onto his forehead. He should have looked boyish. He didn't. Danger radiated from him too fiercely. Danger…and seduction. He looked like every woman's most private fantasy, a god just roused from bed and eager to return.

*We decided not to think that way, remember?* "What were you saying?" I asked.

He rolled his eyes. "I was telling you that you were fired from the café, so you no longer have an income. You should have heard some of your phone messages from Ron."

I sucked in an angry breath, not liking that Rome had listened to messages meant for my ears only. "Did my dad call?" I asked through gritted teeth.

"Yeah," he answered, without hesitation and unapologetically. "We had a nice chat. He's a little miffed at you for not mentioning me, but he's glad you've finally found a man who will put up with your smart mouth. And he wanted me to know that you do have a sweet side, which I'll apparently find if I stick around and search hard enough."

A haze of red flashed over my eyes. "You *talked* to my dad?"

"Yes. Your friend Sherridan, too. She wanted to know why you haven't called her in the last few days, and asked if you were mad at her about the twins. I told her you've been expending your energy trying to win me over, and she told me to tell you to wear black leather and carry a riding crop. Interesting girl. Is she single?"

Oh, this was too much! Did my childhood friend and the man responsible for my creation not think it was weird to chat with a strange man I'd never talked about or introduced them to? So what that Rome had been in my apartment and answered my phone. For all they knew, he could have sneaked inside with every intention of killing me. Wait…

"Anyway," Rome said with a wave of his hand, "you might love them, and they might love you, but I'm all you've got right now. I'm the only one who can help you."

The grim warning washed away my anger and brought fear. Cold, very real fear that froze the tips of my fingers. Since anger caused flames, it made sense that fear caused ice. Too quick on the emotional trigger, Rome had said. He was right. About everything. "What should I do? Hide?"

"No. You have no experience in that arena. You'd be caught before you reached the end of the block. No, what you need to do," he said, tapping his finger against the counter, "is get OASS off your back. The best way to do that is to find the scientist who created the formula. Dr. Enrich Roberts."

I stared at Rome, incredulous. "That sounds great, but how am *I* supposed to do that? I have trouble finding my keys."

"I'll help you. Maybe he can reverse what's been done to you. If not, well, we can trade him—or pretend to trade him. His life for yours. I can't actually let Vincent have him again. He convinced the good doctor once that working for him would benefit the world. I can't take the chance of Vincent convincing him a second time."

What I got out of Rome's speech: There was a chance I could be me again. Normal, average me. The thought was intoxicating. Wonderful. Heady. Except…a stray thought intruded upon my happiness, and I frowned. "What do you get out of all this, Rome? You had orders to take me in. If you're telling the truth, you've disobeyed direct orders. You'll be working against your boss. Why would you do that for me? A stranger."

His jaw clenched and he shrugged, the action stiff.

"Maybe my boss changed his mind. Maybe he now thinks you're of better use in the field."

"And maybe you're full of shit," I said. He probably expected me to accept his explanation without comment. Well, he could stuff his stupid maybes. "Maybe you aren't really working against anyone but me. Maybe you plan to find and kill Dr. Roberts and blame it on me."

Rome remained silent.

"Before your boss let me loose, he would want to see what I could do."

More silence.

"Wouldn't he?" I demanded. "Tell me the truth, Rome. Do you really want to help me? Or are you trying to trick me so that I'll take the fall for something?"

Again, he kept his mouth closed and uttered not a sound.

Anger sparked inside me, but thankfully, I didn't start a fire. I continued to work the rope at my wrists and ankles, my hands and feet becoming as hot as my rage. My life was at stake here, and I couldn't risk my survival on the hope that Rome meant me no harm.

"You'll get no help from me," I declared.

"I don't want to frame you for a crime," Rome finally said. "And my employer doesn't know that I have no intention of bringing you in. Satisfied?"

"No." And I wasn't. "Does this employer of yours have a name?"

Another heavy curtain of silence fell, then he said, "John Smith."

Puh-lease. "Yeah, like a thousand other men. Fine. Don't tell me. I wouldn't know him, anyway. But why won't you take me to him? Give me a good reason to believe you. Tell me why you'd suddenly want my help in saving my own life when you were so determined to hurt me before?"

His dark brows arched, and our gazes locked. "You won't simply trust me?"

"No. *Nein.* Nay. Shall I say it in another language?"

He ran a hand over his face, pausing to pinch the bridge of his nose. "I'm not going to give you to my boss, and I'm not going to let you fall into Vincent's hands," he said. "Not now and not later. I give you my word. If we can't find the doctor, I'll find another way to get Vincent off your back."

"Why would you do that?"

"Because..." He paused, as if confessing was a painful chore. "Because—damn it. This isn't information you need right now."

I stopped working at the rope, poised at the edge of my seat. "Tell me anyway," I insisted.

"Because," he repeated, glaring at me. The heat of that glare nearly singed my skin. "Because I need to take my daughter into hiding, and you're the only one who can help me do that."

# CHAPTER SEVEN

IMMEDIATELY AFTER dropping that little bomb on me—*Rome has a daughter. A daughter!*—he shoved to his feet, skidding his stool backward. He prowled to the far counter and withdrew something from one of the drawers. He kept his back to me. "You're going to help me, right?" he asked.

"Whatever you say, boss," I said uncertainly. What was he doing?

"Good." He pivoted on his heel and came toward me carrying a—ohmygod! He was holding a knife!

Gasping, I jolted backward and tumbled off the stool. I landed with a thump, the cold linoleum floor doing nothing to cushion my fall. A sharp pain shot up my arms. Air shield, air shield. I needed a freaking air shield. But my hands were tied, literally! I tried to scramble back, pushing with my feet, but I wasn't fast enough. Rome reached me and tsked under his breath.

"So suspicious," he said.

"How can you do this?" I cried. What I wouldn't give to hold out my arms and blast him with an air shield. If only I could will that power to work without the use of my hands. "I'll—I'll fry you. I'll rip you apart with a tornado. You said I'd be able to command a tornado, and I'll do it."

Unconcerned, he tossed the knife in the air and caught the hilt.

"You need my help to hide your daughter," I reminded him. "How can you—ummph!"

Without a word, he flipped me onto my stomach. Through my shock and fear, I registered the sound of metal slicing through cord. Once. Twice. My mouth fell open as I realized he was cutting me loose, both wrists and ankles.

"You're free," he said. "Trust me now?"

I swung my arms in front of me; I parted my legs and drew my knees toward my chest, then jumped to my feet. With freedom came a surge of bravery. I whipped around, pointing a finger at his chest and growling, "Don't you ever come at me with a knife again."

One of his brows arched in an insolent salute. "Or a needle?" he asked drily.

"That's right."

"No sharp objects, eh? You're taking all the fun out of our relationship." He tossed the knife in the sink with expert precision. The tip embedded right beside the drain, and the hilt swayed back and forth. "There are a few things I have to do," he said, capturing my gaze with his own. His stare was intense, gauging. "Can I trust you to stay here?"

I batted my lashes innocently. "Of course. You can trust me as much as I can trust you."

"I'll take that to mean you *can* trust me," he snapped. A frown pulled his lips tight. "Don't bother trying to call anyone. There are no phones here. Do not leave this apartment, either. You *will* be hunted. I covered our tracks, but that doesn't mean you're completely safe."

My chin rose, and I regarded him with all the bravado I

could manage. "That's assuming they'll be able to capture me, even knowing my location."

He rolled his eyes and stepped toward me, closing precious personal space. I stood my ground, not backing away as I wanted—or rather, should have wanted. Heat radiated from him, and it made me shiver deliciously.

"You're vulnerable, Belle. Until you learn how to control your abilities, you aren't the amazing Periodic Table Chick, and you'll be defeated. Every time."

"Don't call me that!" I said, stomping my foot. The title seemed to drive home the fact that I wasn't *me* anymore. I was someone else, someone different and dangerous and hunted.

"Vulnerable?" he asked, lips curling. "Or Periodic Table Chick?"

"Both. I'm not some superhero. I *will* find a way to get rid of these powers, and then everyone will have to leave me the hell alone." Nothing was worth this kind of trouble. Nothing was worth being experimented on and/or killed.

"For your sake, I hope we do find the doctor." His tone had lost all traces of amusement, emerging grave and sad.

Wait. Something wasn't right here. Something... My eyes slitted and my hands fisted on my hips. "You're contradicting yourself, Rome. If we find him and he helps me get rid of my powers, I won't be able to help you hide your daughter, now will I? Not that I understand just how I'm going to help, anyway. And you can't just tell me your daughter needs to be hidden and then tell me nothing else. I need details. Why are you going to hide her? Is someone after her?"

He closed his eyes and rubbed a hand down his face. "You like the sound of your own voice, don't you? That's why you ask so many questions."

"Answer me. I'll just keep asking until you do."

"Fine. No, she's not being hunted. Not yet. But she's a little girl and she deserves a normal life. She'll never get that here. She'll never have any kind of life if I don't hide her, because she'll be drafted by one of the paras. With or without my approval." His voice was stark, pain-filled. "And I never said anything about *when* I'd let you try and get rid of your abilities."

I scowled. "Let me? Did you really freaking just say *let me?*"

"Have you noticed that you often repeat what I say? Yeah, I said let you. Unless you want to make something of it, which I don't recommend, I need to go."

Okay, he was seriously testing my (practically nonexistent) restraint, but it was a test I aced. I didn't blast him with rapid-fire curse words (bastard, son of a bitch, Nazi commando) and I didn't slap him until he dropped to the ground and blubbered like a baby. I did change the subject, not disclosing the fact that I would do whatever the hell I wanted the moment he was gone.

Still, I couldn't act too eager for him to leave.

"Where are you going?" I frowned. "Someone really could try to sneak in here while you're gone."

"I'm picking up a few things we'll need, and to be honest, I'd rather risk someone sneaking in here than risk taking you out into the world. You might burn it down."

I threw up my hands in exasperation. "How many times do I have to say it? People are not in danger from me." The more disastrous the deeds he thought me capable of, the easier it might be for him to do his job and take me to his boss. I hadn't been able to call a wind, for God's sake. And

so what that I'd set my fingers on fire? I hadn't hurt anyone
or anything. "This is—"

"That's enough from you," he said, cutting me off. "One
more word and I'm going to tie you up again."

I gasped. He'd do it, too, I thought, my fury increasing.
He claimed I was no longer his prisoner, that we were going
to help each other, but he was already threatening to bind me.
If he dared pick up that cord, I'd...I'd—

A short blast of fire spewed from my eyes and slammed
into the far kitchen wall.

I screamed the moment I realized what had happened.
Rome dived to the floor. He was able to avoid direct impact,
but several sparks danced on his cheek, singing the flesh. My
eyes widened in horror as I stared at the growing inferno.

"You were saying?" he asked, arching those insolent
brows again. He rubbed at his burned cheek.

My horror growing with the speed of the fire, I rushed to
the sink and filled a cup with water. I tossed the contents over
the flames, then repeated the actions over and over. It didn't
help.

Rome managed to contain the damage with a fire extinguisher—but not my mortification. My God. I *was* a menace.
I was dangerous. Maybe Rome and the others were on the
right track, wanting me rubbed out. The scent of burning
paint and wood filled the air. Black plumes of smoke curled
upward, making me cough.

After setting the extinguisher aside, Rome jumped up and
jerked the smoke detector from the ceiling before it could
erupt. He tossed it in the sink and gave me a pointed stare.
"Still think the world is safe from you?" he asked, showing
no mercy.

"No," I said softly, dejectedly. "I'm a freak."

"But you're a cute freak. I won't be gone more than an hour, okay? Try and control yourself."

"I will." My shoulders slumped. I could have killed Rome, could have set him ablaze. I wanted to escape him—didn't I?—but I didn't want to destroy him. Not when he'd never really hurt me.

Rome released a soft sigh. In the next instant, he was cupping my jaw in his hands and forcing me to face him. His fingers felt wonderful. Rough and abrasive, but utterly provocative. Sensual. Hot and strong. But most surprising of all, they felt comforting. I tingled. The warm, prickling lances seeped past skin, sinking right into bone.

"Belle," he said, his voice as gentle as his touch.

Slowly I gazed up at him.

He lowered his head. Breath caught in my throat, burning. Blistering.

I had time to protest as he slanted his lips over mine, but I didn't. I couldn't, not when I suddenly craved his kiss with everything inside me. He was dangerous and exciting, and with everything going on, I might not have a tomorrow. Actually, an hour from now looked pretty iffy. I would allow myself this pleasure without guilt. Without hesitation. Without pause. I'd take it, savor it, enjoy it, no matter how bad it was for me. It could very well be the last good thing to happen in my life.

He brushed my mouth once, twice. Perhaps he'd had every intention of leaving it like that, a brief, innocent touch, but I didn't let him. I opened my mouth and gave him my tongue.

Instantly it was all systems go. For both of us. No more lassitude. No more gentleness. Only undeniable need. Moaning low in his throat, he claimed me. His tongue swept past my teeth, sinking deep, demanding total surrender.

He angled his head to the side for deeper contact. His fingers tangled in my hair, clamping tight. He tasted like hot, virile man. And something raw. Something utterly carnal. I couldn't name it, not exactly, I only knew it was like nothing I'd ever encountered before. I wanted more, so much more.

Our tongues thrust together, eager and needy. I found myself gripping his shirt, holding him to me as if I feared he would slip away. Heat was building inside me, so much blissful heat. It began as a tiny flame, licking over my every cell, then spreading and branching through the rest of me.

My nipples hardened and strained against my shirt, abrading with my every movement. My legs weakened. I ached, yes, I ached. The fire grew. Rome seized my hair in a painful clench, as if he needed an anchor. As if he couldn't stand the thought of releasing me for any reason. Yet in the next instant he growled and sprang away from me.

"Rome?" I said breathlessly.

He stood an arm's length away, his breath shallow. "You were about to burn me up," he panted.

I was aching, burning, as he'd said. I wanted him back in my arms. Wanted his tongue in my mouth again. Wanted his erection pressed between my legs this time, sliding up and down, slowly at first, then quickly pushing me over the sweet edge of satisfaction. Except he'd meant "burn" literally. I'd almost flame-broiled him, I realized, seeing smoke curl from my hands. And still I wanted him.

How could I desire him this fiercely? *Him?*

I inhaled sharply, but that didn't help. Hints of his male fragrance seeped into my nostrils. Another tide of desire slammed into me, making my stomach quiver. Making another flame roar to life there. Damn it, I shouldn't crave him like this. Maybe—maybe we shouldn't have done that. I was vulnerable to him now, more so than before.

My hands fisted at my sides, and I concentrated on my anger. Right now, any emotion was better than desire. He shouldn't have kissed me! "Rome," I said.

"I shouldn't have done that," he said between breaths, parroting my thoughts.

"No. You shouldn't have." I curbed the urge to trace my swollen, pulsing mouth with my fingers.

"I'm not going to say I'm sorry." The words were a throaty growl, cutting through the ensuing silence. "And I'm not going to tell you I won't do it again."

I pursed my lips, fighting a rush of pleasure. *You're angry, remember?* "I didn't ask you to, did I?"

He paused, shook his head. Surprisingly, satisfaction gleamed in his eyes. "Didn't ask if I meant to do it again or didn't ask me to not do it again?"

"Oh, just shut up." I'd basically thrown myself at him, and refused to make it worse by voicing my desires. He had to know that parts of me—the most feminine parts—hoped he *would* do it again. Soon. My nipples were still beaded. The ache between my legs had yet to dissipate.

He reached out and traced his fingertips over my mouth, just the way I'd wanted to do myself, beckoning the fire all over again. "You can trust me," he said. Was that a trace of guilt in his voice? "Despite everything that's happened, or maybe because of it, you can trust me. I'm not going to hurt you. I'm not going to betray you."

Oddly, I wanted to believe him. I wanted to place my life

in his obviously capable (wonderfully wicked) hands. And yet, I couldn't trust my own instincts right then; I mean, look where they'd gotten me so far.

He took my silence for capitulation and said, "I'll check the building and surrounding area. If you stay here, you should be safe." With a final caress of my cheek, he walked away. Or rather, disappeared, leaving behind a deflated, empty room.

My face scrunched, and my gaze jerked from one corner to another. One second he'd stood in front of me, the next he hadn't. In fact, the only sign that he'd been here was the exquisite tingling in my face and the churning heat in my stomach.

"Rome," I called. I should have heard the front door close or at least a window slide. Since I'd heard neither, I padded through the dingy apartment. There was no trace of him.

How the hell had he gotten out so silently? As he'd promised, the door and windows possessed some kind of para-agent, futuristic bolt that spread silver, spiderlike legs through the wood and frame, linking them together. I highly doubted Rome could walk right through them. Or could he? After all, what did I know about the world nowadays?

"He's gone," I told myself. "How he left doesn't matter." Instead of wasting any more of my time on *him,* I trekked through the apartment again, this time searching for a phone. I wanted so badly to hear my dad's voice.

Rome hadn't lied, though. There were no phones.

"Shit." I paced the cramped living room. If I went back to my apartment, would my phones be tapped? The call traced? If I left this building and found a pay phone, would I be followed? Killed?

Taken?

*I'll only be gone an hour,* Rome had said. I had to make a decision *now*. Stay and wait for Rome, trusting him to keep his word and protect me. Or go, doing my best to keep myself safe—and the world safe from me.

Either way, I might make the wrong decision.

Either way, I'd be welcoming trouble with open arms.

Knowing that, I felt frustration and urgency rush through me. I massaged my temples. What I really needed was time alone, time to think this through without worrying when Rome would return. Time to make a decision on *my* terms, not his. Everything he'd said could very well have been a lie meant to lull me into submission. Or not. *Arghh.*

Something about the bargain he wanted to make bothered me, but at the moment I couldn't pinpoint exactly what. Still, the unsettling sensation was there and I didn't like it. Made me twitchy.

I expelled a shaky breath. Until I knew for sure and had this thing figured out, I was going to have to run. Run, just as I'd wanted to in the beginning. I'd be careful. I wouldn't let myself feel a single volatile emotion, which would protect the world. I wouldn't trust anyone, which would protect me.

Of course, I couldn't go back to my apartment. I'd have to go somewhere I'd never been. Somewhere no one would think to look for me.

Determined, I fiddled with the front door for several minutes, unable to loosen it. I didn't have long to escape, I thought, suspecting Rome would hurry back. I stared down at the doorknob. I'd never be able to pry it open.

I'd have to burn it off.

As quickly as possible, I searched the apartment and

located a vinyl bag. Everything of mine, I tossed inside. Thankfully, Rome had brought several pieces of my clothing and many of my toiletries. Of course he hadn't grabbed my ATM card, but the wad of money I found under the mattress made up for that. I stuffed the bills into my pocket.

Ready to face the door again, I stalked to it, glaring. How was I going to summon fire without creating an inferno? Maybe if I allowed myself a little anger. Only a little. Hopefully, the lock would burn and nothing else.

*Please let nothing else burn.*

Drawing in a deep, steadying breath, I dropped the bag at my feet. I popped the bones in my neck, preparing to work up a good (but tiny!) steam. To do that, I needed to think about things that angered me, but didn't infuriate me.

Okay. So. I hated when people cut in line. I also hated rude customers and menial jobs. *Oh, that's good,* I thought, giving myself a mental pat on the back as a kernel of anger sparked. However, the mental pat quickly doused the anger, flooding me with satisfaction.

*Concentrate!* What else did I loathe? *I know! I know!* I hated being chased by bad guys. I hated the fact that people wanted to kill me. I hated that I'd been given an experimental secret formula without my consent. Hated, hated, hated that I was now unemployed, broke, and that my dad's rent would soon be due.

My breathing became choppy as my anger intensified. My fists clenched tightly at my sides. I hated that Rome was so mouthwateringly sexy. Hated that he tasted so good. Hated that I already craved another sampling of him. And what the hell had he meant, blurting out that he had a daughter? A daughter, for Christ's sake. He hadn't been lying about that.

His eyes had been filled with stark, raw emotion. Desperate need and fear. Did that mean Rome also had a wife?

Oh, the bastard! He did. He had a wifey-poo at home. And he'd kissed me as if he couldn't live another moment without cleaning my tonsils. He'd touched my face and made me—

A stream of fire shot from my eyes and slammed into the front door. The force of it knocked me backward. As I fell, fire continued to spew from me and flames erupted everywhere I looked, licking a deadly, orange-gold path from one corner to another. Gasping, I squeezed my eyes tightly closed, cutting off the fire, blanking my mind.

But no sooner did I close my eyes than I felt my fingers heat. Flames began to fly from them. Dear Lord. I'd opened a fiery floodgate that didn't want to close. I felt its singe, its sizzle. The scents of ash and burning carpet, wood and plaster filled my nose.

My heart drummed erratically. *Calm down, Belle Jamison. Right now! Please calm down.* If I didn't, I would burn the entire building to the ground. People might die. Because of me. Me. Deep breath in, deep breath out. The heat continued to wrap around me, and my body responded in kind, enjoying it and producing more.

"I can control the fire," I said, holding out my hands and trying to draw the inferno back into myself. *Let this work, let this work, let this work.* "I can control the fire. I have power over the elements. They must obey me."

I opened my eyes, catching a glimpse of utter chaos before another round of flames burst free. I squeezed my eyelids shut again as panic washed through me. Dear God, what should I do? How did I stop this? *Think good, happy thoughts.* Nothing that miffed me even slightly.

Okay. What made me happy? Sherridan had a date with the twins. My dad was alive. Fifty-percent-off sales. Chocolate chip cookies—they increased my waistline, but I didn't want to go there. The thought of never having to serve coffee to snobs made me ecstatic.

With each new thought, my anger and panic receded and I felt my hands cool. Slowly I cracked open my eyes. A deep exhale became a heavy sigh of relief. An inferno might rage around me, but at least no more flames leapt from my eyes or hands.

I couldn't let the neighbors be hurt by this, though. I raced to the kitchen and was relieved to see the extinguisher Rome had used was next to the stove. Why hadn't I kept it near me? Stupid. As I sprinted back to the door, I sprayed everything in my path. White mist soon thickened the air, and the flames died to a gentle sizzle.

I dropped the now-empty canister, my arms falling shakily to my sides as I looked around, assessing the damage. The couch, TV, coffee table and my bag were ruined. The shag carpet was ruined, too, but that was a cause for celebration.

The front door had burned completely away—except for the freaking lock, which clung to the only beam left standing—leaving a gaping hole that led straight into the hallway. Thick smoke billowed and wafted out. An alarm erupted in the hall, screeching with enough volume to make me cringe.

Within seconds, the neighbors were pouring from their apartments. If one of these people knew Rome, they might call him and tell him what I'd done. He could be on his way back right now. And let's not even discuss the fact that I'd just announced my presence to the bad guys who might not have known where I was.

"What did you do?" an elderly woman demanded, crossing her arms over her ample chest. She wore a cherry-red robe and had blue rollers in her hair. "Does Raymond know you're in his apartment?"

Raymond? Who the hell was Raymond? Maybe the man Rome had stolen the apartment from—if so, sorry, Raymond!—or maybe it was a fake name Rome liked to use. Either way, I wasn't sticking around to find out.

"Turn off that goddamn alarm," someone else shouted.

"Did someone call the super? He's going to be POed."

"No way you'll get your deposit back now."

At least the apartment was so old it didn't have a built-in sprinkler system. Every one of us would have been drenched. "Tell the super I'm sorry," I said, and shoved past the crowd of onlookers.

"Hey, you can't leave," the woman in rollers screeched, momentarily drowning the sound of the alarm. "You almost burned us all. Get back here."

I found the door to the stairwell and slipped inside. Adrenaline poured through me, filling me as if I were drinking it. Urging me onward. The sound of voices and the wail of the alarm faded as I pounded down the steps to the ground floor. Strands of hair slapped at my face, momentarily blinding me. I kept moving and finally made it outside. Morning sunlight streamed from the bright Georgia sky, hot and oppressive. Humidity instantly beaded on my skin; gnats buzzed past me.

People roamed the sidewalks, unaware and uncaring of my turmoil. Cars meandered along the streets. Exhaust wafted to my nose, tickling my throat, and I coughed. The cough continued as I stood in place, trying to figure out which way to go.

I guess I should have thought this through a little more. I

didn't know where I was, where I should go, and had no real plan. I didn't recognize the area, only knew it seemed so *open*. Glancing left and right, I willed myself to calm. I'd be okay. I'd be okay. I'd be okay. No one looked suspicious.

Coughing, I turned right and walked. Just walked, acting as breezy as I could. Hopefully I could lose myself in the crowds until I oriented myself and— Shit! Rome raced around the far corner of a building, his eyes narrowed on me as if he'd expected to see me. His features blazed with fury.

Despite the heat, my blood chilled. And chilled. And chilled as fear bombarded me. I spun and leapt into a desperate run. Buildings whizzed by me, glazing with ice as I passed. People sidled out of my way, and those that didn't froze in place. Literally. I wished I could stop it, but couldn't make the panic go away.

I hadn't come this far to be captured by Rome. Again. If, in the near future, I decided to work with him and trust him, it would be on my terms. On *my* time. I would not be forced. I would not be coerced or manipulated.

Brave thoughts for a girl about to be caught.

The ground beneath my feet developed an icy film, and I began to slip and slide, throwing wild glances behind me. Rome, too, was precarious on the ice, yet he appeared to be closer every time I looked. I blamed my uncontrollable coughing, which slowed me down considerably. What was wrong with me? I'd never reacted this way to car fumes before.

*Get yourself under control. Don't think. Don't feel.* Not knowing what else to do as he barreled at me full speed, I stepped into the street. I got my heart rate under control just as a car honked and swerved into the center lane of traffic.

Another car, a bright red Viper, screeched to a halt right in front of me.

"Don't do it," Rome shouted.

I raced to the passenger side of the vehicle. Thankfully, it didn't freeze. My emotions were leveling out. Music blared from the speakers, but the driver turned it off when I ripped open the door. He wore an expression of utter surprise and white-hot anger. Uncaring, I bent to throw myself inside. In the next flash, a small dart flew past me and embedded itself in the car. Shocked, puzzled, I whipped my head to the side. A man—none other than the very beautiful man who'd questioned me at the café—stood several feet away, holding a gun. And that gun was aimed directly at me.

Ohmygod, ohmygod, ohmygod. I dived the rest of the way inside the car, then quickly shut and locked the door. *Don't think. Don't feel.* Several more darts hit the window, cracking the glass. I nearly jumped out of my skin. At least my coughing stopped.

The car's driver shouted several curses and placed the vehicle in Park. I think he meant to physically kick me out. He was a young man (probably a teenager), with blue hair and an eyebrow full of rings.

"Gas it!" I commanded shakily.

He snarled over at me. "What the hell do you think you're doing? Get the fuck out of my car." Another dart hit the window, cracking the glass a little more. "And who the hell is shooting at my window?"

"Drive. Please drive."

"Get. The fuck. Out! You're covered in ashes and it's ruining my leather. I'm calling the cops." He grabbed a cell phone from the dashboard. "My window looks like a goddamn spiderweb."

I dared a peek out of said window and could see (from multiple reflections) that Pretty Boy—Vincent, I recalled—was almost upon us. Rome, too, his expression dark with rage. Then Pretty Boy began shooting darts at Rome, but Rome easily ducked them. All the while, both continued toward me.

"She belongs to me," I heard Pretty Boy say. "The formula inside her belongs to me."

"Fuck you," Rome snarled in response.

Pretty Boy laughed. "If you want me gone, you'll have to give me the girl or kill me. But we both know you won't do the latter. You can't. *Pussy.* Or maybe you'd like to, at last, join me at OASS. Wouldn't it be nice to finally be on the winning team?"

The driver had been nudging my arm during the entire conversation, trying to get me out of his car, but I maintained a death grip on his dash. All too soon, Pretty Boy tired of Rome and returned his focus to me. He raised his dart gun.

"Drive now," I said to the Viper's driver, more desperate than before, "and I'll make sure you have sex tonight."

The car jerked into gear and we peeled out.

# CHAPTER EIGHT

HERE'S HOW THE NEXT excruciating hour broke down:

After we'd driven a sufficient distance from Rome (leaving him scowling in the street) and Pretty Boy (leaving him to hopefully choke on his dart gun), I asked my punked-out driver to take me to a cheap motel—a suggestion he loved.

I mean, the kid was all smiles. And why wouldn't he be? I'd offered to sex him up hard core. Someone should lock me up in a padded room and burn the key. But I had to go to a random location, as planned, or risk being found, and a cheap motel was the best my stressed-out brain could think up. How I would have loved to go to my dad's, instead, to throw myself in his arms and let him sing me to sleep like he'd done for me as a child. But I didn't want to involve him.

Sunlight poured through the car windows, but the air inside was ice-cold. Not my fault. The kid—what the hell was his name?—had the AC cranked up, blasting it from the vents. I couldn't get warm. My nipples were hard enough to cut glass.

As the scenery whizzed past, I saw a few scattered flower patches and multiple gas stations before the entire landscape was consumed by pine trees. Constantly I cataloged the traffic around and behind us. No one careened toward us or followed—that I could see. To be honest, the only people who seemed to care about us were the angry drivers who didn't appreciate our weaving in and out of lanes.

"Eyes straight ahead," I said when I noticed the kid was staring at my chest.

His cheeks colored. "My little pony needs the road to open up so she can run." He patted the dashboard.

Run. Yes. Forever? How long would I be hunted?

He glanced at me—at my face, this time. "Hey, you all right? You're putting out some seriously funky vibes."

"I'm great." *Considering I'm marked for death.* "What's your name?"

"Tanner, but my friends call me Crazy Bones."

"Uh, that's an…interesting nickname."

"I know. I got it from the ladies." His young chest puffed up. "It's for all the wicked-mad bones I give the girls that make them crazy for more."

I almost choked. "Bones…as in sex?"

"Fo sheezie." He chuckled, a sound of pure adolescent glee. "No one's ever jumped in front of my car like that."

No more "get out, bitch" from this one.

Tanner—I refused to refer to him as Crazy Bones—was cute in a bad boy sort of way. Silver rings winked from his eyebrow, blue hair fell over his forehead and a colorful python tattoo wrapped around the base of his neck. He was a little thin, and his clothes were baggy and ripped. He looked anything but poor, however.

"My dad said the Viper would be a babe magnet, but fuck if I had any idea how much."

"Your dad sounds great," I said drily.

His lips dipped into a frown, and his hands clenched over the wheel. Had I said something wrong? Before I had a chance to ask, he changed the subject. "Who was shooting darts at you, and who was that man chasing you? You were, like, getting it from every angle."

"The dart man is the devil." And I didn't know what Rome was to me. Potential savior? Potential downfall? Potential lover? A combination of all three? "I wish I knew about the one chasing me," I finally answered, choosing honesty.

"He looked pi-issed. I've never seen a scowl that mean."

"Unfortunately, that scowl is not false advertising." Rome's face flashed before my mind. Oh, yes. He'd been pissed. His pupils had been dilated dramatically. His teeth had been bared in a sharp snarl, his nostrils flared. If *he* had been blessed/cursed with power over the four elements, there would have been a spontaneous Belle BBQ there in the street.

Before today, I never would have believed something like this was possible. Anyone who said superpowers truly existed would have been filed in the folders of my mind under "Freaking Insane."

Tanner sneezed once, twice. He rubbed his nose and cut a narrowed glance in my direction. "Those ashes are potent."

"Are they? I hadn't noticed," I said drily, turning toward him. For the first time, our gazes met. His eyes were completely black, as if his pupils had swallowed his irises and— I shook my head, certain my eyesight must be compromised. "Are those eight balls?"

"Hell, yeah." He grinned, appearing younger and slightly wicked. "I could have gone for the tiger eye contacts, but this way the girls know right up front that I've got lucky balls."

O-kay. Too much (creepy) information. I needed to find a

happy place inside my mind and forget I'd ever heard that. *Happy place. Happy place.*

"So, uh, you never told me your name, baby," he said. He leaned back in his seat and stretched out one arm, draping it over my headrest.

I didn't want to give him the real thing. The less he knew about me and my circumstances, the better. "My friends call me…" Crap. Except for the names Hunted and Dead, my mind was completely blank. Surely I could come up with something. My gaze slid over the car, onto the dashboard, and—I grinned. "Viper. My friends call me Viper."

Tanner's brow furrowed. "Like my car?"

"That's right." I didn't try to explain. Whatever explanation he created in his mind was sure to trump any lie I could weave.

"That's not your name," he said, his brow furrowing deeper. "I thought I heard that man call you Elle. Or Belle. Or Nell."

Thinking quickly (and not altogether intelligently), I said, "He was Spanish, obviously, and was trying to say *el stoppo.*" Okay, so that sucked major ass. You try almost dying, being chased, then hopping in a car with a complete (horny) stranger and see what kind of lies you can come up with. Jeez.

A car honked and we swerved, tilting me to the side. I barely managed to hold back my scream. I gasped instead, hand poised over my heart as if such a puny action could slow it down. *No emotion, Belle. Feel nothing.* "Is someone trying to run us off the road?"

"Oops. My bad," Tanner said. He realigned the car, nearly swiping the bumper of a Jeep. "I got distracted."

Did I have to ask what distracted him?

He decided to answer, though I hadn't asked aloud. "Your shirt is so thin." There was a hint of accusation in his tone.

God save me from teenagers. Please. I didn't remember them acting this blatant about their arousal. Maybe that was because I'd been an ugly duckling in high school (and junior high and elementary school) and they hadn't been turned on around me. I'd been too skinny, had a mouthful of silver braces and had been taller than most of the boys (not that I'm a giant or anything). Yes, I'd even had pimples. But I'd been the best dressed, by God!

And just so you know, I wasn't the only voter in that poll.

Finally, the vehicle eased into a smoothly paved parking lot of an elegant motel, and stopped under the covered entrance. Magnolia trees in full bloom surrounded the sprawling structure, their pink tones giving the place a gentle, welcoming ambiance. A patch of wildflowers separated the parkway from the foyer, a rainbow of colors.

"This isn't a cheap motel," I said, frowning.

"Well, it *is* a motel and it's the cheapest one in the area." He cut the engine and unfastened his seat belt.

I released my belt, as well, and bit my bottom lip. The kid wanted to come inside. He expected to have sex with me. How was I going to get out of this one?

Tanner's gaze shifted from the immaculate building to me. "We can keep driving, I guess, and find someplace trashier."

"No." I sighed. My shoulders slumped. I'd be out of cash before the end of the day, and had no way of getting more. Silver lining: the people after me would probably assume I'd conserve my money and stay in a real dump. They wouldn't look for me here. Right? Right. "This will be fine," I said with forced ease.

"Don't worry about money." He wriggled his eyebrows at me. "I'll pay."

I pursed my lips. He thought I planned to rock his world; of course he wanted to pay. While that disturbed me on one level, it overjoyed me on another, solving several problems. One, I'd keep my anonymity. And two, I'd save what little (stolen) cash I had in my possession. I was, as usual, a girl on a budget.

"Okay, thanks," I said, fighting a wave of guilt. "Why don't you get the room? I'll wait here."

He shook his head, causing blue locks of hair to fall over his eyes. "Hell, no. I'm not going in there by myself."

"Why not?"

"Just because." His cheeks burned bright red.

Confused, I blinked at him. "Are you eighteen or older?"

"Yeah, but I'm not doing it alone. That's…embarrassing. Like buying condoms by myself or something. The motel people might think I'm getting a room to pleasure myself."

O-kay. There was no arguing with that kind of dumb-ass logic. I opened the passenger door and eased outside. Humidity instantly wrapped around me, dampening my skin and chasing away the chill. There were more gnats here, but the air was cleaner, fresher than in the city, and layered with the scents of flowers and honey. I inhaled deeply.

Tanner emerged, too, and sauntered to my side. He was a lot taller than me, taller than I'd realized. His pants were so baggy they hung past his waist and revealed the line of his tightie whities. Grinning, he draped his arm over my shoulder.

You had to give the kid points for pretending to be solicitous while covertly groping.

I fought another wave of guilt for lying to him as I pushed his arm off my shoulder. Thankfully, I didn't cause a national disaster—no telling what reaction guilt might bring. Tornado? Tsunami? No way would I sleep with the boy, though. Only one man heated my blood right now and I'd left him panting. And not from satisfaction.

Tanner deserved the truth, but I couldn't tell him yet. I still needed him. If someone managed to track me here, they would be less likely to suspect the gal with the teenager of being, well, me.

"This is so cool," Tanner said.

Our word choices were a wee bit different. What he thought of as cool, I thought of as horrifying. My heart raced as I realized how exposed I was outside, so I picked up speed and rushed to the doors. Tanner stayed close on my heels.

"Try not to stand out," I told him, gaze darting in every direction. "We don't want people to remember us."

"Uh, have you seen me?" he asked, a smile curling the corners of his lips. "I'm unforgettable."

Good point. "Just try not to say anything outrageous. Or do anything shocking."

He snorted, sounding amused and exasperated at the same time. "What can I do in a motel?"

I should have known those words would only lead to trouble.

Glass double doors slid open, and a cool breeze kissed me. The lobby boasted thick, violet carpet, a purple couch and glass table. A kitchen area claimed the right side, complete with sink, microwave and toasters. Several dining tables and chairs were scattered throughout. A long white counter curved in three directions, forming a complete *M,* and blocked the sitting area and kitchen from the offices.

Thankfully, the man behind the counter was the only person inside. He was in his late fifties, with thinning hair and a tall, lanky body. He appeared snobbish rather than menacing.

"How may I help you?" he asked, all business.

The phone rang, but he ignored it.

"We need a room," I said between rings. I tried to keep my face half-hidden with my hands.

Tanner gave the guy a chin nod and eyebrow lift. "That's right. We need a room. The two of us. Together."

I barely restrained myself from punching him in the stomach. Where was his embarrassment now?

The man frowned with nearly palpable condemnation, and asked for Tanner's name, ID and credit card, all the while clicking away on his computer. As he activated a room key, he said, "I hope you and your…mom have a nice stay."

"Very subtle," I said drily. I knew I didn't look old enough to have a child Tanner's age. At least, I better not. That might be reason enough to kill myself. "Let's go, son o' mine."

Turning, I grabbed Tanner's arm. My momentum spun him. "She's my *lover*," the kid called over his shoulder. "And I'm totally not her son."

I groaned and whispered fiercely, "We don't want people to remember us. Remember?"

"He could totally feel the sexual sparks we were generating, and I couldn't let him think I planned to let my mom play with my magic stick. That's just gross."

Outside, I was once again swathed in heat and humidity. I'd lived here all my life, but the oppressive temperatures never failed to shock my system, like stepping from a Frigidaire into an oven.

Birds chirped as we veered right, heading toward room 18.

When a young couple emerged from one of the units, I kept my head down, not wanting them to get a good look at me as I passed. After the dart incident, I wasn't taking any chances.

At our room, I unlocked the door and hurried inside. Tanner followed right behind me. The lights were dim, the air a little stale, but at least the place was clean. A queen-size bed pushed against the far white wall consumed most of the space. Dark purple blankets draped the mattress and blended prettily with the light purple carpet. Two floral pictures dotted the walls, hanging directly over two nightstands.

A pang of homesickness took me by surprise. I suddenly craved my own bed, my own apartment. My dad.

"Let's get this party started," Tanner said.

I glanced over at him, and my jaw dropped. While I'd been studying the room, he'd been removing his T-shirt, revealing a tanned, lean chest. In a few years, he'd probably bulk up like a warrior and the girls would find him irresistible. Skinny as he was now, with blue hair and eyebrow rings, the kid still managed to radiate a certain kind of sex appeal.

Now he was in the process of unsnapping his jeans.

"Uh, Tanner," I said.

"Yeah?" He didn't pause, but gave me a come-hither grin. His jeans fell to his ankles.

I reached out and wrapped my fingers around his wrists before he could discard his underwear. "When I said you'd get sex tonight, I, uh, didn't mean with me."

He stiffened, and his lips descended into a frown. "I don't understand."

"I, well…" I reached into my pocket and withdrew several

precious bills, already mourning their loss. "Here's fifty dollars. It's my pleasure to treat you to a hooker."

Twin circles of color bloomed on his cheeks. He hastily pulled up his jeans and began resnapping them. "I knew you were lying when you said you wanted to have sex with me. I knew it."

I didn't try to deny it. "I'm sorry." With my eyes, I pleaded with him to understand. "I was desperate."

He bent down and retrieved his T-shirt. He jerked the material over his head. "I knew you were lying, but I thought just this once I'd take a chance. Stupid me, huh?"

He sounded sad and angry at the same time, and the combination was like a punch in the gut. "How old are you?" I asked.

A muscle ticked in his jaw. "Nineteen. Why?"

"I just wondered." He wasn't much younger than me, yet in this moment he seemed infinitely so. "If you get the hooker, make sure to wear a condom. Maybe two of them."

"I'm not getting a hooker. Just keep your goddamn money. You'll probably need it." His shoulders slumped ever so slightly. He stuffed his hands in his pockets and simply stared over at me. "So you want me to go or what?"

"You want to stay?" I asked, surprised.

"It's not like I have anywhere else to go," he said, his tone bitter. His jaw clenched.

I flopped on the edge of the bed with a sigh. The kid had been so nice to me, and his expression was so forlorn. My guilt intensified, threading a thick web inside me. "Tanner," I began.

"Stop. Just stop. You're about to go all girlie on me and explain that I can't stay because I'd see it as an opportunity to try and sleep with you."

"Yes. We're strangers and I—" How did you politely tell someone you weren't attracted to him? Sure, men had told me that all the time. Albeit silently. The way they looked right through me said plenty. But it hurt nonetheless, and I didn't want to hurt this boy. "What do you mean, you have no place to go?"

"Forget I said anything, okay?" He turned away from me, but didn't move toward the door. He remained in place, his shoulders hunched. A long while passed in silence, before he softly said, "When you got into my car, you were the first girl to pay attention to me in a long, long time, and I liked it. I don't want it to end."

"What?" I jolted upright, my back straighter than a board. "I thought you were Crazy Bones, the sexual boy wonder."

"I made it up." He faced me again, his jaw tight, his expression defiant. "I wanted to impress you."

Rather than hearing this, I think I would have preferred being kicked in the stomach and having all my money stolen. With a sigh, I patted the space beside me on the bed. "Have you ever had a girlfriend, Tanner?"

His jaw tightened further. He shook his head.

"Maybe…maybe I could give you some pointers or something."

Another blanket of silence fell between us. "Really?" he finally said, his voice dripping with innocent need.

I nodded. Sherridan—a gal who apparently had an affinity for leather pants and riding crops—had once projected this kind of neediness, and still did at times, desperate for someone to love her, to show her attention. I vividly remember the way her parents had ignored her, indifferent to her wild, notice-me antics. She'd calmed down considerably over the years, but the void had never left her.

I wouldn't doubt if Tanner had experienced that kind of childhood, and my heart ached for him.

"Are you sure?" he asked.

"Yes," I said.

"Okay." His expression brightened slightly, and he walked toward me. The bed squeaked as he eased onto the mattress.

"What do you think is the problem? You're a cute kid— uh, guy. Man. You're a cute man."

"I don't know." He shrugged. "I see a girl I like, I approach her and lay my smack down, and she gets all pissy and leaves."

This was worse than I'd thought. "What do you mean by laying your smack down?"

"I mean, I show a woman my best moves and give her my best lines."

"Give me an example of your best line."

He spoke without hesitation. "Hey, baby. You want to take a ride on the Tanner Express?" He did a chin tilt, gave a wicked grin and held out his arms.

Dear God. I tented my hands over my mouth and blinked at him. "You honestly say that?"

"Well, yeah." He lost his smile, and his arms fell to his sides. "It lets the ladies know I'll provide a nonstop pleasure train."

"Uh, no, it doesn't. It lets the ladies know you're a moron and you don't respect them, will only be using them, and you couldn't care less if they have a brain as long as they have breasts and thighs."

"Fine," he snapped. "What should I say?"

"For one, I'd mention nothing about taking a ride on any kind of express." I should not have offered to help him. Even an artist needed something to work with. "You need to compliment women. Tell them how pretty they are. And don't mention that you really love how their nipples poke through their shirt or anything like that."

"I've tried compliments, and that doesn't work." He tumbled onto the bed with a sigh. "It's hopeless. *I'm* hopeless."

I nearly nodded in agreement, but stopped myself in time. "We just need to work on your game a little, that's all. I'm kind of on the run, as you probably guessed, or I'd take you out and show you the ropes."

He turned toward me, his face flickering with genuine concern. "Why are you running?"

"I can't say." I wished I could tell him, though. How nice it would be to confide in someone. "The less you know, the safer you are."

"Are *you* safe?"

"Of course," I lied, with a wave of my hand.

Doubt darkened his expression, but he didn't press me. "Do you want to help me, like, after you're done running?"

"Absolutely." And I did, I realized. He was endearing.

"Promise? You owe me, remember?"

"I promise."

He bounded up and strode to the nightstand, finding a pen and tiny notebook in the drawer. "Here's my number. Call me when you're safe." He paused, looked over at me and frowned. "Actually, call me if you need another ride. I don't like leaving you alone."

"I will," I said, but I knew I wouldn't no matter how desperately I needed him. I'd put him in enough danger already. "Do me another favor. Promise me you'll be careful and won't talk to strangers or hang out in dark alleys."

"Okay, now you *are* acting like my mom."

"I'm serious. What if I've put your life in danger?"

"I need a little danger in my life. Think how much it will impress the ladies."

I anchored one hand on my waist and wagged a finger at him with the other. "It won't impress them if you're dead."

"I can't die," he said, his eyes lowering and lingering on my chest. "I'm invincible."

Spoken like a true teenager. "Get out of here, Tanner, and don't tell anyone you met me."

"I won't." He gave me one of those slow, wicked grins of his. Lord, in a few years the ladies really would not be able to resist him. No matter what he said to them. "I know you told me not to tell potential girlfriends this, but you really do have pretty nipples poking through your shirt."

I slapped his arm, but I was grinning, too. "The girls and I thank you." I got to my feet, clasped his shoulders in my hands and kissed him softly on the mouth. "I think you're a fantastic guy."

He reached around me and pinched my butt. "Don't forget to call if you need me. I'll see ya around, Viper. Stay safe."

ALL ALONE, I locked the door and jumped in the shower, luxuriating in the hot water as it washed away ash, soot and the image of the beast monster I'd been. I washed my clothes, too, and hung them up to dry on the shower rod. Since I had torched my spare clothing, I had to wrap the bedsheet around me toga-style.

Exhaustion settled deep in my bones, and I plopped onto the bed. For half an hour I debated whether or not to call my dad. Would I put him in danger by calling him? What if someone had gone in and tapped his phone, hoping to get my location?

Before today, the most exciting incident in my life had been the bathroom funeral I'd held for Martin, my bastard of a betta fish. Oh, to time-travel back to the good old days. A sigh slipped from me as I stared at the phone. My dad would expect to hear from me sometime soon. If he didn't, he'd worry, and worry wasn't good for his heart.

That convinced me. Decision made. I'd do it. I'd call. Better to potentially give away my location than to cause my dad stress. If he had a heart attack because of me, I'd never forgive myself.

Fighting a yawn, I clutched the phone in one hand and dialed with the other. He answered on the fourth ring, and he sounded out of breath.

"Hey, Daddy. It's me." I strove to keep my tone casual. Breezy.

He coughed and a stream of sizzling static cracked over the line. "Baby doll. Hiya, sweetie. I didn't expect you to call. With your new man and all I thought you'd be busy."

I ignored the comment about my "new man." "Are you smoking again?"

"No, no. Uh—" *Cough. Crackle.* "I went for a little jog. That's why I'm out of breath."

"Daddy," I said warningly. "I do not support your silver fox habit just so you can put yourself in an early grave with cigarettes and cigars."

He sighed. "All right, you caught me. But I had to smoke the cigar, baby. Mary has been giving me the cold shoulder, so I had to find something to do with my hands. You know how twitchy I am."

"Is she refusing to talk to you now?" Their on-again, off-again romance kept me vastly entertained. Truly, I loved that he had a girlfriend. Or two. After my mom died, he hadn't dated anyone. He'd been too busy working and raising me, trying to give me a balanced childhood, acting as both mother and father.

With that thought, I suddenly wondered about Rome's relationship with *his* daughter. I wondered, too, about his relationship with his wife. Or girlfriend. Or whatever the mother of his child was. Did he love her? Did he crave her with every ounce of his being?

"I tried to tell her Janet forced me to kiss her," my dad said, breaking into my thoughts. "But Mary doesn't believe me."

"Janet forced you, huh?" I twirled the cord around my finger and felt my eyelids sink shut, too heavy to hold up. Knowing my dad, he'd probably grabbed Janet by the shoulders and planted a big one on her before she knew what was going on.

"Okay, okay," he said. "Maybe I asked Janet for a kiss. It's not my fault she looked like she needed one. What kind of man would I be to ignore a woman in need?"

I chuckled. "You are an incurable flirt."

"Mary tossed her breakfast bowl at me yesterday morning, and I've been washing oatmeal out of my hair ever since."

Such an exaggerator, I thought with a smile. The man had lost his hair years ago. "Other than the oatmeal incident, how are you feeling? How's your health? Are you taking all your medication? Are you popping Viagra again?"

"Good. Fine. Yes. No. Lord have mercy, my own daughter is questioning me as if I'm a criminal."

Yawning—it was unstoppable at this point—I released

the cord. I couldn't pry my eyelids apart to watch it bounce and twist free. "Don't try that wounded routine on me. You know it doesn't work."

"You sound tired, girl," he said. "How are things with my baby?"

"Good," I lied. Today was the day for lies, it seemed.

"I don't mind telling you that I'm a little upset with you, young lady. You didn't tell me you were dating someone." Exasperation and happiness layered his voice. "Rome seems like a nice guy."

"We only...dated—" any second I'd be hit with a lightning bolt for that whopper "—for a little while, but he wasn't right for me. I dumped him." Hard core. "Listen, Daddy," I said, quickly changing the subject. God, I was tired. "I've decided to take a vacation. You know, get some R and R. So don't worry about me if you call the apartment and I don't answer."

"Like I'd worry." He snorted.

Oh, he'd worry. He loved me as much as I loved him, and he was always looking out for me. I yawned again, this one longer, deeper. My limbs were beginning to shake, my mind forming more mush than thought. "I'm...going..."

"Get some rest, angel, and call me when you get back from your vacation."

"I love you, Daddy."

"Love you, too, doll."

We hung up. I rolled to my side and blindly replaced the receiver in its cradle. My arm flopped on the mattress and I stayed exactly where I was, too exhausted to move anymore. In the span of one day, I'd kissed a (supposed) government agent, developed superpowers, propositioned a teenage virgin and lied to my dad.

"Anything else you want to make me do?" I muttered to the heavens, pulling my knees to my stomach.

*Don't fall asleep yet, Jamison.* I had a lot to sort through, beginning with whom to trust. Not Pretty Boy, the bogus CIA agent who had tried to pump me full of darts. What a bastard. He tortured people. Killed them. I didn't doubt the truth of that. When Rome spoke of Vincent and his experiments, I could practically hear people screaming.

More than that, I remembered the deadness in Vincent's eyes.

Should I go to the police?

If I did, would they just hand me over to the government? To Rome? Hell, would they believe me? I almost didn't believe myself. Para-agencies, for God's sake. What about Rome? I was out of my league with him. He knew it and I knew it. Still, the question remained: could I trust him?

Rome had promised to help me find Dr. Roberts (and maybe an antidote) and make Vincent leave me alone. All I had to do in return was help him hide his daughter. Sounded like a great trade-off. Too good, actually. I guess what bothered me about the situation was that I was just, well, me. No training for this sort of thing. Unpredictable. I didn't know how to hide people, so what help could I ultimately give him?

Obviously, there was something he wasn't telling me. And if he wasn't telling me about it, it couldn't bode well for me.

"Shit." I had no clothes, hardly any money. Maybe I *would* call Tanner in the morning, have him take me shopping, and forget, if only for a little while, all of my troubles. I could give him more date tips and feel normal again.

*And you can put him in more danger.*

A sense of dejection filled me. I'd never felt more alone. More helpless. More tired. I moaned and covered my eyes with my arm, blocking out any hint of light. The hypnotic sound of the air conditioner wafted to my ears.

Lord, the stress of the day had zapped all my energy. Besides that, I hadn't yet fully rebuilt my strength from the effects of the formula. It was clear I wouldn't be making a decision on what to do anytime soon, so there was no reason to force myself to stay awake any longer.

When I woke up, everything would seem clearer.

Yeah, who did I think I was fooling?

# CHAPTER NINE

"DID YOU REALLY THINK you could escape me?" a husky, familiar voice breathed into my ear. "You may be the Periodic Table Chick, but I'm a damn good tracker."

I came awake instantly. A ball of fear slammed into me and quickly sprouted cold, treacherous wings as I became aware of several startling facts. One, Rome's heavy weight pinned my body to the bed. Two, my hands were tied above my head. No, not tied, I realized. Manacled by *him*. Three, a steely palm covered my mouth, preventing me from screaming. And four, the most startling fact of all, Rome had an erection that pressed against my belly—and I liked it.

Did I forget to mention I was naked beneath the sheet?

"Don't be afraid," he said. "You know I won't hurt you."

That should not have eased my worry, but it did. His voice was soothing, gentle. Warming.

Moonlight slithered through the crack in the curtains and bathed his face. His crystalline eyes seemed to glow, all the more vivid in contrast to the shadow beard that dusted his jaw. My tormentor. My rescuer. My...puzzle.

"Are you going to give me to him?" I asked the moment he freed my mouth. I didn't have to specify who "him" was. Rome knew. "He told you it was the only way to get rid of him."

He drew in a sharp breath. "No. That's something you don't have to worry about. I'll never give you to that disgusting scrim. I gave you my word, remember?"

He said it with such force, I believed him. As my fear abated, though, I encountered sparks of anger and dug my nails into my palms. My blood began to heat. How dare he sneak into my room. How dare he lie on top of me. How dare he look so freaking good. How dare he—

Wait. *Calm down. Calm down, Belle Jamison.* I couldn't let myself become upset or I'd start a fire. I just—damn it! He'd found me so quickly. I hadn't had time to decide if I trusted him or not.

Slowly I drew in a breath through my nose; slowly I released it. In the dim light of the room, I stared up at Rome's harshly sexy face. He looked stern, grim, nothing like his tender voice.

He looked wonderful. *I* must have looked ready to scream, though, because he covered my mouth again.

While I *was* upset he'd found me, a small part of me was suddenly glad to see him, all else be damned. It meant I wasn't in this alone, that I had someone to lean on, if only for a little while.

"You left me with a hell of a mess to clean up, Belle. As you well know, the general public doesn't know people with superpowers exist. I had to tell everyone a movie was being shot. Thanks."

"Mmm, mmm mmm mmm—" I narrowed my eyes at him. With his hand over my mouth, my words emerged garbled. I wanted to tell him to stop poking me in the belly with his penis! They should have been the first words out of my mouth, but I couldn't think straight with *it* close to me.

"Yeah," he said, as if he'd understood me. "I'm turned on. Barbecue me if you don't like it." Now his tone held an irresistible challenge.

If I didn't like it—puh-lease. Inability to think because of it did not equal dislike. What, he assumed I had no hormones? I might despise this entire situation, but I was (stupidly) attracted to this man. The part of me that was glad to see him urged me to spread my legs and allow him to fall into the cleft presented. He could rub me where I suddenly ached.

*Come on, Jamison. Show some restraint.* The admonishment from my common sense helped me remain unmoving. Deep inside I knew if I moved the tiniest bit, he'd be on me, kissing me, and I'd be on him, devouring him.

"I'm going to remove my hand again, Periodic Table Chick, and don't you dare think about screaming. I'm pissed at you right now, and you don't want to push me further." Gradually, he did as he'd promised. All the while, he frowned down at me.

"I'll push you further if I want," I said, mouth free a second time. No reason to let him wallow in the delusion that he could intimidate me. "And don't call me Periodic Table Chick."

"I dare you to try something," he said. "You won't like what happens."

"You won't like what happens if you don't get off me. You're crushing me." *Deliciously.* "I can't breathe, damn it."

"If you can talk, Four Elements Girl, you can breathe."

Logic sucked. "I'm dying here, I tell you. And don't call me Four Elements Girl. That's stupid. Besides, I've only used three. Fire, air and ice."

Rome rolled his eyes. "A technicality. I think you like me where I am just fine, and that scares you." His frown deepened. At least he didn't call me by another one of those ridiculous names. "I won't press you, though. Not now. I'm going to move. But if you point your hands at me, I swear to God I'll tie them behind your back and leave them there this time."

"Go ahead," I said smugly. "I can shoot fire out of my eyes."

Intense blue eyes narrowed on me. "Thanks for the reminder. Believe me, blindfolding you won't be a hardship, you little pyromaniac." More exasperated than angry (I seem to have that effect on a lot of people) he shook his head. "I saw the damage you did to the apartment. That's one hideyhole I can mark off my list."

My cheeks colored in embarrassment. "That was an accident. I didn't mean to cause so much damage."

"So a little damage would have been okay?" He lifted off me inch by inch, removing his weight just as I'd asked. Except without him, I suddenly felt cold and empty. He released my wrists, severing all contact, and crouched on his knees at the foot of the bed.

I jolted upright, very aware a thin sheet was all that separated us. Our gazes clashed as I tugged the material up and held it to my chest in a kung fu death grip. My naughty nipples were giving him a happy, so-glad-to-see-you salute, further increasing my humiliation.

"How did you get in here?" I said through clenched teeth.

"I picked the lock." One corner of his mouth curled, but quickly fell back into place, giving his face a dark, menacing cast. "Now you answer a question for me. Who was the boy who gave you a ride?"

Oh, no. No, no, no. Not Tanner. "He's just a kid, and if you hurt him, I'll fry you to a crisp. You'll taste ashes for a year."

He arched an insolent brow. "Embracing our powers already, I see."

"Just trying to survive." Asshole. He made it sound like it was a crime to utilize my new abilities. And can you say *hypocrite?* He wanted me to use them to help hide his daughter, didn't he?

"I'm not going to hurt the kid," he said grudgingly. I heard the word *yet* linger in the air silently, and my fists tightened. "Did you tell him anything about your situation?"

"Of course not."

Rome studied my face for a long while. "I got his tag number, which means Vincent, the man spitting tranqs at you, did, too."

I paled, literally feeling all the color drain from my face. "Do you think Vincent will find him? He's a nice kid and he doesn't deserve to be hurt."

"You should have thought about that before you got in his car."

"I was desperate," I snapped, slamming my fist against the mattress.

Rome sighed. "Don't get mad. Bad things happen, remember?"

I closed my eyes and forced myself to draw in a calming breath.

"The kid lost his tail on the highway with that stuntman driving of his," Rome added. "Happy now?"

I relaxed, but only slightly. "So how did *you* find me?"

"I'm a better tracker than most." There was no smugness

in his tone, only cold, hard truth. "I told you to stay at the apartment, Belle."

My chin tilted, and I know I radiated pure stubbornness. "Hello, did you see the place? It was kind of smoky in there. Not to mention that cops and firemen were on their way."

"If you hadn't tried to escape," he growled, "that wouldn't have happened."

"I needed time to think. *Alone*. Not that I got any," I grumbled. "Listen. We can talk about how stupid you were in locking me up later. We've got to do something to protect Tanner—the boy who drove me here."

"We?" His brows did that arch thing again, an action I was coming to hate.

My jaw clenched, and I glared at him. "Fine. Be that way. Act like a child. I'll do it on my own. I'll find him and I'll protect him." I covered my eyes with my right hand, losing my bravado. "I should have made him stay here."

"You should have done a lot of things." Rome plucked at the sheet, his fingers brushing my calf, my knee, then my inner thigh. It was a casual touch, and all the more sensual because of that.

I shivered, licked my lips, but didn't move or voice a protest.

"Don't worry about the kid." His voice emerged hoarse, strained. "I've stashed his car, and he's now sleeping in mine."

My muscles released their viselike grip on my bones as relief coiled through me. "How—"

"Some of us actually know what we're doing," he interjected drily.

"That's totally unfair!"

"Temper, temper." He tsked again.

"You better watch how you talk to me." Glaring, I leaned forward and pointed my finger at his chest. "*You* asked *me* for help, remember? I can assure you this is not the way to go about getting it."

Without warning, his hand snaked out and gripped my wrist. The touch was electric, erotic. "I'll let you do a lot of things to me with your finger." His voice dipped low. "But poking isn't one of them."

Warm tingles invaded my bloodstream, slipping between my legs and rubbing in all the right places; I gulped and jerked from his clasp. *Happy place, happy place.* "I, uh, need to know some things about you so I can make an informed decision about what I should do." There. A perfectly safe, nonsexual, nonthreatening subject. "Where are you from?"

All hints of emotion drained from his features, leaving him with a blank stare. He remained silent.

I tried again. "How old are you?"

Nothing.

"How old is your daughter?" Again, nothing. *Grr.* "I can't trust you until I know exactly how you think I can help her."

"Your abilities," was all he said, but a flash of guilt filled his eyes for a split second.

There had to be more to it than that, but I didn't press him. *Stop stalling, Jamison. You're going to trust him.* Unfortunately, he was my only option at this point, and I was finally ready to admit it. Though I'd fought against it, denied it, hated it, he'd been my only option all along. I didn't know how to hide myself (obviously). I didn't know anything about tracking people. My talent was getting pissed and accidentally burning stuff down. Can I get a woohoo?

"Once you learn how to use them," he added, and there was that flash of guilt again, "you'll be exactly what I need to ensure my little girl's safety."

"Fine," I sighed. "I'll work with you."

He ran his tongue over his bottom lip, an action more sensual than he'd probably meant it to be. "Maybe I need to rethink working with *you*. You're trouble, baby. A lot of it. And trouble I don't need, especially from someone who's this reluctant. It'd be real easy to knock you out, take you in and wash my hands of you."

Eyes slitting, I squared my shoulders and straightened my back. "It'd be real easy to smoke you right now." That was, if I could still summon fire. I was mad at him, but no flames were appearing. "You're really starting to piss me off."

"I'm trembling."

"You need my skills, Rome. Once I figure out how to use them, that is."

"I'm not so sure you're trainable anymore," he said flatly.

"So you've changed your mind in the last three seconds?" How's that for a twist of the ironic? I now needed to convince my captor to allow me to accompany him. My fists tightened over the sheet, bunching the material. "You can't do it on your own or you wouldn't have asked me for help."

"A moment of weakness, I assure you." He shrugged, but the nonchalant movement couldn't mask the hard, determined glint in his eyes.

"Liar. You were willing to help me escape rather than take me to your boss, and that goes against your orders. You need me. Desperately."

Silence stretched between us. Sizzled. I didn't allow myself the luxury of looking away and easing the tension. His intense eyes studied my features, gauging, measuring. Too bad my new powers didn't include reading minds.

"I said it before, but I'll say it again. You're no good to either of us until you learn to use and control your powers."

Duh! I tossed up one of my hands. The other remained locked on the sheet. "Just how am I supposed to learn? It's not like I can peruse the classifieds for a superhero coach. It's not like I have a lot of time, either. We're kind of on the clock here."

He covered his eyes with the crook of his arm. "I'll practice with you, and we'll just have to pray we don't destroy the entire world in the process."

Would he be a hands-on coach?

The stray thought drifted through my mind, and I frowned. *Hello, my name is Belle Jamison and I have a potty brain.* Geez. Wait. Rome's delectable mouth was moving. He hadn't stopped talking. I hated when I lost track of a conversation.

"—we track down Dr. Roberts, we'll have a better understanding of your abilities."

Since finding the bastard doctor had been on my To Do list, I eagerly agreed to Rome's plan. "Do you have any idea where he is?"

"Not yet." Pause. He shook his head, dislodging several dark locks of hair over his forehead. "God, I can't believe I'm doing this. I should just set myself on fire right now and save you the trouble." Another pause. "I once allowed myself to be taken captive so I could get inside a para-prison and help another agent break free. I was tortured unmercifully, but I have a feeling that will seem like a vacation compared to this."

I didn't like the thought of him imprisoned, beaten up, bleeding. Weird. "I'm not that bad," I grumbled.

"Baby, you're worse. Get dressed. I'll be waiting in the car."

I didn't move. "Where are we going?"

His gaze raked over me, lingering on my breasts, the juncture of my thighs. Heat flared in his eyes, so scorching my skin nearly caught on fire. Breath seared in my throat. "We'll be going to bed if you don't get dressed," he said, his voice laden with wicked intent.

Unbidden, my gaze traveled the path his had taken. I was completely covered, but the sheet was see-through. Even in the moonlight, my nipples were clearly outlined, as was the dark triangle of hair between my legs. I gasped. "You should have told me I was giving you a peep show!"

"What, and let you end it? Do I look stupid?" He turned away from me. "Hurry up. The sooner we're out of here, the better." His legs kicked over the side of the bed, and he stood.

Before I could blink, he strode to the door and opened and closed it without a single noise. Not a whoosh of air, not a squeak of a hinge. He was gone, as if he'd never been inside the room. I knew better, though. I still tingled. Still fought for breath.

I scrambled up, and my knees almost buckled. Would Rome always have that effect on me? Would my body always ache for him? Would every feminine part of me always weep for him?

I hurriedly dressed, my clothes damp and wrinkled from their washing. My shoes were still covered in ash. I would have loved a brush for my hair, but didn't have one. Instead, I quickly finger-combed the dark tangles. So far Rome had only seen me at my worst, and I didn't like that fact. If he found me attractive like this, how would he react if I wore full makeup, a slinky dress and stilettos?

*Not that you want to attract him, right?* one half of me said.

*Shut up, dummy,* the other half replied. If I wanted to take a train out of Denial and visit the harsh land of Reality, so be it. The man rocked my world, and I would dearly love to rock his. *So there.*

Not knowing what I'd find outside, I slowly opened the door and peeked. Six cars, several sedans, a truck and two SUVs occupied this section of the parking lot, barely visible in the darkness of the night. There were no towering street-lights here, only muted beams of moonlight. Where was Rome? Telling me which car belonged to him would have benefited us both.

*I guess he'd been too distracted to think of it,* I mused with a satisfied smile.

Several rooms down, a pair of car lights switched quickly on and off. Surprised, I squinted, narrowing my field of vision. Without the flash of lights, I would never have known the car was there. It was so dark it settled comfortably into the night, perfectly camouflaged. As I studied it and my eyes adjusted, I was able to make out two silhouettes through the tinted windows, one in the driver's seat, one in the passenger seat. I couldn't see actual faces, but was confident I was looking at Rome and Tanner.

I shut and locked the door behind me and moved toward the car, only then hearing the purr of its engine. The night air was cool and clean, and I breathed deeply—but the air froze in my throat as the passenger door opened and light flooded the inside of the car.

My feet froze, too. So did my hands—actually icing over.

Three men were inside the car, I realized, and none of them was Rome. For the second time that day, my gaze locked with Pretty Boy's, who was climbing out of the open door and reaching for me. My hand flattened on the hood, and I pushed myself backward. In a mere heartbeat of time, the entire car glazed with ice.

I shook my head. I'd just frozen a car. An entire car. By touching it. Somehow it seemed more surreal than the other things I'd frozen.

Pretty Boy scowled. "This doesn't have to be violent, Belle." His voice was as unemotional as I remembered. His eyes were flat, not kind in the least as he stepped toward me. "Cooperate and I'll make sure you're kept unharmed."

"You're not CIA," I blurted, stepping backward. Where was Rome? The cold was leaving me for some reason. I didn't think I'd be able to turn Pretty Boy to ice if he jumped me.

"I *am* your only friend at the moment. Rome wants to kill you. I want to help you."

"You're lying." Rome had had plenty of opportunities to hurt me, but he hadn't. Not once. "You're—" A solid wall of muscle slammed into my side, shoving oxygen from my lungs, and strong arms banded around me. I was jolted off my feet and carted away at an insanely swift pace. Rome's male scent enveloped me as surely as his arms. "You should have warned me," I gasped.

"Wait," Pretty Boy called. "Let's talk about this, Agent!" When Rome didn't respond, I heard Pretty Boy curse. "Get the other car," he ordered. "And for Christ's sake, someone catch them. Alive."

"There was no time for a warning." Rome's boots pounded on the pavement and he turned sharply, rounding a corner.

Behind us, I heard a man's curse, then frantic footsteps. My heart hammered against my ribs. "Put me down. I can run."

He ignored me, carrying me all the way to the back of the motel, where a four-door Crown Victoria waited. "Duck your head," he said, barely giving me time to react before he swung open the door and chucked me into the passenger seat.

I caught a glimpse of Tanner sleeping in the back seat a split second before Rome dived into the driver's seat. The car was already running, its front end facing the road, so all he had to do was slip it into gear and stomp on the gas. We peeled out, gravel flying from the back wheels.

*Pop. Whiz. Crack.*

*Pop. Whiz. Crack.*

I screamed as the window beside Rome shattered, spraying glass everywhere.

"Stay down," he shouted.

Our car jolted left, then right, then crashed into something. A body, I realized with the ensuing thump. Someone howled in agonizing pain, but we didn't slow. Didn't stop. We made another swift turn, hopped a curb and went flying across grass. Tires squealed when we finally hit the main street. Wind blasted through the shattered window, whipping inside the car and slapping my hair around my face.

The car's lights were turned off, leaving blackness in front of us. How could Rome see anything? How could another car see us? If we'd escaped Pretty Boy only to die in a fiery crash, I was going to be pissed.

I was having trouble catching my breath—and not in a good way. Fear pounded through me, ice-cold, intense. They had shot at us. Shot at us, for God's sake! We could have died. My heart tripped erratically, and a rush of blood roared in my ears.

Would Pretty Boy ever give up?

Was this how I would spend the rest of my life?

Another icy river rushed over me, lancing at my skin and sinking deep into my bones. I was so cold, mist was forming with every exhalation.

"Calm down, Belle, before you turn the car to ice and ruin the engine," Rome said. Tiny ice crystals were beginning to stream from the car's air vents. "Good thoughts, baby, good thoughts." He grasped the steering wheel and maneuvered us down another road. "Anger causes fire, fear causes cold. So good thoughts should neutralize both."

*Neutralize.* My favorite word.

A tremor cascaded through me. I had no happy place right now. I mean, emotions couldn't be forced. I could no more stop being frightened than I could stop loving my dad. And that meant Rome and I would fail before we'd gotten started. We would be captured.

"Remember when I kissed you?" he asked. "How good it was?"

*How good it was*...as if I could ever forget. An image of his face lowering toward mine, his lips seeking mine, instantly claimed center stage in my head, chasing away all other thoughts. Bye-bye, fear. Hello, desire. He'd looked at me as if I was the most beautiful woman he'd ever seen. As if he'd die if he didn't taste me.

Let's face it. I'm not a grade A specimen of femininity and delicacy. Sure, I'm cute. Some people might call me spunky. (I won't mention the people who call me a bitch.) Cute and spunky do not fill sensual, strong, larger-than-life men like Rome with unquenchable passion.

He'd wanted me, though. That kind of...absorption couldn't be faked.

"You erupted for me," he said huskily. "You were so turned on I could smell your desire, and I liked it. I wanted more. And I'll be honest with you, baby. You've got the hottest little tongue I've ever tasted, and I want it all over me."

My blood heated, and the ice inside me melted. I darted a glance to the back seat; thankfully, Tanner hadn't woken up and I could—

The car swerved again, causing me to careen from side to side. Rome's words faded from my ears, his face vanished from my mind. My hope to engage in an erotic conversation dissolved. The ice erected high walls inside me once again.

"I saw your face afterward," Rome continued, as if he hadn't a care in the world. "You would have come if I'd pushed you much further. You would have spread your legs and welcomed me inside."

I felt myself relaxing for the second time. "Yes," I said, not trying to deny it.

"You were wet for me."

"Yes."

"I was hard for you. I'm hard for you now."

Desire beat through me, and I squirmed in my seat. That he spoke to me like this, erotic and aroused, while danger enveloped us, only added to the thrill. I wanted him. I did. Wanted him naked and inside me, gliding in and out. Hard, so hard.

"If the situation had been different, Belle, I would have stripped you down and loved every inch of you."

"Soon," I breathed, and in that moment I didn't care how easy or foolish that made me.

"Soon," he promised.

After that, I didn't know what to say. I was ready for him. Eager. With only a few words, he'd set me aflame. When he next touched me...

Rome cleared his throat and shifted in his seat. His gaze flicked to me, then hastily moved away. The tips of my fingers were heating, wafts of smoke curling from them. I sank into my seat, hooked my whipping hair behind my ears and blanked my mind, the hardest thing I'd done in a long, long time. Breath shuddered from my lungs. I walked a fine line, I realized. Passion of any sort could cause a fire.

"You calm now?" he asked me.

"Yes." My head flopped against the seat, and I gazed at the moonlight streaming over the trees. *Don't think about Rome. Don't think about that kiss.* "I'd feel better if you'd turn on the car lights."

"No need. I can see in the dark."

No way. "How?"

"A long time ago, I signed up for an experimental...eye surgery where...something akin to night vision lenses were inserted into my ocular lobes."

What was with all the pauses in his speech? Still, the thought of undergoing such a procedure caused me to make a face. "Ouch."

He shrugged. "The outcome was worth the pain—mostly, anyway. Seeing in the dark has saved my life countless times."

I wanted *that* superhero ability instead of the one I had: creating disaster. "That's great and all, but other drivers can't see you."

Softly he chuckled. "That's the point."

"If you cause a crash—"

"Have some faith in me. I just performed a successful rescue. Like I'd really let you get hurt in a collision."

Trees whizzed past, mere slashes of green. "Did we lose Pretty Boy, then?"

"Pretty Boy?" Rome flicked me an irritated glance. "After everything he's done, you think he's pretty?"

I rolled my eyes. "Did we lose him or not?"

"Yeah, about a mile back." He snorted out a laugh. "Pretty Boy."

"So where are we going?"

There was an uncomfortable silence for several seconds. Then, "I have a friend," Rome said hesitantly. "She might be able to help us."

She? Okay, I seriously didn't like Rome having a female friend. A twinge of jealousy ribboned through me, and my hands clenched in my lap. I'm petty, foolish and absolutely ridiculous. I admit it. I'm not proud of it. But really, *she?* She? Somehow, in the last few minutes—yes, minutes—I'd come to consider Rome my property. I didn't like him having a female friend. After all, men and women couldn't be friends without sleeping together. Just a fact of life.

"We'll stay the night with her," Rome continued, "then figure out what to do with our third wheel."

"Third wheel?"

"The kid, remember?" Rome motioned to the back of the car with a tilt of his chin.

I peeked at Tanner again. He had yet to awaken. His lean body was strewn across the cushions, his features soft with dreams. Clumps of blue hair hung over his eyebrow rings.

Why hadn't he woken up during all the commotion? I wondered. My mouth dried as the answer sprang to mind; I whipped around to face Rome. "You didn't hurt him, did you?"

He frowned at me, offended. "I gave him something to knock him out for a while. That's all."

"You and your drugs," I muttered, but I was relieved. "So you neutralized him?"

His frown curled into a wicked half smile he tried to hide. "Something like that."

"What'd you use?" My gaze roved over Tanner once again. "I'm concerned with how deeply he's sleeping."

"I used a perfectly safe combination I like to call the Beddie-Bye Cocktail. He'll wake up in the morning with a light headache, that's all."

Now I frowned. "He's just a kid, Rome. If he's expected home, his parents might call the police when they realize he's missing."

Rome made a fast left turn and accelerated. "I did a quick background check on him. His mom left on his eighth birthday, and his dad, who raised him alone since, died a few months ago. The kid inherited some money, and he takes off a lot to spend it. No one will miss him or suspect foul play."

Dear Lord. No wonder Tanner had seemed needy. No wonder he'd wanted to stay with me. He truly had no one else. He'd lost everyone he loved. I'd lost my mom all those years ago, but I'd been too young to know her. More than that, I'd had my dad to lean on. My heart ached for Tanner, and I found myself reaching out and tracing my fingertip over his cheek. Poor thing. What would I do if—when—my dad died and I was left on my own?

A sharp pang radiated in my chest, leaving me feeling hollow.

In the next instant, a droplet of water splashed onto my cheek, followed quickly by a drop that landed on the side of my nose. Brow furrowing, I wiped them away. "Is it—" eyed the solid roof of the car "—raining in here?"

"Jesus, Belle. Good thoughts. Good thoughts!"

Another droplet. Confused, I turned to Rome. Liquid drops were sprinkling over him, as well, as if a small rain cloud had invaded the car. "I'm doing this, too?"

"Are you experiencing a strong surge of emotion?"

"Yes. Sadness."

"Then you're doing this." His tone was grave.

I covered my mouth with my hand; my eyes widened. "I don't want to do this. I don't want my every emotion to create a change in the weather. I just want to be *me*. I want to feel and not worry that I'm going to burn, freeze or drown someone."

The fine lines around his eyes tightened, and the shadows on his cheeks deepened. In that moment he looked scary, but so comforting I could have thrown myself in his arms. "I know, baby," he said. "The formula sucks ass, but there's nothing we can do about it right now."

"Why did Dr. Roberts create the formula in the first place?" I asked with a gulp.

"From what I've heard, he meant to do America a great service. He wanted to make our military stronger. He just fell in with the wrong people, people who hoped to exploit his ambition." Rome reached over and massaged my neck. "It won't always be this hard for you."

"How can you be sure?" I asked hopefully.

"You'll learn to control the abilities."

"When?" God, when?

"Soon. Let's pray it's soon."

## CHAPTER TEN

WHAT ROME FAILED TO TELL me in the car was that his "friend," Lexis Bradley, was a psychic, as well as one of the most beautiful women in the known universe. She was also hot for his body, and the mother of his child.

I discovered all of that on my own, and then was pissed as hell. Allow me to relive the unfolding of my enlightenment for you.

We rode a plush, mirrored elevator (that was bigger than my entire apartment) to the top of a towering chrome-and-glass building. Below, the doormen and subsequent security guards hadn't given us a second glance when we'd entered—despite the fact that Rome, the caveman, carried a snoozing Tanner over his shoulder. They'd waved at him as if they'd been expecting him.

I guess Rome came here a lot. With strange people in tow.

I wasn't sure what to make of that.

When we reached Lexis's door, she opened it before we could knock. I stood stunned for a moment, gawking at her loveliness. She had sleek, straight black hair that hung down her back like a midnight cloud. Her eyes were a vibrant emerald-green and up-tilted at the corners. Her olive skin glowed to perfection. I swear to God, she looked like a work of art come to life.

I'd like to say she did not threaten my self-esteem. Yeah, I'd like to say that. Too bad it'd be a hideous lie. I looked like steaming dog poo in comparison, and I knew it.

Apparently she knew a lot of stuff, too.

"I knew you were coming," she said, her voice soft and lilting, with the hint of an accent I couldn't place. Definitely not Georgian, though. Her green gaze ate Rome up, devouring him. Mentally stripping him. "Come in. Please."

"Sorry to crash on you so late." Rome swept past her with Tanner bouncing on his shoulder. "How's Sunny?"

"Sleeping." Lexis nearly shut the door in my face.

I caught it with my foot and shoved my way inside. Sunny…I'd heard the name before, I think. It hovered on the edge of my memory. "I'd like to come in, too," I said.

"Oops. Sorry," Lexis said, not sparing me a glance. "I didn't see you."

I mentally flipped her off.

"Put the boy in the yellow room," she told Rome. "I've already made the bed for him."

As I dogged Rome into the hallway, my shoulder brushed Lexis's. She whipped around, her face a kaleidoscope of horror. I stopped. My lips thinned into a scowl. What, did I smell? Did I offend her delicate sensibilities? Did my hideous ugliness ruin the ambiance of her home? *Maybe I should warn her that I'm a dangerous weapon and pissing me off isn't a good idea.*

She tore her gaze from me, reached back with a shaky hand and closed the front door. Her cheeks were colorless by the time she faced me again. "Your name is Belle," she said, a statement, not a question.

"Yeah. Did Rome mention me?" Had that sweet man told people about me already? He must like me, then.

"No. He didn't." She strode to a nearby table, lifted a cell phone and dialed a number. "You need to come over here right now," she said into the mouthpiece, and hung up.

O-kay. Had she just told someone to come and get me? Had she blown my cover? My heart skipped a beat.

Rome emerged from the hall minus his burden. He approached my side, causing Lexis to frown. "I've called your brother," she told him.

At the same time I said, "She called someone—" Wait. Rome had a brother? "Is he an agent, too?" I asked.

Confusion flittered over Rome's face. He ignored me, saying to Lexis, "Why did you call Brit?"

"I want him to take Sunny for a few days." Lexis anchored one hand on her waist. "Why have you not taken Belle to John?"

John. As in John Smith, Rome's boss? Huh. I'd thought he'd been lying about his boss's name.

Rome stiffened and became utterly still, not even breathing. "Is Sunny in danger?" He didn't bother responding to the question about me, I noticed.

"She'll be fine," Lexis soothed, reaching out and stroking his arm. "I promise. Your friend, who should be locked in a laboratory right now, is going to cause trouble. I want Sunny out of the building."

I popped my jaw. Lexis, who should be punched in the face right now, was working her way up my People to Punish When I Could Control My Powers list. But much as I wished I could discount the "cause trouble" comment, I couldn't. Not after the fires, the ice and the car chase. "Who's Sunny?"

"Our daughter," Lexis told me haughtily.

I stopped breathing for a moment. *Our daughter.* As in

Rome's and Lexis's. So. Rome *had* been intimate with this beautiful, perfect woman. Was he still? My hands twitched at my sides. Other than the fact that we'd admitted we wanted to sleep together, I had no claim on Rome. Still, I was feeling very possessive at the moment.

"You want to take me to your *friend's* house, huh?" I said quietly, darkly. "Are you two married?"

"Not anymore," Rome said. That was a relief, at least. I hadn't kissed and fondled a married man. To Lexis he said, "I'll go wake Sunny up and get her things packed." He strode away in the same direction he'd taken Tanner, leaving Lexis and me alone again.

We didn't speak. Not a single word. We didn't even look at each other, just stood there. Uncomfortable. She was the mother of Rome's child, for God's sake.

I used the time to inspect the apartment. I don't think I'd ever been in the presence of so much wealth. A panoramic wall of windows consumed the far edge of the apartment, looking out onto the heart of the city. Vibrant paintings of oriental flowers pulsed with life. Mint-green-and-pearl marble flooring swirled in rivers of iridescence. Scattered throughout were chests and tables composed of bright blue and green lacquer. A crimson velvet couch with silk pillows adorned the center of the living room.

Running out of things to look at, I peeked at Lexis. She was as sophisticated and elegant as her home. She wore a bold green dress that hugged her slender curves, each seam threaded with gold. Gilded leaves adorned the hem. Such loveliness was irritating. And Rome had seen her naked, which was even worse.

He returned none too soon, holding an angel and a bag.

The angel's hair was as black as his and—gag—her mother's, with just a hint of curl. Her eyes were up-tilted and green, also (gag) like her mother's. She wore a nightgown with brown bears scattered all over the fabric. One of her delicate arms was wrapped around Rome's neck and the other clutched a teddy bear. She yawned.

Seeing father and daughter together made my chest ache. Love radiated between them, a shining force of trust, comfort and serenity. A quiet bond that no one would ever be able to break. I had that with my dad, I thought, homesick.

"I missed you so much, sunshine," Rome told her.

"Missed you, too, Daddy," she said sleepily.

She was four years old, was my guess, and the cutest thing I'd ever seen. Until her gaze latched on to me. She frowned. "Who," she said imperiously, "are you?"

"This is Belle. She's a friend of Daddy's," Rome answered for me. Tenderly he smoothed a hand down the girl's hair. "Let's be nice to her, okay?"

"I don't like her," was the reply, stated as conversationally as if she'd said, "My bear needs a hug."

Lexis smirked.

I crossed my arms over my chest. "Mind telling me what I did wrong?" I asked the girl.

"She doesn't like *anyone*," Rome told me. He kissed Sunny's plump little cheek. "Except me."

"It's true," Sunny said, sounding like a college professor. "Oh, I like Mommy, too." She shook her head and her hair swished over her shoulders. "But strangers are bad, bad people who do bad, bad things."

Rome beamed with pride. Sunny had probably quoted him verbatim.

"They sure are," I agreed. "So I guess this means I can't like you, either, since you're a stranger to me."

She giggled, and the sound lit up the room. "I'm not a stranger."

"Are you sure?" I asked, tapping a finger to my chin. "You look like a stranger to me."

"Very sure," she said with a laugh, and Rome smiled. He gave me a soft look that nearly melted me into a puddle.

"Brittan is here," Lexis said, and moved to the front door. She opened it, revealing a tall man whose fist was poised, ready to knock. He wore black lounge pants and a gray T-shirt. His dark hair was rumpled, and if not for the bump in his nose and the fact that his eyes were brown, he would have been an exact replica of Rome.

Brittan's lips twitched. "I thought for sure I'd beat you this time."

"Like that will ever happen." Lexis stepped back and waved him inside. "Come in."

"Hey, bro," Brittan said, walking forward. He clapped Rome on the shoulder with genuine affection. Up close, I could see that Rome was taller than his brother and the younger of the two. Silver was woven through Brittan's hair, and there were fine lines around his eyes.

Brittan saw me and frowned. "Who's she?" he asked, giving me a chin nod.

"Belle Jamison," I answered before someone else (namely Lexis) could introduce me as Troublemaker. "Rome's friend."

"Co-worker?" he asked, but I wasn't given the chance to answer.

"Uncle Brit, Uncle Brit! Stop ignoring me!" Sunny

quirmed in her daddy's arms and threw herself at Brittan. Amid her giggling, he hugged her tightly. "You saw me a few hours ago, squirt, but I like this kind of greeting."

"I need you to watch her for a few days, Brittan. Don't take her back to your apartment, take her out of the building," Lexis instructed. "To our safe house on Peach Street."

Brittan lost all hint of joviality. "Is something going to happen?"

No one doubted a single word out of perfect Lexis's perfect mouth, apparently, even when those words predicted a future no one could know for sure.

Lexis gave Sunny a pointed glance, and Brittan nodded in understanding. Obviously, they didn't want her to know what was going on. *I* wasn't exactly sure what was going on, either. Either Lexis wanted the girl away from me because she simply didn't like me, or Rome really had told her about me and she wanted her daughter out of the line of fire. Literally. That would explain her hostility toward me.

Rome came up to my side, his heat wrapping around me. I don't know why, but just having him near made me feel better. Calmer about everything. Even though the bastard had married Lexis. And slept with her. And given her a child.

Lexis placed little kisses all over Sunny's face. "I'm going to miss you so much, but I know you'll have fun with Uncle Brit as always."

"Daddy said you're going away again," Sunny said. "How long this time?"

"Two weeks," Lexis said.

"Two days," Sunny countered.

"One week," Rome said.

Sunny thought about it for a moment. "Deal."

"Give me a kiss before you go, sunshine." There was a tremor in Rome's voice now.

He was upset that she was leaving, which was heartbreaking. I reached out and laced our fingers. He didn't pull away, but squeezed in thanks. Sunny leaned away from Brittan, who kept a tight hold on her, and stretched past Lexis to plant her lips on Rome's with a loud smack.

"I love you," he said.

"Love you, too."

Tears filled Lexis's eyes, and I admit they filled mine, as well. I felt kind of guilty for intruding on this very personal, very private family goodbye. I felt even more guilty for causing it.

"Get out of here now," Lexis said. "Go on."

"Bye, stranger," Sunny said to me. I smiled and waved.

Brittan anchored Sunny at his side with one hand and gathered her bag with the other. They were out the door a few seconds later, chatting about bears.

Silence filled the foyer until Rome gave me a half smile and said, "What do you know. You not only charmed me, you charmed my daughter."

I'd charmed him? I suddenly felt like dancing (naked).

Before I could, though, Rome turned back to Lexis, his expression sobering. "He'll take care of her," he said, and I think he said it to comfort himself as well. "He might not have powers, but he's trained military."

"Come," Lexis said, wiping away her tears. She held out her hand. "We'll talk in my bedroom."

"Behave," Rome said to me. As if it was totally natural and he'd done it millions of times before, he released my hand and took Lexis's, and they headed down the hall.

I scowled at their backs, suddenly furious and feeling the rims of my eyes burn. "You expect me to wait here? Seriously?"

Rome groaned under his breath and stopped abruptly.

"Yes," Lexis said. "We do."

He released Lexis's hand (a lifesaving action, for sure) and gave her back a gentle push. She tossed me a glare over her shoulder, then flounced away. Rome remained in place, not turning to face me.

"If you think I'll let you go off and have a beddie-bye chat without me," I said, "you're in serious need of an IQ exam." Rome and Lexis, former husband and wife. Alone. Together. Hell, no. Not on my watch.

And this had nothing to do with jealousy. Really. Seriously. My safety hung in the balance, and I had a right to hear any and all conversations about me, my powers, the people chasing me, Rome, his present/past/future (he *is* my partner), Tanner, and a possible relationship between Rome and Lexis. After all, Rome had kissed me and admitted he wanted to sleep with me.

After the way he'd taken her hand... Anger brewed and churned inside me, and I swear tiny curls of smoke wafted from my nostrils. "Well," I prompted.

Finally he gave me his full attention. His lips were pressed together. To keep from scowling? Or grinning? He crossed his arms over his chest, and his gaze cataloged my expression. His brow puckered in confusion, but there was a sparkle in his eyes. Grinning, I realized.

"What are you mad about now?" he asked.

"Nothing," I said in typical girl fashion, while inside I shouted, *Everything!* A part of me wanted him to read my mind and figure it out. Was that too much to ask?

"He can't," Lexis suddenly said.

I hadn't heard her return; my attention had been consumed by Rome. Unfortunately, she now stood beside him. "Can't what?" I asked, frowning.

"Read your mind. Rome can't do it."

How had she known— My mouth opened and closed, and I'm sure I looked like a rabid fish. "Can *you?*"

"Yes," she answered evenly, as if it were a perfectly normal thing to do.

That wasn't possible, I thought, eyes slitting. I stared over at her. *What am I thinking now, you rotten—*

"What am I thinking now, you rotten…what?" She fisted her hands on her hips and pursed her lips. "Please finish that riveting thought."

"Get out of my head," I gasped, horror consuming me. "Right now!" If the woman could read minds, she probably *could* predict the future, too. Great. She'd said I'd be nothing but trouble, and Rome had heard her say it. I didn't want him to think of me as trouble; I wanted him to think of me as sexy. And I'd rather be strangled with my own intestines than allow Lexis access to those most private thoughts.

"One," she said. "That's disgusting." In a perfect imitation of the exasperated look Rome sometimes gave me, she arched her brows. "Two, if you want me out of your head, you'll have to erect some walls."

"How?" My muscles bunched, gearing for a fight. This supernatural world I'd entered really sucked the big one. Hard core. Who else had read my mind?

Lexis glanced to Rome. "You want to explain it?"

His attention, I noticed, had never veered from me. "Have you ever hung a Keep Out sign on something, Belle?"

"Yes." *Keep your mind blank. Keep your mind blank. Show Madam Bitch a blank screen.*

"It was a blank screen, anyway," she muttered.

My nails dugs into my palms, and I took a menacing step toward her.

"Hang a sign in your mind," Rome said, closing the distance between us and gripping my shoulder to keep me in place. "Visualize it."

At this point, I'd try anything. I closed my eyes and began to construct an elaborate block of wood, painting "Keep Out, Bitch," in bold red letters. Then, of their own accord, the words began to smear, dripping up and down, branching left and right, weaving together to form a tightly crafted shield.

I gasped. It had worked. It had actually worked. I blinked open my eyes and watched Lexis shrug as if she didn't care.

"All done?" Rome asked. The hand on my shoulder caressed a fiery trail down my arm. His fingertips brushed my sensitive palm.

I nodded in satisfaction, trying to ignore the intense surge of pleasure such a simple touch elicited.

"There," Lexis said. "She's protected. Shall we adjourn, Rome?"

"I'll be there in a second."

With a frustrated *grr,* Lexis sailed down the hall. Rome cupped my chin and captured my attention. His decadent smell enveloped me, as heady as his touch.

"A little warning next time would be nice," I grumbled, drawing on anger rather than wallowing in desire. "If you had told me she was psychic, I could have worked on that wall sooner."

To my utter delight, he dragged his thumb over the seam

of my lips. A delicious shiver racked me. "What was that all about?" he asked softly. "You're usually snippy, but I've never heard such animosity from you. And don't tell me it was the mind-reading thing, because you were upset before that."

I'm usually snippy? Oh, that grated. "I'm happy, damn it, a joy to be with. I bring sunshine to everyone around me."

He chuckled. "I believe you, but that doesn't answer my question."

I tilted my chin, quite aware I looked inexorably stubborn. "You have your secrets and I have mine." Telling him I craved having him all to myself, telling him I didn't like the thought of him with another woman, no matter the reason, held a high price. My pride. And I wasn't ready to pay such a large sum.

A heavy pause, a heavy sigh. "Fair enough. But you need to understand that's the exact reason I want you to wait out here. *My* secrets."

"No." My chin rose yet another notch.

"You can keep an eye on Tanner."

"He's fine."

"Belle." He uttered another sigh.

"Rome. I'm not staying out here while you have a quickie with your girlfriend, then discuss me to your little hearts' content. Sorry, but my answer is and will remain no."

"Girlfriend?" He snorted. "As if I could handle two of you." Hands slinking to the base of my neck and tightening in my hair, he lowered his lips to mine for a soft, exquisite kiss, a simple but blissful brush of his mouth against mine. "Your thought process fascinates me."

I gulped. "I usually offend people."

"Not me," he whispered, his warm breath fanning my lips, my chin.

My body instantly quickened with arousal, eager, so wonderfully eager, for more of him. It was as if he'd never stopped kissing me the first time, as if stopping had been foreplay for this moment. My nipples were hard, my stomach achy and my legs shaky.

"If I promise not to have a quickie, will you stay here?" His voice was coated with desire, hoarse and rumbling.

A long while passed before I could form a coherent response. "N-no." I finally managed to work the sound past the hard lump in my throat. The man was turned on. Unleashing him into the wild now would be foolish, especially with the piranha waiting for him in the bedroom. Rome might not have romantic feelings for her, but I suspected she still had plenty for him—another reason for her hatred of me.

Can you say jealous? And no, I was not a pot and she was not a kettle. I hated her because she was a bitch, not because she was a rival for Rome's affections.

*Puh-lease. You're seething with jealousy, Jamison.*

"No," I repeated, more for my benefit than his.

Rome rolled his eyes. "Fine. Come on." As he spoke, he intertwined our fingers. "If you learn something shocking, don't say I didn't warn you."

A decadent shiver stole through me at first contact. The feel of his palm against mine...divine. He was strong, so warm and capable, with rough calluses that were a testament to his dangerous lifestyle. How had I ever doubted him?

He pivoted on his heel and led me down the wide hallway. The fragrance of jasmine incense drifted in the air. Instead of the fine art I expected, the coffee-colored walls were decorated with pictures of Sunny.

"Slow down," I told Rome, craning my neck to see a photo of him and Sunny on a swing set.

He ignored me and tugged me into the bedroom.

I stopped, gasped, gawked, drinking in every detail. I'd stepped into a harem. Minus the sexually starved women, of course. Lexis's bedroom was more decadent than her living room. A ginormous bed decorated the middle, wisps of black netting dancing gently around the posts. Red pillows were scattered across the floor, ruby-colored beads sewn into the seams. From the ceiling hung at least a hundred single-bulb chandeliers, illuminating everything in a crown of brilliance. Gold-etched mirrors. A fireplace.

What the hell did Lexis do to afford this stuff? Or did Rome buy it for her? I didn't know government agents were so well paid.

Hair floating behind her like a black cloud, she emerged from a walk-in closet carrying a large black duffel bag and several items of clothing. She carefully placed the bag on the bed.

"Going somewhere?" Rome asked her. He let go of my hand, traced his fingers up my arm, lingering, then withdrew all contact.

Without his touch, I experienced a wave of emptiness.

"Your woman is going to burn this place down," she replied bitterly. She stuffed a green silk dress in the bag. "I figured it was in my best interests to leave before that happened."

There was no time to bask in the acute sense of joy the words *your woman* elicited. Not with her accusation ringing in my ears. "I'm not going to torch this place. Jeez."

Rome's chin dropped to his chest, and he shook his head. "This is great. I'm sorry, Lex. I wouldn't have come if I'd known."

"I know," she said. "Brit will take care of Sunny, so that's one less worry."

"I'm not going to start a fire," I insisted.

"You won't mean to," was the airy reply as Lexis returned to her closet to gather more clothing. "But you will."

"You stay, Lex. We'll leave," Rome offered, his voice taut.

"Too late." She folded a pair of jeans and placed them inside the case. "I can't throw you out, Rome. It's too dangerous. Plus, I'm involved now."

Oh, joy. Just the words I wanted to hear. "You're both acting like me starting a fire is a done deal. But now that I've been warned—" *bitch!* "—I'll be careful." I would have placed money on the fact that she was only trying to make me look bad in front of Rome.

She pinned me with a piercing stare, her emerald eyes taking on an unholy glow, otherworldly and ethereal. "You're still going to cause trouble."

God, I hated this woman. *Do not get mad. Do not get mad.* Trying to control my breathing, I stretched my fingers behind my back—just in case they emitted plumes of smoke. Already I felt the burning, the intense heat.

"Uh, Belle, sweetie," Rome said.

"Not now, Rome. Lexis and I are in the middle of a… conversation."

"Put the conversation on hold. Your fingers are on fire."

Damn it all to hell and back. I whirled on him, pointing a blazing finger at his chest. I growled, "Watch the temper. Think happy thoughts. Well, guess what? I'm on the run, I can't go home, I miss my dad, people want to kill me and/or capture me for reasons I still don't fully understand, your best buddy is a bitch, and I'm starving." My stomach was in danger of eating itself, I only then realized. I hadn't had a decent meal all day. Well, there was that amazing breakfast Rome had cooked me that morning, but already that felt like eons ago. "I have every right to feel emotional."

"I know," he said softly. Features lighting with compassion, he blew on my fingertip, dousing the fire, and snaked his arm around my waist. He tugged me in front of him, then slid his fingers up my back and onto my shoulders, where he began a bone-meltingly delicious massage. "I'm sorry."

Just like that, my anger completely defused. A man who understood—unusual. A man who said he was sorry, and meant it—priceless.

"I'll watch her tonight, Lex," Rome said. "I'll make sure Belle doesn't start a fire."

Lexis hesitated, then nodded. "It's against my better judgment to ignore my instincts, but I'm going to trust you, Rome. We'll leave in the morning."

"Good. Now let's get down to business so Belle and I can eat and get some sleep," he said. His fingers never stopped kneading my sore muscles.

Lexis, who continued packing her bag, avoided glancing in our direction.

I watched her without reservation. Though her motions were stiff, she carried herself with the grace and fluidity of a dancer.

With a flick of her wrist, she tossed another case on the bed. "I'm filling this one for you," she told me. "You'll need some different clothes in the coming days, and we are about the same size."

How…sweet. And completely unexpected. "Thank you," I said, a tendril of guilt drifting through me.

"You're welcome."

"Here's what's going on," Rome said, cutting through the sudden, pregnant silence. "Belle was given an experimental formula."

"Against my will," I added. "A little lower," I told him, moving my shoulders to show him where I needed him. *Oh, yeah. Right there.* My head lolled forward as ecstasy consumed me. "Mmm…"

He inhaled a sharp breath before finishing his explanation. "This formula has changed the alignment of her DNA." His voice began to deepen, a husky edge sneaking into the rich timbre. "It's given her power over the four elements. As you might have figured out when her finger caught fire."

Lexis paused in her movements, a pair of green silk pants dangling from her fingers. Finally she faced us. "So that's the hum of electrical output I feel from her?"

"Yes." Rome dabbled at the top of my butt for a moment, and I bit my lower lip to cut off a moan. "Both Vincent and our boss want her."

Wait. *Our* boss? That meant Rome and Lexis worked together, too. Just great.

"Stop tensing," he whispered to me. "You're the Periodic Table Chick, remember? Keep it calm."

"Don't call me that."

"This is Dr. Roberts's formula we're discussing, yes?" Lexis asked, ignoring me.

Rome nodded. "You've worked with Roberts in the past. You know him better than I do."

"You worked with Dr. Roberts?" I asked. Well, more like growled. I didn't like the man, for obvious reasons.

"Yes," she said. "He's not a bad man. He wouldn't have hurt you on purpose. He's sweet and he means well. But he does have a wild, sexual side, and I think Vincent used it—most likely by blackmailing him—to keep the doctor working on the formula, even after he learned Vincent wasn't the altruist he'd thought."

"Why did you work with him, though?" I asked.

She shrugged. "We heard what the doctor was trying to create, a liquid that could make the weakest of people strong, and we wanted him for PSI. When he chose OASS instead, I was sent in to befriend, monitor, and make sure he failed. But Vincent figured out what I was doing and took the doctor underground."

"Do you think you can get a lock on him?" Rome said. "I need to find him. I promised Belle I would help her search for an antidote and get Vincent off her back."

"What about John?" Lexis asked.

*He can't have me,* I mentally answered.

Rome didn't speak for a moment. "I'll deal with him later," he said, and there was an odd inflection in his voice. An inflection I couldn't decipher. "Tell me about Roberts."

Lexis closed her eyes, a blanket of extreme relaxation falling over her features. For a moment I wasn't sure she was breathing. "Roberts is in the city," she said, completely monotone. "He has not left and will not leave. There's still something he wants to do here."

"What?" Rome asked.

"I don't know," she answered with disappointment. "That is hidden from me."

So Pretty Boy Vincent hadn't captured him yet, I realized. There was still a chance I could find him, talk to him, slap the shit out of him, then force him to reverse what he'd done to me. If that were even possible.

"He's concealed himself very well, and I can't pinpoint his location."

"At least we know he's still in Atlanta," Rome said. His fingers ceased all movement on my back, but remained in place. He rested his chin atop my head. "You're sure Sunny is going to be okay?" he asked, his tone stark. Filled with raw emotion. The words burst from him as if they'd been poised on his tongue all along and he couldn't hold them back a moment more.

Genuine affection and sadness played over Lexis's face, changing her exotic beauty to one of haunting delicacy. "She'll be fine."

Rome's chest was pressed into my back, so I felt the frantic dance of his heartbeat, then the gradual slowing as he accepted her words. My stomach clenched painfully. I reached up with both hands and threaded our fingers together, offering him what little comfort I could.

"We talked about taking her into hiding," Rome said, his voice different than before. Flatter. Like when I'd first met him.

"Yes," Lexis replied. She stilled, gazing over at him.

"Soon," he said. "I have a plan. Belle is going to…help."

Was that hesitation I heard from him? "I'll learn to control the powers," I assured them both. "I won't be a hindrance."

Lexis's eyes widened for a moment and she looked from Rome to me, from me to Rome. "That's why you didn't take her to John?"

He nodded.

Lexis hesitated for a moment—come on, I wasn't *that* bad—then gave a clipped nod. "I appreciate your willingness to help my daughter," she told me stiffly.

*You're sooo welcome,* I wanted to reply snottily. That stilted tone of hers made it clear she didn't expect me to be much help.

"Thank you, Lex," Rome said. "I owe you. For everything."

"No more than I owe you."

They shared a smile, and I had to bite my tongue to keep from saying something dumb. Or mean. Or both. Restraint was my new best friend, it seemed.

"Go," Lexis said, resuming her packing. Her movements were lighter, her expression happier than they'd been since I'd entered the apartment. "Eat. It's getting late, and I need to finish up here so we'll be ready to go in the morning."

*Class dismissed,* I thought, which meant I could drill Rome for answers about himself, his daughter and his relationship with Lexis. No excuses this time. No evasions. He would tell me everything I wanted to know, or he would suffer the wrath of the Fabulous Flame.

I cringed. Eew. No. I didn't like that name any better than I liked the ones Rome had given me. I'd think of a better one soon. If I didn't, I'd be stuck with Four Elements Girl or Periodic Table Chick.

A sigh seeped from me. I did not want to go down in history with a lame-ass superhero name. Not that I thought of myself as a superhero, but I could now see that there was the potential for it. I mean, I was helping Rome track down the doctor who had done this to me, and then I was going to help him hide his daughter.

Yep. Belle Jamison, superhero. I was starting to like the sound of that.

## CHAPTER ELEVEN

I FOLLOWED ROME into the dining room, meaning to question him about Lexis. Instead, I saw food spread out on the table, and my mind went blank. Ham, crackers, cheese—Lexis must have set it out earlier, knowing we were coming and all. By the time I came up for air, Rome had already locked himself in the shower.

I consoled myself with a bottle of red wine (don't ask the brand, I don't know how to pronounce it) and more of the food. It was the perfect midnight snack to top off this long—too long—day. Thirty minutes later, after I'd eaten my fill and given myself a tour of the apartment, Rome still hadn't emerged, so I decided to shower, as well. Alone. In a bathroom that was as expensive and well-maintained as the rest of the apartment, with gold-veined facets and pink-veined marble. Sheesh. I could live in this bathroom.

Afterward, in the guest room Lexis had told me was mine for the evening, I changed into an ice-green silk pajama set she'd loaned me. I'd expected a coarse brown sack or extra-large flannel, so the silk came as a welcome surprise. The material felt ultrasoft against my skin.

I was walking out of the room when I spied a phone on the nightstand. I paused, pressed my lips together. Maybe I should call Sherridan. If she went looking for me at work, found out I'd been fired and I hadn't called her, she'd freak. Would her cell be tapped? I didn't see how it could be. I mean, the woman kept it on her at all times in case a client wanted to see a house in the middle of the night. But...

Should I? Shouldn't I? In the end, I hunted down Lexis and asked her—hating that I had to rely on her for anything. "Would I cause a disaster if I called my friend Sherridan?"

Lexis looked at me for a moment, her pretty features pensive. "No. I do not sense one."

"Thank you." Relieved, I marched back into my room, picked up the phone and dialed Sherridan's number.

"Hello," she said sleepily, and I sat on the edge of the bed.

"Hey," I said. I toyed with the damp ends of my hair. "It's me. You alone?"

"Belle?"

"Yeah."

I heard a crackling static, then, "Why are you calling me at...two in the morning?"

"I wanted to talk. You too tired?"

"No, no. Just give me a moment."

Eager, I mentally counted to five. "You good now?"

"Yeah." She yawned. "So, do you want to talk about riding crops? Or Rome? Let's talk Rome." She sounded more alert with every word. "His voice was sexy enough to give me an orgasm. Does he do phone sex? You should have told me about him when I asked you about the twins."

"You're babbling, Sher."

"I'll stop if you tell me about Rome."

"Rome was sort of a...surprise." Truth. I fell onto the mattress with a sigh. "Oh, Sherridan, I don't know what I'm going to do about that man."

"Have you slept with him yet?"

"No!"

She tsked. "But you want to, you naughty girl. I can tell. Do you remember how to do it or do you need Auntie Sher to remind you?"

"I remember, thank you." I hoped. "Listen, I'm…going away with him for a while." Again, truth. And the real reason I had called her. "I'm going to be unreachable."

Silence. Then, "Wait a second. You're taking time off from work. Okay, this *is* serious. Are you an alien? Did you invade my friend's body?"

"Ha, ha."

"I'm not kidding," she said, deadpan.

"I'd better go," I stated, before she could start asking questions I wasn't prepared to answer. "Rome is probably naked and looking for me." Well, the naked part wasn't a lie.

"Fine. Go. But you owe me major details when you get back. Just do me one favor. Give Rome a kiss for me. With tongue." *Click.*

Little devil. I laughed and replaced the receiver in its cradle. That was done. Next up: Tanner. I tiptoed out of the room and into Tanner's. He was sleeping peacefully, his hair mussed, features relaxed, and a soft snore gliding from his lips. I never should have gotten him involved in my mess. He was just a kid, lost, unsure about his life, and perhaps desperate to find some peace.

I'd shattered that, and I decided then and there to make it up to him. Somehow. Some way.

I left the room and once more braved the labyrinth that was

the apartment. Where was Rome? Surely he'd finished his shower. If not, well, I wasn't above storming into the bathroom and questioning him there—while secretly checking out his goods, of course.

I sneaked into the living room and stopped in a shadowed cubby that separated hall from room. My eyes narrowed. Rome sat on the couch, Lexis right next to him. Their backs were to me. The sound of their whispers drifted in the air, too light to distinguish actual words.

Lexis purred a soft chuckle.

Okay, so even her laugh was feminine and pretty. What kind of mutant was she? No one should be that perfect. My hands tightened into fists. Rome could very well be denying, even to himself, that he loved her. I mean, the woman was the mother of his only child. That kind of bond couldn't be broken. Proof: there was an ease to their relationship, an intimacy that hadn't been shattered by divorce. Proof: he went to her when he was in trouble.

Why had they split, then?

I hated—hated!—that the thought of them together bothered me so much. Rome had seen this perfect woman's perfect breasts and perfect thighs. How could other women compete? What's more, Lexis probably kissed and fucked with the exotic flair her appearance promised. No telling how I compared—and would compare. Not favorably, was my first guess.

"She's going to be more trouble than Daniel," Lexis said, loudly enough that I could hear.

"I remember him," Rome replied with a husky chuckle. "The little boy who could soul-jump, invading people's bodies and taking over their minds. He thought it was a game until Vincent caught him and forced him to soul-jump to rob and murder."

"Getting Daniel out of that lab earned you three bullets in the back." She expelled a sad breath at the memory. "How did Belle survive the formula? No one else did."

"I don't know," he answered. "Maybe the doctor finally got it right. I'm sure blood tests will reveal the true answer to that, but I'm not curious enough to take her in to find out."

Silence.

Then, "Do you ever regret joining PSI?" Lexis asked.

"We've saved thousands of lives and averted hundreds of paranormal disasters."

They weren't called "parasters"? Lord, would I ever learn the lingo?

"But," Lexis said.

"But," Rome repeated. They looked at each other and in unison said, "Sunny."

"That will be corrected soon enough," he stated. He stiffened, then added, "You going to stand there all night or come sit with us?" He didn't face me, but I knew the question was meant for me.

I frowned. "How did you know I was here?"

"I smelled you," he said, keeping his back to me.

Color heated my cheeks, quickly spreading to my neck and collar. I bet he'd never said that to Lexis. "I just took a shower. I do *not* stink!"

"I didn't say you stank, now did I?"

"You said I smelled, and that's the same thing." If he'd been within arm's reach, I would have slapped him.

"Well, you do smell. You smell good. Really good." Finally he twisted to face me, and our eyes locked together.

Sizzled. Oxygen burned in my lungs, and a jolt of desire speared me. "C'mere."

My embarrassment dissolved into absolute pleasure as an invisible cord tugged me forward. *I shouldn't want him this much. I shouldn't need him this much.* I forced my gaze from him and studied the couch. The totally safe, didn't-take-my-breath-away couch. I didn't know where to sit. Between Rome and Lexis? Beside Lexis? Beside Rome?

In the end, Rome took the decision away from me. The moment I was close enough, his arm whipped out, snaking around my waist and dragging me into his lap. I landed with a delighted "Hoomph."

Instantly his strength surrounded me, inexorable and comforting and more arousing than an intimate caress. The strong heat of his thighs pressed into the silk of my pants. My mind beckoned me to rise, to fight against his seductive allure, but I allowed myself to sink into his chest, deepening the contact.

"I will leave you two alone," Lexis said, rising.

I didn't think to utter a token and patently untrue *please stay.*

"You have much to discuss," she added, and there was a tinge of regret in her voice. Hurt. Without another word, she padded from the room.

Rome and I were suddenly alone.

Now that the couch was free, the polite thing to do was get off him. *But I don't want to get off him,* my body whined. *Stay, stay, stay.*

I stayed.

He didn't ask me to get up, I noticed, and with a small smile, I burrowed the back of my head into the hollow of his neck. How I yearned to wrap my arms around him, to slide my lips over his jaw and work my way down his chest. To turn and wrap my legs around his waist, then rub myself against his erection.

"You're going to open up to me now," I told him.

"I am, am I?" He didn't sound upset with that fact. He sounded amused, relaxed. Happy, even. And aroused. Deliciously aroused.

"Yes."

"Or what?"

Biting my lip, I plucked at his pants, twisting the material at his knee. It was softer than it looked and actually tore under my ministrations. Oops. Did I somehow have superhuman strength now, too? I let go. "Do you really need me to list ways to torture you?"

"Depends on what kind of torturing we're talking about."

"The bad kind."

His naughty fingers dipped to the hem of my shirt and rubbed the stripe of skin visible at my belly. "Painful bad or—" his voice dropped huskily "—kinky bad?"

Instantly my nerve endings jolted to life. "Painful?" I said, though it emerged as a question rather than the statement of fact I'd meant.

He chuckled softly. However, his amusement didn't last long. He pushed out a breath, and his fingers stopped their movement. "I figured out what's been bothering you. You're jealous of Lexis. Why?"

I jolted upright, sputtering, unable to form a proper response.

"Careful, baby, or you'll torch the place like Lexis predicted."

He was right and I knew it, but that didn't make it any less frustrating. Truly, if I didn't stay in a constant "happy place" I would unleash a holy terror—or two. How unfair was that? "Everyone deserves a chance to express their emotions, Rome," I said softly.

"I know." Gently he kissed the base of my neck. "I know."

Exhaling, tingling, I returned to my reclining position. I would address the jealousy thing when I had a response that sounded believable.

"Maybe we should get you a stress ball," he said pensively.

I snorted. "What kind of ball are we talking? Asbestos? Or did you have something else in mind?"

Warm breath brushed my skin, and I felt his lips stretch into a grin. "You're a pervert at heart. I don't think I want your hands near *my* balls right now."

The tingling inside me intensified, spreading, growing, stretching from one corner of my body to the other. My mouth watered for a taste of him. My nipples beaded, begging for attention. I closed my eyes, only to see a picture of us in my mind. Me, head thrown back, legs open. Him, gliding his fingers down my stomach, through the fine hair at my pubis and into the wet heat of me.

*Don't forget why you're here.* Questions first. Sex later. Lots of sex. Dirty sex. "Like I said, I, um, have some questions for you, and I want answers." I traced a fingertip over the bumps and planes of his wrist, wanting so badly to guide him to a more intimate caress. "Let's start with your last name. What is it?"

"Masters."

"Are you kidding me?"

"No."

I laughed. What a perfect name for him. "Do you expect everyone to obey your every command, Mr. Masters?"

Slowly he grinned. "Always."

Okay, now for the harder questions. "Why did you and Lexis separate?" He gripped my hips and jerked me against his erection. He moaned. I gasped. Good. So good. "And how long have things been over?"

His fingers spread over my belly again, and my muscles quivered. I bit my lip to keep from crying out in utter bliss. "Why does it matter?" he asked.

"Why are you so secretive?" I countered. Unable to stop myself, I arched my back, grinding my butt into his erection once more.

He sucked in a breath. "The less people know about me, the safer it is. For them. For me."

"In case you've forgotten, I'm a superhero." Up, down, a slow glide. I clutched his knees and continued my bold dance against him. God, he felt good. Big, hard and thick. "I can protect us both." Or kill us both, but that didn't bear mentioning.

"Superhero, hmm?" Reaching around me, he palmed me exactly where I needed him. I nearly shouted at the intense surge of pleasure. "Should I call you the Amazing Matchstick? Sparkie? The Blazing Saddle?"

"Do it, and I'll go four elements on your ass."

His thumb stroked me once, twice. Ohmygod. If I didn't pull away I would come. I would come right then, right there. Just erupt into a thousand satisfied pieces, and that would be the end of our conversation. I'd be too sated to talk, too replete to care what he did afterward.

"I can't do this. Not yet." Stupid girl that I am, I leapt off him and threw myself on the other side of the couch. I was panting. Weak. Empty. *Questions first. Dirty playtime econd, remember?* I didn't look at him. A long while passed *b*efore I caught my breath, and only then did I twist toward *h*im, careful to keep a safe distance between us.

His expression was harsh and dark and utterly captivat-*in*g. Taut lines pulled at his eyes and mouth. I squashed the *u*rge to throw myself back into his arms and offer comfort. *"*How long have you and Lexis been broken up?"

He watched me for a long while, then he said, "This in*f*ormation is important to you?"

I nodded.

"A year." As he spoke, he crossed his arms over his chest. *"*We've been apart a year."

"Why did you break up with her?"

"I didn't." His brow furrowed. "What makes you ask that?"

All my muscles stiffened, and not in a good way. I gripped *t*he red velvet couch arm until my knuckles turned white. "So *s*he broke up with you?"

"Yes."

Okay, I so did not like that fact. Did he have secret feelings *f*or her, as I'd suspected a little while ago—feelings he might *n*ot have admitted to himself? She obviously had feelings for *h*im. Why had she dumped him? Did he want her back? They'd *s*hared their lives, had planned to share their futures. At one *t*ime he'd loved her enough to contemplate eternity with her.

"Is that all you wanted to know?" he asked.

About Lexis—yes. The woman had once possessed every-*t*hing I suddenly wanted. Rome's adoration. Exclusivity. A future with him. The torrent of jealousy coursing through me proved too strong to deny this time. "Will you tell me about *S*unny?" I asked softly. I was treading in dangerous waters, *b*ut I refused to stop myself now.

He pushed a hand through his hair and several strands tumbled onto his forehead. "I don't want to talk about her, Belle."

"I know, but do it anyway. Please."

Several minutes ticked by in absolute silence.

"Let's start with something small," I said. "How old i she?"

"Four," was the reluctant reply. "She's four."

I'd guessed correctly. "She looks like an angel."

"She is. Looks like an angel, acts like a devil, though." A warm chuckle rumbled from his chest as a memory clicked into place.

"Devil? How?"

"Hide and go seek is her favorite game. She'll torment me for hours, misting from one shadow to another, laughing a me all the while."

"Misting?" I blinked. "What does that mean?"

He stiffened, shattering the illusion of relaxation. "Never mind. Forget I said anything." His voice returned to its earlier gruffness.

I shook my head. "You are so secretive."

"The world I live in is a dangerous place. I told you that. The less you know, the better."

"I disagree. I'm part of your world now. The more I know, the safer I'll be. I have a right to understand what I'm up against, just like I have a right to know who you are, who my enemies are, and how I can get your boss off my case."

Rome pinned me with a stare, a stare I couldn't escape. "John's not a bad guy. Not really. Just cautious."

"If he's such a good person, why don't you tell him our plan to find Dr. Roberts? Why don't you let *him* help you hide Sunny?"

"I said he wasn't bad. I didn't say he was an altruist. He loves Sunny like an uncle and would never hurt her, but if he ever found out about her abilities… He still wouldn't hurt her, but I don't want him to draft her. Most of all, I can't take a chance of Vincent finding out about her and developing an interest in her. That's where the true danger lies."

I began to understand what he was really telling me, and it shocked me how easily I accepted it. "When you said she misted into the shadows, you meant it literally, didn't you? She can actually become mist and travel to another location."

"Yes." He nodded stiffly. "Sunny can mist through solid objects, and that's a dangerous ability to have. If she were to accidentally materialize *inside* a wall, she would be killed."

"Was she born with the ability?"

He nodded again. "We didn't know Lexis was pregnant when we both volunteered for some…experiments to enhance our DNA. Unfortunately, those experiments affected Sunny more than me and Lexis."

Poor kid. I sympathized. "Neither of us asked for our abilities, but we got them anyway," I said with a sigh, and Rome looked away from me. My nose crinkled as I said, "What drove the two of you to volunteer for testing?"

"Lexis and I met on the job. We both signed up at PSI at the same time, about eleven years ago. We hit it off from the beginning, dated, got married, and neither of us liked the danger the other was in. When John mentioned that he'd found a way to make us invincible, we decided to go for it so we could stop worrying about each other. It was screwing with our heads, and we were getting sloppy. But in the end, they didn't make us invincible. Just stronger."

Wow. He'd loved Lexis that much. He'd loved her the way

women dreamed of being loved. "You'll have to leave PSI when you hide Sunny," I pointed out.

He waved his hand through the air. "I love what I do, love protecting the innocent, but Sunny comes first. I'll leave and never look back. I want to take my extraordinary little girl and give her the chance at the normal life she deserves."

"I hope, when the time comes, I'll be able to help rather than hinder."

"You'll help," he said, his voice going flat the way I hated. "You'll help."

I liked that he thought I could help protect his girl, just as I'd protected myself from him and his needle that first night. Actually, I was honored that he would place his greatest treasure in my hands. "So what powers do *you* have?" I asked. "Lexis has them. Sunny has them. What about you?"

"I'm just really good at my job." A slow (forced?) grin played at the corner of his lips. "You will be, too. Together, we're going to find Dr. Roberts, stop Vincent and hide Sunny."

I hoped so.

"If—when—we find Dr. Roberts, I'll put the word out that you've taken the antidote—even if he doesn't have one. Hopefully, Vincent will lose interest in you at that point."

*What if he doesn't lose interest?* I wanted to ask, but didn't. "What about your boss? John?"

"I'll take care of him," Rome said, once again looking away from me.

What did that mean, his looking away? He'd done it twice now. "What am I going to do if there's not an antidote?" I wondered aloud.

"Most people would embrace their powers."

"Not me. You were right when you said these abilities of

mine are dangerous. What if I *did* fall into evil hands?" Into Vincent's hands? A shudder raked me as images of mass destruction flashed through my mind. "I would give these powers up in a heartbeat."

Without any warning, Rome reached out and hooked one of his arms under my knees. The other snaked around my bicep. He tugged me back onto his lap, so we were face-to-face. A startled gasp burst from me, but I didn't protest. He cupped my ass and kneaded, then glided his naughty fingers forward and upward, over my hip bones, over the curve of my breasts, and caressed the line of my jaw.

"I think you *would* give up your powers," he said with a husky catch of breath.

Goose bumps beaded my skin. My heartbeat fluttered erratically. Pieces of me that had been asleep for years—perhaps forever—began to stretch and awaken: hope, the first bloom of love. I'd allowed a few men to get close to me, but never close enough for a future, never close enough for love.

I traced a fingertip along Rome's nose, over the seam of his mouth. With him, in that flash of stolen time, I felt completely safe, which was strange because I'd never had more reason to feel *un*safe.

"You continue to surprise me," he said. "I'd read your history before I entered your apartment that first time, and I didn't expect to like you."

My hands dropped to my sides. I caught my bottom lip between my teeth and released it bit by bit, trying to mask my sudden hurt. "Why not?" I asked. Okay, pouted.

"On paper you come across as—and don't shoot me with fireballs for this. On paper you come across as flaky."

"Flaky!" My jaw dropped, and my back went ramrod

straight. I punched him in the shoulder. "On paper I bet you look like a murdering assassin, you rotten piece of shit."

"Ow." He frowned, but didn't release me to rub the tender—really tender, I hoped—area that had collided with my fist. "All I meant was that you've jumped from job to job over the last year. Some of them you were fired from on the same day you started."

"So?"

"So, you asked me questions and I answered them. Now I'm going to ask you some, and you know what? You're going to answer like the good little girl I know you can be. Why were you fired from all those jobs? Your temper?"

Silently I contemplated his expression. He looked curious and interested, rather than insulting. Color bloomed in my cheeks, and I dipped my gaze to his chest, to where his shirt opened in a V. My fingers followed the direction of my eyes, tracing. "I wasn't happy," I said. "On some level I think I sensed that the jobs weren't what I was meant to do, so I didn't give them my all."

"What were you meant to do?" He hooked his thumb on the waist of my pants and gave a little pull, revealing several inches of skin.

"I wish I knew," I said dejectedly.

"Surely there's something." Bare skin to bare skin, he spread his fingers over my lower back. "Did you not want to be a doctor or a lawyer or a candy-maker when you were a kid?"

My blood heated. "Honestly? No." I leaned toward him, closing the small distance between us. *Kiss me,* I silently beseeched. *Kiss me hard and rough, as if you can't get enough of me.*

His breath stroked my cheek, and his grip on my back

tightened. "Have you ever wanted to be a love slave?" he asked huskily.

*Kiss me, damn it.* I traced my tongue over my lips, leaving a glistening sheen of moisture. "No, but I've wanted to own one."

He chuckled, the sound low and rich. "Maybe I can help you out with that. I have connections." He brushed his lips over mine once, twice.

"Yeah?" More. I needed more of him. Any other questions I had for him faded from my mind. I squirmed against him, rubbing myself on the long, thick length of his erection. Total rapture. Exquisite bliss. Our chests strained together, hardened nipples abrading hardened nipples. "What kind of connections?"

"Maybe *connections* is the wrong word." Eyes gleaming with white-hot fire, he cupped my butt again and jerked me against him. Hard. "Maybe I should have said I have the right equipment."

Only a puff of air separated us now, a hated whisper. Had I once told myself that giving in to my lust for Rome would be wrong? Probably. But I'd since told *him* I wanted to sleep with him, and I'd meant it. Then and now.

I wanted this man.

I wanted him desperately. Hungrily. Wanted to know what it would be like to feel him all around me, inside me, skin to skin. Sweating and aching. Filled. By him. By Rome. At the moment, I couldn't even make myself care about his ex.

Rome must have sensed my total capitulation because his fingers slid up swiftly and tangled in my hair. He tugged my face to his. "I'm going to kiss you," he growled. "Not soft like before, but hard."

"Yes."

"And you're going to like it."

"Yes." His eyes were light and fierce, practically glowing. He reminded me of a predatory animal, target in sight, and the idea thrilled me. He was the hunter, I was the prey. "Yes," I said again. *Yes, yes, yes.*

"One day soon I'm going to fuck you."

A shiver of anticipation danced through me. "Yes."

"You'll like that, too. You'll beg for it." As he spoke, his hips arched slightly, creating a dizzying friction. Had I been standing, I would have collapsed.

"No more talk," I said, as ferociously as he had. "Kiss. Now."

Instantly his lips meshed with mine. His tongue thrust inside my mouth, utterly hot, darkly erotic. The heady flavor of him invaded my senses, deepening my pleasure. One of his hands lowered and squeezed my breast, rubbing the nipple through the soft fabric of my silk tank. Rolling. Plucking. Lancing an aching need straight to my core.

He kissed me as if he couldn't get enough—just as I'd wanted. I kissed him as if I'd die without him—as I knew I would. My hands were everywhere, all over him, unable to get enough. Over and over our tongues clashed together. Over and over our hips thrust against each other. My movements quickened, became frantic. Heat, so much heat. I felt it, reveled in it. It flowed through me, as frantic as I was. So close.

I clutched at his hair. I moaned. I purred.

"Belle," he said, the name shuddered and broken. "Belle. Stop."

Stop? *No,* my mind shouted. Almost there. One more thrust and I would—

"We have to stop."

I jerked back from him, panting for breath. My eyelids felt heavy, my thighs ached. "More," I gasped.

"You've started a fire, baby."

Lost in my need for completion, for *him*, I leaned into him, craving another taste of his mouth. "Yes. Burn. I burn."

"Fire," he said again.

This time I heard the urgency in his voice, and I forced my eyes open completely. What I saw made me gasp. Just behind me, a plant flickered with orange-gold flames. The scent of burning leaves filled the air.

"Not again!" I lamented. But at least this wasn't the inferno Lexis had predicted. The woman's psychic abilities clearly weren't as sharp as everyone thought. I'd only torched a measly plant, not the whole apartment!

"Make it rain, baby. Try to make it rain like you did in the car. Remember, you were sad and droplets fell." His movements clipped, he tossed me to the other side of the couch and rushed into the kitchen.

Humming with sexual frustration, I stared at the flames. My cheeks heated with humiliation and regret. What made me sad? Thoughts of my dad being sick and ultimately dying. Thoughts of never seeing Sherridan again. Thoughts of never kissing Rome again.

Oh, God. The realization hit me like a sledgehammer. If I didn't learn to control my powers, I couldn't kiss Rome. Ever. Right now, it was too dangerous. *I* was too dangerous. I might start another fire, a bigger one. An inextinguishable blaze—like the one that had begun churning inside me the day he'd stepped into my apartment.

Sorrow squeezed me, washing over me, dousing my passion. What if I was never able to experience Rome's touch? What if I never learned what it was like to be taken—fucked—by him? To be consumed by him?

What if the kiss we'd just shared was it? All I would ever know of him?

Raindrops fell around me, soft at first, then quickly increasing. Big fat pearls dripped from the ceiling. Shaking, I pointed my hands at the plant and the drops concentrated on that spot. The fire sizzled, spurted, dying just as Rome sprinted back with a fire extinguisher.

He skidded to a stop, looking from me to the fire, the fire to me. "You did it. You put it out." His lips inched into a slow, proud smile, but I saw the lines of tension pulling at his eyes. "You're learning, baby. You're controlling."

I nodded, letting my gaze remain on the floor. My emotions were so raw, I wasn't sure I could speak. A lump coagulated in my throat. "I'm—I'm sorry." There. I'd managed to voice something. I visualized a cold shield around my heart, with a Keep Out sign all of its own, so I would stop wanting Rome. Would stop hurting. It didn't make the pain stop, but it did cause the rain to cease.

Still not facing Rome, I eased to my feet. The carpet squished. With as much dignity as I could manage, I walked away from him. Neither of us said a word. He didn't try to stop me, and I never looked back. I padded to the room Lexis had given me, closed the door with a soft click and climbed into bed.

Only then, alone in the darkness, did I allow myself to cry. After a while, my tears blended with a new fall of rain.

Well, shit.

# An Important Message from the Editors

Dear Reader,

Because you've chosen to read one of our fine novels, we'd like to say "thank you!" And, as a **special** way to thank you, we're offering you a choice of <u>two more</u> of the books you love so well **plus** an exciting Mystery Gift to send you — absolutely <u>FREE!</u>

Please enjoy them with our compliments...

*Pam Powers*

Lift here

Peel off seal and place inside...

**DETACH AND MAIL CARD TODAY!**

# Yes! I have placed my

Editor's "Thank You" seal in the
space provided at right. Please
send me 2 free books, which
I have selected, and a fabulous
mystery gift. I understand I am
under no obligation to purchase
any books, as explained on the
back of this card.

**PLACE
FREE GIFT
SEAL
HERE**

| | **ROMANCE** |
|---|---|
| | 193 MDL EE4Y   393 MDL EE5N |

| | **SUSPENSE** |
|---|---|
| | 192 MDL EE5C   392 MDL EE5Y |

FIRST NAME                 LAST NAME

ADDRESS

APT.#          CITY

STATE / PROV.          ZIP / POSTAL CODE

# Thank You!

(ED2-HQN-06)  © 2003 HARLEQUIN ENTERPRISES LTD.

# CHAPTER TWELVE

STUPID. IDIOT. DUMMY.

I wasn't cursing myself. I was cursing Dr. Roberts over last night's wee disaster. If not for that formula, I could have spent the night in Rome's arms, naked and blissful, rather than tossing and turning. Alone. Miserable. I hadn't set anything on fire the first time Rome kissed me (okay, so my fingers had gotten a little overheated, but that didn't count) and didn't understand why I had this time. Unless…were my abilities getting stronger or were my feelings for Rome simply deepening?

Grrr. "I hate that formula!"

*If not for that formula, you wouldn't even have met Rome, remember?*

"That's not the point," I mumbled.

Men, especially Rome, were off-limits until I learned to control my abilities—or I found Dr. Roberts and he fixed me. Then, and only then, could I kiss Rome like a naughty nymphomaniac. If he still wanted me, that is. After last night, he might never want to touch me again.

"Stupid, idiot, dummy!"

That's what bothered me most and made me angriest with the doctor. Rome probably wanted nothing to do with me now.

Depressed and disheartened, I dressed in the black T-shir
and form-fitting slacks Lexis had laid out for me—which I'
discovered at the edge of my bed when I'd awoken. She'd lef
me a pair of black leather boots. In my size.

*Why'd she have to go and be nice to me, now of all times?*
I thought, brushing my hair and anchoring it in a ponytail
Hating her would have given me a small bit of pleasure or
this crap-infested day. I stepped into the hall. If I'd ever
needed pleasure— I froze. Rome had just strode out of
Lexis's bedroom. Her bedroom!

As he shut the door behind him, our gazes locked. He
moved toward me. I backed away.

"Belle," he said, clearly surprised.

That bastard! I'd cursed and cried all night. I'd agonizec
over him all morning. And he…he…damn him! *I* had turned
him on, and he'd let Lexis finish the job. Disappointment and
fury rocked me, but I quickly extinguished the fury. I would
not react. I *couldn't* react.

*This doesn't matter, Jamison. Don't let it matter.* I swung
away from him and slowly, precisely, as if I hadn't a care in
the world, walked into Tanner's room. After everything that
had happened to him, the kid was probably scared and would
need me to explain the situation.

Except Tanner's room was empty.

I turned, determined to find him and get the hell out of this
apartment. Tanner and I would be just fine on our own.

Rome blocked my path.

"Excuse me," I said stiffly, trying to move around him. I
kept my eyes on his collar.

His arms shot out, gripping the door frame and barring
my exit.

*Remain calm.* "Get out of my way, please."

"Not until you listen to me."

"There's nothing for you to say. Nothing I need to hear. Therefore, there is nothing we need to discuss. Move. Or get a permanent tan from my death ray." *Deep breath in, deep breath out.*

He leaned forward, closing precious space between us. "Why are you acting like this? I did nothing wrong."

My eyes narrowed to tiny slits. "No, you didn't do anything wrong. You kissed me last night, but we don't have a relationship, so we aren't exclusive. You had every right to visit your ex-wife."

"That's not what happened."

When he offered nothing else, I said, "Obviously, it is. It's morning, and you're coming out of her room. I bet you would have liked to hide that from me like everything else so you could screw me at a later date. Or," I added, facing him at last, "maybe you'd already decided I wasn't worth the effort."

"I can't believe you think I'm capable of that."

"I want nothing more to do with you," I snapped. "Now, get out of my way."

He stiffened; his pale blue irises became even paler. His pupils thinned and pointed at both ends, like a cat's. "One, I didn't sleep with her. Two, I didn't spend the night in her room. I went in there to get something, and had you bothered to check you would have learned that she wasn't even in there. She's in the kitchen with Tanner. And three, I think I've already proved you're worth a lot of effort. I didn't want to want you, but the fact is I did. I do."

Without another word, he stalked away from me, leaving

me openmouthed. My hand fluttered over my chest. *You're worth a lot of effort,* he'd said. *I want you,* he'd said. Every feminine instinct I possessed reacted, cheering happily.

He'd meant it, hadn't just been stroking my ego. He'd looked too brutal, too unbending. The ferocity he'd radiated had nearly slayed me. I gulped. And the ache from last night suddenly returned, or maybe it had never left. Beneath my T-shirt, my nipples were hard, my stomach was clenched, eager for a touch, a taste.

Oh yes, he'd meant it. He'd spoken the truth. He and Lexis hadn't had sex. A well-satisfied man did not sport lines of tension around his eyes, did not practically hum with raging need. With savagery. As if he could toss me onto the floor, tear away my clothing and fuck me then and there, the rest of the world be damned.

A delicious tremor rolled down my spine.

Straightening my shoulders, I followed the path Rome had taken. I was smiling, the stupid grin stretched over my entire face, but I couldn't help myself. At least I wasn't skipping. Okay, maybe I was. The boots I wore click-clicked against the marble floor.

The hall opened into the living room, then branched to the dining room I'd been too tired to pay attention to last night. Now, my gaze drank in each little detail. Beyond the low, sprawling glass table were giant, multihued silk pillows that acted as chairs. A towering archway led into a thoroughly modern kitchen of chrome and silver steel. Silver refrigerator, chrome island counter, silver faucet and sink.

Lexis and Tanner stood at the counter. Lexis, of course, looked exquisitely lovely. She wore a bright red and black pantsuit with Chinese symbols scattered on the hem. Tanner wore the same long T-shirt and baggy jeans he'd sported yesterday. Praise the Lord, he'd taken out the eight ball contacts. His eyes were electric blue, almost the exact shade of Rome's. I would have melted under his spell in that instant if I'd been a few years younger.

His features were animated, sinfully intent, as he told Lexis how pretty her skin was, how wonderful her hair smelled, how gorgeously her eyes glowed.

I rolled my eyes. The kid wasn't scared, as I'd feared. He was totally at ease and hitting on the hostess—my would-be nemesis—with moves *I'd* taught him. My gaze strayed farther back, catching sight of Rome. He padded about, gathering glasses and plates. Just looking at him, I felt my chest constrict. *You're worth a lot of effort, too.*

"Did you find the picture of Sunny you were hunting for?" Lexis asked Rome.

"Yeah," he answered curtly.

A twinge of guilt beaded in my chest. He'd wanted a photo from his ex, not wild monkey sex. I'd have to apologize. "I'm sorry," I said. He didn't answer. I'd tell him again when we were alone. Perhaps I'd give him a swift kiss that wouldn't start a fire.

I looked to Tanner. "You seem to be taking this in stride," I told him. I walked to the island. "I'm surprised you like your prison so well." *And the warden,* I added silently.

Blue hair tumbled over his forehead as he quickly faced me. "Viper!" A huge grin broke over his face. He threw his arms around me and squeezed tight. "Dude, this place rocks. What's not to like?"

"Did Commando over there hurt you when he knocked you out?"

"Nah," Tanner said, cheeks reddening. "I'm, like, impervious to pain."

One of my brows arched. "Impervious?"

"Yeah. You know, pain can't—"

"I know what it means, Crazy B, I just didn't expect you to use a word like that."

"Toilet paper word of the day," he said, his eyes narrowing on Rome. I needed to get me some of that toilet paper. "He didn't hurt me, but he did steal my car and I want it back."

"You drive that car now, you die. Bad men will be all over it." Rome stepped up to my side. No part of us touched, but I felt the heat of him. The strength. The patent stillness of his predator soul. He pushed a glass of apple juice in front of me and leveled me with a curious frown, finally giving me his full attention. "Viper?"

I lifted my shoulders in a shrug. "It was the only name I could think to give him." To Tanner, I said, "My real name is Belle."

"I knew it. El stoppo, indeed." He slapped his hand on his thigh. "You'll always be Viper to me, though, my sex-starved babe on the run. Hey," he added with barely a breath. "Lexis told me what's going on. Is it true? Can you really start fires with your mind?"

I hesitated to answer. Would he fear me? Turn away from me? Want nothing more to do with me? Only one way to find out… I bit my lip and nodded.

"Do it!" he said enthusiastically, surprising me. "Start one right now."

Relief weakened my limbs. "No."

"Ah, come on. I'll give you a dollar."

"No! I'm not a circus freak who performs for a little cash." I anchored my hands on my hips. "You have to pay at least a hundred if you want to see actual flames."

His eyes brightened and the irises appeared to deepen, to swirl, like a crystalline pool of magnetic power. "Do you take checks?"

"That's enough. No fires," Rome said. There was a hint of amusement in his tone, as well as exasperation.

He plopped an array of fruits onto the counter, and I plucked a grape. The sweetness filled my mouth, but it wasn't altogether satisfying. I liked fruit and all, but please. Just please. What was up with this healthy meal crap? Ham and crackers last night. Fruit this morning. Where were the doughnuts? The burgers and fries? Hello, I'd almost died— several times in the last day alone. I had a new appreciation for the finer things in life. Like sugar. And fat grams.

"So what's the game plan today?" I asked Rome, then grudgingly stuffed a strawberry in my mouth. It was tarter than the grape and actually contrasted nicely.

"We're going to take the kid—"

"Crazy Bones," Tanner interjected. "Call me Crazy Bones. Or CB. I'll answer to CB."

"We're going to take Dumbo to a safe house."

"That shit is whack, yo." Tanner swallowed a bite of melon and bared his teeth in a scowl. "My name ain't Dumbo, and I ain't going to no safe house. Lexis says I'm, like, an empath. And this empath wants to kick some bad guy ass."

"You're an empath?" I said with a disbelieving shake of my head. "You know what people are feeling? Like on TV?"

"Empaths, like psychics, are born," Lexis said, "not created. Tanner was indeed born with such an ability."

Was I some sort of magnet for the paranormal now? What was next, a vampire? A demon? "I agree with Rome," I said. The thought of Tanner hurt—or worse—was enough to give me hives. He had yet to really *live,* and I wanted no part in helping him die. "I think you need to be somewhere safe."

"I'm not a fucking kid," he snapped.

I frowned over at him. "You don't know what we're dealing with."

"Do you?" he countered, reminding me I hadn't been able to give him answers the day he asked. Which was yesterday, I realized then. I'd only met him yesterday. Wow. Already it seemed as if an eternity had passed.

My shoulders squared, my chin rose and I pierced him with a stern stare. "I know that you're an innocent in all of this, and I never should have gotten you involved. I know—"

"You don't know shit."

"Children." Rome clapped his hands twice. "You may be an empath, Tanner, but you don't have the necessary skills to survive. You'll just get in our way."

"Actually," Lexis said. She flicked her black hair over her dainty shoulder. "He'll aid you more than he hinders you. One day, with practice, he's going to be a human lie detector. But more than that, he's going to be able to sense when Belle needs him. They're bonded in some way. I'm unable to see how, I just know they are."

Rome's focus whipped to Lexis. "Shit," he said.

"Why do you think he was driving down that particular street at that particular time yesterday?"

"I wanted to buy condoms," Tanner said.

Expression soft, Lexis patted him on the shoulder. "No.

On an unconscious level, you'd already sensed Belle's desperation and the heroic part of you forced you to be there so that you could help her."

"Hear that?" Tanner grinned slowly. "The heroic part of me. I'm a hero. A hero, goddamn it, and I want to kick bad guy ass." He punctuated his words by pointing at his chest. "You need me."

He was so excited by his newfound abilities. I wished I could feel that enthusiastic about mine.

Rome glared at Tanner. "Kicking ass could mean getting hurt. Or worse, dying. Are you really prepared to do that?"

"Like I'd die." Tanner snorted.

Kids and their immortality complex, I thought, rolling my eyes. Kids with supernatural abilities were, obviously, even worse. I remained silent while I sucked the juice out of a plump strawberry. The tangy sweetness ran down my throat. If Tanner was connected to me, maybe he could help me regulate my emotions or something. That would be cool, except I would rather Rome had that ability. That way, I wouldn't need Tanner in the room, there to control my reactions, when I next kissed the man.

Whoa. Wait. *What are you doing, Jamison?* I'd decided not to make out with Rome again until after I was back to my normal self, and I needed to stick with that (horrible) plan so I didn't accidentally kill him.

One of Rome's hands suddenly snaked around my wrist. With his free hand, he plucked the strawberry from my fingers and tossed it onto the table. "No more strawberries for you," he said hoarsely, staring at my undoubtedly red, moist lips.

Oh, oh, oh. What was this? Desire from him? Because of

a piece of fruit? Forgetting my plan already, I very delibe[r]ately lifted another strawberry, placed it between my lips an[d] bit. Rome's nostrils flared. My knees weakened. Holy hel[l] His eyes locked on the half-eaten strawberry. I welcomed the rest of the way into my mouth and chewed slowly.

Tanner whistled. "No wonder you wouldn't sleep with m[e] Viper. You're hot for Superagent. Girls go wild for that con[m]mando shit, don't they? Well, guess what? I want to be Age[nt] Crazy Bones. Lexis said her boss, John, will want to hire m[e] and I'll get to go on missions and protect important peopl[e] and uncover evil schemes."

Rome swiped his glass and drained the contents, the[n] turned his attention to Lexis, giving her a look that clear[ly] said, *Why did you tell him all of that?* Her lips twitched.

I bit my tongue at their ease with each other. Was [it] childish of me to want to jump in between them and retur[n] Rome's attention to me? I didn't like that they were so in sy[nc] they understood each other without words.

When Rome's grip on my hip tightened possessively an[d] he pulled me closer to him, I lost my jealousy of Lexis. [A] blissful thrill tingled through me. I forced my gaze to Tann[er] before I melted into a puddle on the floor. "How come yo[u] aren't upset about any of this? We could very well hav[e] ruined your life."

He lost his smile and looked away, past the kitchen, pa[st] the living room. "My life was already ruined." His voic[e] held no humor. Only despair.

"That doesn't mean more danger will make it better[,] Rome said.

"I want to have some fun and get some girls, okay? There['s] nothing wrong with that."

No, there was nothing wrong with that. I just prayed his desires didn't get him killed. "What's our game plan?" I asked again.

"I vote for kicking ass and not dying," Tanner said.

"You're such a comedian." My gaze flicked to Rome. "Well?"

He picked up the strawberry he'd taken from me, and popped it into his mouth. Chewed slowly, purposefully. Savored, then swallowed. "I'm still in shock. I've gotten used to working alone. I'd just resigned myself to using you, baby, and now I've got the kid to contend with."

"Hey," Tanner said, frowning. "I'm not a kid, and I, like, totally resent you calling me that. Men tremble in my presence. I can be dangerous. I have mad skills with a bo staff."

"Sure you do, Napoleon," I said drily. "Did you hunt wolverines this summer, too?"

"You do *not* know how to use a bo staff," Rome said.

"Yes, I do! I've killed people, man. Killed them dead."

Rome scrubbed a hand over his face. "Did you kill them with laughter?"

Tanner scowled, his eyebrow piercings glinting in the overhead light. "You want a piece of me, Double-O Asswipe? Go ahead. Go for it. I said I wanted some action, and I don't mind getting it from you."

Rome flashed a snarl, showing teeth that were surprisingly sharp. The pointed tips gleamed in the light. I double-blinked at them and gulped. Holy hell. They were monster teeth. Had they always been so long, and I simply hadn't noticed? Reaching up, I fingered my lips. When we kissed, those teeth of his should have sliced through my mouth.

"Are you a vampire?" I blurted out. It made sense in a para normal sort of way. He'd denied having any type of powe last night. In light of those fangs, I didn't believe him anymore.

He hastily closed his mouth and turned away. He drew in a deep, shuddering breath. A long while passed before he spoke. "No, I'm not a vampire."

"He's a—"

"Lexis," Rome warned.

She, too, pressed her lips together.

Aha! So he *did* have a power. "Aw, come on." Exasper ated, angry, I threw my arms in the air. "You can tell me." Lexis knew and I didn't, and that needed to change. Right now. "I have no room to judge."

"Get your bag," Rome said, not offering any kind of an swer or explanation. "Lexis left it on the couch for you We're going. I want to visit Dr. Roberts's house and look fo clues. He's an old man. Surely *I* can find him."

"He's old, but he's smart," Lexis warned. "No one has been able to find him yet."

"Wait just a damn minute." I gripped Rome's shoulder and spun him around—and he let me. He could have resisted, bu he didn't. I poked him in the chest and glared up at him. "You know what I am, so I have every right to know about you."

"Yeah." Tanner crossed his arms over his chest. "Me, too."

"Shut up," Rome and I told him simultaneously.

"I'm trying to help you, Viper. Rome's afraid to tell you." Suddenly Tanner ceased all movement. A grin spread over his face. Jumping up and down, he clapped his hands together and whooped. "Lexis. Lexis, did you hear what I just said? I can feel his fear. I can feel his fear!"

"Shut the hell up," Rome growled before Lexis could respond. "I'm not afraid."

"Is that true?" Craving contact, even slight, I traced my fingertips up his torso and cupped his cheeks. "Are you afraid to tell me?"

"Didn't you just hear me?" His jaw clenched, and those taut lines I hated branched from his eyes. "I'm not afraid. This simply isn't something I talk about. Ever. With anyone."

"Lexis knows," I pointed out.

"She was part of my…change. It happened during the experiments we volunteered for."

"Tell me." Inside, my stomach was churning and I felt sick. So sick. I hated that he was blocking me out like this. Did he think I would reject him? Did he think it would disgust me? Or did he simply not trust me with the truth?

"I'm not going to discuss it, so drop it. What I am, what I can do, is not something people like you can tolerate."

My teeth ground together. "People like me? By that you better mean smart, wonderfully compassionate women."

His lips curled at the edges, and he lost some of his dark aura. "Yeah, that's what I meant. Now, end of discussion. We've got some breaking and entering to do today."

Hurt by his continued refusal, I let my arms fall to my sides. "I'm not going to let this subject drop, you know."

Now he cupped my jaw, and his eyes bored into mine. Slowly, languidly, he brought his lips to mine, only a heartbeat away. "Yes, you will, Pyro Chica." He kissed me then. Hard and rough. Delicious, wonderful. A quick thrust of his tongue before he strode out of reach, acting as if it had never happened.

Lexis turned away sharply.

"Pyro Chica?" Tanner grabbed my arm to prevent m
from chasing after Rome. "Is that your superhero name? N
fair. I need a name, too."

I whirled on him, needing an outlet for my frustration
"That is not my name, and if you dare call me Pyro Chica o
Periodic Table Chick or Four Elements Girl I'll singe th
hairs right off your balls." Once I learned how to do tha
without destroying the world, that is. "Got it?"

"Fine." Backing away from me, he held up his hands
palms out. "I'll just call you Homicidal Tendencies Wench."

Rome, who had his back to us and was a good distanc
away in the living room, barked out a laugh. "That's the firs
intelligent thing you've said, kid. It's the perfect name for her
no doubt about it."

I flipped both of them off.

Tanner blew me a kiss, the rebellious teenage jackass.

"Rome," Lexis suddenly exclaimed.

The sound of her voice, nearing panic, caused Tanner an
me to shut up. Rome spun around, his expression dark, dangerous. "What's wrong?"

"They're here," Lexis said softly. "Vincent's men are
here."

## CHAPTER THIRTEEN

HAVING A PSYCHIC on our team provided a distinct advantage. We knew the bad guys were going to burst into the apartment before they actually did. However, having a psychic on our team also proved to be a distinct disadvantage. For me, at least.

Because Lexis was right. Damn it. That plant fire the previous night was only the beginning. In the end, I did, indeed, torch her place.

"How long do we have?" Rome demanded.

"Not long," was Lexis's whispered response. "A few minutes."

A blank screen descended over Rome's features as he faced me. "Catch," he said. He tossed the bag Lexis had packed for me. I slung the strap over my head, anchoring it across my middle, the pouch at my back. Adrenaline rushed through me, hot and stinging, and my palms began to sweat.

Tanner paled, and his cheeks hollowed. "What should I do? What should I do?"

Rome stalked toward us. His motions swift, deliberate, he went to the drawer by the sink, opened it and withdrew two knives.

"I'm not using those." Tanner shook his head for emphasis.

"They're not for you." Rome didn't spare him a glance. "Lexis," he said, then he tossed her the blades.

I sucked in a hiss of air, only exhaling when Lexis caught them, hilts clasped tightly in her hands. In one fluid motion she sheathed them at her waist.

"You know what to do," he told her.

"Yes."

"Take the kid, and we'll meet up later."

Lexis's piercing green gaze swept over Rome, a little sad, a little wistful. I'm no empath, but I could feel the love she felt for him, and I couldn't help but wonder, again, why she'd ever let him go. "Be careful," she whispered.

He nodded. "You, too."

Lexis grabbed Tanner's hand and tried to usher him out of the kitchen. The kid ground his heels into the floor. "Viper? You gonna be okay?"

"I'll be fine." God, I prayed I spoke true.

His gaze slid to Rome, to the lethal picture he presented, then back to me. "Maybe you should come with us. Let Rambo handle the—"

"She stays," Rome said curtly. "We have questions, they have answers."

"I stay," I said, my voice shaking. I didn't know what we were up against, only that it would be bad. And that I wasn't close to being prepared.

Still Tanner didn't move.

"We must go," Lexis said, tugging on his arm. "It's almost too late. Rome won't let anyone hurt her."

That was all the assurance Tanner needed. He allowed Lexis to lead him down the hall. His tortured gaze remained on me until the last second.

*Oh God, oh God, oh God.* "Do you have a gun or something for me?" I asked Rome.

He palmed another knife, but kept this one for himself. It was larger than the other two, with a sharp gleaming tip. "You know how to use a gun?"

"No."

"Then, no." Like his ex, he slid the blade into his belt buckle.

I crisscrossed my arms over my stomach in an attempt to bolster my courage and draw some strength. "What can I do to help?"

"You have powers, remember?" he said, his tone grim. "Use them."

I liked that he trusted me. I did. But I didn't trust myself. If he was hurt because of me, because of my lack of skill… "My powers are dangerous, Rome. I can't control them."

He wasn't given the chance to respond.

The sound of breaking glass erupted. I nearly jumped out of my skin. A millisecond later, wood from the front door splintered. Black-clad men rushed inside the apartment. More glass broke; more men burst inside.

"Get down," Rome whispered fiercely, pushing my shoulders until we were both crouched behind the counter, hidden from immediate view. A look of savagery passed over his features, as if he relished what he was about to do. "Just be careful not to hurt me, okay?"

His mouth slammed against mine for the barest of seconds, lighting a small fire in the pit of my stomach. My passion was melded with fear, though, so the fire lacked any true heat. Footsteps pounded in the living room, followed by still more breaking glass.

Rome rushed forward, staying low.

Gunfire erupted. *Whiz. Pop.* I cringed, and my breath froze in my throat. Dear God. This was real. Terrible, real and in your face. I'd known that during yesterday's car chase, but it once again hit me, with a force I couldn't dispute. The man I desired had just thrown himself headlong into danger. A part of me wanted to stay crouched in the shadows as I was—the part of me that recognized fight-or-flight syndrome and eagerly embraced flight.

I forced myself past the debilitating fear, however, while trying to allow it to help me. I had to work with what emotions I could, and right now, all I had was fear. But fear brought ice, as I'd learned running from Rome and touching Vincent's car, and ice could be a powerful weapon.

"Come on," I muttered. "You could *die*, Belle. Rome could die."

More gunfire. A man screamed.

Terror rushed over me, cool, cold, then frigid. *Welcome the fear. Welcome the fear, but don't let it keep you immobile. Welcome…* A numbing cold pricked at my fingertips, barely noticeable at first. *Welcome the fear, welcome the fear.* Frost formed on the end of my nose, and the air around me misted. *Good girl.*

Another scream.

*Welcome the fear.* Wave after wave of it slammed into me, each one colder than the last. Trembling, I stared down at my hands. As I watched, a ball of ice began to form. I could hardly believe it, but there it was all the same. I shoved to my feet and drew back my hand, searching for a target. I spotted several. Multiple men raced through the room, kicking over furniture.

Rome suddenly flashed into my vision. He spun, striking a man in the chest with a razored boot heel. His victim screamed and clutched at his now-blood-soaked chest before slouching to the ground. Someone spotted Rome and dived for him.

"Rome!" I shouted. "Look out." I released the ice with all the power my arm would allow. The gleaming white ball flew through the air and slammed into my target. The moment it touched him, the ice spread over him, enveloping his entire body.

I'd expected it, but the sight still gave me a jolt.

"Get down, Belle."

I did as Rome had commanded. Gunfire peppered the counter I hid behind, and I curled into myself. A cry rent my lips. Weren't these people supposed to keep me alive for experimentation? My terror deepened, and several more balls of ice formed in my hands.

Two disharmonized screams blasted my eardrums, and then the bullets stopped flying. Rome, I suspected, had killed the men shooting at me. I leapt up, found targets and tossed the ice. I missed one, but a ball slammed dead center into the second, a black-clad assailant who froze in place.

Wide-eyed, I studied the bodies littering the living room floor. Some were moaning, some were writhing. Some were lifeless. The ones I'd frozen were still blocks of ice. Rome danced around those who remained standing. He was kicking, slashing. Killing. How long could he hold them off? Not long, I realized with horror as I watched someone bolt from the shadows and stab him.

Horror pounded through me, and I shouted, *"No!"* Blood dripped from Rome's side, soaking his shirt. Without reacting to the pain he must have felt, he bent and lashed out with his left arm, sinking his own blade into the man's stomach.

"Come on, come on," I whispered frantically to my hands. Nothing. No more ice. My fear was gone, dissolved in the wake of an intense surge of determination to save the man who had saved me over and over again. These goons were here to take me, perhaps kill me, and obviously meant to kill Rome in the process.

That, I couldn't allow.

Fury invaded me then, more powerful than ever before, completely melting away every ounce of chill. I burned. No. No, I couldn't let myself experience anger. I didn't want a fire. Rome might be hurt by *me*. But the fury wouldn't leave me—how dare they hurt Rome!—and flames began to lick the ends of my fingers and burn the rims of my eyes.

From the corner of my gaze, I saw someone sprinting around the counter and straight toward me. His determination to immobilize me was evident with his every hurried step. Underneath his black mask, I suspected he wore an expression of cold, unfeeling intent.

Instinctively, I stretched out my hands to ward him off. No air shield this time, but flames shot from me and engulfed him. His screams were agonizing, howls and pleas for help. He dropped to the floor and rolled. My stomach churned with sickness, and I gulped. Ohmygod. I'd done that. *I'd* done that. I covered my mouth with a shaky hand, fire dying.

In the distance, I heard Rome grunt, and my thoughts immediately focused on him. I stepped around the counter, moving straight into the center of the action. I didn't see him. Where was he? Had he fallen? White-gold sparks flicked from my eyes. Even my hands began burning again.

As the remaining assailants aimed their guns at me, I raised my hands and twisted my body in every direction, desperate to find and save Rome. Fire sprayed everywhere I turned, trailing paths of deadly flame. Metal liquefied. Wood crackled. Smoke thickened the air, and I began to cough. My fire never ceased, though. Around me, men howled and dived for cover.

From the back rooms, I heard the infuriated growl of a wild animal. A…jungle cat? "Rome," I shouted. I wanted to see him, to assure myself that he lived and breathed.

An alarm suddenly screeched to full, startling life. A heartbeat later, the sprinkler system kicked on, and showers of cold water burst from the ceiling. Droplets rained on my face, caught in my eyelashes and trickled down my nose. But the flames on my fingertips refused to be doused; they sizzled hot and blistering. If they'd hurt him further…

"Rome!"

I blinked the water from my eyes and noticed the room's blaze was not as resilient as my own; already the fire lessened. Using this to his advantage, one of the men hurdled over the couch and dashed toward me. He didn't have a gun, so he made use of another weapon—his legs. He jumped up and slammed his feet into my stomach. Air burst from my lungs as I was propelled backward; pain exploded inside me. I hit the floor, a wall, I didn't know. My head thudded into something hard, and my gaze went black for several seconds.

When my vision cleared, I caught sight of a large black object—a jaguar?—flying through the air and landing on top of my assailant. The cat went for the flailing man's throat. When it finished, blood dripped from its mouth. A scream tore from my own throat, and I found myself throwing a stream of fire at the cat. No, not flame. Ice. The ball barely missed its left shoulder.

It faced me dead-on, stalking forward, blue eyes slitted. Water rained upon us, splashing like tears. Panicked, I scrambled backward. Instead of attacking me as I feared, it jumped over me, a streak of black lightning, and knocked down a man I hadn't known stood behind me.

Limbs shaky, I pushed to my feet and batted the wet hair out of my eyes. I had seen this same animal in my apartment. Hadn't I? It hadn't hurt me then, either. Had Rome—Rome! Dear God, had it already gotten Rome?

I stumbled through the rooms, searching each and every one, leaping over body after prone, unmoving body. In Lexis's room, I found Rome's clothes—without his body. They were ripped down the center, mere rags. And they were splattered with blood.

My fire had died, and now the ice left me, too. I was suddenly empty inside. "Rome!"

A violent fit of coughing doubled me over. Despite the cascade of water, the smoke became so thick and black I had trouble navigating, and had to lean on the wall for support and guidance.

"Rome!" Weakness drifted through me, a phantom at first, easily ignored. But as the coughing fit refused to lessen and the smoke burned my throat, the weakness became a tangible entity.

My knees suddenly lost all strength, and I dropped to the floor. Had to…find…Rome. I didn't know what I'd do if he'd…if he'd… I couldn't finish the thought. In the distance, I heard the wail of sirens. Thought I heard the scramble of footsteps, the panicked shouts of men.

"Rome." His name was nothing more than a hollow, ragged whisper between coughs.

"Here, baby. I'm here." His arm snaked around me, and he dropped to my side.

Sobbing in relief, I buried my face in the hollow of his neck and wrapped myself around him. "Where the—" cough "—hell have you—" cough "—been?"

"I'll explain later. Right now, we have to get out of here. Can you crawl?" He didn't wait for my answer. The palm of his hand settled on my shoulder and pushed me down. That same hand then slid to the small of my back and urged me forward.

"Can't...see," I said. Pools splashed around my knees, causing me to slip and slide.

"Hold on to me. I'll lead the way."

A whoosh of air, the brush of his arm, the sprinkle of water. I tried to clasp his shirt, only then realizing his chest was bare. I opened my mouth to ask why he'd ripped off his clothes, but he hissed in pain and the question evaporated. "Sorry."

"Here." Not breaking stride, he guided my fingers to his naked hip bone.

With one hand I held on to him, and with the other I crawled. God, the smoke was so thick. Even down here. Tears from my eyes blended with the drops falling from the sprinkler. Nausea welled in my stomach.

"Look out...for the...cat," I managed to wheeze. There was something odd about that jaguar, something I knew I should guess but couldn't seem to place at the moment. The fog in my mind proved too great. I only knew it hadn't been a dream; it wasn't a hallucination.

"Don't talk, baby. Save your breath. Try not to inhale the smoke."

The bag strapped to my back bounced against me with every movement, bruising, and I winced at the soreness. Finally we reached a small doorway. No, not a door, I realized as I stretched out my arm and patted it, but a hatch.

"Get ready to slide," Rome told me. Without any more warning, he clutched my waist, lifted me and chucked me inside.

I didn't have time to prepare. One second I was on the ground, the next I wasn't. Down, down I toppled. My arms flailed, my legs stretched behind me. I would have yelled or shouted, but my throat was too raw. Black walls surrounded me, hemmed me in. Stifled me.

I smacked onto a solid foundation, and my bag smacked into me.

The force of both blows vibrated through my bones. Dizzy, I remained immobile, prone, trying to breathe, trying to see, trying to will strength into my trembling limbs. At least the air proved clean and fresh, a welcome contrast to the smoke-filled rooms above.

Rome plowed on top of me, his bag slapping me in the face. The only oxygen I'd been able to draw in rushed out of me unbidden.

"Sorry, baby." He scrambled off me, blood dripping down his side. Grimacing, he rifled through his bag.

He was naked. I had known it before, but hadn't grasped the actuality. Rome was naked, as in not a stitch of clothing covered his magnificent body. Why? Wait. Did it matter? He was tanned and toned, and even in my weakened condition I could appreciate his hard (large) strength. I almost cried when he whipped out a pair of pants and tugged them on.

"No underwear?" I managed to sputter. A girl had to embrace a good distraction when it came along.

"I don't wear them." He fastened the button. "Ever. Come on. Firemen are here, and we can't afford to be detained or spotted."

"We didn't—" shallow breath "—question any—" another breath "—of the bad guys."

"There were more than I anticipated. Taking one would have slowed us down or gotten us killed."

He helped me to a shaky stand and pulled me into motion. I wanted so badly to fall to my face, to close my eyes and sleep forever. It took a conscious effort to place one foot in front of the other. Water dripped from my hair onto my already soaked clothing. I scanned the surrounding area. Plain gray walls. Some type of machinery. The scents of soap and oil. Were we in the basement of the apartment building?

"Faster, Belle. You can do it."

I tried to keep up with Rome, I really did, but I'd inhaled too much smoke. Racking coughs plagued me. Utter weakness had taken root in my every cell. When I tripped over a cord, I didn't have the strength to right myself. Darkness blanketed my mind before I hit. No. Not hit, I mused groggily. Floated. Rome had caught me, his strong arms banded around me. His voice drifted through my subconscious. "I've got you, baby. I've got you."

If he kept calling me baby, I thought, just before darkness consumed me, I really would fall in love with him.

"COME ON. Take a drink."

Cool liquid touched my lips before descending my raw, aching throat. I coughed and sputtered and dragged my eyelids open. Hazy light stung my eyes, and I blinked.

"Drink," Lexis commanded, her expression stern. Sh
loomed over me, the plastic cup in her hand poised at the edg
of my mouth.

Had I died and gone to hell? I raised myself as best
could and drank. The liquid's tart flavor filled my mout
before scraping at my throat. I winced.

"There," she said. "Don't you feel better?"

"No." The word was hoarse, barely audible.

She chuckled, easing down beside me and setting the cu
aside. "You scared us pretty badly."

Images of the fire, of the men I'd hurt—probably killed—
flashed through my mind, and I pressed my lips togethe
They were bad guys. I shouldn't feel guilty. They'd tried t
hurt me, tried to hurt Rome. Rome! His image filled m
mind next, his chest bloody. Panic slithered through m
How was he? *Where* was he?

I tried to sit up. "Where's Rome?" Gaze wild, I searche
my surroundings. Lexis and I were the only ones present, an
we seemed to be inside a cabin. Wooden walls, woode
floors. Only the barest amount of furniture: a bed, a lamp,
table and a few chairs.

"Settle down," she said. "Rome is fine."

"He had a deep cut."

"No, it was a paltry wound that has already begun to heal.

"There was a cat, a jaguar—"

"I'm sure there was, but Rome wasn't hurt by it. I promise
Just lie back and relax."

"Tanner—"

"Is fine," she said, cutting me off. "Everyone survived. Al
is well. It was *you* we worried about. You've been asleep al
most an entire day."

"A day?" I allowed her to ease me back onto the mattress. God, I hated being this weak, this vulnerable. I stared up at the domed timber ceiling. "Where are we?"

"My cabin. It's on the outskirts of Madison. But don't worry," she added. "No one knows about it, not even John. Rome built it for occasions such as this. I made sure Tanner and I weren't followed, and knowing Rome as I do, he did the same."

"Where is he?"

"I sent him and the boy to gather supplies. They were driving me crazy with their concern for you, and the cave is only a short walk away." She busied herself tucking the plain brown covers around me. "Rome found the cave years ago and has stocked it with every item a person in hiding might need."

Lethargy beat through me, beckoning me to sleep a little longer. My eyelashes fluttered shut, heavy with exhaustion, but I forced them open. Forced myself to concentrate on her words. "Why were they concerned for me?"

"Well…" She paused, cleared her throat. "You stopped breathing several times."

Stopped breathing? My hand fluttered to my aching throat. Dear Lord. I'd come close to dying, and I hadn't known it. I wouldn't have had the chance to tell my dad or Sherridan goodbye. Wouldn't have gotten to see them one final time. "I want to call my dad," I said, suddenly filled with the need to hear his voice.

"Before you do," Lexis said, an odd inflection in her voice, "Rome would like to talk to you about him."

"Why?" I jolted upright, and the hasty action cost me dearly. Dizziness and nausea blasted me; bright lights winked in front of my eyes. I rubbed my temple with one hand and clutched my stomach with the other. *He's fine, he's fine, he's fine.* "Why?" I repeated, the word no more than a tortured moan.

"There's no reason to worry. Your dad is alive and well. I promise."

My heart drummed in my chest, and cool prickles rolled in my veins as I stared into the green depths of her eyes, trying to glean the truth. She appeared sincere, and I decided to believe her. Slowly relaxing, I flopped back against the pillow. "What's wrong with me? Why am I so weak?"

"Smoke inhalation is our guess."

I frowned. "Shouldn't I be immune to that? I mean, I started the fire."

Her delicate shoulders lifted in a shrug. "Rome said you're probably ultrasensitive to pollutants now. While you can withstand the fire itself, the ensuing smoke devastates you more than other people because you are now one with Mother Earth. Pollutants now hurt you as much as they hurt the world."

That made sense. I didn't like it, but it made sense.

Lexis turned away from me and walked to the room's only window. She separated the brown curtains, peeking out. Whoever picked the brown color scheme needed a serious spanking. Talk about bland. Must have been Rome, since Lexis's taste—as proved by her apartment—was colorful and expensive. So, Rome needed the spanking, did he? My pleasure.

"Is someone coming?" I asked.

"No."

A thick blanket of silence descended over us. I shifted uncomfortably on the bed. What was she—

"I love him," she blurted out.

O-kay. Going there, were we? Better to get it out in the

open, I guess, than to let it fester between us. "I realized that within an hour of meeting you. So why did you cut him loose?"

She laughed bitterly. "I'm psychic, which is both a blessing and a curse. I—I knew before I married Rome that I wasn't meant to be with him, but I did it anyway. I hoped I could make him love me the way I loved him."

My brow wrinkled in confusion. "I don't understand."

She tossed me a sad half smile, and my chest actually constricted in sorrow for her. The pain in her eyes was staggering. "We were together for several years, married several more, and then I got pregnant. Yet all along I knew, deep down, that if I didn't walk away from him, he would be tied to my side when he didn't really want to be there."

"I'm not usually this dense. I hope. But I don't get what you're trying to tell me."

I didn't need an empath to help me read her emotions at that moment. Her shoulders slumped as her sadness deepened. "Rome likes me. He might even love me, but it's not the kind of love a man should have for a wife. I knew, I always knew, that there was someone else for him. He didn't. He thought I was the one, but he would have learned the truth soon enough. And he would have stayed with me despite wanting—no, craving—this other woman." She wiped a tear from her eye with a trembling hand. "I couldn't have endured that."

Her words were both wonderful and terrible. She wasn't the right woman for him, but was I? I couldn't kiss him without starting a fire. Trouble followed me everywhere. I was currently jobless. Not exactly great girlfriend material. Still. I wanted to be the right woman. Badly. If I wasn't... My stomach twisted.

"Who *is* right for him?" I found myself asking. M
fingers clutched the sheets as I waited for her answer.
hoped; I dreaded.

"Maybe you. Maybe someone else. I don't know who."

So there was still hope, but there was also doubt. A sharp
ache tore through my temples. Cringing, I covered my eye
with the crook of my arm. Best to change the subject before
I induced a brain aneurism from overanalyzing. "I'm sorry
about your home. You were right. I torched it."

She waved her hand through the air. "It was only a building. Rome and Sunny are safe. That's all that matters."

I didn't want to like her, I really didn't. After everything
she'd revealed, however, I found that I did. Despite my (al-
leged) jealousy. She could have railed at me for holding the
(temporary) affection of the man she loved. She could have
thrown me out. Instead, she gave me that sad smile.

"I think you have two admirers," she said, wistful. "Tanner
was so worried about you."

"Well, I like Tanner, too. He's a good kid."

"He's not a child. He's a man who just has a bit more maturing to do."

Her affection for him was clear.

"His abilities are raw," she added, "hardly developed, but
I think with the proper training he could do great things." A
warm chuckle escaped her. "Rome almost knocked him out."
Her smile spread all the wider as she returned to the bed.
"Tanner kept saying you would have been perfectly healthy
if Rome had let you leave with him, and I think it hit Rome
hard. He has always been a protector, yet he had enough faith
in you to utilize your...skills."

There was just enough hesitation in her voice to suggest

I didn't really have any skill, but I still experienced a tendril of pleasure because Rome *had* trusted me. The pleasure was quickly followed by prickles of disappointment. "I hate that I did so little to actually help, and so much more to hinder. The only reason he and I stayed around was to question one of the men, but I ended up freezing or barbecuing everyone there. And then—"

Lexis suddenly straightened, and she lost her good humor. My words ceased abruptly. "What? What's wrong?" I demanded. I guess I was coming to rely on Lexis as Rome and Brittan did.

"The door is…" Frowning, she closed her eyes and an aura of stillness came over her. Several seconds passed, and her smile returned. "The men are about to return. As Tanner would say, Rome is pi-issed."

# CHAPTER FOURTEEN

AS PREDICTED, the door burst open. Rome stalked inside, dragging a protesting Tanner behind him. When the door closed in their wake, he pushed Tanner into a chair and dropped a heavy bag at the boy's feet.

"I'm not afraid to use my lethal kung fu moves on you," Tanner growled.

"Stay," Rome growled back. "And don't speak for the rest of the day." He pivoted toward me, and when our eyes met his expression softened. "You're awake."

I sat up slowly and finger-combed my hair, wishing I had a mirror. I probably looked like crap, while he looked edible. He wore one of the black T-shirts he favored, and black slacks. I would have liked to see him in stone-washed jeans, but he only ever wore pants. And no underwear, I suddenly recalled, my cheeks heating.

He approached me and settled at the edge of the bed, a whisper away. My heartbeat accelerated, nearly exploding from my chest when his arm brushed mine. Always there was this electric tingle between us.

"How are you?" I asked, drinking him in. His face glowed with healthy color. He didn't appear strained or hurt. In fact, he looked perfectly normal. Well, as normal as a dark angel could look.

"I'm good. Just a twinge in my side. How are *you?*"

"Better."

He reached out and smoothed a hand over my cheek, his gaze becoming fierce. Lethal. "You scared me. Don't ever do that again."

I shivered at the savage intensity he projected. "I won't."

His blue, blue eyes bored into mine as he laced our fingers together. "When you passed out..."

I squeezed his hand.

"Ah, look at the little lovebirds," Tanner cooed. "Want Lexis and me to leave?"

"Yes," Rome said, not switching his focus from me. They didn't leave, unfortunately, but stayed where they were. With absolute tenderness, Rome's thumb played across my palm. "Belle, do you feel well enough to go outside and practice using your powers?"

At the moment, with his strength seeping into me, I felt capable of anything. "Sure."

"Good. After yesterday, I need to know how you'll hold up. Besides, I don't want to head into the city until dark, so we've got time to kill." He turned to Lexis. "Did you tell her about her dad?"

I stiffened with renewed fear and felt a cool draft gust through my veins.

"No," Lexis said. "I knew you would want to explain."

"Someone better tell me what's going on with my dad before I freeze this entire place."

With his free hand, Rome hooked a strand of hair behind my ear. "He's fine, but I'm afraid Vincent might try to use him to draw you out."

A lump formed in my throat, and my hand flew to my

mouth. If my dad were in danger, I'd—I'd…I'd simply die, and take everyone responsible with me. "We can't move him from the center. His medication is there. His nurses are there."

"I know. That's why I'd like to send Lexis to guard him."

"I don't know." Automatically, my attention moved to the woman in question. Yes, I'd seen her catch the knives Rome had thrown to her, but could she fight off armed men? Would she kill to protect my father, a man she'd never met before?

Her lips twitched in genuine amusement. Before I could blink, she unsheathed a knife and tossed it straight at me. I heard a whoosh, immediately followed by a thud as the blade embedded in the wall behind me. I gasped out, "Holy shit!"

"I can take care of him," she said, her confidence a palpable force.

"Way to test my bladder control," I said drily. My pulse hammered hard and fast. God knows I didn't have enough excitement in my life. Having a knife thrown at me was like contaminated icing on an already poisoned cake. "She's perfect," I told Rome. "I'll have to call the center and ask if they'll allow her, but—"

"No need," he said, cutting me off. "The kid here apparently does have some uses. He's very good with a computer and already hacked into their system. They are now under the assumption that a specialized cardiac nurse has been ordered to give him twenty-four-hour care."

"Okay. Good. I'll just call my dad and—"

"No phone calls. No telling who's been tapped." There was an apology in his tone, but the command was clear, unrelenting.

Besides, I'd told my dad I wouldn't call him. I'd told him I would be away on a fabulous vacation, relaxing. *I wish.*

"Unlike what you see in the movies," Rome said, "phone calls can be traced instantly. If your dad is under any type of monitoring, I don't want you in contact with him."

"I understand." Sighing, I glanced at Lexis. "Can you keep me updated on him? Secretly? He thinks I'm on vacation, and it would be best to let him keep thinking that."

"Of course."

I eased back against my pillow. "I'll shower and eat, then we can go outside for our practice session. Okay?" I asked Rome.

He leaned down, pressing his cheek against mine, but not before I caught a glimpse of his wickedly sexy smile. "Belle Jamison naked and in the shower. I like that image."

I gulped, and peered once again at Lexis, who had already turned away from us to busy herself in the kitchen. I didn't want to hurt her more than necessary. Look at what the woman had done—and what she was *going* to do for me. I don't think Rome realized his ex still loved him. In his realm of male understanding (aka limited), he likely figured Lexis didn't care who he was with.

"One day I'll be able to join you in there—and not just in my mind." His breath fanned my cheek, then my ear, and he added softly, "I've been thinking about this, and I think the shower is the perfect place for us. If things get too hot, the water will cool us off."

Or turn us to steam, as hot as I was for him. "One day," I replied just as softly. God, I hoped that day came soon. "I want you so much."

His nostrils flared, and his eyes gleamed with heat. He looked, in short, like a man who was battling a savage need to claim me. "Get in there. Hurry. I've been worried about you, and if you don't get in there I'm going to take you here and now."

Oh, I loved it when he went all alpha on me. I lumbered from the bed. My knees were wobbly as I hobbled into the bathroom. For my own sake, I locked the door.

I showered, lingering in the hot, steamy water and letting it clean me inside and out. I felt stronger with every second that passed. The damp, misty air soothed my throat and swept the soot from my lungs. A part of me worried about Pretty Boy Vincent finding us and bursting in on me, catching me with my pants down. I'd been surprise-attacked too many times in the last couple of days. Still, the other part of me simply luxuriated in this totally *normal* act. The cabin was a safe haven, and one I desperately needed at the moment.

When the water became too cold to bear, I exited and dressed in the black shirt and jeans Lexis had packed for me—which someone had laid across the toilet. Someone who had picked the door lock and entered the bathroom without my knowledge. Whoever the lock picker was (cough, cough—Rome!) hadn't brought me panties or a bra.

I was unwilling to wear the dirty ones—if I had them, that is, which I didn't. The aforementioned *someone* had taken them with him. So, as this *someone* had obviously planned, I dressed without them. No panties. No bra. My lips inched into a smile. Lecherous man.

Rome was a true male, even in the face of danger.

When I emerged, a cloud of steam followed me. Rome, Tanner and Lexis were at the table, eating breakfast. Seemed weird, since the last meal I recalled was the breakfast in Lexis's apartment. I guess that's what happens when you sleep an entire day away. I strode to them, meaning to claim the empty chair next to Rome, but he tugged me onto his lap and plopped a buttered biscuit in front of me, all without pausing in his speech.

"—forces are divided while they search for both Belle and Dr. Roberts. Now is the perfect time to strike."

Sitting in his lap aroused me. My nipples instantly pearled; my stomach quivered in anticipation of a touch. Maybe I was a slut and a harlot (a slot?). Or maybe, just maybe, Rome emitted lethal pheromones no woman could resist.

"I'm not saying I disagree with you," Lexis said, slathering her own biscuit with strawberry jelly, "but you have to consider the fact that we're divided, too. I'll be with Belle's father, while the three of you evade capture from Vincent. And John, if he's looking for you."

"John might be looking for us?" I asked. I smeared honey on my biscuit and then proceeded to inhale it. "I thought Rome took care of him."

"He has to know you're helping Belle now," Lexis said to Rome.

He plucked the last nibble from my fingers and popped it into his mouth. "For all he knows, she escaped me and I'm still hunting her down."

Lexis snorted. "No one intelligent will believe she escaped you."

"Hey! For your information," I told her indignantly, "I *did* escape him."

"And I helped," Tanner added. His chest puffed up like a peacock.

"I know you did, honey, and I'm proud of you." Lexis patted his back. "Truth is stranger than fiction, I suppose, but no one will believe Belle defeated Rome."

"I called John and told him she was a wily little thing and

had gotten away," Rome said, "but that I'd find her soon and bring her ass in."

Both Lexis and I gasped. "You did?" we asked simultaneously. Our tones were different, though. She sounded surprised. I sounded pissed.

Rome's hand squeezed my waist. "Yes, I did."

Okay, I was totally feeling betrayed here. Did Rome truly plan to bring me in after I helped him with Sunny? I couldn't stand it; I had to know. I *deserved* to know. "Are you going to be an asshole and give me to John when you no longer need me?"

"John didn't say much," Rome said, ignoring me. "Just told me to find her before Vincent did."

Lexis sighed. "Knowing John, he's probably got other agents looking for her."

"Stop ignoring me. I'm getting mad, and we all know that's not a good thing." I pinched Rome's leg. "You better answer me."

"We'll talk about this later, Wonder Girl," he said.

Wonder Girl. Hmm, I liked it. I just wished he had answered me. Frowning, I sipped at my water. "Why later?" I finally asked, unable to help myself.

He sighed. "You'll get mad. I'd rather talk to you about it in the shower."

My stomach twisted. "Why will I get mad?" There was only one answer that would make me mad, and that was that Rome did indeed plan to betray me.

He ran a hand through his hair. "I did plan to turn you in, okay? After we got Vincent off your back, I planned to dangle you in front of John so he'd be distracted, and I could take Sunny safely into hiding."

Tanner and Lexis became quiet, and all hint of moisture left my mouth. "But…but I thought you said you needed my powers to help hide her."

"I did, just not the way you assumed. John will want you even more when you're able to control your abilities."

"You bastard!" I tried to jump out of his lap, but he wouldn't let me. He held on tight. "You told me to trust you, and you even said specifically that you wouldn't betray me," I yelped.

"If it makes you feel any better, I've felt horribly guilty for double-crossing you. I was only able to comfort myself with the thought that you'd be able to take care of yourself."

"You—you—" Words failed me, I didn't know what to call him. I'd never felt so betrayed in my life—not even when I'd discovered that the Prince of Darkness had cheated on me.

"I'm not going to do it," Rome said, squeezing my waist again. "I can't. I realized that last night. I'll think of something else."

I started to relax, but forced myself to stay on guard. "What changed your mind?" I demanded.

"Yes, what changed you mind?" Lexis echoed.

I whipped my gaze to her. "You knew?"

She nodded.

Bitch!

"I didn't like seeing you hurt," Rome admitted. He watched me. "I'm sorry, baby. I am. I can't stand the thought that I could be the cause of anyone hurting you. Including myself. Do you forgive me?"

Yes, I realized. I did. I was hurt, but I did forgive him. He had wanted to protect his daughter and had been willing to do anything necessary. I would have done the same for my dad. "Yes," I said.

He let out a relieved breath. "Good. You're as innocent as Sunny, and I'd like to keep you that way, Wonder Girl."

"That name is totally lame," Tanner interjected, clearly trying to bring back our earlier jovial mood. "She's Viper, plain and simple—unless we decide to go with Homicidal Tendencies Wench like I suggested earlier, that is."

I threw a glob of egg at him. The small white-yellow missile nailed him in the nose and tumbled onto his black shirt. I looked down at myself, looked at Rome, then looked at Tanner again. "Hey, we're all wearing black."

"That's because we're going to break and enter tonight," Rome said, his voice as calm as if he'd told us we were signing up for a massage and pedicure.

"Dr. Roberts?" The fact that I didn't protest the actual breaking and entering spoke volumes. I was becoming a hard-core criminal. An outlaw who obeyed no rules but my own. *A little dramatic, don't you think, Jamison?* I'd never broken into a place before, and was a bit scared about the prospect now. Scared and, I admit, excited.

"Yep. We're touring the doc's place," Tanner said. "Uninvited."

My lips dipped into a frown. "It's probably being watched."

"I'm counting on that," Rome replied. "This time we'll make sure we leave someone alive to question. Which reminds me. If everyone is done with their breakfast, we need to help Belle learn to control her powers."

GOOD THING THE SUPPLIES Rome and Tanner had fetched earlier were a fire extinguisher, raincoats, gloves and an industrial-size bottle of Tylenol. Not to mention the supplies

Rome had acquired when he'd left me in that "safe house" I burned down. Guns, guns and more guns. Large guns, small guns, guns that didn't look like guns.

I'd never fired one before, but vowed to learn. If people were going to shoot at me, I was damn well going to shoot back. Dirty Harriet, that's me.

Rather than practice with us, Lexis left for the city. The sooner she arrived to guard my dad, the better. Tanner, Rome and I trudged into the forest, not stopping until we reached a small clearing. We spent an hour practicing. I say "we" loosely. I practiced, Rome yelled and Tanner cracked jokes.

None of us had made any progress at that point, but at least they were the only witnesses to my…mishaps.

Sunlight glared overhead, heating the air, making it thick and sticky. The trees provided some shade, but it wasn't enough. The heat, combined with Rome's snarls, put me on edge. The birds had stopped chirping and flown away. The insects had stopped singing and buzzing, opting for escape. Smart bugs.

"Concentrate this time," Rome said. "Both of you," he added, shooting Tanner a glower.

Tanner had his arm around my waist on the excuse that personal contact would help him read me, and I felt his muscles tense. "I was concentrating before, Agent Ass. We both were."

"If you're concentrating," Rome said, "why the hell have I doused three fires, been hit with a dirt ball, endured a hailstorm and nearly had my balls frozen off? You're supposed to tell her when her emotions are becoming too wild, Tanner, so she can learn when she needs to take the goddamn edge off them."

Scowling, Tanner dropped his arm to his side and kicked a rock with the toe of his boot. "I've been trying, but I'm new at this, too. I don't know when they're wild enough to cause damage, and I don't know when they're too weak to do nothing."

"Then learn together, damn it!"

"Rome," I said, hands on hips. No way would I allow him to talk to Tanner like that. "I'd like to speak with you privately."

He stopped giving Tanner the evil eye long enough to stalk toward me. "What?"

We stood nose to nose. I glared up at him, strangely excited. Soot darkened his face, trailing black streaks down his cheeks. "What's your problem? You're making everyone miserable when you should be happy for me. For the first time, I formed a mound of dirt—the fourth element—with my mind." Or rather, with my jealousy, the emotion that summoned the earth to me. But I didn't mention that fact because I'd had to think of Lexis and Rome—gag—together. Eek. If I didn't stop thinking this way, I'd form *another* dirt ball. Back to the conversation. "That should have put you in a stellar mood."

His jaw muscles twitched, and he glanced away from me, scowling off into the distance. "I don't like that Tanner has to put his hands on you."

"What?" Of all the things I'd expected to hear, that wasn't close by any means. Could shock kill a person? I think I'd just experienced a minideath. "He's a kid. A horny kid, but a kid nonetheless."

"So. He's old enough to like it."

I rolled my eyes, though I couldn't stop the thrill that tingled along my skin. This strong, sexy man was jealous. About me. Me! "It's not like he had his hand up my shirt. You're being silly." *You wonderful thing, you.* "You better treat him nicer or the moment I'm able, I'll make sure you're followed by a rain cloud for days."

Quicker than the blink of an eye, his arms snaked around me, dragging me into his embrace. "I'll feel better after I've made you mine."

Despite the oppressive heat, I shivered. I licked my lips, unable to stop myself from imagining this fierce man stripping me down, laving his way over my entire body, then branding me with his scent, his taste, his touch.

"Oh, hell. Not this again." Tanner moaned. "I thought we were on a time crunch here. Nowhere in the Kill the Bad Guys schedule did I see a make-out break. You're soiling my innocence with all this romance crap."

I brushed a gentle kiss against Rome's lips—lips that instantly softened and beckoned me to linger. "Settle down and behave," I told him, ignoring Tanner. "We're all hot, tired and cranky. If we finish practicing early and you're a good boy, I might let you kiss me again." Wait. No hard-core kissing. Stop forgetting.

His mouth curled in a small but genuine smile. "You're going to be the death of me, you know that?"

God, I hoped not. My smile dissolved, the thought sobering me. In the coming days, he could be hurt or killed. By me. By someone else. I totally understood now why he and Lexis had offered themselves as guinea pigs when the prize was potential invincibility. Anything to protect your partner. "I'll do better, too. I promise."

Unaware of the complete change in my mood, he slapped

my butt and turned to Tanner. Rome's eyes were lighter, his face more relaxed. "Sorry," he said grudgingly. "Are you ready to try again?"

"Whatever, dude." Tanner rolled his shoulders, sweat painting his shirt onto his skin. "Let's get this over with so I can fill my undies with ice. Your balls might be freezing, but mine are melting off."

"Places, everyone," Rome said.

"We need to do something different," I said. But what? Determined to succeed, I shut my eyes and forced myself to concentrate. In, out, I breathed, and I could hear Tanner doing the same. In. Out. He reached over and closed his hand around mine. His palm was smooth and possessed a quiet strength.

Because the mental thing had worked when I'd needed a Keep Out sign, I pictured our hands fused together. Connecting. Locking. Soon I felt my mind reaching out for his, probing for contact. I almost opened my eyes in surprise. I could feel myself trying to break down the mental door separating us.

"We're melding," Tanner said under his breath. "We're melding. We're actually meld—" As he spoke, I mentally pushed the rest of the way inside his mind. Suddenly he jerked, and I felt a jolt travel the length of my arm. "Shit," he said. "Something just...broke inside me. I can really feel you. I can really feel your emotions."

"Make it rain," Rome commanded.

Rain. I let images of sad things float through my mind. Lost puppies. The homeless. Orphaned children. Soon I hoped to be able to do this instantly, to automatically draw on my emotions without thought or force. As for now, this was the best I could do. World hunger. The amount of fat grams in a Krispy Kreme.

"My God, Viper, your sadness level just spiked to thunderstorm proportions. I can actually feel the storm inside you." Pride and shock laced Tanner's voice.

Even as he spoke, thunder boomed. The clouds opened up and poured a deluge of rain over the forest, soaking the three of us. Cotton and denim became glued to my body. Wet hair streaked my temples and cheeks. Water droplets caught in my eyelashes.

"Bring it down," Tanner said.

*Bring it down, bring it down.* I couldn't do it, though. The sadness was there. Strong and indomitable. Then I felt something—someone—reach inside me and take most of the sadness away. It wasn't Tanner, I knew that. The…essence was different, hotter. My eyelids popped open, and I met Rome's surprised stare.

"How did you do that?" I asked, at the same time Tanner said, "The storm is dying."

The rain slowed to a gentle drizzle.

"Now," Rome said with determination. "Make it stop."

I tried to blank my mind completely, to allow myself to feel no emotion, but random thoughts stubbornly intruded. How had Rome swept through me, taking the heart of my sadness? What was my dad doing at this moment? When would I next eat one of those delicious but fattening Krispy Kremes? Did Rome think I looked like a drowned cat right now?

"Okay, why is your embarrassment level spiking?" Tanner asked me.

"No reason. Now zip it."

Several minutes passed before I successfully emptied my head. The rain, at long last, trickled to a halt.

"Good." Satisfaction gleaming in his eyes, Rome nodded in approval. "Now make it rain again. Faster this time."

My teeth gnashed together. How easy it was for him to issue the order. Following it, however, proved difficult. Emotions did not like being forced. A depressed person would have trouble laughing and smiling. An excited bride-to-be would have trouble shooting her fiancé in a killing rage. Well, unless he really deserved it.

"Come on, baby. You can do it. I know you can."

"I'm trying, damn it," I snapped.

"Uh, I think you're about to start a fire," Tanner said drily.

Bubble baths and chocolate. Champagne and roses. I inhaled slowly, exhaled loudly and long. Calm, I was calm, damn it. Wait. I needed to be sad. Being without Rome—although at the moment, that thought didn't sadden me too much. He was so freaking bossy! Be sad, be happy. Blah, blah, blah. Why didn't he get over here and try to command himself—

"Ow!" Tanner jerked away from me, breaking our connection. "You're burning the shit out of me. If I scar, I'm suing your ass."

I blinked down at my hands. Sure enough, the ends of my fingers blazed. Anger—crap. It would have been nice if Rome had once again swept through me and helped rid me of *that*. Though I still wasn't sure how he'd done so before. I shook my hands and managed to extinguish the fire. "If you scar," I told Tanner, "the ladies will love you."

His face brightened. "Really?"

My eyes clashed with Rome's, hazel against blue. "This

isn't working. I'm an emotional person, but I can't just force myself to feel a certain way. Damn it, I don't want these powers."

He crossed his arms over his chest. "Well, you've got them, so you need to learn how to use them."

"It's too hard."

"The more you practice, the easier it will get."

"That doesn't help me now!"

"We've got plenty of time before we need to leave. We'll keep at it. You'll get it. I have confidence in you."

His praise almost softened me. Almost. "A few more hours isn't going to make a difference. I've connected with Tanner, and he's doing wonderfully, gauging my emotions. But *I* can't control them."

"I am good, aren't I?" Tanner interjected with a grin.

"Stop whining, Belle." Rome showed me no mercy. "Just close your eyes and try again."

Had he always been this much of a task master? This determined to get his way? "No."

"Tanner isn't giving up," Rome said.

My eyes narrowed. Oh, how low. I didn't appreciate being compared to someone else. Especially a smart-mouthed kid. I crossed my own arms over my chest. Let's see if he liked payback. "You want me to keep at this, then you'll damn well tell me about your own powers and how you mastered them."

"Belle," he said warningly.

I'd issued the ultimatum and I wasn't backing down, wasn't taking it back. I wanted to know. Hell, I deserved to know. And if I had to force his hand like this, I would. "Fine. Don't tell me. We'll see you inside the cabin." After blowing him a saccharine-sweet kiss, I turned on my heel. I grabbed Tanner's hand and moved toward the cabin.

Surprisingly, the kid followed me with dragging feet. "I want you to burn my hands again," he whined. "I need a scar."

"Keep it up and I'll burn your entire body."

Rome growled low in his throat. "You want to know, I'll show you."

I froze. Inch by inch, I turned and faced him. My heart slammed against my ribs.

"Go inside, Tanner," he said, eyes leveled on me.

"I want to see, too."

"Go in the house. You've mastered your job already. Now I'm going to master mine. I'm going to filter for her. Go in the house," Rome repeated.

"Without me, you won't know when or how much to filter."

"Tanner. Go."

"But I want to see your superpower. I'll just look out the window, so you might as well—"

"I tried to be nice, Tanner." Rome's face was dark with fury. His nostrils were flared, his irises were glowing crystalline blue and his pupils were a mere slash of black. "This isn't a joke. This isn't a game. Go in the house, or I'll kick you in."

Tanner raced inside without another word.

I had to force myself not to follow the kid. A lump formed in my throat as Rome stalked toward me. True frissons of fear unfurled, chilling the air around me.

"I'm going to show you my ability," he said through suddenly sharp teeth, his tone deceptively quiet, "and you're going to wish to God I hadn't."

## *CHAPTER FIFTEEN*

A SMALL PART OF ME (on some level) expected what Rome did next, and the rest of me, well, was an idiot. I should have figured it out. How had I not guessed? Selective common sense?

The fact that I should have known didn't lessen the impact, though. My eyes widened in shock, and I inched cautiously away. My stomach bottomed out. "You're—you're—"

Changing. He was changing.

His face elongated. His bones rearranged themselves, until he was stooping over the ground. The clothes he wore ripped from his body, and shiny black fur sprouted from his skin, covering him in mere seconds. His teeth sharpened even further, and his pupils thinned, pointing at both ends.

Dear God, he was a jaguar. A jaguar! No, *the* jaguar. The one I'd seen in my apartment. The one who'd invaded Lexis's home. The one who'd protected me against assassins.

The one I'd almost iced.

Had Rome simply told me of his ability, I might have tried to deny it. I might have called him a liar, might have told him to stop joking around. Seeing it, *watching* his transformation, offered irrefutable proof.

And it brought home the fact that there was an entire world out there I hadn't known existed until a few days ago.

Rome growled up at me, the sound fierce and pure animal. Total danger. I backed another step away, my hand fluttering over my throat. Not once had he hurt me while in this form. But…a girl couldn't be too cautious.

"Holy shit!" Tanner shouted from the cabin. "Rome, the badass, is a pussy. Woohoo!"

The jaguar's fierce attention never deviated from me. Its— *his*—gaze continued to pierce me, daring me to say something. Daring me to *do* something. He expected me to run, I realized, to rebuke him. He probably expected me to faint, as well.

No wonder he had been so adamant about keeping this part of himself secret. Did he fear rejection, too? Did he think I would find him disgusting? Silly man. This was weird, yes, but hardly a relationship killer.

I'd dated worse.

Besides, I started fires—with my freaking eyes. Like I really had room to judge. I crouched, lowering myself to his eye level. "Here, kitty, kitty. Come to sweet, sweet Belle."

His long, black lashes swept down, back up. Then, slowly, he prowled toward me, closing the distance between us inch by animal inch. I reached out and stroked the softness of his fur. He purred.

"I guess this means I get to call you Cat Man."

He bared his teeth, his lips quivering over them as he uttered a feral snarl.

"No? What about Agent Fur Ball?"

Another snarl.

My own lips twitched. "You should have told me about this," I admonished. "It would have saved me a near heart attack and you a near icing."

His snarling ceased, and he blinked at me again. I

scratched behind his ears. Hesitantly, he licked my arm. The warmth and smoothness of his tongue surprised me.

"Are you letting him lick you?" Tanner called. "Gross."

"Shut up!"

"Belle and the pussycat sitting in a tree," came the sing-song reply.

With a roar, Rome prowled menacingly toward the cabin. Realizing he'd just been placed on the dessert menu, Tanner finally shut his big fat mouth.

"This actually explains some things," I said, cupping the cat's jaw and forcing him to stop and face me. "Your never wear jeans, probably because they won't rip when you change. You don't wear underwear, either. For the same reason, I'm guessing." I recalled how easily his pants had torn that day I'd twisted them. So much for my theory that my superhuman strength had been responsible. "Sometimes you act like a total animal. You get this savage gleam in your eyes, like you could eat everyone in sight. And not in a good way. Then there's the way you kiss—"

Another growl erupted from him, this one different from the others. Hope and desire deepened the timbre. He stretched his front legs, then his back. My hands dropped to my sides. His bones elongated instead of hunching. Fur shed, falling from him as if it had been nothing more than a temporary suit. His teeth retracted; his face reformed into hard planes and angles.

The muscles of his chest roped, corded. His penis—oh my holy Lord, his big, hard, *erect* penis… I forced myself to turn away from him. My cheeks overheated, and I had to fan myself. The sun seemed brighter somehow. I'd seen him naked before, but I'd been too weak to feel the effects. Surely I'd start a fire if I looked at him now.

"Belle…"

"You're naked." Ah, stating the obvious. My specialty.

"*That's* what you have to say to me?" Shock and laughter, anger and relief dripped from his voice. "You don't blink at my…animal form, but my nakedness intimidates you?"

"Not your nakedness, exactly," I hedged, glancing down at my feet. I kicked a pebble with the toe of my boot.

"Then what?"

"Well, your penis." Duh. "It's big. And hard."

He barked out a laugh. "You need to get used to it, baby, since you're going to be seeing a lot of it in the future."

My cheeks heated another degree. "Just put a leash on that thing for now, okay?"

A pause. The crackle of grass. "I just showed you I can shape-shift, and all you care about is my dick. I don't think I've ever experienced this much shock."

"Well, I think I mentioned how big it is." Thankfully, my newfound superpowers didn't, like, cause the world to explode with the force of my awe. And lust. There was definite lust here, making me all tingly and breathless. "I don't want to start a fire."

I'd never seen a man so well formed. So rippled with muscles and tanned skin. Rome was the epitome of total masculinity. He reeked of power. Oozed it. "Can you put some clothes on?"

I didn't have to see him to know he rolled his eyes. "No. I've finally managed to intimidate you. I'll probably remain naked for the rest of my life."

Lalalala. The trees were lush and green. The sky, what little I could see of it through the leaves, was a bright, vivid blue. Hardly any clouds. The scent of pine filled the air.

"We gonna stand here like this all day or are you going to turn around and talk to me?" Rome asked comfortably.

"Stand like this all day. Duh."

"Belle."

"Rome." I crossed my arms over my chest. If the man hadn't yet figured out I possessed a stubborn core, it was past time he did so.

"You've seen a naked man before, haven't you?"

I liked the way he'd snarled that, as if he couldn't stand the thought of me with another man. "Yes, I have." I shifted from one foot to the other. "I just hadn't seen *you* naked before—at least, not when I was strong enough to do something about it."

Another pause. "And that's different how?"

"Well, it's you."

"Me?"

A slight breeze danced past, cooling my skin somewhat. "That's right. You. You make me feel things."

"I'm glad," he said. His hands settled atop my shoulders and gently squeezed. I hadn't heard him approach, but suddenly he was there. The scent of virile man enveloped me.

"Me, too," I said softly, "but that doesn't mean I'm looking again. Not now, at least. I mean, if I turned around we wouldn't be talking, now would we?"

A third pause, then, "No, I guess not."

"Like I told you, I'm in serious danger of starting a fire. Not a good idea when we're standing in a forest." I needed to change the subject before I forgot exactly why not talking would be a bad idea. "How did you end up a…cat? Ohmygod, you didn't really have that eye surgery, did you? You have night vision because cats do."

His chest pressed against my back (earning a slight gasp from me) and he deepened his massage of my shoulders. "No, no eye surgery. Remember those experiments I told you about? My DNA was spliced. They—the scientists who work at PSI—did other stuff, as well, but I've never fully understood it."

My mouth fell open, and I floundered for the right words. When they came, they choked out of me on infuriated breaths. "How could they do that? Mix human and animal, which could have kill—"

"While I like that you're outraged on my behalf, you shouldn't be. I volunteered, remember? I wanted the kind of skills that would make me invincible. I can do things, see things, *hear* things others can't."

I toyed with the ends of my hair and shifted my feet again. My heartbeat had yet to slow down, and his touch was only making it worse.

"And you're right," he added. "I don't wear jeans because they don't rip easily. The underwear, well, the first time I changed, all of my clothes stayed on my...cat body. They stifled my movements, but I was able to tear them off with my teeth—all except for the underwear. As you can imagine, I made quite a spectacle. A hard-core predator wearing nothing but Hanes."

A laugh bubbled from me. "Why did you expect me to be disgusted by the change?"

"Other people have been." His fingers tightened for a moment, and I knew it was because he wanted to take the conversation down a different path.

I persisted anyway. "Like who?"

"Like Lexis." Inch by inch, his fingers descended the

length of my spine. "She vomited the first time she saw it happen."

"She probably had a virus."

"Wrong."

"Morning sickness, then."

"She'd had Sunny by that point."

Fine. Besides, did I really want him to reevaluate his ex's reaction? "I'm not Lexis."

"No." His soft lips brushed my neck, eliciting all kinds of erotic sensations. "You're not."

Heat sizzled between us, and I became hyperaware of his every action. I heard every intake of his breath like a battle drum; I felt every naughty glide of his fingers like a live wire.

He was naked, and I wanted to touch.

No. *No, no, no.* With Tanner watching from the cabin window, me needing to practice controlling my powers, and my inability to stop the fires that lust caused, we simply could not allow ourselves to indulge in each other. Much as I might want to.

"Well. Hmm." I coughed. What should I do now? Walk away?

"Why didn't the change bother you?" Rome asked. The question was hesitant, as if he feared the answer.

Okay, I could handle this topic without succumbing to his sensual assault. "I don't know. It just didn't."

"Why?" he insisted.

"I've done a little changing myself recently. I don't want to be judged, either. Besides, I'm the amazing Wonder Girl and—"

"I'm not calling you that," he interjected with a laugh.

"Why not? You're the one who thought of it."

"I've since decided that name is all wrong for you. You're the Naughty Siren, and that's that."

I failed to suppress my grin. "Well, you're Cat Man, no doubt about it."

"Don't call me that." He gave another laugh and gently pressed me forward. "Go get me some clothes and we'll finish your practice."

"Without Tanner?"

"Without Tanner."

"He's not going to like that."

Rome shrugged. "He deserves a break. Go on." He swatted my butt.

Laughing, I forced myself to walk away from him, from his sweet touch and sweeter scent. I didn't allow myself to look back as I entered the cabin. The moment the door closed behind me, cool air surrounded me. I breathed deeply.

Tanner was waiting for me, standing at the door and jumping up and down with excitement. "Did you freaking see that? He's a cat. A cat! With fur and everything."

"I saw." I slipped past him.

"Did he purr? Tell me he purred."

"No." Where was Rome's bag? My gaze scoped the small cabin.

"Think of the fun we can have with this." Tanner tangled his hand through his hair. "My God, the jokes are already rolling through my mind. What's the difference between a cat and a frog?" He didn't wait for my reply. "A cat has nine lives but a frog croaks every day."

"That's not funny." Finally I spied the edge of black vinyl peeking from the side of the bed, and strode to it.

"What do cats eat for breakfast? Mice krispies."

My lips twitched. "Better." Hunched over, I dug through the bag. Not a single piece of clothing offered any type of color. They were all black. "You better not crack these jokes in front of Rome. He's kind of sensitive."

"I felt his hesitation, remember? He needs to get over it, and joking about it is the best way to help him do that."

"You want to be eaten?" I withdrew a T-shirt and pants. I didn't bother with shoes. Those had fallen off during the change, but they hadn't been damaged. "You weren't close enough to see how sharp his teeth are."

"Rome wouldn't hurt me. He's all bark and no bite. Wait. He's all purr and no bite. Damn." Tanner laughed. "They just keep coming. I'm unstoppable. I'm the Joker. Hey!" His eyes widened, and he clapped his hand on his thigh. "That can be my superhero name. The Sensitive Joker."

I snorted. "Except you're so not sensitive."

"I am, too. I'm sensitive to other people's feelings."

"I think your new name needs to be the Amazing Ass."

He grinned in agreement. "I *do* have a cute ass, don't I?"

God, I loved this kid. I straightened and tucked Rome's clothes under my arm. "Why don't you fix lunch or something? It's time, right? Breakfast was, like, hours ago. I'm starved."

He arched a brow, the one that was pierced, and the silver rings winked in the light. "Or we could make out before you take Rome those clothes."

I slapped his shoulder, but I was having a hard time maintaining a stern expression. "How have I not fried you up like battered shrimp?"

"You'd be lost without me, and you know it. I can feel the love. Don't try to deny it."

I flipped him off and strode outside. His laughter followed me. Instantly, heat wrapped me in its sticky claws. Rome was standing in the exact place I'd left him. His arms were at his sides, and he made absolutely no effort to cover himself.

He was smiling, daring me to look. Responding to the challenge, I did. I looked. Finally. I'd wanted to all along, anyway. I stopped a few feet away from him and allowed my gaze to linger. My mouth watered, and as I'd feared, my blood heated. He was, without a doubt, a prime specimen.

"One day you'll have to return the favor," he said huskily.

Stand naked in front of Rome, in front of such perfection when I was far from perfect? "I don't think so."

"You will."

"Maybe," I hedged.

"Definitely." The long, hard length of his penis twitched.

"Almost definitely." I tossed him the clothes.

As he deftly caught the garments, there was a tenderness to his expression that hadn't been there before. I mentally applauded myself for noticing. It was quite a feat, considering that his manly assets held me in thrall.

I gave him absolutely no privacy as he dressed, starting with the pants he worked over his strong thighs and hips. I'd already looked, so there was no going back now. I didn't really want to go back. I just wanted this man. Oh, how my skin tingled, heated.

"When this is over—" I said, then caught myself and pressed my lips together. *Don't go there, Jamison.* All the heat died.

He was in the process of jerking the shirt over his head, but he stilled. His fingers poised over his chest, at the hem of the shirt. His tanned, rock-hard abs remained visible. "What?" he demanded. "What were you going to say?"

"Nothing. Hurry up, and we'll start practicing."

With a final flick, he had the shirt in place, had his delicious body covered. I felt a twinge of loss. What kind of idiot was I to insist such a delectable morsel cover himself? He closed the distance between us, grabbed my hand and escorted me out of the view of the cabin. When we stopped, he faced me and tipped my chin with a hot fingertip.

Our gazes locked. "What were you going to say, Belle?"

I gulped. What if he didn't want to see me when this was over? Yes, he was attracted to me now. And yes, he seemed to like me. A lot. But he could be one of those guys who abhorred all mention of a future. After Lexis... He could be one of those guys who freaked out at the first mention of the dreaded *R* word. *Relationship*. As if the word were synonymous with *hell* and *evil*.

"Nothing," I insisted. My jaw clenched stubbornly.

"Then I'll take a few guesses. When this is over do I want to sleep with you? Yes. When this is over do I want to see you again? Yes. When this is over do I want you to spend some time with my daughter? Yes. When this is over do I want to smear you in chocolate syrup and lick it off? Yes." He paused. "Did one of those cover your question?"

I nodded, unable to speak past the sudden lump in my throat. He really did want to see me again. Tendrils of happiness slithered through me, making me grin like a loon.

Expression fierce, he tangled his hands into my hair. "You fascinate me, but I've told you that, right? I've wanted you since the first moment I laid eyes on you, and the want has only grown."

My jaw fell open in wonder.

He took that as an invitation.

His lips swooped to mine. His tongue immediately thrust inside, and that addicting flavor of feral man consumed me. He released my hair, cupped my chin and tilted my head, angling me for deeper contact. I moaned in ecstasy. My hands rained down his roped chest, wishing like hell the shirt would suddenly disappear. I wanted skin on skin. Man on woman.

I wanted the animal in him unleashed.

But damn it all to hell, I was already heating again, and the consequences could be deadly. I jerked my lips away, panting, "We shouldn't. I could cause a fire."

"Give your emotions to me." Dark arousal pulled his features taut. His voice was a honeyed purr. "Give your passion and fire to me."

My teeth sank into my bottom lip. "What if you're hurt? Tanner's not here to tell me when it's too much."

"Give me."

Rome crushed his mouth to mine. I was helpless to resist. As I licked him, sucked him, bit him, he hauled me against him, lifting me high, and I wrapped my legs around his waist. The hard length of his erection pressed against me, somehow bigger, somehow hotter. Pleasure speared me right where I needed it most. I trembled; I burned. I tried to hold the fire inside me. My blood boiled; my skin pricked with red-hot heat.

If I wasn't careful, the raging inferno inside me would burst free, consuming the forest. Consuming Rome. I didn't want to hurt Rome. I didn't want to scare him away, make him determined never to kiss or touch me again.

"I've never been so desperate for a woman in my life. Give me your fire, Belle. I'll control it."

"How can you be sure?"

Through our clothing, he rubbed his penis against my clitoris. Friction. Desire. Absolute pleasure. I gasped at the ready sensations. He sucked my tongue, hard. "Give it to me."

"No." I couldn't stop moving. I arched against him, the action utterly necessary for my peace of mind, but dangerous. So dangerous. The fire inside me speared all the hotter, threatening to devour. I grasped at it, trying, trying, trying so hard to hold it inside me.

"Give." Bite.

"No." Nibble. "What if you're wrong? What if you can't control it?"

"Let me try. Give it to me, and I'll make you come," he promised. He carried me until the cool bark of a tree pressed against my back. His erection slid up and down, the fabric of my jeans adding to the delicious friction.

"Rome…" His name was ripped from my throat, hoarse and needy. A plea.

"I was watching you earlier, when you made it rain, and you looked so sad my chest actually clenched. I wanted so desperately to take your sadness away, and suddenly I was. Trust me on this. Let me try." He shoved against me, hitting directly, and I was lost. "I think I can do it again."

It had worked once, and he was right: it could work again. Gradually, I allowed myself to relax my guard. The heat and flames I'd tried so diligently to control rushed from me as if floodgates had been opened. They swept over Rome, who groaned. Instead of burning him, however, the flames were absorbed into him.

Had I not been so distracted by his seduction, I would have jerked in shock. As it was, I could only tighten my hold on him. His tongue moved against mine more frantically. His hips arched more deliberately. My head fell back. I simply didn't have the strength to hold it up. He bit at my neck, nipping the flesh, then licking the sting.

"See?" he said, his voice as hoarse as mine had been. Tension bracketed his eyes, but it was aroused tension. Aroused pleasure-pain. "We did it. I'd hoped I could filter the flames, take the most violent of the heat, and it worked."

"I don't understand how you're able to do that," I managed to moan as I squeezed and kneaded his back. Time slipped out of reality. Here, now, I had Rome and I had pleasure and I hadn't started a fire. Nothing else mattered.

"If I hadn't learned to cage the animal inside me, it would have overtaken me. I would be only animal. I thought, hoped I could cage your fire, and so I have. One day you'll do it on your own, but until then…"

I kissed him again. Our teeth scraped together as our bodies strained and arched. He palmed my breast, pinched the nipple.

"Speaking of one day, we're going to do this naked," he breathed.

"Yes."

"In a bed."

"Yes."

"One day you'll be mine."

His hand dived inside my pants, past—nope, no panties because this naughty, pleasure-giving thief had hidden them—and into the wet heart of me. Instant contact, exactly where I needed him most. His fingers buried deep, pounding, pounding. "Yes."

I jumped over the sweet edge and screamed. Stars winked

behind my eyes. My whole body tensed, relaxed, tensed, spasming as intense pleasure rocked me.

I held on to Rome, afraid to let go lest I fly away to the heavens. Images raced through my mind. Images of Rome naked and inside me, his cock replacing his fingers as he claimed me from behind, then took me from every position possible. Images of—

"Viper?" a familiar voice called. "What's wrong? Are you okay? Hold on a minute, I'm on my way out. You better not have hurt her, Rome, or there will be serious hell to pay."

## CHAPTER SIXTEEN

WHILE I BATTLED A plethora of desires (namely, to kill Tanner, strip Rome, scream, cry, beg for more of his loving) Rome pulled his fingers from me, then moved away from me entirely. His expression was taut—no longer in a good way— and pained as he readjusted his pants.

Trembling, I righted my clothing, unable to draw in a steady breath. "I finished, but what about you?" I whispered. My gaze flicked to his swollen fly. "You're—"

"Fine. I'm fine. Nothing we can't take care of later." But his gaze lingered on my hardened nipples, dipped to the apex of my thighs, caressing. A hot, wistful gleam appeared in his eyes. Then he did something unexpected and wholly erotic. He licked his fingers—the fingers that had been buried inside of me.

His eyelids closed in surrender. I almost came again, the action was so arousing. Almost wicked. Definitely naughty.

Tanner raced around a tree and spotted us. "Belle?"

"I'm good," I said, my cheeks reddening. "Nothing's wrong."

He ground to a halt and studied me, studied Rome's back. "Oh. *Oh*. You guys were having sex. Gross. Just gross. Cat sex. I'm going back inside. Try to keep your mind on the objective, you two. Jeez, am I the only one here with a work ethic?" He turned on his heel and marched back to the cabin.

Rome looked at me, and we both burst into laughter. "That kid," he said.

"I know."

"Now that I know what you taste like, we can get back to work." He spun away from me, his shoulders stiff. It was only then, with distance between us, that I realized the extent of what had just happened. I studied him, searching for signs of damage. There were no red marks, no blisters. It had worked. Ohmygod, it had really worked! Rome had actually taken my fire into himself and completely tamed it. He'd kept it from raging, kept it from hurting anything—or anyone.

We could be together.

We could make slow, languid love. We could enjoy hard, fast, raunchy sex. All without the fear of consequences. Just the thought was enough to reawaken my desire. Soon I'd have him inside me. Completely.

A shiver of delight coasted up my spine as I prepared for our next practice session. I'd get to start a fire, just not the kind I wanted. Not yet.

Without stopping for a lunch break, we spent the next two hours creating flames, rain, snow and wind whirls. I actually did a good job. Rome stood at a distance, filtering my emotions. Without Tanner, he didn't know how much to filter, but that wasn't what he needed to work on. *He* had to practice filtering without becoming aroused.

With every distraction, I had to start over—but overall, I made progress. Hopefully, in a few more weeks (probably months, sigh) I'd be able to create the desired results instantly, even with distractions all around. Even when Rome was aroused.

What frightened me, though, was that as I improved I began to enjoy my abilities. Wielding and controlling such power was heady. Intoxicating, like an addictive drug. A wild adrenaline rush. I started to picture the things I could do once I truly mastered these powers. If someone pissed me off, I could burn off his hair. If someone threatened me, I could ice her home. Who wouldn't enjoy dishing out that kind of revenge?

I mean, a few weeks ago, I'd borrowed Sherridan's car for a job interview. Ten minutes into my drive, I'd been pulled over by the most egotistical, I'm-above-the-law cop ever allowed on the force. Officer Ken Parton was his name. As if I'd ever forget.

I hadn't driven in a long (long) time, so of course my license had expired. Guess what? He arrested me. Yep, the stupid prick cuffed me and hauled me down to the station as if I were a hardened criminal. He booked me and everything. (Maybe my comment about his Dolly man-boobs pushed him over the edge. Who knew?)

So yeah, I now have a record. All because one jerk-off got his jollies from intimidating women. Am I bitter? Hell, yes. If I'd had these powers then I could have drowned that miserable bastard in a hailstorm, could have frozen his balls to his thigh, could have twirled him in a violent tornado.

*Note to self: look up Officer Parton when I return to the city.*

"What the hell are you thinking about?" Rome said.

I blinked and shook my head, scattering the dark thoughts to the back corner of my mind. However, that failed to extinguish the small fire kindling at my feet. I stomped on the embers.

Black plumes curled upward and slithered around me. I coughed, only then realizing what I'd been doing. Planning to hurt someone. The officer deserved it, sure, but that didn't make it right.

Damn. This was what Rome had feared would happen to me. That I'd grow to love my powers and be unable to give them up. Wasn't that what he had said? People killed for power. People craved it, became monsters for it.

I'd wanted so badly to give up my powers when they were uncontrollable, but now that I was beginning to see exactly what I could do—and would be able to do—I wasn't sure I really wanted to return to my normal self. Officer Parton had clearly been enamored of his own power. Would I be just like him?

I sighed and my shoulders slumped.

"You okay?" Rome asked. He strode to my side and wrapped his arms around my waist. He rested his chin on top of my head. "That was a pretty heavy sigh."

"Hey, are you guys going to start kissing again?" Tanner called from the cabin window. He pretended to gag. He'd been watching us the entire time, throwing out bits of unneeded advice and unwanted orders like "try to make a naked ice sculpture."

"Did you ever make lunch?" I retorted. Or was it dinnertime now? Either way, I was starved!

"I do *not* cook."

Exasperated, I threw up my arms. "Then how do you eat?"

"Takeout." Tanner shrugged. "Maids."

"Maids?" I expected him to laugh, but he didn't. He was totally serious. Great. I'd invited a Richie Richerson to join the Squad of Doom. Wait. Never mind. *So* not a cool name for us. "Just make sandwiches or something. We'll join you in a minute." I hoped. My stomach rumbled.

"Fine." Scowling, Tanner stomped away from the window. I heard him mutter, "I'm just the empath, so I get the grunt work."

Rome maneuvered behind me to block me from view, wrapped his arms around my waist and said, "You never answered me. What brought that sigh on?"

"I was just thinking." A slight breeze wafted past us, cooling my sweat-beaded skin. His body sizzled against mine, eclipsing the coolness, but no way in hell I'd ask him to move. I liked him where he was.

"About?"

"Powers." I paused, considering my next words carefully. "If you could give up being a cat—"

"Jaguar."

"Jaguar. Whatever." Jeez. Like there was a difference? "If you could give up that ability, would you?"

He offered no hesitation. "In a heartbeat."

"Even though you can get into places normal humans can't? Even though you volunteered for the DNA splicing? Even though you can—"

"Even though," he interjected firmly. "Whatever the advantages, there are far more disadvantages. Like the fact that Vincent would love to recruit me for OASS by any means necessary, which puts my family in danger."

Somehow I'd known he would say that.

"I'm not saying I hate everything I can do." His hands rasped down my arms, up my chest, and cupped my breasts. The man obviously liked to touch me. "I'm not saying that at all."

"Then what are you saying?" I asked breathlessly. His

hands were big and calloused, and I felt the abrasion through my cotton shirt, felt the phantom imprint that branded my very soul.

I'd had other boyfriends; I'd always enjoyed sex. But something was different with Rome. His slightest touch excited me like nothing else ever had.

"I'm saying the good doesn't outweigh the bad. Yes, I'm able to see more clearly in the dark. Yes, I can smell things I couldn't smell before." He paused, the silence laden with sinful intent. "Yes, I know when a woman is aroused before she does."

"How?" I squeaked, suddenly embarrassed. Heat spread and branched from my cheeks. I'd been aroused by him so many times I'd lost count.

"I can smell her desire."

"Is that…part of the good or the bad?"

"Good." His voice dipped to a wine-rich whisper, a whisper that caressed my still-hot cheeks. "Very, very good."

Holy hell, this man knew how to seduce. My knees were weakening at a rapid pace. It didn't matter that the cabin was behind us and Tanner could be watching from the window. It didn't matter that we were outside. Nothing mattered but Rome.

"I love all of those abilities." He pinched my nipples, and I arched backward. "I can find the unfindable. Stalk the unstalkable."

"But…?"

"But these abilities have not helped me do what matters most. They haven't given my daughter a normal life. No, they've brought the evil of the world to her door. Because of that, I can never drop my guard. I can never fully trust. People want to examine me, bad people, just like they want to examine you. They want to test me, experiment on me, and they don't care how painful it is. They want to make more like me. More like you. More like Sunny. I can't keep her off Vincent's radar forever. If the bastard ever tried to experiment on her…" The last was said in a growl.

I quivered when he glided his wicked hands down my stomach again, this time gripping the hem of my shirt and allowing his fingertips to dabble with the exposed skin.

"Do you trust me?" I asked breathlessly.

"Surprisingly, yes." He bit the shell of my ear, then licked away the sting.

"Rome." I groaned in need. My head fell onto his shoulder. I wanted him to lick my neck. Bite it. Something. Anything. Except…

He released me with a low, guttural growl. "Come on." He pushed out a shuddering breath. "I can't fuck you the way I want right now, and holding you is torture. Let's go inside and eat."

He strode away from me without another word.

*Happy place, happy place.* "I'll be there in a minute," I called. "I need some alone time to decompress."

He nodded but didn't look back.

Even though I was famished, I needed time to calm my racing blood. I was panting (a little) and aching (a lot). I didn't think I'd find complete satisfaction until that man had me penetrated. Right now I didn't fear I'd start a fire or anything like that. It was just, well, I feared I was giving Rome more of myself than was wise. Frissons of love had already sprouted, but giving him any more of my heart was completely idiotic.

I plopped onto the grass, which was damp from the rain-storms I'd produced. The wetness seeped through my jeans, but I didn't care. Every minute I spent in Rome's presence, I fell a little deeper under his erotic spell. He was animalis-tic (obviously), addictive, charming when he wanted to be, sexy without meaning to be, and protective.

Who could resist that?

Not me, I thought with a small twinge of dejection.

I kind of understood now why Lexis had walked away from him. To love him, but have him love another…was there any greater torture? No, probably not. When a woman looked at him, she wanted all of his focus to be on her, all of his strength under her hands, all of his passion directed at her. She simply wanted him to be hers.

He pulled you into his essence, and you were helpless to resist.

I was in serious danger of falling completely, I'm-in-deep-shit in love with him, of losing myself to him, and I knew it. I was too excited by him, too aware of his every touch. I plucked at several strands of grass. I wasn't going to walk away from him—it was too late for that, and I was honest enough with myself to admit it. But I needed to erect better guards against him.

How did a girl do that, though?

If it involved rejecting Rome's touch and not getting naked, then no, I couldn't do it. I *had* to know what it felt like to make love with this man. I'd always had a strong fantasy life. This time, however, I needed the real thing. After the way I'd exploded for him, I knew that everything else I'd ever experienced would pale in comparison to Rome.

He'd given me an orgasm while we were dressed, for

God's sake, not a single stitch of clothing removed. A first for me.

"Belle," he suddenly called, breaking into my thoughts. His deep, rough tone made me shiver with remembrance. "You okay out there?"

"Yeah." I pushed to my feet. "I'm coming in."

"Lexis phoned. She's with your dad and he's doing great. He even tried to hit on her."

That was my dad, I thought as relief flooded me. I hadn't realized how deep my worry was until just that moment. I wished I could have talked to him, but it was enough for now that my dad was alive and well, with no bad guys lurking around him.

"The, uh…sandwiches are ready," Rome added.

From the hesitation in his voice, I suspected Tanner had done something to the food. *It had better be something good, by God.* The noises my stomach made were deafening. I trudged up the porch steps and past the front door. Cool air caressed my bare skin and cooled the damp flesh under my clothes.

The cozy scene that greeted me had me blinking in surprise. Both Rome and Tanner sat at the table, their elbows propped on the surface. A plate of sandwiches rested in front of them. Neither was eating. Like gentlemen, they were waiting for me.

Rome didn't look at me. He radiated a supreme arousal he couldn't quite manage to hide.

Tanner grinned wickedly when he spotted me. "I prepared a meal, just like you told me."

Mouth watering, I plopped into the chair beside Rome and gazed at the food. My jaw dropped. Sure enough, Tanner had

repared dinner. Sandwiches, just like Rome had said. Except
hese sandwiches were cut into round globes and each was
opped with an olive.

"They look damn good," Rome said.

"Yes," I said, "but they also look like—"

"I know." Tanner's grin widened. "I was inspired, what can
say? You asked for food, and I delivered."

"You are such a punk," I replied, but I, too, was grinning.

His black brows wiggled up and down, momentarily hid-
ng under his hair. The silver piercings winked. "Now you
an tell everyone you've sampled grade A boobies."

Rome snorted, but he leaned toward me and whispered,
'I already have."

Grade A? Ha. More like A-cup. Still, I shivered at the in-
ensity of his words. Instead of allowing myself to jump him
is I always seemed to want, I reached for a sandwich. Rome
and Tanner reached for one at the same time. The boys were
ucky they didn't pull back bloody stumps, I was *that* hungry.
Apparently, the more I used my powers, the hungrier I became. With my first bite, I almost died and went to the pearly
gates. Turkey and Swiss. Mmm. I ate three pairs of breasts.

"So, Rome," Tanner said, after swallowing a gulp of milk.
'How'd you get Belle into bed so soon?"

I choked on the olive currently in my mouth.

Rome fought a grin and slapped me on the back.

"I mean, you guys have only known each other, what? A
few days? And you're already going at it like rabbits. I wish
you could have seen yourselves. She was moaning, you were
groaning. Live porn for sure."

The moment I could breathe, I shouted, "Are you calling
me easy?"

"Close your pie hole, Viper. I'm not meaning no disrespect okay? Rome obviously has some skills I need to know about and since you haven't exactly given me any tips that work…"

I scowled at him. "They work when executed properly."

"Oh, really?" He leaned back in his chair and folded his arms over his middle, the picture of disbelief. "I told Lexi she had pretty hair and you didn't see her stripping and falling into bed with me, did you?"

"You've got to try it on someone your own age, moron."

Rome slammed his palm against the table surface. The plates jostled and clanked. "You're teaching him to con women into bed?"

What was this, dump on Belle hour? "Not con. Exactly." I shifted uncomfortably in my seat. "Seduce."

"There's a difference?" He studied Tanner, letting me off the hook for a minute. "You shouldn't sleep with a woman unless you care about her."

"That's easy for you to say," Tanner grumbled. "You're getting some."

"Not really." This time, Rome was the one grumbling. His eyes darkened with savage need.

My nerve endings reacted to that need, springing to instant attention. Again. Why couldn't I have civilized men in my life? Instead I was stuck with a horny teen determined to nail some booty and a horny adult determined to nail *my* booty.

Never mind that I liked the latter.

And never mind that I planned to offer said booty freely and eagerly.

*Just remember to guard your heart,* my mind piped up.

"Well?" Tanner banged his empty glass on the table. "Are you going to share your expertise or not?"

"Not," Rome said succinctly. "We have more important things to do than talk about your lack of a sex life."

"Hey, now. There's nothing more important than my sex life." The kid straightened, adamant and offended. "All we're doing is eating. Nothing wrong with a little erotic conversation during a meal. Especially when we're eating booby sandwiches."

No way to refute that.

Flustered, Rome pushed his plate away. "Fine. I'll talk to you about sex and how I—how I got Belle to like me, but I'll do it later. Right now I need to talk to you guys about tonight. Have either of you ever broken into someone's home?"

"No." Me.

"No." Tanner. Although his admission came more reluctantly, as if he didn't like revealing he wasn't a criminal.

"I thought not." Rome glanced to the heavens. For guidance? "Usually the best time to go in is during the day. People are at work and less likely to be home, and if you're dressed right, the people who *are* home won't notice you. But Belle was sick and I needed to see how much she could handle, so I postponed for—"

"Dressed right, how?" I interrupted. Had people broken into *my* house that way?

He popped a nipple (aka an olive) into his mouth and shrugged. "Repairman. Deliveryman. Doesn't matter, though, because we're going in at night. *This* night, to be exact, and it's a whole different story. Dr. Roberts's house is, I'm sure, being watched by Vincent's men. And Belle is a wanted woman," he continued, "so we don't have the luxury of hiding in plain sight."

A wanted woman. I liked that. Well, when it pertained to

Rome. Not Vincent. "What exactly are we looking for?" *The antidote, please say the antidote.* "We know the good doctor isn't home, and we're risking a lot by going there."

"Papers, books, anything that will give us information about where Dr. Roberts is hiding and whether he has an antidote."

Excellent! "Wouldn't Vincent have already found those things, though?"

"Not necessarily."

Okay, what did Rome mean by that? I was about to ask him when Tanner said, "If the house is being watched, how the heezie are we going to get in? You mentioned breaking and entering, but we can't do that if our every move is monitored."

Confused, I shook my head. "Heezie?"

"You know. Hell. Don't you ever listen to the Snoop Dogg?"

The Snoop Dogg? Dear Lord, another superhero? "If heezie means hell, then why the heezie don't you just say hell? Jeez."

"Doesn't sound as cool," he said with a pout.

Rome covered his mouth with his hand to keep from laughing. Or possibly to keep from strangling us. "You want to hear my plan or not?"

"Yes, please." Me.

"Totally." Tanner.

"All right. Here's what we're going to do." Rome launched into a speech worthy of any army commander.

I listened, growing pale. God help us. The more he talked, the more it sounded like he wanted us to die.

Actually, I think that was Plan B.

*CHAPTER SEVENTEEN*

THAT NIGHT, after I'd changed into clean clothes—with panties and a bra!—we made the hour-long drive to Dr. Roberts's house in silence. I was too nervous to speak. The men, well…I think maybe Rome was getting into his zone. His kill-or-be-killed zone, that is, weighing possibilities and probabilities, mentally preparing to do whatever was necessary to obtain the desired results. Tanner's features were pale, and he looked ready to pass out at any moment. Oddly enough, he also exuded a palpable air of excitement, like he could high-five some of his buddies while bragging to the ladies.

"Duck," Rome said conversationally.

Tanner and I didn't hesitate; we ducked. Since we were both in the back seat, Tanner smashed his face against the seat and I covered his body with my own. My heart rate burst into hyperspeed.

"What's going on?" I whispered, then mentally chastised myself for whispering. I didn't have to be quiet yet.

Our car slowed, turned gently, straightened out and eased over a speed bump. "I'm going to park several blocks away from the doctor's neighborhood. We'll enter on foot."

Great. Walking. Exercise. Making a target of myself. My

favorite things. Perhaps I should just hang a neon sign around my neck that read Shoot Here.

"Why are we ducking?" Tanner said, whispering as well.

"Vincent's agents are patrolling the area," Rome said.

"What the hell?" Tanner, I noticed, was too nervous to say "heezie." I did my best to comfort him by giving his arm an I'm-here-for-you squeeze. I only prayed he didn't notice the nervous, swamplike nature of my hands.

"You didn't mention *that* in the plan," he continued. "You said they'd be watching the house, not the whole goddamn state of Georgia."

"I did mention the fact that you could be shot at or knifed, and *this* is what you complain about?" Rome blew out a heavy breath, and through the crack between the seats I watched as his hand inched from the steering wheel and curled around the handle of the gun resting in the passenger seat.

That gun was the reason I'd been relegated to the back seat. He'd wanted it at the ready, and he hadn't wanted me near it. *You might accidentally nail me,* he'd said. And I'd replied, *I thought you* wanted *me to nail you.* He'd shut up after that.

A few seconds passed—or were they minutes?—before he parked the car in a shadowed corner. "I saw four agents in four different cars, and they're diligently watching this lot." He tucked the gun in his ankle holster and covered it with his pants. I knew he had knives (and other guns) strapped to several parts of his body, too.

"Park somewhere else," I said. *Please.*

"Every shop, house and building is going to be watched. Dr. Roberts got away. We got away. And they're determined to find us. This is as safe a place as any." Rome paused, turned off the car and palmed the keys. "This is what we're going to do. I'm going to head toward the store and create a distraction, as well as draw the agents to me and, well, you can guess. When I've done that, you guys get out, stay in the shadows, and meet me behind the Dumpster on the west side."

I gulped. "I could try to start a fire somewhere in the distance."

Before I spoke the last word, he was shaking his head. "Too risky. One, we don't know if there are innocent people in the area, and two, you might accidentally start the fire in the car, and we need a getaway vehicle. I'll create the distraction."

"With what?"

He patted his slacks pocket. "You'll see."

Frustration clawed at me. "How am I supposed to develop my powers to the point that I can help you with Sunny if you're always making me hide and duck?"

"I told you I was no longer sure how I'll want you to help with her, so that question is moot right now."

I hated that Rome was taking so many risks, but didn't see how I could truly aid him at the moment. "Be careful," I said softly.

"No worries, baby." He didn't turn to look at me. "I'll be fine. You just make sure *you* don't get hurt." With that, he exited as casually as a man intent on shopping for eggs, milk and biscuits. But I could see the muscles bunched under his shirt, the tension that he tried so hard to hide. Had I once thought him impossible to read?

The door shut, leaving Tanner and me in complete silence.

Wait, no, not complete silence. I could hear the raggedness of our breathing, the rush of blood in my ears. "I'm so sorry I got you into this, Tanner."

"It's okay." He uttered a nervous laugh. "It'll be one hell of a story for my bitches."

"You could leave. You don't have to stay with us."

He paused. Groaned, sighed. "I'll stay." The edge of firmness in his voice left no room for argument. "What kind of man would I be if I abandoned you? You're, like, my family now."

"I feel the same way." And I did. I loved this kid. He was smart and brave, a dear friend I hadn't known how desperately I'd needed until now. "Wait till you meet my dad. He buys Viagra on the black market, so I know he'll love you."

"I like him already. Hey, can I tell you something?" Tanner asked, his voice going soft, sweet.

"Of course. You can tell me anything."

"I can feel your boobs pressing against my back."

I choked back a laugh. "If we're family now, that comment is completely incestuous."

He didn't reply. Our nerves were frayed, our minds heavy with the coming events. It was odd, really. I'd lived my entire life craving adventure, wishing for it, depressed that I didn't have it. Now that it was here, a part of me wanted the return of my staid existence. Normalcy, the ordinary, were the gates to paradise. Weren't they?

"How will we know when Rome's created the distraction?" I asked.

*Boom!*

I gasped and jolted upright. Tanner did the same. We stared wide-eyed out the front window as flames consumed a small patch of trees. "My God," I breathed. Moonlight bathed the area, then was chased away by the glow of the fire.

"I think we know," Tanner said, his tone awed.

Tires squealed. People raced in every direction, their expressions panicked.

"Let's go." I bounded out of the car, Tanner close behind me. "He said to meet him behind the Dumpster on the west side." But, uh, which way was west? I'd always had a hard time with directions. Did the sun rise or set in the west?

"This way." Tanner pointed.

My gaze followed his finger and lit on a dark blue bin at the far side of the grocery store. "Come on." I grabbed his hand and we were off, heading in the same direction as the frantic crowd.

There were more cars in the lot than I'd anticipated, and I didn't know who to avoid. At least my hair was hidden under a baseball cap. I tried to stay in the shadows as much as possible, but no matter what I did, I felt exposed. Vulnerable. Finally we reached our destination, and I pressed my back against the cool metal.

Smoke was beginning to thicken the air, burning my lungs and throat. I coughed. My eyes watered.

"Shit! Not again." Tanner pushed on my shoulders, forcing me to the dirty, trash-laden ground. "Lie down. Stay as low as you can and cover your nose with your shirt."

I did as he commanded and was thankful to discover the air was thinner, cleaner when filtered through the cotton. My coughing subsided. Only a few minutes passed before Rome sprinted around the corner, stopping abruptly. His gaze narrowed when he spied me lying prone.

"What's wrong with her?" he asked Tanner.

"Smoke got to her."

Rome reached down and hefted me up over his shoulder, fireman-style. Without protest, I let him carry me. A coughing fit from me would slow us down considerably.

"This way," Rome said. "We're good to go, but I want you to stay behind me."

Tanner moved to the rear. In the distance I heard the wail of fire truck sirens. We entered a field behind the store, careful to avoid security lights. We raced across it. Well, the boys did. I was just along for the (bumpy) ride.

When we reached the beginning of a gated community, Rome gently lowered me. His hands cupped my jaw, and our gazes locked. "You okay?"

I allowed the shirt to fall from my nose, and inhaled deeply. The air was sweet and clean. The cords in my throat relaxed, and the irritating tickling sensation subsided. "I'm good."

"Okay. We've got a public street on one side of us and a fence that peeks into rich people's backyards on the other. Try to look casual, at ease. Belle, you're going to hold my hand. Tanner, stay beside Belle. We're a family out for a nighttime stroll. Nothing more."

He didn't wait for our reply, but gripped my hand in his and leapt into motion, leading us closer to Dr. Roberts's house. Tanner quickened his step until he paced at my side. "If we're staying in the shadows," he asked under his breath, "why do we need to look casual?"

"There are people who can see in the shadows, not to mention a little thing called night vision goggles. If we're spotted, I want people to think we have nothing to hide."

"Won't they shoot first and ask questions later?" I asked.

Rome gave my hand a squeeze. "Hopefully, they won't expect us to come out in the open. Anyway, there's really no place for us to hide."

"Thanks for that," Tanner said drily. "You could have lied, at least. How the hell am I supposed to act casual now?"

Yes, it *was* hard to act as if we had nothing to hide when we were each loaded with weapons. Did I forget to mention that part? Rome hadn't wanted us to rely solely on our superpowers—and let's face it, an empath like Tanner couldn't slay a bad guy by understanding he was angry. Rome hadn't wanted us to rely solely on *his* weapons, either, in case we became separated. So he'd given me and Tanner each a Taser, a flashlight and several knives, which were now strapped to our thighs, waists and wrists.

I wasn't sure I'd have the balls to actually stab anyone. Fry them or ice them, maybe, even though I still wasn't one hundred percent comfortable with the fact that I'd already deep-fried a few people (bad guys though they were). But there was something so personal about stabbing someone.

I guess we'd see if I could do it (on purpose) when the time came.

A car honked in the distance, startling me. I gasped and jumped about a foot in the air.

"Easy," Rome said.

I drew in a steadying breath, trying to relax. I kept my attention straight ahead, absorbing Rome's strength and assurance.

"At the next street, we're going to turn left," he said.

Tanner ran a hand through his hair, looking anything but casual. "How do you know the way?"

Rome shrugged, and I think he answered just to keep us

distracted. "A while ago, Lexis had to pretend to be Dr. Roberts's friend. She told you that, right? Our boss wanted the formula for himself. I followed her each time she came here, making sure she was safe."

Oh, that he would always look after me like that. What a tantalizing thought. Oh, that he still looked after Lexis like that. What a…not so tantalizing thought.

We had to stop and hide behind bushes for a bit as a black SUV slowly prowled the street, followed by a car filled with shouting teenagers. Thankfully, no one spotted us.

"Well," Tanner said, "I think we should have slammed the car through the security fence and into the house, run in, grabbed what we needed and hauled ass."

Rome's brows arched into his hairline, and he shook his head. "And risk destroying our getaway vehicle, not to mention wiping out any possible paper trail?"

"We could have driven two cars," I suggested. "One to smash and one to drive away."

"Now that's a plan, Viper."

"What about the destruction of files or information about the formula?" Rome didn't give us a chance to answer, grumbling, "You two are ruining my concentration." He released my hand and wound his arm around my waist, drawing me closer. "I'm supposed to be on the lookout for the people who want to kill us. I swear, this is why I never work with amateurs."

The reminder sobered us, and silence reigned until we came to a section of the fence Rome approved. I glanced uneasily at the tall iron bars that stretched skyward, pointing sharp tips toward the heavens.

"This it?" Tanner asked, his voice shaking.

Rome nodded. "This is it. More shadows. No dogs around. And we're not too far from the doctor's house."

The shadows *were* darker here. Thicker. Consuming the small enclosure. I swallowed. Yes, this was it and there would be no turning back now. Several pines stretched toward the gate, but they weren't close enough for us to climb.

"You ready, Belle?" Rome faced me. I couldn't make out his features very well, only the occasional flash of white teeth. But I drew comfort from his presence.

I nodded, realized he might not be able to see me, and said, "Ready." God, I was nervous. I did *not* want to be the weak link that let this team down.

"Then get us past it."

Breathing in and out slowly, precisely, I squared my shoulders and turned to the gate. I held out one of my hands, palm out. The wind, I was learning, was the hardest element for me to call. It required a combination of feelings. An emotional cocktail, if you will, of fear (check), desperation (check), and, as I'd figured out during the day's training session, some type of affection. Love worked, though I didn't know why.

All I knew was that it was hard to maintain such a sweet, positive emotion while drawing from the other two, the negatives.

As before, in the clearing, I allowed images of my dad to spill across my mind. My heart swelled with love for him. To strengthen the emotion, I allowed Rome to enter the picture, envisioning the two men slapping each other on the back. I didn't want to—God, I didn't—but I forced the images to twist. To darken. To become a nightmare I never wanted to come true.

"Whatever you're doing, it's working," Tanner said proudly. "I can feel a tornado forming inside you."

In my mind, I saw the two men I held so dear being hurt. Gunned down. Bullets whizzed and popped with startling realism. I saw both men flinch in pain. Saw blood escape from their many wounds.

"Yes, yes," Tanner praised. "It's getting stronger."

Rome cupped the back of my neck and massaged. "Good girl. You're doing great."

Around me, a fierce wind began to blow. My hair whipped from the ball cap and slapped at my cheeks. The trees danced, leaves swaying. Twigs and dirt swirled up from the ground, whirling round and round. I closed my eyes, saw myself running toward the fallen men, screaming their names.

"The wind is too strong, Viper." Concern laced Tanner's voice. He was suddenly shoved into the bars. "It's going to blow us away."

"Give some to me," Rome said.

I visualized the fierceness of my emotions traveling out of me and into Rome, giving him pieces of the positive, pieces of the negative. He tensed the moment they hit him, and hissed in a breath.

Instantly, the churning sea inside me calmed. The emotions were still there, but they were manageable. The violence of the wind eased slightly.

"That's it," he said. "I've got it."

With my free hand, I motioned for the wind to churn at our feet. After only a moment's hesitation, it obeyed. We were lifted an inch or so in the air, the force of the moving current creating a solid foundation beneath us.

"Higher," I whispered. We rose sharply, and I almost dropped my hand to my side. Almost commanded the wind to leave.

"Steady," Rome said.

"Are you concentrating?" Tanner said. "I don't think you're concentrating."

"I'm concentrating!"

"You're doing good, baby." Rome slapped Tanner upside the head. "Can you get us over the wall, Belle?"

To do that, I needed to make the wind swirl. What should I do, what should I do? I twirled my finger in a circle, mimicking a whirlwind, but that didn't help. I closed my eyes and visualized it, but—no, wait! The wind began to rotate. Up, up we went.

My stomach twisted in progression with the wind, but I kept my mind on the chaos. Besides, if I opened my eyes and looked down, I might vomit or scream or any number of other things. I wasn't afraid of heights, far from it, but my God, we had nothing but air holding us up. Wind, which was invisible. I only hoped there were no onlookers.

The top spike of the fence suddenly scraped the bottom of my boot. I gasped, but managed to keep my mind on the task at hand. My finger never stopped twirling.

"We cleared it," Rome said.

Happiness flooded me. I'd done it. I'd done it!

"Uh, celebrating a little too early," Tanner said, a split second before the wind ceased and we tumbled to the ground.

I hit with a hard smack. My feet absorbed most of the shock, but my body vibrated painfully. My teeth rattled, almost slicing into my tongue. Tanner humphed and rolled to his side. Rome landed perfectly, without sound, without bouncing. Just thump, he was crouched on his feet.

Damn cat reflexes.

For several prolonged seconds, I sucked air back into my lungs. "Oopsie," I said between pants. "My bad."

"We'll practice the landing next time." Rome tugged me to my feet, then did the same for Tanner. "Let's move out."

Once again we were in motion, remaining close to the fence, striding along its shadowed edge. We didn't try to pretend nonchalance this time. We simply stayed out of sight as much as possible. I was so ready for this night to be over, and would have sold my soul for a little of Lexis's psychic ability. If I knew what was going to happen before it actually happened, well, I could make sure Rome and Tanner emerged unscathed.

Row after row of sprawling homes came into view. Lights gleamed from the streets, from garages, from gardens. "Rome," I said uncertainly.

"Just keep your back to the fence."

When we rounded a corner, he stopped. Crouched. I glanced at Tanner, Tanner glanced at me and we both crouched beside Rome.

"That's Dr. Roberts's home." He motioned to a pretty Victorian with an unkempt yard and overgrown bushes. Wraparound porch. Hanging wind chimes. Blue shutters.

I experienced a tiny flutter of shock. This beautiful mansion housed the man who'd made me what I am. No lights were on inside it. I guess I should have asked if Dr. Roberts had a family here we needed to worry about awakening.

"Is anyone there?" Tanner asked.

Rome didn't answer. Instead, his gaze slowly scanned left and right, searching, intense. Minutes passed. Insects chirped.

Finally Rome whispered, "See that black SUV?" He pointed to the right, to a car parked in a driveway several homes away from Dr. Roberts's.

"Yes."

"Definitely belongs to Vincent's men. Be careful. No telling what kind of scrim agents he has inside."

"How can you tell?" I studied it, but it looked like every other expensive car in the neighborhood.

"One, I know Vincent well enough to be sure he'd keep men here to watch for Dr. Roberts. Two, his agents are still inside the car. If you look closely, you can see the exhaust fumes. I'm betting they've been turning it on and off for the air conditioner. Plus, I can smell the amount of coffee they've consumed."

Ugh. Coffee. After what had been done to my grande mocha latte, I'd probably never want to drink the stuff again.

Tanner pressed deeper into the darkness, his gaze darting nervously. "What should we do?"

"Belle, do you think you can make it rain? A hard-ass storm just like we talked about at the cabin?"

"It will hail," I warned. "We won't be able to run through it without getting hit."

His lips lifted in a slow smile. "That's exactly what I want. Lots and lots of hail. Trust me. It'll be okay. Just make the storm as fierce as you can without blowing the houses away."

"The weather channel is going to have a field day with this," Tanner said drily. "I hope you both realize that. Everyone who knows about the formula will suspect Belle was here."

"It's a chance we have to take." Rome turned back to the house.

"What about the people in the SUV?" I asked.

"I'm going to leave them to you," Rome stated.

"What?" I said, surprised.

"What?" Tanner seemed equally taken aback.

"I'll disable their car and knock them out." I knew what that meant. Kill. "If one of them wakes up," Rome continued, "you two are to take care of him."

Tanner and I shared a wry look. Yeah, he was really letting us take care of the bad guys in the car. We got his leftovers, if there happened to be any. Knowing Rome, there wouldn't.

"This is going to work out, baby, you'll see."

I admit it. I love it when he calls me "baby," and he seemed to do it more when we were in dangerous situations. "Be careful, okay?" I wrung my hands nervously. "There could be armed men in the house, too."

His lips twitched. "Could be? No, there are."

My mouth fell open. He said it so casually, as if it was perfectly normal. "Maybe we shouldn't—"

"Create the storm, baby, and I'll signal when it's safe to enter the house."

"You going to distract everyone with another explosion?" Tanner asked drily.

"Hopefully not" was the only answer Rome gave.

I wanted to protest, but didn't. He was the expert here. He knew what he was doing. He knew how to survive. After all, he'd been doing it for a long time. Forcing my attention from him, I blinked up at the night sky. Stars twinkled from the black velvet. I didn't ask Rome to filter for two reasons. One, once the storm erupted he needed to leave. And two, I didn't want him to diminish my sadness in any way. The more intense it was, the more intense the storm would be.

My emotions were already frayed from their use and abuse

today, but I dragged them front and center once more. Concentrating on all the things that saddened me, I drew forth a large wave of sorrow, plumped it with more depressing images, encouraged it to grow. It sprouted wings inside me, spreading. Spreading.

"That's it, Viper. Let it flow."

Overhead a crash of thunder boomed. Lightning bolts lit the sky, one after another. Fat droplets of rain began to descend, slowly at first, then gaining in speed and density. My chin trembled and tears flowed down my cheeks. I'd never been this sad in my life. I verged on total depression. Feelings of aloneness swamped me. Feelings of helplessness consumed me.

"Stay safe," Rome breathed into my ear. He kissed my lips and was gone, disappearing into the darkness like a nocturnal phantom.

Rain pounded the ground, soon joined by the hail I'd predicted. The golf-ball-size ice smacked everything in its destructive path.

Tanner and I huddled under a tree. Its thick branches shielded us from most of the ice, but the rain managed to slip past the leaves and soak us. I shivered with cold as I searched the streets and houses for any sign of Rome, but I couldn't see him. The SUV stopped humming with life, I noticed, the black plumes of smoke disappearing. The rear wiper stopped in the middle of its glide.

I didn't see any movement in the car, though. Several more minutes passed. I didn't see any movement outside the house, either, but suddenly I heard the growl of a jungle cat echoing off the walls and into the night.

I gripped my stomach, hoping the puny action could prevent it from twisting painfully. Obviously, Rome had discovered his prey. *He'll be okay, he'll be okay, he'll be okay.*

Another growl.

A tortured scream.

Tiny flickers of light flashed from Dr. Roberts's windows, as if someone—or multiple someones—were firing several rounds. The rain stopped as fear held me in its tight clasp, but I forced my sadness to return. Rain fell again.

"He'll be okay," Tanner whispered, voicing my thoughts. "He has to. I mean, he's Agent Kick-ass, isn't he, with an impenetrable force field or some kind of shit. Right?"

"Yes." The word sounded broken, hollow. A tremor raked me. Two men stumbled out of the SUV, blood dripping from their necks. Both had weapons drawn.

Without thought, I stretched out my hands. I don't know what I expected to happen, and wasn't given a chance to ponder. A bolt of lightning instantly slammed into the first man, throwing him backward and into the other man. The two sailed several feet before hitting the SUV. Both slumped to the ground.

"Holy shit, Viper. How did you do that?"

"I don't know!" I said, pointing my hands toward the ground before they could do any more damage. "Come on. Rome needs us."

"He didn't give the signal."

"I know."

"Oh, hell."

I sprinted into action, racing into the thick of the rain. No, not rain. With my fear, the rain had turned to snow. The cold infiltrated my bones.

When I reached the porch, I withdrew the Taser Rome had

given me. If I'd had a gun, I would have pulled it out, too. I would have shot someone, with no hesitation. And yes, now I knew for sure I'd stab someone, if necessary. Anything to protect Rome.

Tanner stepped up beside me, panting. Water dripped from his hair onto his face, and ran like a river from the clothes now plastered to his body. "We opening a can of whoop-ass now?"

"Fo sheezie," I said.

He paled, but slid a gun from the waist sheath hooked to his side. He rolled the…whatever the hell that was called. Cylinder? I don't know.

"Locked and loaded," he muttered.

I hadn't realized Rome had given him a gun, and blinked at it, stunned for a moment.

He kissed the barrel. "I'm a wild man, Viper, and I'm ready for action. Let's get this showdown started."

I positioned myself beside the front door. It was opened slightly, so getting in wouldn't be a problem. "Guard my back, you hardened outlaw. Okay?" I could hear the scramble of feet, the scrape of furniture. At least there was no more gunfire.

Tanner closed in behind me. "I used to hunt with my dad. I'll hit anyone who aims at you, promise."

I couldn't believe I was doing this, but I didn't want to leave Rome in there alone. No telling how many men he was up against. "On three. One. Two. Three." I kicked my way inside, Taser raised and ready for action. The lights were out, but my eyes had already adjusted to the darkness so I could make out the total chaos. Overturned tables and chairs, pillows strewn in every direction.

It was oddly silent now. The sound of footsteps had faded.

Suddenly a huge, black blur sprang at me. A part of me realized it was Rome in his jaguar form, but the rest of me acted on pure, terrified instinct. Those lethal claws were coming at me, and Rome might not realize exactly who it was he was attacking.

When he hit me, his massive body knocking me down, I allowed my instinct free rein and nailed the beast with the Taser, shooting volt after volt of electricity into his heart. We fell to the ground, the cat roaring and convulsing.

Behind me, a shot suddenly rang out, the sound so loud it nearly busted my eardrums. In the next instant, a human man (who, I would discover, had been about to shoot *me*) collapsed on top of me and the now-immobile cat.

## CHAPTER EIGHTEEN

SO I'D TASERED MY boyfriend. Other girls have done worse. I felt bad, really, but I wasn't going to beat myself up over it. He'd come at me, claws and fangs bared.

Anyone else would have done the same thing.

Yeah, he'd been in the process of saving my life. Had I known that at the time? No. Had he given me any type of warning? Again, no. I might feel (slightly) bad about this, as mentioned above, but I wouldn't accept blame. Rome was the only one at fault. Well, the assassin who'd been behind me was at fault, too. But not me!

Tanner switched on his flashlight and moved it over Rome, whose body still vibrated from the electrical charge. What did that mean? Crap, maybe I needed to examine him or something, and make sure I hadn't damaged him worse than I'd thought.

While I scooted out from under him, as well as the dead body draped over his back, Tanner's babbling assaulted my ears. "I shot him. I shot him dead. One bullet, just *boom*. Did you see me?"

"Don't beat yourself up about it," I said. God, Rome weighed a ton. "He was a bad guy, and he wanted to hurt us. You had to kill him."

"Beat myself up?" Grinning like a loon, he whooped. "Did you see my kick-ass aim? I had my eyes closed, but it was dead center—excuse my pun—and he went down like a horny boy in a whorehouse."

The implication of his words slammed into me harder than a bullet, and I gasped, my mouth agape. "You're telling me you aimed that gun in my general direction and your eyes were closed?"

Some of his excitement waned, and he gulped. "Well, yeah."

"The fact that you could have hit me doesn't bother you?" My eyes narrowed on him, the rims burning. "The fact that you could have hit Rome doesn't freaking bother you?"

Tanner's chin raised stubbornly. "What would a bullet have mattered? You Tasered him."

My jaw clenched. "For God's sake, he was coming at me."

"Yeah, to help you. And how did you repay him? By frying him up like an egg."

"Shut up and get over here. I need help. My legs are trapped under two tons of cat."

Tanner kicked the dead guy off of Rome. "I think the pussycat's coming around." He bent down and clutched Rome by his—its—head and shoulders, lifting. "My God," he grunted. "You weren't lying. What kind of cat chow has this heifer been eating?"

I wiggled free and glanced at the cat. He'd stopped shaking, at least, but his eyes were slitted on me. His lips were pulled back from his teeth in a lethal snarl. I'd never been Tasered, but I knew the electrical currents had rendered him immobile. Thank the Lord. He might have pounced on me for real if he could move.

"What?" I said to him, all innocence, with fluttering eye-lashes and a dainty shrug. "This is your fault, and you know it."

Tanner released Rome, who thumped to the floor. "Oops. Sorry."

Licking my lips, I glanced around the room—anything to keep from looking at Rome. "Are there any more bad guys in the house?"

"Not that I can see," Tanner replied.

"So…what should we do next?"

"Aren't we, like, supposed to question someone and look for information about the doc and his evil potions?"

I nodded. "Yes, of course. While Rome's recovering, why don't you look for a survivor and I'll search for the informa-tion."

Tanner's head canted to the side, and he surveyed the de-struction. "Uh, I'd rather search for information."

"Fine. Jeez. Let the delicate woman search the menacing criminals for signs of life."

"Thanks," he said, flouncing off, his flashlight in hand, leaving me in the dark.

"Tanner!" I shouted at his retreating back.

"Don't make an offer you don't want accepted," he threw over his shoulder. He disappeared down the hall.

"Smart-ass," I muttered. To Rome's prone body, I said, "We really need to teach that punk some manners." I reached toward the wall, feeling blindly for the light switch.

Rome growled.

My hand stopped in midair. "No light?"

Of course he didn't answer.

"Blink once if you want me to leave the light off, twice if

I can turn it on," I said, turning on my flashlight—duh, I'd forgotten I had one, too!—and shining it in his face. Well, I needed *some* light, whether he wanted me to have it or not.

He blinked once.

Great. I got the privilege of finding a live body/killer with only a flashlight. Yippee for me. "Growl or something if you need me," I sighed. I planted a kiss on his nose and scampered off, only thin beams of amber illuminating my path.

The house had wide, spacious rooms that looked very much like the foyer, with furniture overturned and broken glass scattered in every direction. I counted nine of Vincent's agents, both upstairs and downstairs. Rome had made short work of them, and though he'd wanted to keep one alive, none had survived. The ones I'd heard moaning earlier were now quiet.

I bumped into Tanner in the master bedroom. He *oomphed,* but didn't remove his attention from the far wall. He had something long and blue in his hands. When I saw what held him enthralled on the wall, though, I forgot to ask him about the blue thing.

"My God," I said.

"Do you think I could, like, take some of this with me?"

"Eww. No. That's gross." The good doctor obviously enjoyed S and M. Whips, spiked collars, crops and black leather abounded. Not to mention the silver chain harness hanging from the ceiling. No wonder Lexis had said the man had a wild sexual side. Just how "friendly" had she pretended to be with him? I shuddered.

"Look at this." Tanner held up the long, blue thing. "What is it? What are the beaded things?"

"Tanner!" My cheeks heated. "That's a *vibrator.*" I whispered the last word, embarrassed even to be saying it.

"Really?" Grinning, he shook it. The batteries rattled. "Cool."

"Put that down right now!"

"Hell, no. I found it on the floor, in plain sight. Finders keepers." Grin widening, he rattled it some more—and the end fell off. A sheet of paper drifted to the floor. "Hey, what's that?"

I frowned, bent down and pinched the paper between my fingers, shining my flashlight over it. When I realized what it was, I gasped. A note. From Dr. Roberts to…me. Well, to the Person Who Drank the Formula—my name wasn't specified. Still, my mouth fell open in shock. He'd known I would come here. Or maybe he had hoped.

"What does it say?" Tanner asked.

"It says 'I'm sorry.'" I swallowed and read the rest. "'I've done a terrible thing to you. I was weak and let a threat to ruin my public reputation influence my work. I should have destroyed the formula when I first discovered how dangerous it was. By the time I realized the error of my ways, it was too late—the formula had been perfected, and was just about to fall into the wrong hands. Evil hands. Unfortunately, the best hiding place I could think of on such short notice was…you. You were convenient, nearby. Please don't hate me. I've left you a present in my office, which is in a secret lab directly across from Utopia Café. Watch for prying eyes.'"

I paused, looking around. I could almost feel those prying eyes on me just then. "'P.S. Sorry about the sordid hiding place. I couldn't risk OASS finding this note, but I knew PSI would be hot on your heels and I hoped they'd know where to look.'"

"Wow," Tanner said. "You'd think since OASS knew he was a sex fiend, they'd have looked in the vibrator, too."

"I wonder why they didn't."

"They're dumbshits, if you ask me."

"Hey! Lexis told me the doctor was a pervert, but I didn't think to look in the vibrator, either." Tanner opened his mouth to comment, but I pointed a finger at him. "Don't say it."

He grinned. "Hey, this means the good old doc considered the employees of PSI pervs." He wiggled his eyebrows. "Belle hooked up with a perv," he sang.

"That means you're a pervert, too, since you're the one who actually found the note," I shot back.

His grin widened. "I know! Isn't it great?"

I shouldn't have been surprised by his happiness, the hornball. If I didn't change the subject, though—vibrators, for God's sake—we'd never get anything done. "So how'd Dr. Roberts get back into his house to hide this note?" I said, thinking aloud. "How'd he get past the OASSholes?"

"The who?"

I waved my hand through the air. "Never mind. Just ignore me." He could have planted it before he made his escape, knowing he was going to give the formula to someone.

Tanner shrugged. "Maybe there's another note around here, with more instructions." He began searching the rest of the "toys," whistling in tune with his movements.

I tapped a fingertip to my chin, wondering just what kind of confession was left for the doctor to make in a second note. I'd cause a world-wide flood if I wasn't careful? I'd have to live in an igloo for the rest of my life just to control the fire inside me? There was a depressing thought.

"I doubt we'll find anything else," Tanner said a few minutes later, his voice heavy with disappointment. "None of the other toys open."

"Just keep looking," I said.

Tanner ran his hand over the inside of a drawer, probing for a hidden compartment. "Have you found a live body yet?"

"No," I grumbled. I had to admit, in all my many jobs, many interviews, many hours spent scouring the classifieds, I'd never pictured myself doing this. Was there even a title for it? Certified Body Finder?

I should have preferred serving coffee to snobs. Should have preferred tweaking the odometers of used cars or making stupid balloon animals for ungrateful kids. Hell, I should have preferred sweeping disgusting balls of hair off the salon floor.

I didn't.

I kind of liked my current position, I realized. Maybe I *wasn't* ready to go back to my normal life. Sighing, I stuffed the doctor's note in my pocket. What would Rome say when he saw it? Maybe it would bribe him out of his Taser-induced bad mood when he finally came around.

As I trudged down the stairs, I ran my fingers over the bullet holes in the wall. Where was I going to find a living bad guy? The answer came to me instantly, surprising me. Grinning, I hopped over Rome's body—which had begun the slow process of returning to human form. Big patches of fur had fallen out, leaving gaps of tanned skin and sleek muscle. At the moment he resembled a hideous man-beast. I tried not to grimace.

"Be back in a jiff," I told him with a false, breezy air. I sailed outside. The neighborhood was calm, as if the shootout had never happened, but the man next door was standing on his porch, scratching his head as he stared out at the hail and snow covering the ground.

He saw me and said, "You one of Roberts's girls?"

I was very thankful the two sleeping (or dead) agents were hidden by the SUV. "Yep." I wiggled my eyebrows suggestively, as I thought a hooker might do.

"Always weird stuff going on in that house." He motioned to the ground with a tilt of his chin. "You ever seen anything like this? Snow this late in spring, of all things."

"Very weird," I said, just standing there.

After a moment, he shook his head and went back inside his house.

*Hurry, hurry, hurry! Before he comes out again.* I raced the rest of the way to the SUV. The two men were slumped at the tires. One of them, the one I'd hit directly with lightning, was in the same condition as his cohorts in the house.

I lost a little of my giddiness. I'd killed him. Another victim of my powers. *Don't think about it, Jamison. Remember, he was one of Vincent's men. He wanted to kill Rome. And capture you.* With shaky hands, I checked the second man for a pulse. At the first touch of my fingers, he moaned. I sighed in relief. He, at least, was alive.

I anchored my hands under his arms and dragged him toward Dr. Roberts's house. He weighed a freaking ton (more than Rome, even, the fatty), and I strained under the burden. He had black streaks on his face and shirt, as if the lightning bolt had ricocheted off his friend, frying him, too.

By the time I heaved him onto the porch, gooey mud covered him from head to foot, splattered over his skin and clothes. I huffed and puffed from exertion. Amid his moans, I held him up with one hand and opened the front door with the other. Thankfully, the neighbor never came back out.

My gaze immediately sought Rome. Except he no longer

lay in the entryway. The only sign that he'd been there was the mountain of fur he'd shed.

Should I call for him or not? He might be searching for me, ready to attack the moment he saw me, in retaliation for what I'd done. He might—holy shit—round the corner and storm toward me, death gleaming in his expression. He was in the process of jerking a black T-shirt over his head. A pair of black slacks already encased his lower body. How many spare pairs of clothing did this man have?

His eyes narrowed on me, then flicked to the man I held. "Don't say a word," he snapped, his steps never slowing.

"I wasn't." I shook my head for emphasis. "You look great. Really."

"How. The hell. Could you stun me?" The words left him haltingly, filled with the dark edge of his fury. He stopped just in front of me, our noses touching. Hot breath fanned my chin.

Better to go on the offensive, or he'd stomp all over me with guilt. "I think a better question is how could I not?" I released my burden, and the body thumped to the floor. I wagged a finger at Rome. "You came at me as you would a target. You should be commending my excellent reflexes in taking down an assailant."

His nostrils flared. "Commending? Did you just say commending?"

"Your hearing is excellent, Cat Man."

His pupils elongated, the black growing thinner, pointing on top and bottom. "What happened to waiting outside like a good little girl?"

"Tanner and I wanted to protect you. You're not invincible, Rome."

"But I'm damn close." He spread out his arms, motioning to the bodies lying around us. "You wouldn't have almost gotten yourself killed if you'd stayed where you were told."

"And you might have died if we had stayed. There was a man about to shoot you." I rose on my tiptoes, putting us on more level ground. "And like it or not, you've got partners now. We're supposed to look after each other. That means *we* look after *you,* just the way you look after us. Don't try to do this all on your own."

"If stunning me is how you look after me, I'd rather you didn't."

The man behind me moaned. "Look. I brought you a present. Two, actually. A live body and a note from the doctor."

Rome brushed past me, crouched beside the man and hefted him effortlessly over his shoulder. "Lock all the doors," he grumbled. "We might be here awhile. And what do you mean, a note from the doctor?"

I fished out the paper and held it toward him. "It was stuffed in a vibrator, of all places."

Rome reached for the note, but suddenly stilled. One corner of his mouth lifted, as if to say *are you kidding me?* Then he shook his head, muttered, "God save me," and grabbed the paper. He shifted the body over his shoulder as he read it. His expression became grim.

"You wanna put him down?" I asked.

"That bastard knew what he was going to do to you, and he did it anyway," he said, ignoring me.

"What do you think he left me in the office?"

"I don't know, but we *will* find out."

His voice was so ominous, I shuddered.

"What if someone called for backup?" I asked, only then thinking of the possibility.

"That's a chance I'm willing to take, rather than drag this guy with us." He rubbed a hand over his eyes. "Stand watch at the back and have Tanner guard the front. We'll do this quickly and get the hell out."

"Tanner," I called.

The kid trudged down the steps. "There's nothing else, just like I feared," he said, throwing his arms in the air. "No papers, no diary. Nothing. Hey, did you guys decide to stop arguing?"

"Yes," Rome said at the same time I said, "For the moment."

I opened my mouth to give Tanner his new orders, but his eyes lit on the unconscious man, and he clapped excitedly. "Is he breathing? Awesome. We get to question him, don't we? We'll torture some answers out of him for sure."

"I need you at the front, since you're our expert marksman," Rome said, hefting the body into the living room. "Stop anyone from entering."

Tanner's grin widened. "Did you see me take down that guy? Did you know I took him down in one shot? Just one shot?"

"You did real good," Rome praised. "If I hadn't been immobilized, I would have told you sooner," he added darkly. "Belle, right a chair for me."

As Tanner strode to the front door, I grabbed an overturned chair from the kitchen and dragged it to the center of the living room. Rome plopped the man in it and strapped him down with strips from his torn clothes.

"Should I turn on the lights now?" I asked.

"No. I don't want anyone outside to be able to see in or to know there's activity in here."

"The neighbor is awake. He was surprised by the snow."

"Did he seem suspicious?"

"Not at all. He just thought I was one of Dr. Roberts's regular hookers, and that the two of us were having one hell of a party."

Rome pinched the bridge of his nose. "Just…" he waved a hand through the air "…get me a glass of water. Please," he added after a moment's hesitation. "And hurry."

Okay, so I was no longer Wonder Girl. I was Errand Girl. That was fine. I didn't want to torture the guy, anyway. "You don't want me to put poison in it, do you?"

"Just water. Cold water."

"Why not just have Belle conjure some raindrops?" Tanner wondered aloud from his post at the door.

"We don't want to emotionally exhaust her," Rome said. "We should only use her powers when absolutely necessary."

Amen to that. I quickly found a glass in one of the kitchen cabinets, filled it at the sink and rushed back to Rome. "Here."

He tossed the contents in the man's face. Sputtering, our victim began to stir, blinking open his eyes. Rome and I leaned toward him expectantly. Seeing us hover around him must have shocked and frightened him, because he belted out a little-girl scream.

I winced. Rome grabbed a pillow to stuff over his face, and Tanner ran into the room and slapped him. "You should be ashamed of yourself!"

"Don't hurt me," the man cried. "Please don't hurt me."

"I locked the front door," Tanner told Rome. "Can I stay?"

Rome rolled his eyes. "Why not. Why stick to plan now?"

"I'll tell you anything you want to know," the terrified guy said.

I'd never been to a torturing session before. I'd seen several on TV, of course, so I had kind of expected resistance. Maybe threats, maybe cussing. Instead our guy blubbered like a baby. "Is he faking?" I asked, confused.

"No," Tanner said with disgust. "He really is this much of a pussy. No offense," he added wickedly, looking at Rome. Then, exasperated, he threw up his hands. "How are we going to work in these conditions?"

Rome looked like he wanted to flip Tanner off, but instead crossed his arms over his chest. "What are you doing here?" he asked our victim.

"Waiting for Dr. Roberts," was the hasty reply.

Rome gave Tanner a pointed look.

"What?" Tanner said.

"Is he telling the truth?"

"How the hell should—oh, wait." Tanner hopped to the man—who screamed again—and placed a hand on his shoulder. He closed his eyes. "Yes. Truth." His lips stretched into a full grin. "This is so cool. I'm a human lie detector, just like Lexis said. I mean, once I opened the gate to my superpowers—"

"You're an empath, not the Hulk," I said. Jeez. "And we need to get on with this." I admit, I was nervous and wanted to leave ASAP.

Tanner splayed his arms, an action that said, *Look at me and look your fill.* "Don't pretend you don't like the Tanner flavor. Like I was saying, once I opened the gates to my powers, it's been a constant stream of emotions and new abilities. The guy spoke and I could totally feel his fear recede."

"Good," Rome said. "Now, if you two don't mind, I'd like to resume my questioning. That is why we're here." He frowned at each of us before turning his attention back to the man. "Does Vincent know where Dr. Roberts is now?"

"No, no. I swear he doesn't."

Tanner nodded. "Truth."

Finally taking up my post, I walked to the nearest curtained window. I sank to the floor and crossed my legs, propping my elbows on my knees. There was a slight crack in the brown material, and I was able to see outside. The men had the interrogation under control, and we needed a lookout. Thankfully, everything appeared calm.

"What are Vincent's plans for Belle?"

"He—he wants to test her. See what she can do, then use her in the field."

"Truth."

"Does he have an antidote for her?" Rome asked.

"No."

"Truth." Tanner glanced at me. "Sorry, Belle."

Was *I* sorry? Part of me was, I think. Part of me…wasn't.

Rome pushed out a frustrated breath. "Let's try this from a different angle. Does Vincent have any leads on the doctor's whereabouts?"

The man shook his head, his dark hair slapping his forehead. "Dr. Roberts tried to break into Vincent's lab yesterday, but he was spotted before he got inside. He was chased, but managed to escape again."

"Truth."

"Now we're getting somewhere." Rome planted his hands on the chair arms and leaned down. "Why did Dr. Roberts want back inside the lab?"

I suspected the answer was that he'd been leaving me that "present" he mentioned in his note.

Inching backward, the man babbled, "I don't know. No one knew."

"Lie," Tanner said triumphantly.

"Do I really need to torture you?" Rome asked quietly, leaving no doubt he would do whatever was necessary. "The animal inside me—allow me to introduce you to him." For a split second, Rome's mouth and chin stretched forward, his teeth gleaming long, sharp and menacing. "The animal inside me is hungry. Very, very hungry."

The guy squealed. "We think he left a written copy of the formula in his office," he babbled. "But we haven't been able to find it."

"Truth."

The formula—that's what he was giving me! What better present, in his mind, than the one thing that could possibly make me, well, *me* again?

Rome ran his tongue over his teeth. "How many men does Vincent have chasing Belle?"

"I don't know the exact number, I swear, I just know he wants her. Bad. Every day he sends more men searching. If he studies her blood, he can make more like her and his agents can begin killing off everyone who opposes him. He'll run the most powerful para-agency in the world. He'll decide which countries win wars. He'll decide who to help, who to destroy. Please, just let me go. I want to go home."

"Truth," Tanner taunted. "He just wants to run home to Mommy."

The man risked a glare in Tanner's direction, but cringed again when Rome snarled. "He'll never stop searching," the man added pitifully. "Like you, he'll do whatever it takes."

Great. What a fan-freaking-tastic thing to hear. My shoulders slumped. "Has Vincent given the formula to anyone else?" I asked. "Who survived," I added, remembering Rome had once told me others had died.

The man shook his head. "You're the only one," he said. "That makes you all the more valuable to him."

"Truth."

I rested my head against the wall and stared out the window, groaning inwardly. Thanks to the doctor's note, I now knew I'd survived ingesting the formula because he had finally perfected it, not because I was some sort of mutant freak with unusual blood. Would Vincent believe that, though? Probably not. That man was all about experiments. "I wouldn't work for him even if he captured me."

"If he caught you, you'd work for him," Rome said, his tone bleak. "He'd make sure of it, even if he had to destroy everything you love."

*My dad,* I thought, panicking.

*Lexis is with him,* I reminded myself, and calmed. *He's protected.*

"What about the formula's ingredients?" Rome asked. "Do you know them?"

"Roberts deleted the files," the man answered, "destroyed the paperwork and fled. There's no way we can duplicate the formula. Not without the written recipe. Or Belle. The hope is that the molecules in her blood will spell out exactly what she was given."

"Truth."

Rome straightened. He stood there for a moment, saying nothing, doing nothing, his expression raw, harsh.

"I cooperated." Tears streamed down the man's cheeks. "You're going to let me go, right? You're not going to hurt me? I won't tell Vincent what we talked about. I swear I won't."

Tanner didn't say anything, but he gave Rome a pointed stare. What was going on between them? Moving faster than the blink of an eye, Rome slammed his fist into the crybaby's face. Instantly his wailing stopped, and he sank into unconsciousness.

"What'd you do that for?" I asked, standing. "He was right. He cooperated."

"He would have killed you if he had the chance," Rome said. His voice was low and raspy, and dripped with quiet rage. "He's lucky I don't cut him up."

"Truth."

Rome shook his head. "Enough, Tanner."

"Yeah," I said. "You better not do that truth-lie thing to me. Ever. Or I'll hurt you."

He grinned. "Truth," he said, and I showed him my fist.

"Let's go." Rome picked up his bag and slung it over his shoulder. "We've got some planning to do."

"Wait." My eyes narrowed on the man. Rome was right. The guy would have hurt us if he'd been able. Might still one day hurt us if he had the chance. No one threatened my men and left unscathed.

I drew on my darker, colder emotions, let fear swamp me until my fingers went numb, until a mixture of dirt and ice formed. Just as I had that day in Lexis's apartment, I threw the ball. The moment it hit him, a frozen dirt box encased him. It would melt (I think), but not for a long while (I hoped).

I rubbed my hands together. "Now we can go."

## CHAPTER NINETEEN

THE ENTIRE DRIVE BACK to the cabin, Tanner expounded on and on about how wonderful he'd been, how cool he was, how the girls would be all over him now. I loved that he was so proud of himself. He *had* done a good job (except for shooting blind, the dumb-ass). But I couldn't stop thinking about the note we'd found—and that I might not *want* to find the formula.

I sighed. What was wrong with me?

"—so, like, awesome," Tanner said, again cutting into my thoughts. "The only thing that would have been cooler was if it had been recorded. Think about it. I could break out the DVD on every date, and I guarantee any lady would become desperate to ride the Tanner Express."

Rome reached out and jacked up the volume on the radio. While Gwen Stefani rocked from the speakers, he linked our hands. His warmth and strength and calluses soothed me.

I glanced over at him. He kept his eyes on the road, so I was able to study his profile. He was as savage from the side as he was from the front, with a sharp nose, harsh cheekbones and a hard chin. Cut from glass, chiseled from steel, that was Rome.

He looked as likely to kill people as to speak to them, yet right now he was gently tracing his thumb over the peaks and valleys of my palm. So contradictory, so mysterious. I wanted to crawl inside his brain and learn everything about him. I wanted to know his thoughts, his feelings.

I sounded like a freaking girl, didn't I? But I couldn't help it. He fascinated me.

He was destined to love someone with his whole heart, Lexis had said. More than ever, I wanted that someone to be me. Imagine all that fierce maleness directed totally at you. Oh, just the thought made me shiver. He would be a demanding lover, exacting. He would expect utter faithfulness and wouldn't tolerate anything less.

And he would give the same in return.

Heady knowledge indeed. And yet, if I gave him my heart, gave him everything I had to give, and I wasn't the woman for him, I would be destroyed. Like Lexis, would I have the strength to give him up rather than keep him bound to me, knowing he lusted for another?

My fingers tightened around his hand as I tried to hold him closer, lest he float away from me. I had probably caused Rome more physical pain, not to mention worldly disasters, than anyone he'd ever met. Why be with a girl like me when he could have someone like Lexis? Someone gorgeous, intelligent, wealthy. Someone who could hold a job for more than a few months. Okay, days.

I felt my already raw emotions attempting to create some type of physical reaction—rain, snow, a little of everything. Yet I'd been pushed to the brink today, and nothing happened. I breathed a sigh of relief. I didn't want Rome to know how I was feeling. Not when *I* didn't know how I was feeling.

Rome used his free hand to turn down the music. Blessed silence; Tanner had stopped talking. I peeked over my shoulder, only to see the kid asleep in the backseat. His head lolled to the side. Rays of moonlight streamed over him, and those long eyelashes cast shadows on his cheeks.

"You okay?" Rome asked me.

To ask or not to ask the dreaded where-are-we? question men hated so much… I mean, we hadn't even slept together yet. "I—we—I'm just nervous about my dad," I finished lamely. I didn't want Rome running away from me in terror. I didn't want him afraid to take our relationship to the next level because I expected more from him than he could give.

He squeezed my hand. "Give Lexis a call, then. She has a cell, and it's a secure line." He released me, picked up his cell phone, dialed, then handed it to me.

Lexis answered the moment I placed the phone to my ear. My dad was doing well and was sleeping, she assured me. No one had tried to hurt him. Nothing serious had happened, and she didn't foresee anything bad happening, either. Also, my dad wouldn't stop flirting with her, the rogue. I released a pent-up breath, relief washing through me.

"How's Rome?" she asked me, her voice quiet, hesitant.

I forced my gaze to remain straight ahead. "Good."

She paused. "Take good care of him."

"I will."

We hung up, and I placed the phone on the dash.

"Your dad is doing well, I take it," Rome said.

I nodded, my lips pressed together. "Flirting, as always."

He flicked me a proud glance. "You did good today."

"Aside from knocking you on your ass?" I said drily.

He gave a tiny but genuine grin. "Yeah. Aside from that. You got us over the gate twice. You created the storm that got us inside the house undetected. And you didn't burn anything down."

"Sweet progress," I replied with an answering grin. "So we're going to break into the laboratory tomorrow?"

He nodded. "It will be more difficult than tonight. Way more difficult, actually. There will be security everywhere. Lexis once told me the building has heat sensors, weight-sensitive flooring, motion detectors and eye scanners."

"Getting in sounds impossible. Not to mention dangerous."

"Nah," he said. "It sounds fun."

I rolled my eyes, but I was chuckling inside. What a macho-guy thing to say. What a *Rome* thing to say. "I bet there will be guards. Armed to kill."

"You'd win that bet."

My heart stopped at the ease with which he spoke of facing trigger-happy killers. "How are we going to get in? Tanner and I are—and I shouldn't have to remind you of this—amateurs. We're more likely to get you caught than give any real aid."

"You know that's not true. Did I or did I not just thank you for how wonderful you were tonight? You kicked major ass."

"You could have done it without me," I grumbled.

"Truth," he said, mimicking Tanner.

I snorted. "You're funny. Not." Would it have killed him to say, *No, my sweet beauty. I would have failed had you not been there to save me*? Was that really asking too much?

"This next job, though…" His voice trailed off and he sighed. "I need you, Belle. I really won't be able to do it alone."

That admission startled me. Could he have said it to pacify

me? Yes. Had he? I don't think so. That wasn't Rome's style. He always said what he meant, and never diluted the truth. No matter how much it would hurt. He needed me and he wasn't afraid to admit it. Lord, I really liked this man. More than liked him. I admired him, trusted him, desired him.

"You don't have to break into the lab, you know," I said. "You don't have to put yourself in danger when you'll get nothing in return."

"I *will* get something in return. I help you, you help me. Right?"

"Right," I said softly, "but you haven't figured out how I can help yet."

"I will."

"Whatever you need me to do, I'll do." Now. Tomorrow. It didn't matter. When he needed me, I would be there.

"Thank you." He linked our fingers again. "Don't worry. We'll find a way to succeed. At everything."

A few cars whizzed past us. Rome was making sure to only go a few miles above the speed limit, not wanting to get pulled over or draw any attention to us. Trees flashed past the windows. The moon was high and wouldn't begin its descent for hours yet.

"Where are you going to hide Sunny, do you know?" I asked.

"A safe house in the heartland." He leaned against the headrest with a slight smile. "We'll really live like a family for the first time in years. I'll take her grocery shopping. To the park. Swimming. All the things families do."

Family. His words were a harsh reminder that I wasn't part of his. He didn't ask me to come with him after I'd helped him, and I didn't invite myself. Lexis and Sunny were his top priority—Lexis because she was Sunny's mom—and that was as it should be. Still, it hurt. It hurt badly, and everything inside me sort of crumbled. In that moment, I realized I couldn't possibly be the woman he was destined to spend his life with.

Sharp lances of pain speared me, cutting deep. So deep.

Would I let that stop me from enjoying him? No. Hell, no. I'd take him for as long as I could have him. No regrets. I didn't want to look back over my life and wonder what could have been. What pleasure I could have shared.

"Will your boss search for you?" I managed to ask. Inside I prayed I didn't sound as broken and hollow to him as I did to myself.

Rome didn't seem to notice. "He can look, but that doesn't mean he'll find." He paused for a moment. "He's not an evil man. Like I said, he does love Sunny. I think in time he'll come to realize that this is the best thing for her."

"You'll have to excuse me if I disagree with you about him. I think he's evil. He wanted to neutralize me. *Wants* to neutralize me, that is." *Good job, Belle. Keep it light. Keep it impersonal.*

"He wants that for safety reasons."

"Not mine."

"No. The world's. A few days ago I agreed with him, remember? But you don't think I'm evil."

I ignored the last part of his words. "If a woman has to die to protect the world, no big whoop, is that what you're saying? He could have come to me and we could have talked about it like two civilized adults."

"No, he couldn't. Vincent is after you, too." Rome paused. "Maybe now a meeting is something that would be good for both of you, though. Once John hears what you can do, neutralizing you will be the last thing on his mind. He'll want you on his team."

I snorted. "What if he sees me, pops a cap in my temple first and asks questions later?"

"'Pops a cap'?" A short bark of a laugh escaped him. "Now you sound like Tanner."

My gaze dropped to my feet. Wet mud caked my boots and streaked the floor mat. "If your boss gets to know me and wants to lock me up in Château Villain, what will *you* do? Betray him—or me?"

He paused. A long, horrible pause. Why did he have to think about this? Did I mean less to him than I'd thought?

"You don't have to worry about it," Rome finally answered. "I won't let anyone hurt you or experiment on you or lock you away."

Sweet words. Words that touched me deeply. But what about when he wasn't around? What about when he left me? *You'll take care of yourself, that's what!* Yes, I would. I'd be okay without Rome, I assured myself. So what that my heart felt like it was breaking into a thousand pieces.

The car eased onto a dirt road hidden between two thick groves. The farther we drove, the thicker the trees became, and the less obvious the track. Branches and leaves slapped against the car. Finally there was no road that I could distinguish, and Rome had to twist and turn the wheel to keep from hitting anything. Up and down I bounced.

After a while, the small cabin came into view, illuminated by rays of golden moonlight. Had I not known it was there, I would have thought it was a thick wall of bush and forgotten timber.

Rome parked the car in back. "Wait here while I get rid of the tire tracks."

I nodded. "Be careful."

"Always," he said, flashing me a grin. He exited the car and disappeared into the night.

Turning toward the back seat, I clapped Tanner on the shoulder and shook him. "Wake up, sunshine."

"I am," he said without hesitation. His voice held no trace of slumber. His eyes opened—and not gradually. One minute he appeared asleep, the next he didn't.

"How long have you been awake?" I demanded.

He eased up and brushed the hair off his forehead. "The whole ride. How else was I going to eavesdrop on you and Rome? You really gonna let him leave you behind when he goes into hiding?"

I turned away and stared out the window. "It's not like I'll have a choice, Tanner."

"There's always a choice."

"Not when it comes to someone else's feelings," I said.

"You could fight for him."

I closed my eyes for a moment and leaned my head against the seat. "I want a man who wants to be with me. I don't want to force him to stay, force him to keep me with him."

"Rome cares about you. I can feel it coming off him in waves every time he looks at you."

"Sometimes that isn't enough," I said softly.

He *pfted.* "That's pride talking."

"You don't know anything about relationships, okay?" I twisted the hem of my shirt between my fingers, tightening the material around my knuckles and cutting off my circulation. "So don't try to hand out advice."

"I may not have ever had sex," he said darkly, "but I *have* loved. I may be young, but I've suffered my share of loss. Don't you try to act like I don't know what I'm talking about simply because *you* don't have the courage to keep your man."

Anger and shame tried to spark inside me, but I didn't let them. I didn't need the complication of another fire. Besides, Tanner was right. So right. He'd loved his parents and lost them. He knew pain intimately. And I *was* acting like a coward. "I'm sorry." I turned toward him.

He looked away from me and shrugged. "Don't worry about it."

He was trying to act blasé, but I knew I'd hurt him. I wanted to make it right. He didn't deserve my snippiness. Not after everything he'd done. He was fighting a war for me. Risking his life for me. And young as he was, he *was* a man. As Lexis had said, he just had a little maturing to do. "Tanner—"

The driver-side door suddenly opened, and Rome stuck his head in. "All clear."

My motions were slow and tired as I exited. Tanner was right behind me, and we trudged toward the cabin. He still wouldn't look at me. I would apologize again, but I'd wait until he was more receptive to do it.

Before we reached the porch, Rome strode to my side and clasped my hand, bringing me to a stop. "Tanner, go inside. Get some rest. Belle and I will join you in a little while."

I opened my mouth to ask what was going on, but Tanner muttered, "Take your time," and entered without us.

Rome tugged me into a thicket of trees. "There's a pond out here," he said.

"And?"

"And we're going to swim in it. Alone. Then do whatever else we feel like doing."

Oh. *Oh.* Suddenly I wasn't so tired. Warmth tingled through me. Warmth and lust and a seemingly unquenchable hunger. The rational, keep-me-out-of-trouble part of my brain tried desperately to remind me of what the future had in store. *Rome is going to leave. When this is all over, he's going to leave you.*

Maybe it was foolish of me, but I still refused to let that ruin the here and now. I'd guard my heart, keep my emotions on a tight leash, but I would enjoy this alpha male while I could. No regrets, I reminded myself.

Soon the trees opened up, revealing a large oasis. Dappled water formed a beckoning oval. Boulders lined the edge in a half-moon, and pink flowers bloomed around them, a perfect frame. Bright ribbons of moonlight and curls of mist ghosted over the silvery liquid, making it shimmer like polished glass. Lightning bugs flickered like romantic candles.

The sheer beauty of the area snagged my breath, and I trembled.

"Do you know why I brought you here?" Rome asked me.

"Yes," I answered. And I was more than ready to begin.

## CHAPTER TWENTY

ROME TURNED TOWARD ME, and I turned toward him. When our gazes caught, held, the warmth inside me flared to a low burn. I licked my lips. It seemed as if I'd waited for this moment forever. Maybe I had.

"Nervous?" he asked.

"Yes." I didn't try to deny it.

"Me, too."

My eyes widened. "You? I didn't think anything got to you." Then realization slammed into me, and my shoulders slumped. "I understand. You're afraid I'll burn down the woods or something."

Moonlight couched his features, bathing him in gold. His eyes glowed bright blue, shimmering. "No, nothing like that. I'll filter any heat you create."

"Then what are you nervous about?" I asked, confused.

"I want to be your best. I want to set *you* on fire. Over and over again. I want to make you wet."

Everything inside me tingled with delight, with bliss. With pleasure. Moisture pooled between my legs, drenching me. "You already have," I said.

"More," he replied. His head slowly lowered toward mine.

I went up on tiptoes, meeting him halfway. At the moment

of contact, I opened for him, and his tongue swept inside. The taste I was becoming addicted to—savage man, wild beast— flooded me.

He took his time with the kiss, laving my tongue, exploring me. Enjoying. My blood simmered, my bones liquefied. I melted into him.

"You taste so good," he said. "You smell so good. That's the first thing I noticed about you. You were horribly sick, but you smelled like apples and cinnamon and total woman."

While he spoke, he traced his fingertip down my chest, over the ridged peak of my nipple, the sensitive plane of my belly. Where he touched, I quivered. He gripped the hem of my T-shirt and slowly worked it over my head, then dropped the material at our feet.

I did the same to him, reveling in the ropes of his muscles, the feel of velvet-encased steel. I yearned to lick every inch of him. To savor him, to have his cock inside me, hard and hot and eager. I'd wrap my legs around his waist and he would sink deeper into me.

"Your turn," he said. He reached behind me and unhooked my bra. My breasts sprang free, aching for him. He kneaded them and plucked at the wanting nipples.

I gasped at the heady sensation, the consuming need. "Now you." I worked at his weapon holster. My fingers were trembling, so it took me longer than I wanted, but the thin black strap soon lay in the puddle of clothes.

When I attempted to unsnap his pants, he tsked with his tongue, the sound rough and raspy. "You don't get to go twice in a row." He worked the button of my pants and pushed them over my hips, down my legs. "Step out of them."

I was aching so much I nearly didn't have the strength to

obey. I had to grip his shoulders to hold myself up. Slivers of moonlight illuminated him, my dark angel. He stepped back, his gaze roving over me. Only a pair of lacy panties shielded me.

Usually I was comfortable with my body. I didn't own a car, so I had to walk a lot, which kept me fairly trim. But having Rome see me like this... Did he like what he saw? Did I turn him on?

"Take them off," he rasped. "I *do* get to go twice. I'm bigger."

I hooked my fingers in the sides of my panties. Rome still had his pants on, and if I did what he asked, I would be completely naked. Completely exposed. A daunting thought, yet...

I shimmied them down my legs, stepped out of them and straightened. Nervousness blended with my arousal, a hot and cold combination. I wished he would say something, anything. Wished he would touch.

As if he knew my deepest desires and wanted only to cater to them, he reached out and swirled a finger in my belly button, saying, "You are, without a doubt, the sexiest woman I've ever seen."

My breath caught. The words were so rough I could barely make them out. When I realized exactly what he'd said, any lingering doubt about my decision to be with him died the sweetest death. My nerve endings sparked with desire so complete it nearly slayed me.

He worked quickly, furiously, at his pants, no longer content to slowly strip. Finally he, too, was naked. I drank in the sight of him. The golden rays of the moon paid him absolute tribute. He was a buffet of muscles and corded strength. He was big and strong, utterly majestic, and I needed him inside me.

Neither of us said a word as we stepped toward each other in unison. I gasped; he growled. His arms closed around me; my arms closed around him. Our tongues clashed together, and his breath became mine. I burned for him, just as he'd wanted. Though my emotions were frayed and raw, I felt passion boiling inside me, flooding from me into Rome.

He instantly captured and caged the heat. Wave after wave beat around us. A groan purred out of my throat. My hands were all over him—his back, his stomach, his penis. I allowed my fingers to curl around the long, thick length of him, and my other hand gripped the heavy weight of his testicles.

He hissed in a ragged breath and suddenly I was falling down, falling backward. The kiss didn't break. Instead of slamming into the ground as I expected, I landed on top of Rome. He had twisted, taking the brunt of the fall himself.

"Straddle me," he said roughly.

I did. With pleasure. My legs settled around his waist, placing the core of me at the tip of his cock. The sensation of flesh against slick flesh rocked me. He tugged me down until my breasts rasped against his chest. Oh, delicious abrasion. Then he slid me up until my nipples perched above his waiting mouth. As he sucked and licked, I rode his cock without actual penetration. I arched and strained against it. Sensation after blissful sensation tore through me.

The deliciousness…the riotous intensity…

He captured my other nipple, giving it the same attention he'd bestowed on the first. "Rome," I said, his name a desperate plea. Up and down, I rubbed myself on his penis. The fire in my blood continued to spill into him. "I'm going to—"

"Ride my fingers," he commanded. He reached between us, his decadent fingers gliding over my stomach, past my pubic hair. "Fuck them like you did before. I've thought about it a thousand times since and got hard every time."

Quivering, I lifted slightly and gave him complete access. He sank two fingers into me. That's exactly what I'd wanted, a part of him inside me. I fucked his fingers as he'd requested, like I wanted, riding them, driving myself to satisfaction.

"That's it," he praised.

My head fell back, and a cry parted my lips. Felt...so... good. Flashing lights winked behind my eyelids as I erupted. Pieces of me soared out of my body, to the stars. While my inner walls clenched and released, tide after tide of pleasure pounded through me. I don't know how long I milked the orgasm, but when the last spasm tapered away, I collapsed on Rome's chest.

He flipped us over. Reaching out, he clasped his pants and dug inside one of the pockets. Expression tense, he withdrew a condom.

"When did you put that in your pocket?" I asked breathlessly.

"After meeting you, I put a condom in every pair of pants I own."

I arched my brows and chuckled. "That sure you'd get laid?"

"That hopeful." Sweat trickled down his temples. With muscles bunched, poised for release, he rolled the condom over his length, and then his mouth was covering mine. Consuming. Feeding me kiss after kiss.

I wouldn't have thought it possible, so replete was I after that mind-shattering climax, but in seconds I began to heat up again. I arched and writhed against him. I strained. I purred.

I gasped his name.

He shouted mine.

"Inside you. Now," he growled.

"Inside me. Now," I commanded. I spread my legs, anchoring my ankles on his back. God, yes.

He slammed into me, all the way to the hilt. No more foreplay. No more going slowly. We were too far gone for that. My back arched. I cried out. My nerve endings caught on fire. Flames licked at me.

Rome drew them inside himself, and I think that must have increased his own pleasure because he pulled out of me and drove home again. Hard. In and out. Over and over. We strained against each other. As the pleasure increased, his strokes quickened. My nipples rubbed against his chest, a decadent friction.

He kissed me again, our tongues battling, following the same in and out pattern as our bodies. My eyes squeezed shut as I savored a frantic thrust, then I opened them—forced them open, really. I wanted to watch him, watch his face when he came.

I saw glimpses of the beast inside him, flashes of fur and fang, and God help me, it excited me all the more, pushed me over the sweet edge for a second time. Another orgasm blasted through me.

"Belle," he roared, as he, too, erupted. "Belle, Belle, Belle."

AFTERWARD, I LAY in Rome's arms for a long while. Thankfully, the only fires I'd started had been inside us. The trees were intact. The animals went about their business without interruption.

My body ached with satisfaction. It had been a long—

long—time for me, and never like this. Sweat beaded our skin, sticking us together. I stretched languidly. "I'm going for a swim," I announced.

"Mmm, but I want you to stay in my arms."

I planted a kiss on his mouthwatering chest and eased to my feet. My bones protested, but I forced myself to remain standing. If I lingered in his arms, I was more likely to allow myself to think about what we'd done, more likely to fall deeper in love with him. I was already addicted to him.

"I do like the view," he said, his tone heavy with admiration.

I tossed him a grin over my shoulder as I stepped into the water. The coolness of it lapped at me, making me shiver. I dove under, soothing my overheated cheeks and staying there as long as my lungs would allow before coming up for air. The pond was deeper than I'd thought. And tranquil. I treaded water, staying afloat.

"You should come in here," I said. He was bathed in shadows, and I could barely make him out from my vantage point.

"No, you should come out," he said, his tone deadly serious. Without a hint of teasing.

"You just want to see me naked again."

"Actually." His shadow grew taller as he stood. "I don't want to be eaten by that alligator."

I screamed—an ear-piercing, end-of-the-world scream—and scrambled out of the water as quickly as I could. I threw myself in Rome's arms, my heart pounding so fast I thought it would burst from my chest.

He was laughing. The ass!

"That's what you get for Tasering me."

I pressed my lips together to keep from laughing, too. "You play dirty, Mr. Masters."

"You were right." He nuzzled my cheeks with his nose. "I really did want to see you naked again. I'm sorry I scared you."

"You'll be sorrier when I never let you see me naked again." I dressed, and he reluctantly followed suit. "Catch me if you can," I said, and raced to the cabin.

Rome jogged after me, his laughter echoing through the night. I loved the sound of it; he didn't laugh often enough. He wrapped his arm around my waist and led me to the cabin's threshold, where he shouldered the door open. "You're going to—" He stopped abruptly and sniffed the air. A strange look crossed his features, chasing away his good humor. He stiffened. "Get in the car," he said quietly.

What the hell was going on? I turned, but—

"No need to leave," an unfamiliar voice called from inside the cabin. "You might as well let her come inside, since I'll shoot her if she takes a single step toward the car."

The voice startled me, and I spun back around. I expected Rome to morph into cat form. Attack, at the very least. Instead, he strode blithely inside, pulling me behind him and keeping me shielded from the stranger with his big body.

Trying not to panic, I searched for Tanner. The kid sat on the couch, and our gazes locked. He was pale, but he was alive and looked unhurt. I relaxed a little.

When Rome ground to an abrupt halt, I didn't stay behind him. I moved to his side. He cast me a surprised glance, as if he couldn't believe I'd chosen to fight with him rather than stay protected, but there was also pride in his eyes. Then his gaze narrowed on the intruder. Mine did, as well—and my mouth fell open at the vision the man presented.

He was an angel, fallen straight from heaven. The most gorgeous man I'd ever seen lounged in the cabin's only recliner. His hair was so blond it was nearly white, almost silvery. His eyes were freaky—amazingly freaky. They were metallic silver and seemed to…spark. Yes, spark. Pop and crackle with energy. His features were perfectly proportioned—a sloped nose, high cheekbones, full pink lips.

"He doesn't have a gun," I told Rome through the side of my mouth. "He's unarmed."

"Oh, he's armed, but his weapon is much worse than a gun." With barely a paused, Rome nodded his head in acknowledgment and said, "Cody. I wish I could tell you it's nice to see you again."

So. They knew each other. I didn't know whether to take comfort in that or not. For all I knew, this guy could hate Rome and want him dead.

"I parked a ways out and wiped my tracks," Cody said. "I hope you don't mind."

"I happen to have a big problem with that." I folded my arms together and prayed I appeared strong and menacing.

His angelic lips lifted in a menacing grin. "Too bad." He returned his attention to Rome. "I'm glad you two finally decided to join us. We were about to come looking for you. Why don't you and your woman have a seat with the boy." It was a statement, not a question.

I glanced at Rome. He gave a nearly imperceptible nod of his head. His mouth was compressed, firm. His jaw was clenched. Should I wait for him to give me a deep-fry signal or not? If I created a distraction, he and Tanner could escape.

"Should I start a fire?" I whispered. If I could. I wasn't sure I had the energy.

The man, Cody, uttered a short laugh devoid of humor. "If you want a fire, sugar, *I* can start one."

"Sit," Rome told me. "Do nothing."

I eased reluctantly onto the couch beside Tanner. The boy squeezed against my side and gripped my hand. "I'm sorry about earlier," I whispered.

He nodded in acknowledgment. "Do you know this loser?" he asked me quietly.

I shook my head.

"Rome and I work together," Cody supplied, as if Tanner had asked the question of him.

Oh. *Oh*. Shit! Not good, not good at all. Most likely, Cody was here to apprehend me and take me to John. A hard lump formed in my throat (how many of those things had I swallowed lately?). I released Tanner's hand and buried my own between my knees, covertly stretching my fingers. Drawing on my emotions would be difficult. I was tapped out, so to speak. But I wasn't leaving this cabin. Not without a fight. Rome's orders be damned.

Cody eased to his feet, squaring off with Rome. The two men stood nose to nose. "John wants to see you. My job was to find you, then the girl. But I see you saved me some trouble." He motioned to me with his chin, then turned back to Rome. "You haven't phoned in a while. We were worried, but now I see there was no need." Accusation laced his tone.

"I won't allow her to be taken," Rome said with deadly calm.

Cody arched a black brow, the harsh color a surprising contrast to his pale hair. "So it's like that, is it?"

Rome nodded. "It's like that. I don't want her recruited."

"You know the rules. You know how things work. You took the assignment. Now you have to finish it or it will be finished for you."

"She didn't volunteer like we did, Cody."

"That doesn't change the strictures of your assignment."

"She stays."

"They won't do anything to her that they didn't do to us," Cody said, exasperated.

"I told you. We volunteered. She didn't."

"Doesn't matter. Word is, she's dangerous. She can start fires."

"So can anyone with a lighter," Rome countered.

"Lighters can't cause thunderstorms," Cody replied. "Nor can they freeze buildings."

"You want her to freeze your ass, keep talking," Tanner piped up.

The men ignored him.

I shifted nervously on the couch, wavering between attack and patience. They were discussing me as if I weren't in the room, and I didn't like it.

"Rome, don't give me shit about this," Cody said. "I've been ordered to bring the two of you in and that's that. If she's not taken to John and trained it will only be a matter of time before Vincent and his men find her. All John wants to do is test her and put her in the field. She'll be doing the world a public service, taking down the bad guys."

Should I maybe try to freeze him? Give Rome time to decide what we should do with him? I mean, it wasn't like the icebox would kill him. "Rome," I interrupted.

He knew what I was asking. "No," he said. "Do nothing."

"She may not be able to help herself," Tanner muttered. I elbowed him in the stomach and he *hmphed*.

Cody grinned. "I'm an electrophile, sweetheart, and Rome's afraid I'll hurt you." I must have worn a blank look because he added, "I have an affinity for electricity. I wield it, control it, and if you attempted to use your powers against me, I'd have to give you the shock of a lifetime."

"You know that Taser you used on me?" Rome asked without turning to face me. "Cody can send a thousand more volts than that through your body."

Cody's grin widened. "She took you down?"

Rome gave one jerky nod.

"Good for you, sweetheart," the gorgeous (traitorous) man said to me.

"You won't think so when I do it to you." I gave him a confident smile—a smile I wished I actually felt.

Cody laughed. "I see why you want to keep her, Rome. Not many are so brave and foolish at the same time. She's perfect for PSI."

Rome gave no reply.

"Right now, John doesn't realize you've decided to walk. He just wants you and the girl delivered safely."

"What will happen if Rome refuses?" I asked.

Cody shrugged, lifting his big, wide shoulders. "That's assuming I'll *let* him."

"I'll be hunted," Rome told me, "as will you."

"The government can't afford to have people like us running loose with no one to pull our strings," Cody added. "We either work for them or against them. And working for them isn't a bad deal. I once got to neutralize a woman who sucked the soul right out of a man during orgasm. Literally."

"You killed her?" I gasped.

He frowned. "No, I put her to sleep and she was locked in Château Villain with the other scrims. Anyway, if you're a good girl and do grunt work for a while, like chasing down the fake psychics and crap, you'll eventually get to handle gems like the little sex fiend. Best assignment of my life. If you continue running, well…" He shrugged again. "It's the whole can't-let-anyone-else-have-you thing."

Rome would be hunted if I didn't cooperate. I didn't care about myself. Well, I did, but not as much as I cared about Rome. If he was at risk, that would put Sunny in even more danger. Rome must have expected that. Accepted it, even. But…

Maybe the best way for me to help him with his ultimate goal was to turn myself in so he wouldn't be blamed for my escape. That would take some of the heat off him. I closed my eyes for the briefest of seconds, unable to believe what I was about to do. But I forced the words out. "I'll go in," I said.

Rome whipped around, facing me, finally taking his attention off Cody. His eyes glowed with fury. "Don't say another word," he snapped.

"I'll go in." I stood, squared my shoulders, all the while eyeing Cody. "Do you have to handcuff me or anything?"

His silver eyes gleamed wickedly. "I will if you ask sweetly."

"You don't have to do this, Belle," Rome said. "And for fuck's sake, Cody, quit flirting with her!"

"Yeah," Tanner reiterated, standing beside me. "What he said."

"I want to do this," I said softly. These men had done so much for me already. Rome had chosen me over his job. He'd helped me break into Dr. Roberts's house. He needed me now, and I wouldn't let him down. "Cody said it wouldn't be very bad for me," I offered, trying to soothe him.

Rome sighed. "Then I'll go with you."

"Me, too." Tanner assumed battle position, arms locked behind his back, feet spread.

"Excellent." Cody's tone sounded gleeful, but his expression was one of surprise and confusion. "We can have a celebration on the way."

"You're not taking us to headquarters," Rome said, turning back to Cody. "I don't want her anywhere near the lab."

The blond angel lost his smile. "I know what you're trying to do—"

"Just shut the hell up and call John. Unless you want a fight, those are my terms."

There was a long pause; a heavy tension. Then Cody shrugged. "Fine."

"Tell him we'll meet him at the park near his house in two hours. And no agents. Got it?"

"No one knows where he lives," Cody said, brows arched.

"I do."

Admiration sparked in Cody's expression. He nodded. "I'll make the call."

WE DROVE FOR AN HOUR. Tanner and I sat in the back seat of a very comfortable sedan. The interior was leather, the standard black that seemed to be preferred by all types of agents. Overall, pretty nice. As far as prison vehicles went, that is.

"How much of a fight did John put up?" Rome asked as he steered down the winding roads.

Cody chuckled. He'd made Rome drive so he could keep his own hands free. The better to subdue us with. "I've never heard him so angry. How'd you find his place, anyway? He's so guarded I doubt his wife knows where he lives."

"I tracked him one day." Rome's tone suggested his words were no big whoop, but I sensed his pride.

"That'll teach him to make a jungle cat, eh?"

Dawn tinged the sky, lighting it up with pinks and purples. I yawned. I'd been without sleep for…what? I couldn't remember. Seemed like forever. But then, these last few days hadn't exactly been tame. And on the bright side, I was too tired to be scared of the approaching confrontation.

"Stop there." Cody pointed.

Following the direction, Rome eased the car to a halt near a beautiful park. Flowers bloomed, a sea of yellows, reds and blues. There were two swing sets and a merry-go-round. Several slides.

No people.

I had a tingling sensation at the back of my neck, though, as if I was being watched. Probably John. I started to unbuckle.

"We've been spotted," Rome suddenly said, "and not by John. See the two SUVs? Black? Tinted windows?"

Cody glanced out the passenger mirror. "Vincent. God, the man is a walking cliché."

"He wants Belle just as bad as John does," Rome said.

"Well, we can't let him get near John. If John were hurt, PSI would be placed in major upheaval and Vincent could try to take over. Again."

"Pussy," Tanner mumbled, acting brave, as if he could defeat Vincent single-handedly. "No offense, Cat Man," he added.

"Cut it *out,* Tanner." Rome thrust one hand through his hair and gripped the steering wheel with the other. "Shit. Are you ready for another roller coaster ride, Belle?"

"Floor it," I said, dread filling me from head to toe. And here I thought I'd be too tired to fear my fate. I glanced skyward. *Thanks a lot for proving me wrong.* To my way of thinking, this proved beyond a doubt God was actually a man.

# CHAPTER TWENTY-ONE

IT WAS A CAR CHASE to end all car chases. Several times we almost crashed—into parked cars, moving vehicles, trees and buildings. The object didn't matter; nothing was safe from our rampage. I was surprised the police weren't involved yet. Maybe Vincent had convinced them to look the other way, as he had at the café. I just didn't know. All I knew was that my stomach churned and was very close to heaving.

As we soared down the highway, a black SUV pulled alongside us. I gasped. "Uh, guys. Look to your left."

"Can't," Cody said, chuckling. He hadn't stopped laughing since the chase had begun. Either he was a danger junkie or completely insane. Maybe both. He leaned out the window, aimed the gun he'd taken from his ankle holster, and fired off a few shots. "We've got a tail on the right, too."

"What?" I whipped around and gasped. Sure enough, another black SUV had closed in on our other side.

The sound of bullets—with which I was now intimately acquainted—erupted, followed by a loud thump, thump. I whimpered, okay. Like a little girl. I'm not ashamed, but I had to keep my fear to a minimum. I didn't want ice in our car's engine.

Logically, I knew I should cause a thunderstorm, shielding us from their view. I just didn't have it in me. I couldn't forget my fear, couldn't force sadness to come. If I'd been offered a million dollars and a one-way ticket to heaven, I still wouldn't have been able to make it rain.

"Everything's going to be fine," Rome said, suddenly hitting the brakes.

The momentum threw me forward, but my seat belt shoved me back again, saving my life. The SUVs sailed ahead of us. Cody fired as Rome jerked the wheel, steering us into oncoming traffic.

"Someone could have hit us from behind," I squeaked out. Tremors raked me. "We could have died."

"I checked before I stopped, baby, and there was no one behind us. Have a little faith."

"Yeah, have a little faith," Tanner said. Brave words, marred by his pale face and trembling hands.

One civilian car after another whizzed past us, honking and swerving to avoid hitting us as we traveled the wrong freaking way. I squeezed my eyelids tightly shut, desperate to drown out the sights. "How did Vincent find me?" There. Conversation. Now maybe I could pretend I was at home, with my dad, sipping hot chocolate and watching cartoons.

"I'm sure he had men all over town, and one of them spotted us and called in the others," Rome said.

"I don't want you to talk, Rome," I said. "I want you to concentrate. Cody can answer me."

"I'm sure he's had men all over town," Cody repeated with a chuckle. His damn chuckling! "Someone spotted our car, figured you were with us, and hello, B movie scene."

"They're gaining on us again," Rome said, ruining the mirage I had going. "Use your goddamn powers, Cody, and let's finish this."

"If I do, I'll cause a power outage in this area."

"So?"

A pause, then, "Fine." Cody leaned out the window again, stretching out his hands. Electricity sparked from nearby poles and lanced toward him in orange-gold streams. He gathered the crackling, flickering energy in his palms and hurled it at the SUVs. The surrounding streetlights, which were already muted upon the arrival of the dawn, darkened completely.

*Crash!*

The cars lit up like a Fourth of July fireworks display. One flipped, careening down the highway. At that point, I shut my eyes again and anchored my head between my knees. *Deep breath in, deep breath out.*

Finally, blessedly, we lost them and traveled back to the park where we'd originally arranged to meet John. When I called Rome and Cody stupid for going there, they laughed at me.

"Vincent won't think we're 'stupid' enough to return, so he won't show up himself," was the answer Rome gave me.

"Tanner, you okay?" I asked. "You're so quiet."

"Just wishing for babes," he answered with a nervous smile.

Cody jerked a phone from his pocket and speed-dialed John. He informed him of our whereabouts and what had happened. When Cody hung up, he turned to Rome and said, "He's on his way. And he's bringing protection."

Half an hour later, a car parked beside ours. Same make, same model. Four men exited. We did the same. Rome came up beside me and took my hand. There were kids on the swing set a short distance away, parents watching over them.

"You trust me?" Rome whispered.

"Yeah. Thanks for asking," Tanner said drily. And not quietly.

"Yes," I whispered back. I studied the man obviously in charge. He was the only one who didn't look as if he'd just come off a beefcake calendar. He was about five-eight, with thinning gray hair, glasses and a slightly rotund belly. Yet he radiated power.

"Belle Jamison. Finally we meet," he said to me.

"Yes." Here he was in the flesh, one of the men who wanted to control me. He was somehow more menacing than the males around him, who were tall and muscled. One had red hair, one black and the other highlighted brown. They oozed strength and mysterious power as they surrounded the old man. The redhead was smoking, and that smoke wafted to me. I coughed, the ashes tickling my throat.

"Put that out," Rome snapped. He wasn't content to wait for the man to obey. He strode to him, plucked the butt from his mouth and tossed it on the ground, stomping it out.

Slowly my coughing subsided. John watched all of this with interest.

"Strong aversion to pollutants," he said with interest. "Were you always like that?"

How could this grandpalike figure have ordered painful experimentation on me? "No," I said hesitantly. "Just recently."

"Interesting." A faraway look glazed his eyes, as if he were mentally calculating an equation.

"Let's get this over with," Rome barked.

"All right, then." The old man's features creased with anger, and yes, power more intense than the young men around him, giving me a glimpse of the tyrant who could hurt me without blinking. "Why don't you tell me why you failed to bring Belle in when you found her? Why don't you tell me why you stopped all communication between us?"

Expression unreadable, Rome stepped in front of me. "You've always wanted Vincent out of the picture, but the government wouldn't let you take him out. Well, I'm willing to do it, and I'll make sure it's never linked back to you. But I'll need to use Belle as bait."

John's eyes narrowed. In unison, his shadows crossed their arms over their chests and flanked him. "I can't risk it. Besides, I want her tested."

"There's no time for that. You either want him gone or you don't."

"What makes you think you can get him and not have the blame fall on me?" John asked staunchly.

"There will be no evidence. Not while Belle's at my side," he answered. "I'll give her over to him, and she'll burn his lab to the ground."

The conversation finally clicked into place for me, the part of Rome's speech that affected me most. "You want to dangle me in front of that madman?" I gasped, then pressed my lips closed. *Trust him.* At least he hadn't mentioned Dr. Roberts's letter.

Rome reached behind him and gripped my hand, squeezing. "We plan to break into his lab tonight," he said. "Believe me, Vincent will come to us."

A long pause ensued, blanketing the sound of insects, the rustle of wind. Then, in the distance, I heard a helicopter. Dear God. Would it never end? The bad guys knew we must be in the area, I guess, and were desperate to find us.

"Yes or no, sir?" Rome splayed out his arm. "We can't stay here, they'll spot us. Either take her or send us on our way."

I trusted Rome, I did. But jeez, thanks a whole hell of a lot. Just gamble with my life, why don't you. No biggie.

A muscle ticked in the old man's jaw. "I don't have any men to spare right now. Everyone is out on assignment, and I can't give up my guards with Vincent so close."

"We'll be fine on our own," Rome said.

John paused. Sighed. Then mumbled, "Use her. But Cody is going with you. Get in the lab, kill Vincent and bring Belle to me. Understand?" His eyes glinted in warning, telling Rome the consequences if he failed to obey.

I gulped.

Rome nodded.

Without another word, we pounded back to the car, and Cody claimed the driver's seat this time. He gunned it, shooting into a nearby thicket of trees. I looked back, but John's car had already disappeared.

"VINCENT'S LAB HAS an internal security system that is not reliant on outside electrical units," Rome said to Cody.

I knew that Vincent's lab was the place Dr. Roberts had worked, the building across from Utopia Café. And night had, unfortunately, fallen, which meant we were about to head straight into that lab. Into danger. Right now, we were several blocks away, standing near a deserted intersection. Already I wanted to vomit. Danger sucked.

"That won't be a problem." Cody patted the lamppost beside him. "The lights *do* use outside currents. I'll be in before you know it."

I kid you not—Cody climbed the pole, reached out and grabbed two of the wires. Sparks flew around him a split second before he *became* the sparks. He seemed to melt right into the wires. I watched from the ground, wide-eyed, as those sparks traveled along, disappearing from sight.

"My God," I breathed.

"He's a good man to have on our side."

"Are we really going to draw Vincent out and try to kill him?"

"Yes. First we need the formula Roberts left in the building, though, so *it's* the bait rather than you. Can you make it rain?" Rome added with barely a breath, wasting no time.

"Yes." *Maybe.* How many emotions could one girl endure before spontaneously combusting? Or better yet, killing herself?

At the moment, I wanted nothing more than to soothe my stomach and embrace numbness. Maybe experience total anesthetization. Maybe sedation. Even the thought of happiness bothered me right now. I wanted nothingness, damn it.

Tanner gripped my hand and gave a comforting pat. "You can do it. I know you can."

I guessed we'd find out. I forced sad thoughts into my mind, but the emotion didn't touch me. It was kind of like standing on the edge of a dream, watching, unable to do anything. Rome linked his fingers with mine, forming a three-person circle.

Tendrils of strength suddenly curled through me; thunder boomed. I straightened. Wait. I hadn't been sad. I'd simply—ohmygod! Did I actually not need to feel sad to create a storm? Maybe…maybe I just needed the *power* of the emotion. Like seeing a rainbow in the distance, but not having to touch it to experience its beauty.

There were reservoirs of emotion in everyone. Perhaps if I could tap into specific feelings and experience their effects at a distance… Hopeful, I searched for and found the sadness buried deep inside myself without letting it flood me. I drew on its strength, milked it.

Another clap of thunder boomed. I grinned. Yes! Lightning lit the sky with jagged gold bolts. The already dark sky turned a swirling, churning black. Droplets of rain began to fall, already hard, already fast.

"You're doing good," Tanner praised.

Rome said, "We need to get to the lab, baby. Try to keep the rain up as best you can."

I nodded. I was excited by what I'd discovered, but also very ready to get this over with.

We hiked on foot, rain pelting us the entire way. We remained in the shadows as best we could, avoiding streetlights and businesses. Very few cars were on the road. My wet clothes were soon plastered to my skin, and water trickled into my eyes as I passed Utopia. I barely spared my former workplace a glance. It felt like a lifetime had come and gone since I'd last been there—the day I drank that fateful latte. What would good old Ron the Pervert think if he could see me now?

By the time we reached the laboratory, I think I carried more water weight than at prime PMS season. At the doorway, Rome jerked wires from a metal box with one hand and withdrew a card from his pocket with the other. He twisted a blue and a red wire together and flashed the card in front of a scanner. Obviously he'd done this type of thing before.

The doors slid open.

He entered. I followed close behind him, Tanner on my heels. The entryway was plain and unremarkable. I'd kind of expected computers, maybe a robot. Definitely armed guards.

"Dr. Roberts's office is this way." Rome grabbed my hand, I grabbed Tanner's, and like a train, we started moving through a winding corridor. Rome stopped along the way and jerked cameras out of the walls. At the last camera we could see, he froze, sniffed. "Someone's coming."

"Yep, and he's got a gun!" Tanner shouted. "Duck."

In unison, Rome and I dived for the floor. During our fall, he jerked me underneath him. The guy fired at us and missed. Tanner had already aimed his gun and squeezed the trigger. A muffled whiz and crack rang out, barely audible over the roar of blood in my ears. The bullet slammed into the uniformed guard, and his big body crumbled to the ground, just to the right of the Rome-Belle huddle.

"Come on." Rome stood, grabbed my arm and helped me to my feet. Maybe I was about to pass out, because I saw sparks shoot from an outlet, lights flashing, crackling...and then Cody was there, standing just in front of me. I blinked, shook my head. My heart had yet to calm from everything that had already happened, and seeing him suddenly appear didn't help.

"Well?" Rome said to him.

"I did damn good," Tanner exclaimed.

Rome replied, "Not you, little boy. How many guards, Cody?"

"I counted only three. I disposed of two..." Cody's silver gaze flicked to the blood-soaked tile and to the gun in Tanner's hand. "Looks like the kid took care of the third, so we're good to go. The building has been emptied out. Maybe Vincent feared discovery and ran. The whole place is under surveillance, though."

"I took care of the cameras," Rome said, "but this seems easy. Too easy."

"We'll look at the office and get out fast." Before Cody finished his sentence, he was moving down the hall.

The rest of us followed, flying along abandoned hallways. We soon entered a large room, where the sound of our breathing echoed. The walls were covered in chalk marks. Some were symbols I didn't recognize, other were clearly depictions of the four elements. There was a periodic table, as well. Several floorboards had been ripped up. Vincent and his men *had* been searching for something here. Had they found what they were looking for? I turned full circle, wondering what to do, where to look when there was nothing to look through.

"There's nothing here," I said, disappointed.

Rome's face scrunched as he studied the walls. He appeared curious, disbelieving and shocked at the same time. "No, there's something. I thought it'd be easy to find him since he's only one man, and old at that, but he's a wily thing. The present is hidden. Belle. Use your powers."

"What? Why?"

"Use your powers, baby. Please."

"Uh, sure. Okay." I didn't understand, but there wasn't time to argue. Tanner reached out and linked our fingers, offering comfort. "Which one? Rain? Fire? Ice?"

"Someone please explain what's going on," Cody said, tossing up his arms. "Rome knows something I don't, and I don't like it."

Holding out his arms toward the walls, Rome spun around. "The formula is here, in this room, waiting for Belle." He stopped, facing us dead-on. "If ordinary people can't see it, it must need some sort of catalyst to become visible."

"And you think changing the weather is going to be that catalyst?" Skepticism tinged Cody's voice. "That would mean Roberts wanted Belle to find the formula."

"That's right." Rome nodded. "He does."

"Why would he want to help her?" Cody asked.

"To make amends." Rome's blue gaze pierced me. "Try. For me."

Anything for him. I closed my own eyes. *Concentrate, Belle.* Okay. What element would Dr. Roberts have been most likely to utilize? Not fire, surely. That would torch the place. Rain? Maybe. It was worth a try. I'd start with that.

Once again, I did not summon sadness. I summoned the power behind the emotion, remaining distant from it, simply drawing from my deepest reservoir and projecting out of my body. A clap of thunder echoed in the room, blending with the sound of the continuing storm outside. My lips curled in a proud grin. Having succeeded for a second time, I knew without a doubt that I'd been right.

"Ease up a little," Tanner said. "It's becoming very strong."

Rome mentally reached out and captured some of its edge. Physically, he clasped my free hand in his. I immediately relaxed.

"Good, good," Tanner said.

A trickle of rain began to fall inside the room. Fat droplets splashed my face and my already wet clothes.

"Shit," Cody said, scrambling to the doorway, away from the rain. "Who would have thought?" he breathed, awed by his first viewing of my abilities. He shook his head in surprise. "With this power, she'd be able to kick my ass in a heartbeat. Water fries the hell out of me."

Holding on to my optimism, I looked around the room. The rain continued to fall, but nothing became visible, no clue, no object.

"Rain isn't the answer. Fine. But what next? He wouldn't have wanted me to use fire," I said, voicing my earlier thought. "Nothing could survive that." I paused, frowning. "Or maybe that's exactly what he wanted people to think."

"We'll save that for last." Rome kissed the back of my hand. "What about wind? An increase in dust circulation or simple air pressure might work."

*Wind,* I mentally called, not changing the focus of my emotions. As before, I pulled from my reservoir. The wind answered immediately, chasing away the rain. Strong gusts swirled and churned, whipping my wet clothes around me. I shivered from the chill. The precarious floorboards shook and danced. Paint peeled from the walls.

Still nothing.

"Try snow," Tanner shouted over the roar.

I shut off the wind and pictured a snowstorm. "Don't filter," I told Rome, pushing his presence from my mind. "Not yet. Let it rage for a bit." The air chilled, and I shivered again, this one reverberating through my entire body. Huge white flakes fell from the ceiling. The wet floor froze into a sheet of ice. I'm pretty sure icicles dripped from my nose.

Several seconds ticked by. Wet as I was, the cold seemed unbearable. Shivers continued to rack me. My blood crystallized. The air began to solidify.

Rome cursed under his breath. "You're going to have to set the place on fire, Belle. Don't be afraid. We'll get you out before the smoke hurts you."

I was just about to summon the flames when the walls changed color, going from white to blue. As if by magic, words began to appear on them. Giddiness thrummed through me. "Rome, look. Look!"

"My God," he breathed, his hot breath creating a mist. "He must have used some sort of chemical that reacts to cold."

At least I wouldn't have to burn the building down. "What does it say?" I asked, doing my best to maintain the level of chill.

"It says, 'You're being watched, and I'm sorry for that. Maybe the wood will make up for it.'" Tanner's brow puckered. "We know we're being watched, but what does he mean, the wood will make up for it?"

"Could there be a secret ingredient in the wood that will make me normal again?" I asked.

With the water frozen and no longer able to harm him, Cody stepped back into the room. He laughed and bent down. "Smart bastard. Look at this." The chill had changed the wood panels, as well. Words covered them.

We all crowded around him. "It's the formula," Rome said, something unreadable in his tone. Happiness? Resignation? A combination of both? "Maybe we can make our own batch and find an antidote for Belle."

Though I'd been unsure earlier today, yesterday, about giving up my powers now that I was coming to wield them properly, I realized then that I *needed* to give them up. I needed an antidote. Rome would be off the hook with John, my dad would be safe and I wouldn't be chased anymore.

It was funny, in a horrible way. If we were able to make an antidote, I would most likely lose my powers and Rome within the same week. Hide Sunny. Kiss Rome goodbye. Take antidote. Yin and yang: a bad for a good. Wasn't that how things usually balanced out?

"Let's pull up every floorboard." I bent down and lifted two, the wood heavy in my hands. "We'll take them with us."

"Shit," I heard Rome mutter. I paused and looked up. He'd stood and was now studying the wall and rubbing a small black dot. "Another camera."

"We're getting good at this clandestine crap," Tanner said as he blithely gathered more boards.

"No, we're not." Rome faced us, his features pained, tortured. "We just walked into a trap."

"Yes, you did." The amused voice floated from the doorway. "You can drop the boards. We'll take care of them now."

# CHAPTER TWENTY-TWO

THE ARMED MEN I'd expected when we'd first entered the building suddenly flooded the room, weapons cocked and ready. Vincent was, of course, shockingly beautiful to gaze upon, as always. Young, too, for such an asshole.

He was tall and lean, and his angelic features rivaled Cody's. Only his eyes gave away his despicable nature. They lacked any kind of emotion, making his physical beauty haunting and eerie.

"It certainly took you long enough to come here," he said with a humorless grin. Without another word, he stretched out his arm and shot Rome. I covered my mouth with shaky hands, gazing wide-eyed at the only man I'd ever loved. He was still standing. I didn't see any blood, only a red dart in his neck. Motions jerky, he plucked it out and tossed it onto the ground. He wavered on his feet.

I summoned fire, letting flames spark from my hands. I didn't point my fingertips at the bad guys, however, not yet. I pointed them at the floorboards. I wanted the formula, but even more, I wanted to prevent Vincent from having it. He would not win. He would not gift himself with these powers.

The flames hit the wood and sprang to instant life, melting the layer of ice, spreading, raging. Someone screeched. Cody used the distraction to race to an outlet, sparking and disappearing inside it within seconds. No one seemed to notice his vanishing act. Rome stumbled forward, trying to morph. Small patches of fur sprouted from his skin.

"Put out the fire, Belle," Vincent said, monotone. "Or I'll kill your father." Just then, my dad was shoved inside the room, Lexis right behind him. My dad's features were pale and his cheeks were hollow. His clothes were wrinkled and dirty, but there were no signs of injury.

"Belle, sweetie," he said, apologetic. Scared.

I paused. Rome paused, all hints of his cat self receding. "Dad, don't move," I said, trying to tamp down my panic. I couldn't let him worry. "Everything's going to be fine."

Rome's knees buckled and he slammed onto the floor. I gasped and bent down.

"Don't even think about helping him," Vincent told me. "Just stop the fire."

Despite the intense heat, breath froze in my throat. I straightened. *Rain,* I mentally called. *Rain, come to me now.* My fingers cooled, but nothing else happened. Fear and fury were overriding everything else, making it impossible to draw from my reservoir of emotions. They were trying to consume me, to bring ice and more fire, a combination that produced no results. I needed rain, damn it.

*Rain!* Tears filled my eyes and spilled onto my cheeks. I stared at my dad. He looked confused, withered. "Rain," I screamed, desperation riding my shoulders. I reached so deeply inside myself it caused true, physical pain. My stomach cramped. "I command you to fall." Slowly, tiny drops descended. I squeezed my eyes shut, ordering the droplets to thicken and multiply. They obeyed, liquid splashing over my face.

The fire sizzled, crackled and finally surrendered. Thick black smoke curled in the air, tickling my throat. I coughed.

"There. The formula is still intact." Satisfied, Vincent nodded.

I coughed again, unable to stop. "Belle," my dad said. I was unable to respond.

"I'm so sorry," Lexis cried. "I should have known they were coming, but they had some sort of mind shield. I'm sorry. So sorry."

"Lock everyone up." Vincent motioned to our group with a wave of his fingers. "I'll need them later. And keep a gun on the old man's temple, just in case Belle decides to start another fire." His chin canted to the side and he glanced down at Rome. "If Agent Masters sprouts a single patch of fur, kill him. Since I'm now the proud owner of the psychic *and* the formula's carrier, I don't really need him anymore. Understand?"

"Yes, sir," several of the guards said in unison.

"The rest of you gather up the floorboards and take them to the lab."

Men grabbed Tanner, Lexis and my dad. I started to reach for him, but dropped my arm to my side. I didn't want him playing the hero and trying to come to me. *Just do what they say,* I told him with my eyes. The rest of the guards hauled Rome to his feet and held him up. I continued to cough, more afraid in that moment than I'd ever been in my life.

"Please," I managed to gasp. "Take the…gun off…my… dad. I'll be good."

One of the men latched on to my upper arm, but Vincent shook his head and I was released. "I'll take care of her myself," he said.

I watched, helpless, as my unconscious lover, my dad and my friends were escorted away from me. Anger and fear continued their wild course inside me, and I barely managed to control them. I wanted to scream, to rant, to rail, to cry. To kill.

"This way, Belle." Vincent hauled me out of the room and ushered me down the hall, away from the smoke. The farther we traveled, the more my coughs subsided.

"Where are we going?" I asked, my throat raw.

"The lab is underground." He answered without hesitation, because he believed, I'm sure, I would never be able to escape and use the information against him. A chilling thought. "I want to get the preliminary data on you—which I should have had days ago."

Did he have a heart? A smidge of compassion? I guessed I'd soon found out. "Let my dad go, and I'll do whatever you want. I swear."

"You'll do whatever I want, anyway."

"He's sick. His heart is weak and he needs his medication."

"You be good and cooperate, and I'll make sure he gets his meds. Misbehave and I let him die. How do you like that for a bargain?"

About as much as I liked him, the bastard. The man was as cold and unfeeling as his eyes proclaimed. If I ever had the opportunity, I was pretty sure I would kill him and not experience an ounce of guilt. I might even dance on his grave. "What are you going to do with me?"

We had reached the end of the hall, and he pressed a series of buttons. Elevator doors slid open. He pushed me inside, following close on my heels. "I can't wait to see everything you can do." He opened a panel on the wall and held out his hand for a scan. A blue light glowed between his fingers, and the elevator began a smooth downward glide. "We gave the formula to some others, but they died. Hopefully, once we've studied you, we'll be able to discover why you didn't."

I tried not to grimace. He painted a gruesome, painful picture. Maybe—maybe I should try to kill him now. Freeze him, smoke him, anything to stop him.

*Will you be able to save the others in time? If you can't...*

Fear held me immobile. Then the opportunity passed and the elevator doors opened, revealing a room bursting with equipment, people in lab coats and cages filled with animals. And humans. I gasped. *Humans* were locked in cages, and they were in bad shape. Some had missing limbs, with wires hanging from sockets. Others had metal plates in place of skin. All of them were bloody and ragged. They all watched me with pity, as if they knew what was about to happen to me.

"What did you do to them?" I said, unable to keep the horror from my voice.

He shrugged, unconcerned. "I'm in a competitive business. If I don't have the strongest, most powerful agents, customers will go to someone else. Customers will pay someone else to protect them or find a missing item. Customers will pay someone else to kill their enemies. One day the people in those cages will have supernaturally strong robotic limbs and indestructible skin. They'll thank me."

"And you don't care that you're hurting them?"

"No."

I scanned the rest of the lab, trying not to look at the cages. Toward the back, I saw my friends and family locked inside a glass cell. I gulped hard and stumbled. Vincent righted me. Even from this distance, I could see that my dad shook with fear. Lexis had her arm around him, offering what comfort she could. Tanner radiated hatred and fear, and glared at everyone who approached him. Rome was propped against the wall, slumped and weakened by the tranquilizer. His expression held no emotion.

How long would they be allowed to live? Damn it! I had to save them.

Vincent thrust me at an older woman who looked as prim and proper as a librarian. "Strap her down," he said, eyes alight with eagerness—the first real emotion he'd displayed. "And take some blood."

"How much?" Her fingers curled around my arm in a viselike grip.

"Whatever you need. I want to know what's in her blood that isn't in anyone else's."

"You don't need my blood. You have the formula now," I protested.

"You survived. I want to know how."

"I survived because the formula was perfected!" I pressed my lips together. I hadn't meant to admit that out loud. I didn't want to help Vincent in any way, but the words had spilled from me of their own accord, unstoppable.

*You can't lie to Vincent,* Rome had once told me. Holy hell, I was in trouble.

"We'll see for ourselves," Vincent said. "I'm going to conduct my own tests. And believe me, they'll be like nothing you've ever experienced. Let me know if she gives you any trouble," he added to the evil-looking lab tech. Having pronounced my sentence, he sauntered away.

*Ding, Ding.* Let the torture of Belle begin.

WHAT FOLLOWED WERE endless hours of poking and prodding, and it hurt like hell. I felt drained, but at last Martha, my prim and proper tormentor, finally decided to let me rest. She wanted me fresh for tomorrow's torment, I suppose, when the initial test results would come in. These scientists were, in my expert opinion, concerned only with their experiments. Mercy, compassion and morality played no part in their actions.

Wanna bet tomorrow's adventure would make today's seem like a five-star vacation?

I lay on a cot, inside my own glass cell, and stared at the monitor on the far wall. To keep me docile, Vincent wanted me to see my dad and my friends and know that at any moment their lives could end. Though sleep beckoned me sweetly, I remained awake. And though my bruises begged me to sink into oblivion, I watched the screen, unable to glance away.

How could I save everyone? What could I do? Helplessness bombarded me, taunted me. Where was my hope now? Lost, my tired mind supplied, with all the blood that had been taken.

Rome suddenly stepped into the center of the screen, staring into the camera expectantly. In that moment, it was as if our gazes locked on to each other. He blinked. Surprised, I sat up and studied him. Was he trying to tell me something? He blinked again.

Damn it, what did he want me to do? What *could* I do? *Think, Belle, think.* I couldn't start a fire. There were sprinklers above me that would douse the flames instantly. I'd be stopped and my loved ones would then be punished for my escape attempt.

If Cody were here, I could— My eyes widened. Cody! I'd

forgotten about him. I pressed my lips together to prevent a victory shout. Streams of hope hit me. Cody might still be in the electrical system.

Vincent had turned on a secondary power source that didn't rely on electricity, yet Cody didn't need to physically touch the power. He could create his own from the wires, as I'd seen during the car chase. And maybe, just maybe, he'd gone for help.

If I could get back into the lab and draw Cody to me, he and I could incapacitate the guards. I looked out. Night must have fallen because fewer people were around. *Now is the time.* I pushed myself to my feet. Cameras followed my every move.

I paced, allowing my gaze to circle the room, searching. My cot was anchored to the floor. The walls were thick glass. The floor was concrete. The only door (that I knew of) was the kind that slid open when it had the proper sensor. I'd never be able to pry it open.

How was I going to get out? I kept pacing. If I attempted to melt the door sensor, I might jam the door in place, closed permanently. If I froze the glass— Wait. Wait!

A memory flashed through my mind. Weeks ago, I had decided to go on a vegetable diet. Not that it lasted. Anyway, I cooked said vegetables in the microwave. In a glass bowl. When I'd taken it out and seen the mushy results, I had lost my appetite, but placed the bowl in the refrigerator just in case I changed my mind later. The hot-cold change of temperature had caused the bowl to crack in half.

I could do that now, to the wall. Heat it, cool it, crack it, then kick my way free. I would have to move and act quickly lest someone realize what I was doing, and stop me. Plus, I'd have to be careful not to use too much heat and activate the sprinklers.

I stared into the laboratory and met the gaze of several scientists. I flipped them off. They frowned and scribbled in their notebooks. What were they writing? "Subject displaying unhealthy sassiness?"

Could I heat the air without causing any actual flames? Without Tanner here to tell me when I was becoming too violent, and without Rome here to filter, that seemed like an impossible task.

I didn't care. I had to try.

Still pacing, I dug deep into my emotions. I summoned desire, desire for Rome that was buried in my every cell. Drew on it. I let thoughts and images of Rome consume me. Rome—naked. Me—naked. Rome kissing his way down my body. Stopping to lave between my legs.

My body heated, my eyes heated. The air heated.

After Rome tasted me, I'd kiss my way down his body. I'd take him in my mouth. I'd suck him. He'd moan, shout my name.

Both the air and I sizzled, rising another degree.

Tiny flames nipped at my fingertips. I hid my hands behind my back and faced the wall, gaze focused on the glass. My nipples were hard, my knees shaking.

Rome—telling me he loved me.

A tremor stole over me. The warmth from my eyes intensified, hitting the wall. It began to heat, a fine steam covering the corners. *Freeze it,* my mind shouted. *Freeze it now.* I switched the direction of my emotions, still remaining deep within myself. The heat from my eyes chilled, getting colder, colder still. The steam hardened into frost.

A loud crack echoed through the cell.

Like a spiderweb, the crack spread over the glass. On a wave of victory, I raced to the wall and kicked. My foot made contact, and the glass shattered around me, sharp, tiny diamonds. Panicked voices greeted my ears as I rushed into the lab.

Someone shouted, "She's escaped," over the intercom.

"Cody!" I yelled. "Cody, we're in here." Hopefully, my voice would lead him to me.

A silent alarm must have been tripped because armed guards rushed into the lab, shoving the doctors and scientists out of the way. The people in the cages cheered loudly and reached through their bars, grabbing at those responsible for their pain.

"Cody!"

Guards were sprinting toward me. Not knowing what else to do, I held out my hands and iced them all, just as I'd done to the glass. Then, in a cloud of sparks, Cody materialized from an outlet. Without pause, he shot a blast of electricity at the men I hadn't seen behind me. Their bodies convulsed and they collapsed to the floor.

"Get the others," Cody shouted. "I couldn't leave the building to get backup. I'm sorry, sweetie, but it's just you and me."

I rushed toward the other cell. Rome was standing, his strength returned. He had wakened everyone and they, too, were on their feet. But just before I reached their door, Martha grabbed me, whirling me to a stop. Her weathered face was determined.

"You're not going anywhere, Miss Jamison."

I punched her in the nose. Blood squirted from her nostrils, and she slumped to the floor. "Wanna bet?" Bending down,

I removed her badge and with a shaky, aching hand, held it to the sensor. I expected it to open, but it didn't. Shit! It probably needed a finger ID, as well.

Behind me, I could hear footsteps shuffling. Women screaming. Men groaning. Cody laughing. He enjoyed his job. I caught a glimpse of him freeing the human lab rats, and they sprang from their cages, attacking the scientists who had yet to escape.

A few muffled gunshots erupted, and I ducked. My gaze snagged on the unconscious Martha. Ah, hell. I slid my hands under her shoulders and hefted her up as best I could. Trying not to drop her, I forced her hand to the ID pad. Blue lights winked over her skin, and the door to the cell slid open.

I dropped her with a thump.

Rome rushed to me, and our eyes locked. His fingers tangled in my hair. "You okay?"

"Never better. You?"

"Good to go. Your dad needs you. I'll take care of Vincent." Off he went, jumping into the fray, using anything and everything in the lab as a weapon.

Relieved, ecstatic, I ran to my dad and threw my arms around him. His heart drummed erratically against my ear, but the beat was strong. What a sweet sound. When his arms wrapped around me, the world felt like a better place. "Daddy, tell me you're okay. Tell me your heart's all right."

"I'm fine, doll. Just fine." He weakly cupped my face with one hand and lifted the necklace he wore with the other. "I always carry nitro. What about you? Lexis told me what's going on. Are you okay?"

"I'm good. I'll tell you more about it later." I looked up into his hazel eyes, into his sun-wrinkled face, and tears streamed down my cheeks. "Right now, we need to get out of here."

I spun around—and came face-to-face with a scowling Vincent. He pointed a gun at my dad's head. I reacted instantly. Fury, potent and intense, sprang to life inside me, and I shot out my hand, blasting him with fire. I didn't have to summon it. I didn't have to rely on any reservoir inside me. My rage was too strong. Vincent managed to squeeze out several rounds as he erupted in flames, screaming.

Time seemed to slow as the bullets hurtled toward me. I shoved my dad out of the way just as Rome jumped in front of me. The bullets slammed into him.

After that, everything happened quickly. Rome hit the ground with a thud. I whimpered. Lexis screamed. Both of us dropped to the floor beside him. Blood poured from his chest. He tried to speak, but no words emerged. Our gazes locked for a split second before he closed his eyes.

"Ohmygod," Lexis cried.

"Rome," I shouted. "Rome, open your eyes. Talk to me!" He didn't respond.

"Open your eyes, goddamn it!" I screamed.

No response.

The others rushed to my side, but not before Cody shot Vincent in the head, ending the man's pain-filled moans, ending his reign of terror.

"We have to get Rome to a hospital," I managed to say, my voice trembling. *Stay strong, Belle. Don't crumble. Not yet.*

Desperate, I placed my hand over his wound, letting my fear consume me. The edges of the injury began to freeze. The blood loss stopped. I just hoped I hadn't given him hypothermia.

"I've taken care of the guards," Cody said, "and the scientists all scattered and ran." He gathered Rome in his arms.

Frantic, I whipped to Lexis. "Is he going to live? Tell me he's going to live."

"I don't know." Her chin trembled. Tears ran down her cheeks like crystalline rivers. "I only see darkness."

"Wasn't...just a few...bullets," a weak voice suddenly said.

"Rome!" Thank God. Oh, thank God. Relief pounded through me, relief and hope and dread. "We're taking you to a hospital, Cat Man. You're going to be okay. Just relax. I managed to freeze the wound and stop the bleeding."

"Good...girl. Not...bullets, though. What did...he use?"

"Probably a chemical reagent," Cody said gravely. "Poison."

I covered my mouth with a hand to keep from whimpering again. No. *No!* Bullets could be removed. Could poison? I could live without this man if I had to—but only if I knew he was alive, healthy, happy and whole. He couldn't die. He couldn't. He was too...vital. I needed him. He was my man, and I was his woman.

Cody must have seen my stricken look, because he added, "But the ice should stop the poison from spreading, as well."

Finally, I had used my powers to help someone. To help Rome, no less—the man who'd saved my life over and over again.

"Belle," Rome panted. "Get the...formula, then burn...the place down."

"I'm not leaving your side."

"Do it," he said weakly. "You...owe me."

I knew what he was telling me to do. Take the formula and

run. If I stayed with him, Cody would give the formula to John, and I'd probably never see it again. Probably never be able to use it to find an antidote. Definitely never be able to use it as a bargaining tool or take the heat off of me and keep my dad safe. So I had a choice, it seemed. I could (possibly) have the return of my ordinary life or I could try and save Rome's life. Maybe he would live, maybe he wouldn't.

I didn't even have to think about it. "Cody," I croaked. "Let's get him to the hospital."

# CHAPTER TWENTY-THREE

INSTEAD OF RUSHING Rome to the hospital, Cody drove us to a chrome-and-brick building on the edge of the city. Of course, this was after he'd gathered up the floorboards. I'd almost burned him to a crisp in my rage over that. Time was our enemy.

During the drive, Rome's pulse became threadier, his breathing more shallow. He stopped moaning at every bump and bounce in the road. He kept morphing between human and cat. Unfortunately, my dad, Tanner and Lexis followed us in another car; I could have used their support just then.

"Think of Sunny," I whispered to Rome as we drove. "She needs you."

He was sprawled out in the backseat, his head resting in my lap. I sifted my fingers through his dark hair. My fallen angel. That's what he was. My savior, my love. Yes, I loved him. With all of my heart. He was my everything.

"Where are we, Cody?" Worry twisted my stomach as the building came into view. "This isn't a hospital. If you don't drive to a fucking hospital, I'll kill you myself."

"The doctors here can help Rome better than the ones at a hospital. Look at him. Regular people will not want to touch him if he's in cat form. This is the lab where Rome was created."

"Okay, okay. You're right." *Please, Lord, let Rome live.* He was strong, a fighter. The car eased to a stop, and a group of men rushed forward. They wheeled a stretcher to the curb.

"I called ahead," Cody explained.

Rome was gently lifted onto the stretcher and carted inside the building. I tried to hurry after him, to follow, but Cody latched on to my hand. Without looking back, I attempted to jerk myself free. "Let me go!"

John strolled out of the sliding doors, perusing the scene. "Bring Belle to me, then take the kid and the old man to a secure area," he snapped. Cody pulled me forward as the others piled out of their car and rushed to my side.

"We stay with Belle," my dad and Tanner said simultaneously. They grabbed on to me and tried to jerk me away from Cody.

"Cody, you better let me go," I snarled. "I'm furious right now, and my fingers are starting to burn."

"I know," he muttered, but retained his grip. Tanner and my dad kept holding on, too.

"Lexis, you may go see Rome," John said, "but you, Belle, will stay with me. We have much to discuss."

"I'll keep you apprised of his progress." Lexis rushed out, already running for the door.

I scowled at John. I wanted to go with Lexis, but was too afraid my dad or Tanner would be punished in retaliation. So I stayed where I was. For the moment. "I'm not talking to you or allowing you to test me until I know Rome is okay."

John's eyes narrowed. "Allowing me?" He snorted and reached out to clamp my arm in an iron grip. Only then did Cody release me.

*Fuck it,* I thought darkly. And after all, Rome had once told me John wasn't an evil man, that he didn't hurt innocent people. I'd take him at his word. "That's right, allowing you," I said. "Daddy, you and Tanner stay here, okay?" They nodded. "You have to let go of me now," I added.

The moment they did, I froze John's hand without much effort—I was getting damn good!—and when his grip on me slipped, I took off without another word in the direction Lexis had gone. *Rome,* my heart shouted. *I'm coming.* I managed to catch up with Lexis in the elevator. She held the door open for me, and I flew inside before it closed, catching a glimpse of John's shocked face as he chased after me.

She knew exactly where to go, and ushered me into a sterile-smelling hallway. John soon arrived, scowling, but he didn't protest. He must have sensed that I'd fry him if he tried to come between me and Rome right then.

Rome was being wheeled into—an operating room? A lab? I didn't know which. Thick silver doors flapped shut, blocking the sight of his gurney. He'd been deadly silent, though, and I gripped Lexis's hand.

"He's going to be all right," she said.

"You're sure?"

"I'm…hopeful."

My chest constricted. Hours passed. We paced. More hours passed. John watched, observed us. He even relented and allowed my dad and Tanner to wait with us. They sat on the only couch, their expressions equally troubled.

Lexis eventually sat next to Tanner and rested her head on his shoulder. He put his arm around her and she cried. He cooed and comforted her, and she finally stopped. She raised her head, and they stared at each other for a long moment, then she leaned forward and kissed him.

I stopped pacing long enough to watch Tanner eagerly respond. I was shocked, but happy for them.

John pinched the bridge of his nose, much as I'd seen Rome do whenever he was truly exasperated. "What next?"

"Come sit by me, doll," my dad said. "You're not doing Rome any good by worrying."

"No. I'm too upset." I leapt back into motion. I felt so helpless. I could control the elements, but not save the life of one lone man. I couldn't help him, and I would have given my own life to do so.

"You love him?" John asked me.

"Yes." God, yes. I'd given the man my whole heart.

"Belle, sweetie," my dad said. "Please sit down. Rome will—"

"He's going to make it," a man said, stepping past the doors. He had dark red hair and so many freckles he appeared to be one big brown spot, but at that moment he was the most beautiful, welcome sight in the world. "Rome is going to make it. Whoever froze the wound saved his life. We almost lost him a time or two, and would have if the bleeding hadn't stopped."

"Thank God." I slumped to the floor in relief. Lexis pulled away from Tanner and threw her arms around me with a laugh. Tears trickled from my eyes, then the dam burst and I gripped her and sobbed. My dad and Tanner were suddenly at our sides, trying to offer comfort. Though I was experiencing intense sadness and worry, it didn't rain or freeze. Yes, I really was getting good at controlling my powers. I would have loved the knowledge yesterday. Right now, I couldn't make myself care.

When I finally quieted, John said, "Will you speak with me now?" Exasperation filled his voice.

I gazed at him through the watery shield of my lashes. "I need to see Rome first."

Silence descended like a thick, oppressive blanket. John nodded to the redheaded doctor. "Let her see him, then take her to the spare room."

Whatever he had planned for me in that spare room, I didn't give a shit. I was too eager to glimpse my man. Lexis bid Tanner a tentative goodbye, then she and I were led down another hallway. Around us, scientists—nurses?—meandered in and out of rooms. There were computers and some type of beeping machine along the walls. Definitely a lab. A short, round man in a white coat stopped me when I tried to enter Rome's room, and pointed to an observation panel.

"You can't go in yet. We're sterilizing the air."

Beside Lexis, I pressed my nose to the glass, my hands at my temples, and looked inside. Rome lay on a bed, completely still, but I could hear the steady beep of his heart monitor, could see the bandages on his chest and the color dusting his skin. A bright blue light was shining on him from the ceiling.

"He's okay," I breathed. "He's really okay."

"Yes," Lexis said, her voice trembling.

"Lexis, you may stay here," the redheaded man said. "Belle, I need you to follow me now."

I wanted to refuse, but didn't. The time had come. I'd promised. I blew Rome a soft kiss and followed the doctor. John waited in an empty room, leaning against the far wall. When I stepped inside, he crossed his arms over his chest. "Shut the door," he said.

My hands trembled as I obeyed. "What exactly is it you want from me?"

His thick, silver brows arched. "I've worked at PSI for a long time," he began. "I've seen more evil than most people know exists. There are vile scrims out there, like Vincent, intent on claiming a piece of the world pie for their own. They don't care who they hurt or what they destroy."

"I thought you didn't, either," I said, laying it all out. "You were—are—willing to experiment on me. To hurt me."

"For the good of the world," he said. "By now you know there's a paranormal realm out there, people who have powers as deadly as yours. That's why agencies like mine exist, to keep them under control. People like you could destroy us all."

"I don't want to cause harm," I insisted.

He studied me for a long moment in silence. "Good. Cody told me how you defeated Vincent, a man who has been a thorn in my side for many, many years."

"I helped," I admitted.

"Would you like to do it again?"

I blinked in confusion. "Do what again?"

"Destroy another thorn in my side. There's a woman— Desert Gal, we call her. She dries everything in her path, destroying life."

I blinked again, shook my head. "You want me to fight her?" Even as I said the words, excitement worked through me. Actual excitement. I'd had fun with Rome these past couple of days. Yes, we'd been chased and shot at and almost killed, and at times I'd hated the danger. But for the first time in a long time I'd felt content, all hints of restlessness gone.

Maybe I'd found my true calling. Maybe I'd found the one job I could stick with.

Maybe I was as bad as Cody, finding joy amid the danger.

"What about neutralizing me?" I asked. "What about testing me?"

"Oh, I still want to test you. You survived a formula that killed everyone else who ingested it, and I want to know why. So yes, I *will* test you. But there's no reason to neutralize or imprison you if you work for me. You'd be a real asset to PSI."

"But there's nothing special about me! Dr. Roberts finally perfected the formula, that's all. He told me so in a note."

John hesitated for a moment, then said, "I'll need to verify that."

"By talking to the doctor or by testing me?"

"Both."

*Grr!* Was there no getting out of the testing? "We have no idea where Dr. Roberts is," I said.

"Don't worry. We won't give up the search."

I threw up my hands. "I don't know why I'm even discussing this with you. My answer has to be no." I had other, more important things to take care of: my dad, my promise to Rome. I couldn't forget those. I *wouldn't* forget those. No matter what excitement presented itself.

John's eyes narrowed. "You're a superhero, Belle, and there's no better job for you."

"There's a chance an antidote can be made from the formula," I gritted out.

"Maybe," was his reply. "I already have my men working on it. Until then...I'm offering you the chance to make the world a safer place."

I ran my tongue over my lips. So Cody had already given him the floorboards. Fine. That didn't mean I was completely powerless in this situation. "I can find Dr. Roberts on my own and get my nice, normal life back."

John laughed with genuine amusement. "Even if you weren't working for me, you'd never have your life back. When other paras hear about you, and they will, they'll come after you. Maybe your family. My agents can protect you."

"And my dad?"

"Of course. Perhaps Rome can even be your partner," he added, the sly bastard.

Oh, the thrill of that suggestion. But Rome didn't want to be an agent anymore—John just didn't know that. Rome wanted to disappear with his family. A long pause stretched between us as John studied my face and I studied his.

He wanted me to work for him. Badly. It was there in his eyes, gleaming, glowing, a desperation he couldn't hide. I guess my powers really were desirable, even with their destructive tendencies. An idea struck me, scary but welcome. "If I decide to work for you," I said, "you have to understand that I'll only take assignments I want. *I* pick and chose what I do. Not you."

"Done," he said eagerly.

"I want my dad protected twenty-four hours a day, seven days a week."

"We already agreed to that."

"I want Tanner left alone."

John hesitated. "From what Cody tells me, the boy makes a good sidekick. You might reconsider that one."

*Truth,* as Tanner would say. Wait until he learned what I'd gotten him into. Hell, he'd probably be thrilled. "Fine, I'll reconsider, but I want you to let Rome go."

"What?" John straightened, his arms falling to his sides.

"You heard me." I tilted my chin and straightened my shoulders. "Cut him loose. Fire him."

"I thought you loved him," John snapped.

"I do." And this was what he'd wanted more than anything. To escape this dark world and show Sunny how ordinary people lived. I'd lose him, yes. But he'd been willing to give his life for mine. I could do no less. "I'm sure you've been able to make other cat men, but you and I both know there's only one Wonder Girl." For the moment.

A long while passed in silence. "Fine," John finally said, reluctantly. "He's gone. Anything else?" His voice held an edge of sarcasm.

"Actually, yes. I won't start my new…duties for another month. There are a few things I need to do." Like keep my promise to Rome. Get my shit together at home. Cut out my heart so it would stop hurting.

"Fine, whatever." John sighed. "But you have to come in at least twice a week for testing, whether we decide to test your powers and abilities or your chemical makeup."

I gulped. "Will it hurt?"

"Not too badly," he said vaguely. "Are those all of your demands?"

"Yes." I half expected my fingers to freeze from my nerves, but they remained warm. Yep, I was damn good.

His mouth slowly inched into a smile. "Good. Welcome aboard, Wonder Girl."

WHEN ROME WOKE UP a week later, I was right by his side. The world was back to normal—in a weird sort of way. My dad had returned to the assisted living center, but now he had several guards. Including Cody, who was a new favorite with the "silver foxes" and now the bane of my flirtatious dad's existence, since his harem of women were all interested in the gorgeous younger man.

Bizarrely enough, Lexis and Tanner were hanging out all the time now, and were constantly seen kissing. Once they'd started, they had a hard time stopping, I guess. Lexis told me she was tutoring him in the art of loving, helping the "man" mature. Tanner had put it another way: they were getting their freak on. Either way, they both seemed happy with their Demi/Ashton romance. And I was happy for them.

I'd told Sherridan about my superpowers—had to prove it to her, actually, by blow-drying her hair at fifty paces—and she'd been ecstatic. "Think of the men you can freeze in place and we can fondle!" she'd said. "I'll need to stock up on riding crops."

That woman and her riding crops…I swear.

Brittan and Sunny had returned from their temporary safe house, and Sunny no longer called me "Stranger." I was now "Daddy's friend." Warmed my heart every time the little angel said it. Maybe one day she'd call me Belle. Or…I didn't dare think the other word I wanted her to call me. The *M* word.

Lexis had taken a leave of absence from PSI to spend more time with her daughter, and, I was sure, to get ready to go into hiding with Rome. I wanted to cry just thinking about it.

From his hospital bed, Rome moaned.

"Stupid man," I chastised him. He had saved my life by almost giving up his own. Since I'd frozen his wounds, though, we were even, so I could call him names if I wanted.

He blinked at me, those crystalline eyes filled with tenderness. Bandages were wrapped around his chest. IV tubes and electrodes protruded from him. Monitors beeped.

"Belle," he said groggily. "My sweet Homicidal Tendencies Wench."

"Hey, Cat Man," I said with a slow grin, suddenly so happy I could barely breathe. He was alive and on the mend. "How are you feeling?"

"Like shit."

I chuckled. "You're alive. That's all that matters."

"Thanks to you." Gingerly, he reached out and our fingers intertwined. "Did you get him?" he asked.

I didn't have to ask to know he spoke of Vincent. "We got him, sweetie. We got him." I'd helped kill the bastard, and was glad of it. Anyone who threatened Rome's life deserved a painful death.

"Thank you for taking those bullets for me, you big stupidhead," I said. Tears suddenly burned my eyes. "You saved my life, but you also pissed me off. I would rather have taken them myself."

"I'd never let anyone hurt you. Ever."

I leaned over and kissed him softly on the lips. My chest ached then, and my stomach knotted. "You need to hurry up and get better. It's time to get you and Sunny to safety."

With a trembling arm, he reached out and caressed my cheek. "What's wrong?"

"I guess now is as good a time as any to tell you that John fired you."

His brow puckered and disbelief flashed over his face. "What? Why would he do that?"

"I'm, uh, sort of taking your place." I looked away.

"What!"

"You, Sunny and Lexis can leave now. You can be a family. An average, normal family. But you'll probably have to take Tanner with you, since he and Lexis are seeing each other now." I forced a happy tone.

"Tanner and Lexis are…*dating?*" He flicked a glance to the ceiling. Praying for divine intervention? "And you, without consulting me, signed up to work with John. You did this so that I would leave the agency."

O-kay. He'd sounded incredulous about the dating thing, but he'd sounded pissed as hell about the other. He should be slobbering all over me in thanks.

"Yes. On both counts."

Silence.

"I'm not going to address my ex-wife's romance with a teenager right now. The shock might kill me. What I want to know is why you want me gone so badly," he finally said, his voice quiet.

"I don't want you gone." I faced him. "I just, well, this is what you wanted. This is what your daughter needs. And by taking your place at PSI, I'm fulfilling my end of our bargain. You helped me, I helped you."

He reached up to pinch the bridge of his nose, but grimaced when he moved his arm, and quickly stilled. "I can't believe you. You're completely unpredictable and you're a huge pain in my ass."

"Gee. Thanks. That's just the reaction I hoped for." Tears once again filled my eyes. "Don't you know this is hard for me? I don't want to lose you."

"Then don't," he said, his tone now raw. "Come with us."

My eyes widened. With those words, he'd just offered me everything I'd wanted. Him. A life together. As a family. "I can't." It was the most difficult thing I'd ever had to say. "If I go back on my word, John will expect you to work for him. He'll probably send Cody to hunt us both down."

"Damn it, Belle. I never planned to fall in love with you."

Rome reached up and wiped away my tears. "But you snuck past my defenses."

"What?" I demanded. That was the first I'd heard of love.

"I love you, okay? I suspected I was falling for you when you passed out after the fire. I mean, I'd never been so worried about a woman in my entire life, not even Lexis. But I knew it for sure when you saw me transform into a cat—"

"Jaguar," I corrected.

"Whatever," he said. "The point is, you didn't give a shit."

"That's the sweetest thing I've ever heard," I said, covering my eyes with my hand. But I didn't want to hear those words. Not now. Not when I couldn't take what he was offering. Still, I owed him the truth. "I love you, too." The admission was hoarse, broken and unstoppable. "I love you so much."

"I don't know why you're upset. It's not like I'm going to leave you here to fend for yourself."

My mouth fell open. "What?"

"You've got yourself a partner, baby. Get used to it. No way in hell I'm leaving you to your own devices. You need a keeper."

"But…but…"

"Vincent's dead, and he was the biggest threat to Sunny. Besides, you'll help me keep her safe from the rest of the world," he said. "And if anyone can ground her in normalcy, it's you." His tone was dry, but overflowing with affection.

*Ohmygod, ohmygod, ohmygod.* He wanted to stay with me, was going to stay with me. All of my dreams were coming true. *What if you're not the woman for him? Lexis wasn't.* The thought drifted through my mind, but I quickly squashed it. I couldn't predict what the future would bring, but I knew that I loved him. I now knew that he loved me, too.

"What if I told you Tanner will be working with us, too?" I asked.

Rome said, "I'd still want to stay with you. One big happy family."

Tears of joy cascaded down my cheeks and I climbed onto the bed and lay beside him. Careful of his injuries, I buried my face in the hollow of his neck. "I love you so much," I said again.

"I love you, too. God help me." He sighed. "Did you already agree to a specific mission?"

I traced a figure eight over his chest. "John *did* mention that there's a scrim named Desert Gal who needs neutralizing."

"You've learned to talk the talk, I see."

"Yep. I've even learned to neutralize parasters."

He regarded me as if I were crazy. "Parasters?"

"Haven't you heard? It's the new, hip word for paranormal disasters."

Rome shook his head, but wrapped his arm around my waist and held me tight. "What have I gotten myself into?"

"Heaven," I said, and he laughed. "We need a name for our partnership," I added. "Maybe we could call ourselves the Wonder Cats."

He snorted, a sound that was followed by a grimace of pain. "Don't make me laugh anymore."

"Don't let me go," I whispered, suddenly serious.

"Never." He kissed my temple. "One thing's for sure. Life is going to be interesting. But we'll have each other."

Yes, we'd have each other. A girl—even Wonder Girl—couldn't ask for more than that. I could hardly wait to see what life brought us next.

### Résumé of Belle Jamison,
### aka "Wonder Girl" (Final Draft)

**OBJECTIVE:**

To kick major scrim ass; save the world from parasters; mentor my smart-mouthed sidekick, Tanner; track down the elusive Dr. Roberts; and, um, learn to control the flying dirt balls that keep mysteriously hitting any woman who checks out Rome.

**EXPERIENCE:**

• Many hours of (hot and heavy) practice with Rome, aka "Cat Man"
• Totally successful elimination of the evil scrim Pretty Boy
• Roasting marshmallows with my bare hands (and eyes)
• Watering the flowers at my dad's assisted living center (without a hose)
• Orchestrating a snowball fight in the middle of summer (Tanner so got his ass kicked!)

**EDUCATION:**

• The School of Rome
• Awarded straight A's and aced all "extra credit" assignments

**INTERESTS:**

Long walks on the beach (with Rome), sunsets (watching them with Rome), romance novels (acting out the love scenes with Rome), cold winter nights (snuggling with

Rome), Rome in kilts/uniforms/calendars (or nothing at all), and massages (given by Rome).

## REFERENCES:

"If you're looking for trouble, Belle is the girl for you. P.S.— Hurt her and I'll kill you."

—Mr. Rome Masters, aka "Cat Man"

"Need a gal who can fry the bad guys but still give your hair the perfect blowout? Wonder Girl's the one for you!"

—Miss Sherridan Smith, best friend

"You'll never find a sweeter, harder-working gal than my baby Belle."

—David Jamison, father

"Once you get to know her, she's not a stranger."

—Sunny Masters, friend and one day,
perhaps, stepdaughter

"I predict she'll do great things. Just don't leave home without a raincoat, a fire extinguisher and moist towelettes."

—Lexis Masters, aka "Know It All"

"I've never met a nicer, more wonderful woman—with such great cleavage!"

—Tanner Bradshaw, aka "Mr. Sensitivity"

*If you've enjoyed Gena Showalter's*
*PLAYING WITH FIRE*
*don't miss the author's next enthralling*
*paranormal romance*
*THE NYMPH KING*
*available February 2007 from HQN Books*
*Turn the page for a sneak preview!*

"I SHOULD HAVE KNOWN you'd act this way," Shaye's mom snapped. With an angry flip of her wrist, she tossed a dark, shoulder-length tress over her shoulder and glared out at the water. "All I've ever wanted was a nice, normal daughter. Instead I'm stuck with you. You won't be happy until you've ruined my wedding."

"Which one?" Shaye asked drily, pushing aside her hurt. She didn't like emotions. They were messy. She much preferred the icy numbness she usually surrounded herself with. That numbness had saved her during childhood, sweeping her away from depression and desolation and into a life of satisfaction, if not contentment.

"All of them, damn it." Tamera didn't face her, but continued to stare out at the pristine water. Another splash sounded, this one closer. "You're jealous of me, and because of that you've never wanted me to be happy. Every time I'm close, you do something to hurt me."

"Don't blame me for your misery."

"Connor and I wanted this day to be perf—" Her eyes widened, glazed with instant lust, and her words cut to an abrupt halt. "Perfect," she sighed. "Hmm. So perfect."

The way her voice dropped to a husky purr, as if she

wanted to peel off her dress and dance naked in the moon-light, had Shaye blinking in confusion. "What's with you?"

"Man." There was a hypnotized quality to her words, an entrancement that left her unable to elaborate. "My man."

"What the hell are you talking about?" Shaye dragged her gaze to the ocean. She sucked in a shocked breath. "Holy—"

There, rising from the water like primitive sea gods, were six gloriously tall and muscled barbarians. The moon settled reverently behind them, enveloping them in a golden halo. Each carried a sword, an honest to God, I'll-slice-you-into-a-million-pieces sword, but she couldn't seem to make herself care. They also carried scuba-clad men under their arms and draped over their backs. Again, she couldn't make herself care.

The warriors were shirtless, and all of them possessed sinewy washboard abs, skin so tanned it resembled liquid gold poured over steel, and faces any male supermodel would have envied. Only better. So much better.

Unbelievable…surreal…magnificent.

Shaye gulped, and her heart skipped a beat. Heated air snagged in her lungs, burning and licking her with white-hot flames. All six of the warriors were staring at her as if she'd make a tasty meal, no silverware required. Strangely enough, she wanted to splay herself on a table, naked, offering her body as the dinner buffet. All you can eat. For free.

She moistened her lips, her mouth watering, her skin tingling, her stomach clenching. *I'm turned on. Why the hell am I turned on?* More importantly, why wasn't she running?

Closer and closer they came. So close she could see the silvery water droplets sliding down their hairless chests and gathering in their sexy navels. The water slid lower, lower still….

*Snap out of this, dummy,* she thought dazedly. Her gaze snagged on the one in the middle, and for a moment she forgot to move. Forgot to breathe. *Dangerous,* her mind supplied. *Lethal.* He was taller than the rest, his dark blond hair hanging in a wet tangle around his wickedly mesmerizing features. His eyes…oh, Lord. His eyes. They were blue-green, neither color blending with the other but standing alone, and so erotically seductive she felt the pull of his gaze all the way to her bones. Her nipples hardened, and an ache throbbed between her legs.

There was something wild about him, something untamed and savage, a deceptively calm glint in his expression that said he did whatever the hell he pleased, whenever the hell he wanted. And as she stared at him, he stared at her. He studied her face, a fleck of searing arousal flittering into those magnificent eyes of his, deepening and mixing the blue-green to a smoldering turquoise, followed quickly by a glint of anger.

Anger? Was he mad? At her?

Either way, he cocked his finger at her, summoning her to him.

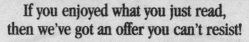